PINK
CHIMNEYS

Center Point
Large Print

**This Large Print Book carries the
Seal of Approval of N.A.V.H.**

PINK
CHIMNEYS

ARDEANA HAMLIN

CENTER POINT LARGE PRINT
THORNDIKE, MAINE

This Center Point Large Print edition
is published in the year 2019 by arrangement with
Islandport Press.

The text of this Large Print edition is unabridged.
In other aspects, this book may vary
from the original edition.
Printed in the United States of America
on permanent paper.
Set in 16-point Times New Roman type.

ISBN: 978-1-64358-398-3

The Library of Congress has cataloged this record under
Library of Congress Control Number: 2019946806

TABLE OF CONTENTS

*For Janet Elliot Danforth, for believing,
and Cathryn Piippo Marquez, for caring*

Thirty Years with Pink Chimneys

I had no idea what the fate of *Pink Chimneys* might be after it was originally published by Harpswell Press in 1987. I assumed it would have a moment of interest then fade gracefully away. That seemed to be the fate of most books.

Almost immediately, I received letters from readers telling me how much they enjoyed *Pink Chimneys*. One of the first notes came from Roxanne Moore Saucier of Bangor. She wrote, "When a reader can shed a tear by page 36, the author has quickly made her care about the characters. . . . Based on the first six chapters, I don't want the book to end, so will you proceed promptly to the second book, please?"

Little did she know that it would take nearly twenty-five years before *Abbott's Reach*, the sequel to *Pink Chimneys*, was published. Little did I know that fifteen years after Saucier's note, she would be my editor on The Weekly desk at *The Bangor Daily News*, and through her mentoring, I would learn the ins and outs of newspaper writing.

For years—even still today—I received letters, notes, and emails from readers who loved *Pink Chimneys*. The book's fans lived not only in cities and towns throughout Maine but other states as well: New Hampshire, Maryland, Florida, California, Arizona, Hawaii, Maryland, Pennsylvania and Texas.

Pink Chimneys quickly took on a life of its own. The book traveled to places I never have been nor am I likely to go—Great Britain, Russia, Bolivia, Africa, Israel, and Canada. In my imagination, I watched the book ride on airplanes, buses, cars, burros, motorcycles, horses, yachts, or rowboats to cottages, camps, haciendas, apartments, bungalows, beaches, parks, and business conferences—always tucked into handbags, attaché cases, and tote bags.

Pink Chimneys did other things I never dreamed it would do. It made the reading list of an American studies program at Searsport High School and a women's studies course at a college in Virginia. It was included in the Maine Women Writers Collection at the University of New England in Portland. It was even optioned for film, a project that unfortunately never materialized.

When I began writing *Pink Chimneys* in 1983 I had one hope for it—that my sister, Nancy, would like it. She had suggested I do something with the family and local historical information I had researched and stored in cardboard boxes under my bed. "I think you ought to write a romance novel," she said. She loved reading romance novels.

Although I had never written a book, it never occurred to me that I couldn't. Whether or not it would be published was quite another matter. Not that I fretted about it—I wasn't writing to be published, I wrote because it made me happy. I loved what I learned from reading musty diaries, antique obstetrics textbooks, and the handwritten records at the Penobscot County deeds office. I loved listening to the voices in my head and putting the words on paper.

Pink Chimneys wasn't the romance novel my sister hoped for. It turned out to be what I think of as popular fiction with history running through it, dictated by characters who had ideas of their own about what they thought the book ought to be. Sometimes, as I wrote, it was as if an insistent spirit whispered, "Pay attention, smarten up, write this down, do it now."

When my sister read *Pink Chimneys*, she said, "It's not as good as *Gone with the Wind*, but it's pretty darn good." Even the guy laying carpet at a friend's house got so caught up in the story when he overheard me reading chapters aloud, he wanted to hear more. I thought that was a good sign.

Years passed and people still asked for *Pink*

Chimneys, still read it, still recommended it to others. It appeared on local bestseller lists in Maine and was even named one of the ten must-read Maine books. It went through another paperback edition after Harpswell Press became Tilbury House. It made its "bigness," as my mother commented.

A fourth edition of *Pink Chimneys*, marking its twentieth anniversary, was published in 2007 by Bookmarcs Publishing.

I don't know what has given *Pink Chimneys* its longevity, but I believe readers find in the story something that moves them, that makes them care about Maude, Fanny, and Elizabeth, that causes them, as Saucier wrote in her note, "to shed a tear by page 36." Something in the story stirs in readers a sense of historical place, particularly as it concerns women and the Bangor region. Perhaps the story reveals to them how history flows around, away from, and toward us in a never-ending stream, inundating us, whether we know it or not, in an aura of the past.

At a book signing a few years ago, a reader told me that when she was learning to read as an adult, one of her goals was to read *Pink Chimneys*. She said it was the first novel she ever read, but not the last. It filled me with pride to know that my writing had played a part in helping someone move along the path to literacy.

Then, there was the *Pink Chimneys* tour in the 1990s. Fans filled a pinkish-colored bus embellished with white daisies, an excursion organized by Searsport Public Library as a fundraiser. Participants were driven to Stockton Springs and the Bangor area to view locations used as settings in *Pink Chimneys*. The last stop on the tour was BookMarc's bookstore where I worked. As tour-takers strolled in carrying books to be autographed, or to purchase new copies, I felt, for a few brief moments, like a writing rock star!

In the early to mid 2000s, at a book talk at Bangor Public Library, a *Pink Chimneys* reader in her 80s asked if I planned to write a sequel. I said I never had given any serious thought to a sequel, but perhaps after I retired I might consider it. The woman said, no, I must do it soon, otherwise, she might not be around to read it. I took her suggestion to heart. The sequel, published in 2011 by Islandport Press, turned out to be *Abbott's Reach*, the story of a young woman in the 1870s on her honeymoon voyage aboard her sea captain husband's ship. *The Havener Sisters*, the story of China, India, and Persia, women of a certain age who must reinvent themselves in the early 1880s, became the sequel to the sequel, published in 2015, also by Islandport Press.

I wrote other books during the twenty-five years

between *Pink Chimneys* and *Abbott's Reach*, including the self-published *A Dream of Paris*, and several other as yet unpublished novels. I also worked full time writing feature stories for *The Weekly* and *The Bangor Daily News*, and for ten years I penned the BDN weekly "By Hand" column about knitting and needlework. My keyboard was never idle.

Now, here it is 30 years later, and a new edition of *Pink Chimneys* has come into being. This could not have happened without the support of publishers who believed in me as a writer, or without booksellers who recommended *Pink Chimneys* to readers and kept it on their shelves. It couldn't have happened without the expertise of local and state librarians who provided essential research assistance. It couldn't have happened without the support of my family. Friends, too, were strong fans of *Pink Chimneys*, serving as first readers, asking questions, making suggestions, wanting to know what I was thinking and imagining. They believed in *Pink Chimneys* before I wrote a single word.

Pink Chimneys would, indeed, have faded away, had it not have been for thousands of appreciative readers—you know who you are. I am deeply grateful for the part you have played in making a 30th anniversary edition possible.

I hope *Pink Chimneys* will continue on its path

into the future, and will engage a new audience of readers who will find—in its pages—a reason to laugh out loud.

Ardeana Hamlin

Prologue

Local historians do not mention the house on Oak Street called Pink Chimneys where sexual secrets were kept. There is no record of the events that led Fanny Hogan to become Joshua Stetson's notorious mistress.

If Maude Webber, the midwife, left a diary giving accounts of her personal association with Pink Chimneys and its occupants, it has not been found.

Nor are there any letters from Abner Giddings, the master mariner, addressed to Elizabeth Emerson, the seamstress at Pink Chimneys.

You will not find their graves at Mount Hope Cemetery. Nor will you find Pink Chimneys sitting behind the green discretion of a cedar hedge. The house no longer stands.

Some say the house had blue chimneys. Some say it never existed. Others say the women whose lives were affected by the events at Pink Chimneys aren't worth including in any brick-and-mortar local history.

But the ghosts of the past are persistent. Eventually, they find a voice and tell their story.

Part One: Maude

1.

Maude Richmond shivered as she hurried into the house close behind her father, Eli Richmond. She was small of stature, not above five feet tall. Her dark blue, high-waisted dress swirled and snagged at her feet, but she did not stumble. She moved with quick determination, intent on keeping as close to Eli as possible.

At fourteen, her face still contained the rounded contours of childhood. Even after she grew into her final face, it was evident she would never be called beautiful. She resembled her father too much for that. She already knew this about herself and it did not daunt her. Her chin held lines of stubbornness and her nose was straight and finely made, giving her face a look of refinement. Her eyes were large and dark—black, some said. Everything she felt showed in her eyes. Her feelings often remodeled the contours of her pretty mouth, and dictated the way she carried herself.

It was early September 1814. Maude shivered, not because she was cold, but because she was frightened. There had been rumors for days that war had come to the villages along the Penobscot

River, but she had ignored them. The fact remained though, that Eli was all she had. She did not want him to go to war.

The messenger who brought the news to the Richmond house in Bangor had come across the Penobscot on a raft from the Brewer side. The militia, he said, was mustering to go to the defense of Hampden, five miles downriver. The *Adams*, an American privateer, lay at anchor there. The *Adams* had captured several British vessels since the United States had declared war two years ago. In retaliation, the British were on their way to Hampden from Castine, which they occupied, to capture the *Adams*. The messenger had come to alert the militia. There was going to be a battle.

Eli was the only physician in the Penobscot region who belonged to the militia. He had to go. Maude knew this and though it grieved her, she made no attempt to deter him.

Maude watched silently as Eli packed his medicine chest with instruments she'd never seen before, which surprised her. She had supposed Eli had taught her everything he knew about doctoring, except, of course, for childbirth. Childbirth was attended by midwives, and Eli believed midwifery was not a skill that belonged in the realm of simple doctoring. Eli added a generous supply of bandaging material to the medicine chest.

Eli was thin and spare, a head taller than Maude. He moved with intense concentration. A worried expression deepened the lines of his mouth. His hair had turned gray after his wife's death, when Maude was five. His eyes were dark like Maude's, almost black. He had kind eyes. He was quick to sense pain of the body or the soul.

"What are those?" Maude asked, pointing at the instruments. She lifted one. It felt cold and menacing in her hand.

"Probes and forceps. For extracting musket balls," Eli answered in clipped tones very unlike his usual manner of speaking.

As a young man, before he had come to settle in the frontier District of Maine, part of the state of Massachusetts, he had served with General George Washington's troops during the War of the Revolution, though he rarely spoke of it. He rolled several bottles of rum in thick towels and added them to his stores. He used rum to ease pain.

"I don't suppose I can go with you," Maude said. It was not a question. She already knew the answer. She laced and unlaced her fingers, rested her hands in the folds of her dress, trying to keep them still. She fingered the fabric, picked at it like a chicken pecking the ground. She hung her head in misery and a hank of dark brown hair slid out from the narrow band of the white muslin cap she wore. The expression on her face mirrored the concern etched in the lines of Eli's.

"War is no place for a child," Eli said. He snapped the lid of the medicine chest shut and buckled the leather straps, pulling them tight. Maude regarded him intently, trying unsuccessfully, to conceal her feelings. She wanted to contradict him, to tell him she wasn't a child anymore. She was a young woman. She wanted to point out to him that she had nursed several people through serious illnesses. She had even set and splinted a broken arm not long ago— she possessed the sense to know the limb was broken. But she kept still. She knew perfectly well why she couldn't go. It had to do with a snatch of conversation she had overheard between Mrs. Howard, who kept house for them, and a neighbor lady. Their talk had been about what British soldiers did to women in times of war. Rape, they had said, in hushed tones.

Maude knew what that was. Some of the women whose ills she had tended talked of sexual matters in those same hushed tones. She remembered listening with a curious mixture of keen interest and sheer outrage that women could be so used.

Maude sighed heavily, more than a little hurt that Eli had spoken so curtly.

Eli sensed her feelings, took her hand, patted it, and reached for his old gray jacket. Maude had sewn a button on it the day before.

"Someone has to stay here and tend the sick while I am gone, Maude," Eli said. "You are quite capable of bandaging a cut or dispensing a cough elixir without my supervision. People won't stop getting sick just because President Madison's war is about to arrive downriver."

His face was grave, a little pale beneath the wisps of gray hair drooping on his forehead. He was fifty-two, but his anxiety over the impending invasion added years to his looks.

In spite of her concern, a small smile of self-pride crept across Maude's lips. She knew how to crush medicines into powders with the big wooden mortar and pestle. She knew how to strain the leaves from the herbal tonics Eli prepared in the tiny dispensary next to the kitchen. She knew how to tie on a bandage as neatly as if she had been born knowing how. She had read Eli's medical textbooks, the few he owned, and she had delved into the heavy volume of his pharmacopeia.

Eli gathered his things together. Maude's small smile faded. She bit her lip and sniffed back the tears stinging her eyes. It unsettled her to see Eli leaving, looking so old, so worried, so distant from her. Suddenly, she was no longer a young lady of fourteen. She was five years old and her mother lay cold and silent, distant, in the upstairs chamber, her life snuffed out in the wake of a stillbirth. She was terrified, to the point of hysteria, to let Eli out of her sight.

"Take me with you, Papa," she pleaded in a little girl voice. She flung her arms around Eli's neck. Her cap fell off as she dove into the safety of her father's arms. "Please take me with you."

Eli pried Maude's arms off his neck with gentleness, but left a comforting arm around her shoulders. She shook with fear.

"Listen to me, Maude. I'll be in no danger. I'll set up a hospital in the town hall, at the academy, or in someone's barn if need be. I won't be where musket balls are flying. I'll send word to you as soon as I can. I'm counting on you to look after Mrs. Howard and to take care of things until I return. Will you do that for me, Maude?" Eli's eyes pierced through her fear. His worried expression was replaced by one of caring and concern.

Maude composed herself for his sake, reminded herself that she was a grown up young lady with serious responsibilities. Eli needed her to be strong.

As Eli rode away, Maude memorized the slight stoop of his shoulders, his gray hair laying against the darker gray of his jacket. She stood on the granite rock that served as a doorstep and waved as he disappeared down the Atlantic Highway toward Hampden. She smoothed her dress and brushed back the hank of dark hair that had worked loose. She put her cap back on.

A warm, damp breeze blew the crisp smell of September across the river and lifted a fold of her dress. She stood watching a long time after Eli was out of sight.

2.

The next day dawned fair and promised to be warm. It seemed impossible to Maude that, barely five miles down the road, men were shooting muskets at one another, and that British soldiers were invading her small corner of the earth.

Eli had not returned, nor had there been any word from him. Maude went about her duties with a sense of unease that set her jumping at the smallest sound. By tacit consent, she and Mrs. Howard avoided one another. Neither wanted the other to see how worried they were.

Mrs. Howard had kept house for Maude and Eli ever since Mrs. Richmond's death. She had taken a dim view of Maude reading Eli's medical books and visiting the sick with him. She had held to the beliefs of her own generation. It was far better, she maintained, for a girl's sensitive brain to remain uncluttered with book learning. Girls ought to concentrate on the things suited to the female temperament such as baking, brewing, spinning, and weaving. And keeping a decent house. She had taught Maude all these skills and Maude did them willingly and well.

But Maude simply refused to accept that her lot in life, according to God's plan because of Eve's indiscretion, was only to marry, keep house, and raise children. She did not share Mrs. Howard's belief that intellectual pursuits were best left to menfolk.

Maude paused in her application of linseed oil to the pine table in the kitchen. She thought she heard several dull, heavy thuds coming from the direction of Hampden. She went to the window. The river was devoid of shipping, an unusual and curious occurrence. The Atlantic Highway, which ran by the front door, was deserted, too. It was mid-morning and no people had passed by yet.

Maude spied a lone figure trudging past the house, coming from the direction of Hampden. She dropped her dust cloth and ran out to the yard to stop him. It was old Hatevil Colson, an itinerant laborer some said was touched in the head. He lived from hand to mouth in old barns and never stayed long in one place.

"Mr. Colson," Maude called, "is there news from Hampden?" The sun warmed her bare head. Her dress was too short in the sleeves and she tugged at them absently.

Hatevil grinned a toothless greeting. He clawed his battered hat off his stringy hair and made a courtly bow.

"Oh, there is, Miss, there certainly is news."

There were holes in the elbows of his black jacket.

"Please, Mr. Colson, I must know . . ." Maude gripped the fence rail. She was wearing a pale blue muslin dress. It laced up the back. The waist was high according to the current mode. It was not only too short in the sleeves, it barely covered her ankles. She tugged the narrow sleeves again. Maude had little interest in fashion.

"Well, now I tell you, Miss, there's been a battle, and there's some as been killed and some as haven't. And some, and that's the most of them, yes, indeedy, that has run all the way from the Penobscot to the Kennebec." This amused him and he cackled with laughter.

"But who won, Mr. Colson?" Maude asked. Her voice was urgent.

"WON! Why, the cussed Redcoats, Miss. And threatening to burn Hampden to the ground. On their way to Bangor, too, I heard one of the devils say. I'd hide in the cellar if I was you, Miss. I've heard tell those Redcoat soldiers ain't very particular about how they treat handy little ladies like yourself." He scratched his scraggly beard and leaned wearily on the fence rail. The knees of his britches sagged around his ragged wool stockings.

"I'm waiting for news of Eli Richmond, the physician. Did you see him by any chance?"

"Oh, aye, I saw him all right. He was took

27

prisoner along with all the other townsmen. Held for a ransom, too. On a prison boat. I was lucky to get away when I did. You'd better run, Miss. That's what I be doin'! Good day to you, Miss." Hatevil plunked his battered straw hat on his head and went off up the road toward Bangor village.

Maude hiked up her skirts and ran.

"Mrs. Howard! Mrs. Howard!" she screamed.

The widow appeared at the door with an alacrity quite out of keeping with her stout figure. She was dressed in the old style in dark red linsey-woolsey, a white gauze fichu folded around her breast and tucked into the band of her skirt. She had come to the Penobscot as a bride in 1775. She could remember other encounters with the British. Her husband had been killed at Bunker Hill. She had never remarried and had no children.

"Lord in heaven, Maude, what has happened?" The pads of flesh around her jaws trembled. Her small green eyes were wide with fright.

"It's Papa! The British have taken him prisoner! What can we do? We must do something!" Maude's skirts snapped and swished as she moved.

Mrs. Howard wrung her hands. Her pale knuckles had bits of bread dough stuck to them.

"Oh, dear heaven," she breathed. "I'm all aflutter, Maude. Help me to the kitchen." The ruffles on her elbow-length sleeves fluttered too.

Mrs. Howard lowered herself into a chair by

the pine table. Everything in the kitchen shone. Everything had a place and was in its place.

"Now you listen to me, Maude. There's no sense in flying off the handle. Let's think about this. If he's been taken prisoner and held for ransom, then he'll go free when the money is paid. That's how it works, isn't it? And there's money in Hampden. Why, John Crosby alone is worth thousands. And Jeremiah Herrick, the merchant. I've heard he's already made his fortune. And Simeon Stinson, the trader. They'll pay, never you fear, Maude. Your father will be home safe. Never you fear." But she didn't sound like she believed it.

Maude laid her head on Mrs. Howard's lap and wept.

A timid rap sounded outside and a small boy stuck his head in the open doorway. He was about nine years old and barefoot. His expression was serious, too serious for so young a child.

"Can the doctor come, ma'am? It's me little sister Samanthy. She's been cut and bleedin' fit to die. Ma says come quick 'cause she's afeared Samanthy is gon'ta leave this world."

Maude wiped her eyes with the back of her hand. Mrs. Howard got up and reached for a dipper of water to give to the child. The boy was dressed in patched and faded blue linsey-woolsey. He was one of Nathan Thatcher's brood and Maude knew the family. There would be little

29

else but water in the boy's house to do with, she knew. Her fear for Eli abated. He had told her to take care of things until he got back, hadn't he? Now she would have something useful to do. She hurried to the dispensary, chose salves, bandages, other things she thought she'd need.

"I'll be back as soon as I can, Mrs. Howard," Maude said.

A look of horror formed on Mrs. Howard's face. Her small mouth pursed and unpursed.

"But you mustn't, Maude. The Thatchers live right at the edge of the river. The British are coming. You'll be in harm's way!"

For a moment, Maude thought Mrs. Howard would have one of her spells. The widow's face was flushed and beads of sweat appeared on her upper lip. Maude patted Mrs. Howard's arm.

"I'll be all right, Mrs. Howard. There's nothing at the Thatchers' that the British would want. I won't be gone long. Besides, there's no sign of the British. We would have seen their ships on the river. I'm needed." Maude's fingers were busy with bonnet strings. "I expect to be back by noontime. If I'm delayed, I'll send this boy back with word when to expect me."

3.

The Richmond house stood a little ways back from the Penobscot on the river side of the

Atlantic Highway. It was barely a half-mile from the Bangor-Hampden town line. Long pastures rolled away to the river's edge, each one bounded by sturdy rock walls. The house was built in the snug Cape Cod style preferred by most. Large elms drooped leafy pools of shade into the dooryard. Already the landscape had taken on its autumn aura of red and gold. The sky was intensely blue. A few asters, a little paler than the sky, grew by the door rock. The river sparkled in the sun.

Maude, with Nathan Thatcher plodding along beside her, walked away from the house, up the Atlantic Highway. Despite its grand name, it was hardly more than two rutted tracks thick with dust. The day was unseasonably warm, just as Maude had anticipated it would be. The boy trudged along without speaking. His white-blonde hair lay in damp clumps on his skinny head. If he had any worries about the British, he kept them to himself. In fact, Maude thought, no one seemed unduly alarmed about the British. Some of the men had gone to fight, of course. Others had not. There had been no exodus from town.

Perhaps, Maude thought, the danger had been greatly exaggerated. Hatevil Colson was not a reliable source of news. Perhaps the British had subdued Hampden and were content with that. Perhaps they were on their way back to Castine and Eli was on his way home. Her spirits lifted then settled back to earth like a feather.

Before the War for Independence, everyone had been a British subject. Maude understood the reasons for fighting for independence, but she didn't understand, entirely, the politics of the present war with Britain. She knew it had something to do with forcing captured American seamen to serve on British vessels and an Embargo Act which barred any kind of commerce with Britain. It seemed, on such a pleasant day, to have little to do with her. She tried to imagine cannon balls flying through the village, and failed. Yet, there was an unusual stillness to the day, a wariness, a waiting feeling. She scanned the river again. There were no ships on it. If the British came, she would be safely back at home before they arrived.

The Thatchers lived at the very end of Exchange Street where Kenduskeag Stream met the Penobscot River. Their dwelling was small and mean, one of the last of the log cabins that had housed Bangor's early settlers. The Thatchers, like nearly everyone else, had come to the District of Maine from Cape Cod right after the War for Independence to take up the land granted to them for service in the Continental Army. Most of the log cabins had been replaced by more desirable frame dwellings. The Thatchers had not prospered and could not afford to make the change.

Mary Thatcher leaned heavily on the door frame. A clutter of children clung to her skirts. They moved in and out of the door in a swarm of flies and shrill voices. She had the broad beam and heavy breasts of a woman closely acquainted with lying-in. Her hair was a shade darker than her son's. Her apron, tied high to accommodate her bulging belly, was bloodstained. She was far gone with the child.

"I told you to bring the doctor, Nathan," Mary said. Nathan squeezed through the clutter of his brothers and sisters and went inside.

"My father went to Hampden yesterday, Mrs. Thatcher. I came in his place."

Mary's red, work-roughened hand flew to her mouth. Her lips tightened into a small round O. She stepped aside and let Maude into the cabin's one room. The place looked as if a mad bull had charged through. The floors were unswept. An iron kettle sat like a black mushroom on the hearth. It was caked with the remains of baked beans. Maude cleared a space on the table and set her basket down.

"Samanthy is over there," Mary said, and indicated a small trundle bed near the big bed in the corner nearest the hearth. "Mr. Thatcher went to Hampden, too. He said I was to take the young ones and head for the Kennebec if the British came upriver. But I'm too far gone to do that. Then Samanthy fell and hurt herself."

33

Samanthy Thatcher was, Maude judged, upwards of four years old. She lay in a pale spindly huddle, blonde braids coming undone, all arms and legs like a new foal. She closely resembled the rest of the Thatcher brood. A clumsy bandage fashioned from a wad of linen toweling was tied around her leg. It was soaked with blood. Maude undid the bandage carefully and found that the cut was long and deep, but clean. It bled in a slow ooze of dark red. Not so bad as she had feared. Still, she had never treated so serious a wound all by herself. She had watched Eli and assisted him a number of times and she knew how to proceed. She asked for a basin of water and soap. She cleaned the wound and applied a fresh bandage from strips of an old sheet, making certain that the edges of the wound were drawn closely together. Samanthy whimpered and buried her head in the small remaining space of her mother's lap.

"It's in a bad place," Maude said. "Every time she bends her knee, the wound opens and begins to bleed. It ought to be stitched closed, but I don't have the skill for that. I need two good solid laths for a splint to keep her from moving the leg."

Mary called to Nathan and sent him to forage for the laths. She spoke to her other children. They dispersed and settled in various places in the room.

"Ma! Ma!" Nathan cried as he spilled through

the doorway waving the two laths. "There's six big ships on the river. It's the British! Mr. Barker has put up a white flag out the window of his store!" Baker's store sat on a small rise of ground right at the very edge of the river.

Maude reached instinctively for her basket. Her feet moved her toward the door. The thought of home, of Mrs. Howard, and safety canceled all other thinking. But before Maude could do more than rise from the side of the trundle bed where she sat, Mary took charge.

"Nathan," she commanded, "shutter the windows and bolt the door." Nathan's small frame moved quickly. The other children sprang up to help. Mary grabbed the basin of water Maude had used for washing Samanthy's wound and doused the fire with it. It was a drastic action. It meant, once the danger was over, walking to a neighbor's house to ask for live coals to rekindle a blaze. It meant, in the meantime, no cooked food, no lighted candles, no warm water. "If there's no smoke going up in the chimney, maybe the British won't bother us."

Maude sat down by Samanthy again. She set the laths against the child's leg and busied herself with bandaging them in place.

Mary reached for a pitcher and drew out two plain silver spoons. She ran her thumb along the bowl of one. She handed them to Maude.

"Quick," Mary said, "wrap these in Samanthy's

35

bandages. You young ones go to the loft and lay down. And stay quiet or I'll take a stick to you!" Many pairs of small bare feet scuffled up the loft ladder. Then there was silence.

Mary tucked a tattered quilt around Samanthy.

Maude and Mary exchanged glances, gauging one another's fright. Mary steered Maude to the settle and made her sit. For a long while the only sound was the hiss of the coals on the hearth as they slowly turned cold. Gradually, the distant shouts and curses of men replaced the hissing. Oars dipped water. Ships' rigging creaked and groaned. There came a bedlam of screeching chickens, bawling cows, and barking dogs. Then, beneath the sounds of frightened animals, came the unmistakable tread of marching feet.

Maude twisted her hands in her lap. She tugged at her too-short sleeves. She picked at the fabric of her gown.

Mary's hands rested on the bulge of her belly. She fidgeted, as if she were not comfortable. She leaned close to Maude and whispered, "What do you know about lying-in?"

Maude's stomach flopped like a frog in a dried up bog. She had never attended the birth of a child. Most girls her age had witnessed and assisted at the lying-in of elder sisters, in-laws, mothers, aunts, and in some cases, grandmothers. But Maude had no near female relatives. She was ignorant of practical experience in the matter.

Nor had Eli ever spoken to her about childbirth. Eli believed, and often said as much, that midwifery was a profession best suited to women. He felt a man's presence at childbirth was immodest, unnecessary as long as there were skilled childbirth operators to summon. Childbirth was not a subject a father discussed with his daughter. That was woman's work.

Embarrassment colored Maude's face. "I don't know anything about childbirth, Mrs. Thatcher," she whispered.

"You're about to learn then, Miss Richmond. It won't be long. I'm always spry around the house until the last minute. This one's my ninth. About all you have to do is catch it when it comes out. Tie the cord, then cut it. I'll tell you what to do." Her whisper had gotten a little louder.

Maude tried to remember what she had heard other women say about childbirth. Her mind was blank. All she could think of was what Eli had told her about cleanliness.

"I'll need water. For my hands. And to wash the knife and twine with." Her whisper was just a little stronger than Mary's.

Mary frowned. Her blonde eyebrows puckered over her pale eyes.

"No need to go to all that trouble. I never heard of such a thing." Mary spoke out loud.

"Oh, it's no trouble, Mrs. Thatcher. My father says it's like cheeses. If you didn't wash your cheeses carefully, they would go bad and you couldn't eat them. It's the same way with people. Uncleanliness causes sickness, makes one's health go bad."

The frown left Mary's face. "Now that makes sense. I lost all my cheeses once and I never could figure out what it was I'd done wrong."

Time inched on. The din of British feet invaded the silence in the room, ebbing and flowing around the cabin, but the sound stayed well away from the Thatcher home.

Eventually, the young ones in the loft rebelled at the long spell of inactivity. Their restlessness rustled and scratched like a nest of mice. Mary gave them cold porridge to eat. She gave them bits of charcoal and told them to draw pictures on the chimney bricks to amuse themselves. Shortly after, Mary retired to her bed. Samanthy was asleep.

Worry rode Maude's heart like a heavy stone. Could she be of use to Mary when the time came? But surely, she thought, childbirth was no worse than Samanthy's bloody wound. Or gutting chickens for supper. Or cleaning hogs' intestines for sausage casing. Or emptying chamber pots every day. Those things did not turn her stomach. It was her lack of skill that set her heart racing with fright. The one story she remembered hearing about childbirth had resulted in the death of the mother and the deformity of the infant.

But when Mary's travail progressed to the point of bearing down, of panting and perspiring, Maude's misgivings about her lack of skill fell away. The delivery of Mary's infant was accomplished without any difficulty. The child breathed by itself and did not wail. Its eyes were wide open, searching for something, then found Maude, and she was caught in the infant's amazement of the newness of life. They regarded one another with soft intensity. Maude was mesmerized.

Mary reached for the infant.

"Another girl. I'm glad for that. I've already got six boys. You did a fine job helping me, Miss Richmond. I'd be pleased if you gave her a name . . ."

A loud banging came at the door. Male voices, shouting in British accents, demanded to be let in.

4.

"Open up in the name of the King or we'll break the door down!" a man called. Shoulders battered at the door.

"Quick!" Maude called to Nathan. "Help me push the chest against the door!" Nathan jumped down from the loft to help. With the chest firmly across the door, Maude dashed to the loft ladder and climbed up halfway. She poked her head into the loft. The children huddled fearfully near the chimney. Their faces, streaked with charcoal, were as white as goose down. They had drawn a fierce looking soldier on the chimney bricks. Joseph, the littlest boy, leaped up and held out his arms. Maude gathered him up. "Hush!" she commanded the children.

The thudding against the door increased. Mary drew the bedcovers up around her chin to hide her infant. The Thatcher brood whimpered and cried out in terror. The cabin went up in a wave of screams and wails. The door splintered and cracked, and gave way with a sickening crash. Four British soldiers tripped over the chest and spilled headlong into the cabin. They lay scattered on the dirt floor like discarded lobster shells.

Maude stood frozen on the sixth rung of the ladder. Joseph clung to her neck and screamed in her ear.

The soldiers scrambled to sort out a maze of arms, legs, and dented hats.

Joseph stopped screaming in mid-wail and stared. His small, narrow face relaxed into a beaming smile, showing his four new teeth. He threw up his grubby little hands and crowed, "Aw faw down."

Joseph's innocent assessment of the situation and the sight of four soldiers divested of their composure, struck Maude as ludicrous. A quick grin flashed across her face. The children saw it. Abruptly, their cries turned to giggles.

The soldiers glanced sheepishly at one another.

The one with the red hair spoke with as much dignity as he could muster, "You are to surrender your weapons and make all the food stuffs available to the quartermaster, ma'am." His tone was firm, but polite.

"We have no weapons, sir," Maude replied. She regarded the soldier from her perch. "And no food. There's little enough to feed the ten mouths that live here. There's nothing to give you." She was no longer frightened.

"Sorry, ma'am," the red-haired soldier replied. "We've got our orders. Captain Barrie wants troops quartered here. You all have to clear off." He shoved the chest aside with his foot.

Anger rose in Maude like a high tide on a full moon night.

"Sir," she said carefully, as if the soldier were slow-witted. "You cannot turn an injured child, a newborn infant, a lying-in woman, and eight young children out into the dooryard with nowhere else to go and no food. It is uncivilized. We will not leave. You tell that to your Captain Barrie!"

Joseph squeezed Maude's neck more tightly. She nearly lost her footing on the ladder. She set Joseph back on the loft floor.

"Please don't divide them, Miss Richmond," Mary pleaded. She was sick with fright.

The soldiers shuffled their feet. They were ill at

ease and unsure what to do. The Soldiers' Manual did not cover all situations concerning civilians. They milled around, tripping over one another.

Maude jumped off the ladder. She picked up a few pieces of the splintered door and flung them in the soldiers' direction. "Shoo," she said firmly. The men ducked and retreated as far as the doorway.

"Now we're in for it," the red-headed soldier said. "There's Captain Barrie." The soldiers stiffened to attention and saluted with precision.

Captain Barrie's protuberant eyes had pouches beneath them. They contrasted oddly with the sharper lines of his nose and cheekbones. His sword clanked ominously as he strode toward his men.

"Sir," Maude said, "I beg you to order your men away. They have made a mistake . . ."

"Mistake, ma'am?" Captain Barrie cut in harshly. "There has been no mistake." His pouchy lids narrowed around his flinty eyes. "You are the enemy. My orders are to burn and destroy. Private Williams, carry on."

Williams, the red-headed one, snapped a salute.

Maude's mind refused to work coherently. She did not think about the consequences of her action. She rushed back into the cabin and reappeared with the infant in her arms and Joseph by the hand. The infant was wrapped in a quilt with dark red sashing. Joseph's dress was grimy at the hem. She planted Joseph squarely in front of Private Williams. Joseph lurched, tripped on his dress, and sat down heavily.

"Faw down," he sang.

Private Williams reached down instinctively to break Joseph's fall.

Before Captain Barrie could do more than open his mouth to protest, Maude thrust the infant into his arms, shocking Barrie into inaction. His mouth hung open. He stared at the wailing child. The infant's tiny fists waved in jerky, impotent circles.

Sweat trickled down Maude's back. Her bodice stuck to her skin. The laces at the back of her dress felt as if they had shrunk. She was terrified. She was furious. She pulled her spine into a rigid straight line and faced Captain Barrie.

Captain Barrie's lips compressed into a thin line. His sword rattled.

"Very well then, sir," Maude said evenly, "you do it. You throw this babe, hardly an hour old, into the road. There's an injured child inside, too, who will bleed to death if she is moved. And a lying-in woman. And seven young children. You throw them into the road, sir, for I'll be damned if I'll be part of any such goings on."

Maude turned on her heel, appalled that she had resorted to profanity. She was so agitated she did not see the other British officer. She crashed into him, lost her balance for a moment, was quickly righted by a firm hand. The officer bowed slightly from the waist. His uniform accoutrements far outshone those of Captain Barrie. He was very tall, his dark hair misted with gray at the temples. A white plume waved jauntily in his hat. He did not wear a sword.

"Colonel John, at your service, ma'am," he said. "Your name, please." His tone was respectful, yet implied he had a duty and would not hesitate to perform it.

"Maude Richmond." Her voice was tight. She knit her fingers into the fabric of her dress to hide their trembling.

"And this is where you live, Miss Richmond?"

"No, sir," Maude said as she tugged at her too-short sleeves. She was acutely aware that her dress did not quite cover her ankles.

"Then what are you doing here?"

Maude explained. Colonel John turned to his men.

"We're not barbarians, gentlemen. You are dismissed."

Colonel John took the infant from Captain Barrie and handed the child to Maude. Nathan crept out of the cabin and hauled Joseph back inside.

Captain Barrie's face was unreadable. He stalked off, his sword clanking. His boot heels left deep prints in the ground. The four soldiers marched smartly, at double time, after him.

"You are very courageous, Miss Richmond,"

Colonel John said as soon as his men were out of earshot.

"No, sir," Maude replied. "I'm just mad as a wet hen at such unjust treatment."

A smile played around Colonel John's mouth. Maude stared at the ground. She waited for Colonel John to arrest her.

"Is everyone in Bangor this poor?" Colonel John asked. He peered into the dim interior of the cabin, inspected the dirt floor, the sparse furnishings, the huddle of thin children clustered around Mary in the big bed.

"No, not everyone. Most are. The embargo beggared many."

The Embargo Act had been enacted in 1807. It prohibited trade with Great Britain. After the Embargo Act, the British had stepped up their interference with American shipping. In retaliation for that, American privateers such as the *USS Adams* increased their harassment of British ships. Businesses of all kinds had declined because good markets for lumber and dried fish, the primary products of the Penobscot River settlements, could not be reached without extreme danger of capture by British ships. A few of the wealthier shipowners got around their dilemma, and managed to salvage their fortunes, by registering their ships under flags of neutral countries. They continued to do business with the British. Others simply had ignored the embargo

45

and smuggled much-demanded British goods from Canada into Bangor. Still, most people had suffered. Maude remembered Eli telling about dwelling houses left unfinished—how local merchants had found themselves hopelessly in debt to the Boston merchants who supplied them with goods and capital. Even Eli had to be content with fees paid in bushels of apples, a pair of shoes, or a few pounds of raw wool.

"My orders from General Sherbrooke are to evict all inhabitants on the Penobscot and burn every village I find," Colonel John said quietly.

Maude leaned heavily against the cabin. The fight had gone out of her. Tears flooded her eyes. One great drop rolled down her cheek. She hid her face in one hand for a moment before she dared to look at Colonel John again.

He regarded her from his great height. He shifted his gaze to the river. Maude followed his glance. The fires consumed the ships that made up Bangor's small merchant fleet.

"I had no choice but to burn the ships. The villages are another matter. General Sherbrooke will accept my recommendation if I advise him not to destroy the towns. If the inhabitants pledge not to take up arms against us, they will go unmolested. The prisoners will be released. Would you say that is fair, Miss Richmond?"

Maude nodded dumbly, yes, not quite believing what he said.

"How old are you, Miss Richmond?"

"Nearly fifteen, sir." Maude eased away from the cabin's support and stood erect. She shifted the infant to her other arm.

"I thought as much. Barely out of the walking strings. I pray my own daughter will never be faced with the necessity of defending her home and the people in her care at so tender an age." Colonel John paused, as if uncertain of what else to say.

Maude was speechless. She had never imagined that her defense of the Thatchers would result in the salvation of the Penobscot villages.

"War is a beastly business," Colonel John said. He swept his hat off his head and placed it over his heart. He bowed deeply, replaced his hat, and turned to go.

"Wait," Maude said. It was another of her impulses. "What is your daughter's name?"

"It's Sarah." Colonel John's face softened into an expression that Maude interpreted as home-sickness.

"This babe hasn't been named yet," Maude said. "Mrs. Thatcher asked me to choose a name. I'd like to call her Sarah, if you don't mind, sir. Sarah John Thatcher."

The colonel's face softened into an expression Maude interpreted as gratitude. He bowed deeply again. The fringe on his epaulets trembled.

"I should be most honored, ma'am. If this

wretched country you call America ever comes to anything, it will because there are ladies like you in it. Good day."

Maude knew she would never see or hear of Colonel John again. She had the distinct sensation that a new page in her life had been written, the new page turned. She could not name the feeling, but she felt as if something deep within herself had taken root and already was sending up strong new stalks. She felt a blooming that she had never imagined possible. She touched Sarah John's tiny fist. The child opened her eyes, found Maude's face, and made a bond with her.

"Nathan," Maude said with a new confidence, "you go get some wood and run over to Barker's store and ask for some live coals. I want the fire going as soon as you get back. You little ones come here and see Sarah John, your new sister. The soldiers are gone. You can come outside. One of you bring a bucket of water. Watch after Joseph." She took command of the Thatcher household as if she had been giving orders all her life.

The cabin hummed and thrived and settled back into a rhythm of its own.

5.

By evening, the British had burned every vessel capable of floating. Dark billows of smoke blotted the sky. Nathan told Maude he had seen some soldiers help themselves to goods from John Barker's store. He had heard Mr. Barker say that Captain Barrie's men were getting soused on rum at Hatch's Tavern. The news put Maude ill at ease, but no citizen was molested, no house burned. Colonel John kept his promise. At dawn, the British ships sailed back down the Penobscot, leaving the villages intact.

Maude sent Nathan to Mrs. Howard to say she was safe. Nathan brought back word that Eli, too, was safe and expected home by evening. Three British soldiers and a man from Frankfort had been killed in Hampden.

Eli arrived at the Thatchers' early the following morning. He was unshaven and his cravat was slightly askew. A button was missing on his coat. The lines from his nose to his chin curved into a smile. Still, his eyes showed concern. Eli had a face that was easy to trust. He had a knack for not interfering if it wasn't warranted. It was one of the things Maude loved most about him.

Eli surveyed the room. The Thatcher brood eyed him solemnly. They were eating a breakfast of cornmeal porridge sweetened with molasses Maude had prepared. She had baked bread and churned butter from the gill of cream she had discovered hanging in the well. She had washed the children's hands and faces. They fairly shone in the dim light. The room was neat and tidy. Mary, sitting up in bed with her hair neatly plaited and covered with her best muslin cap, nursed Sarah John.

Maude did not rush into Eli's arms with sobs of relief as she would have done only two days ago. Instead, she strode purposefully toward him and kissed his cheek.

"I am quite well, Papa," she said with great calm and dignity. She carried herself with a new assurance and Eli noticed the change.

"Well, Maude, I see everything here is in good hands."

Maude led Eli to Samanthy. The child's leg was propped comfortably on a wadded up quilt and she sucked her thumb contentedly.

"I want you to look at Samanthy's leg," Maude said.

Eli stroked Samanthy's smooth blonde braids. He inspected the wound and bent to sniff it.

"No odor. No putrefaction. I'd say you've done a fine day's work, daughter." His eyes were filled with pride.

"And that's not all, Papa, I helped Mrs. Thatcher with her illness." Maude adjusted Mary's pillow.

"Aye, that she did," Mary said. She removed Sarah John from her breast and held the infant up for Eli to see. "Your Maude was as handy as any I've ever come across. Gentle as a lamb. I'll send for her again when the time comes. The cradle is never empty for long in this house."

Maude sent the children outside to play. She settled Samanthy for a nap and Mary for a rest. She jiggled Sarah John in her arms. She and Eli sat down at the table. Eli crossed his legs. He folded his hands across his spare middle.

"And what of you, Papa?" Maude asked, "What happened at Hampden?"

"The militia got there all right. Most of them without weapons except pitchforks or flails. None of them trained to know what they were supposed to do. The whole kit and caboodle ran the minute the first British soldier came over Academy Hill. They scattered from here to Belfast and back again on both sides of the river. Morris, the captain of the *Adams*, put the ship to the torch before he and his men got away. I thought I'd be spared the prison ship because a few men got banged up in their haste to get away and needed my attention. But a British officer by name of Barrie said he had no humanity for any of us. Several dozen of us were locked up in the hold of the *Decatur* without food or water. The man had no decency whatsoever. We spent a pretty cramped night. The people of Hampden raised the $30,000 bond the British demanded. None of the townspeople suffered any hurt. But the British dumped molasses and feather ticks in the wheel of Mr. Crosby's grist mill. Made an ungodly mess. Some cattle and sheep were killed.

Some property trespassed on. But the British were put in their place a time or two. I saw Judge Kinsley's wife empty a chamber pot onto the heads of some British officers. And I heard Hatey Colson went up to a colonel and asked if it was true that his name was Gosling. The colonel said it was and old Hatey said, 'Then damned it be the goose that hatched ye!' "

At the mention of Captain Barrie, Maude and Mary exchanged significant glances, a tacit agreement passed between them. Maude turned the conversation to other things. She was not yet ready to tell Eli of her adventures with the British.

Shortly thereafter, Nathan Thatcher, the elder, returned and Maude and Eli started for home. They walked slowly. The golden September weather had held. Red and amber leaves dappled both sides of the river. Maude tugged at her sleeves. Her basket swung from her left elbow. People came out into their dooryards to pass on and receive news of the Battle of Hampden. One woman rushed up to Maude and grasped her arm.

"I heard how you put that brute Barrie to shame. Why no one's talking of anything else but how you won Colonel John's heart and made him promise not to burn the roofs over our heads," the woman said. Her nose was, Maude thought, exactly the right sharpness for delving into other people's business. Maude protested that she had done nothing of the kind.

"Well," the woman sputtered, indignant that she had been contradicted, "that's not the way John Barker told it. You are much too modest, Miss." She sailed away in a flurry of brown skirts and red petticoats to pass on her gossip to anyone inclined to listen.

Maude dreaded to think what kind of tales would be tacked onto the story before it got done making the rounds of the Penobscot villages. Not that it mattered. Better the town should think she had captured the affections of a British soldier, which she had not, than accuse her of acting foolishly and bringing harm to the Thatchers.

"Apparently, Maude," Eli commented quietly, "your adventure was somewhat more entertaining than mine." He wore his stern father face. His mouth was firm. His eyes searched hers, neither teasing nor chastising.

Without embellishment or omission, Maude told Eli the story of her encounter with Captain Barrie and Colonel John.

Eli closed his eyes a moment and shook his head.

"I thought you had more sense than that, Maude."

"Please don't scold me, Papa. If I hadn't acted the way I did, Samanthy might have died. Or

53

Mrs. Thatcher's condition could have become dangerous. The children were hungry and dis- comforted enough as it was. No one should have such authority over anyone else. Especially over the women and children. It isn't right." Maude hesitated. She tried to think of a way to say what it was that had infuriated her when Captain Barrie had ordered them away. "Women," she went on, "have little enough to say about what happens to them as it is. It seemed to me that I had some rights. I simply could not submit without a whimper." The set of her face grew stubborn and determined.

Eli's face softened into the quizzical expression Maude had noticed several times since he had come to conduct her home.

"Where do you get such ideas, Maude?"

"The last parcel of books you had sent from Boston had *A Vindication of the Rights of Women* in it, by Mary Wollstonecraft. She believes women ought to have power over themselves, that they ought to be educated, and have the same rights as men to determine the outcome of their lives. It sounded very sensible to me."

Maude had read the book twice.

"I thought it was a collection of learned essays on the proper sphere for women. The household arts. Raising a family. Those things."

They had had similar conversations before. The idea of spending the rest of her life beating rugs and dusting tables made Maude uneasy. She wanted something more. She had not been able to make Eli understand.

Eli chewed on his bottom lip. He was thinking. They walked more slowly.

"I was some upset," he said, "when Mrs. Howard told me you'd gone to the Thatchers'. Poor lady, she's been fit to be tied ever since you left. All I could think of was how my little girl was in danger. I didn't know what to expect when I got to the Thatchers. That you were harmed in some way, I guess. I certainly didn't expect to find a very capable young woman completely in charge of the situation." He paused and looked hard at Maude, appraising the difference he sensed in her attitude. "Forgive me, Maude, for not realizing that you have grown up."

Maude was touched, but she saw how difficult it was for him to adjust his perception of her. Her instinct was to protect him because all they had was one another.

"Oh, Papa, you know I'm grown up. I take very good care of you and help you very much."

"No, Maude. I'm serious. Until this very moment, I hadn't dared to admit to myself that you are no longer a child." He drew a deep breath. "You've followed me around since you were five years old. Mixing medicines. Reading my books. Learning the doctoring trade. I never once thought that one day you'd be able to do, all

55

by yourself, the things I've taught you. And even a few I didn't."

Eli clasped his hands behind him as he was apt to do when he was in a reflective mood. They walked in silence a few moments, letting the immensity of what he had said sink in. Maude matched his contemplative stride and did her best to match his mood. It puzzled her.

"I suppose you'll be wanting a husband and have no need for a father before too long," Eli said thoughtfully. He kept his eyes fixed on the road.

"I want to be a physician like you, Papa. The husband can wait." She had said as much to him before. He had merely smiled indulgently and given some vague answer that neither encouraged nor discouraged.

Eli stopped in mid-stride, wiped his brow with his handkerchief, and sat down in the shade of an elm.

Maude put her basket down. She pulled on her sleeves.

"Rest a minute, Maude. I'm not as young as I used to be. This will surprise you, but I always hoped that one of your brothers would follow in my footsteps. That's the way God meant it to be, a son learning his father's work. I always expected you'd be like your mother, well versed in the housewifely arts, glad to share the yoke of matrimony with a strong husband of your own choosing." Eli took Maude's small, square hand in his. He sighed deeply, pained by the memory. "Your brothers went off to sea and went down with their ships. Then your mother died. And you have been the one to follow me around to visit the sick. You read my medical books as easily as you read a recipe for gingerbread. I never gave any thought to whether or not it was seemly for a young lady. I just liked your company very much. I liked watching you learn. But you weren't a boy and I didn't take your interest too seriously. It seems you have become my apprentice and I scarcely know how it has happened."

"I've only done what I want most in the world to do, Papa," Maude said earnestly.

"You're certain you wouldn't rather be at Miss Stanley's Young Ladies' Academy learning the gentle art of embroidery or the genteel way to step a reel?" His tone was teasing. Eli released her hand and wiped his forehead again.

"No, Papa. I want to be a physician like you."

"Some men won't want a woman to doctor them."

"I know, Papa. But some women will not want a man to doctor them either."

The quizzical look registered again on Eli's face. He had never thought of it that way.

"You have a caring heart, Maude. I saw that very clearly at the Thatchers'. I guess that's what set me thinking. Mary Thatcher is right.

Women will be glad of your presence when their travail begins. You have the makings of an excellent midwife. Midwifing is a proper sphere for women. More so than simple doctoring. Would you consider the art of midwifery a proper calling?"

"Yes," Maude said simply. She thought of the amazed questing of Sarah John's eyes. She thought of Mary immersed in the intense work of her travail. "Yes," she repeated.

"When you're eighteen, I will apprentice you to Sally Cobb Robinson, the midwife across the river at Orrington. Does that sound agreeable?"

"Yes," Maude said again, more strongly.

"You wouldn't rather have a husband? Perhaps one in a militia uniform who calls himself captain or general?"

"Perhaps, Papa. Someday. If the right one comes along."

Maude picked up her basket. Eli pocketed his handkerchief. They walked on down the rutted, grass-tufted track of the Atlantic Highway, in step, heads tilted slightly down, hands clasped loosely behind their backs.

6.

"This is Miss Anne Stinson, Miss Richmond. She has lately become engaged to my dear grandson, John, of Hampden. She is staying with me while her parents journey to Boston," Mrs. Crosby said.

Old lady Crosby was as wide as she was tall. She was gouty, spoke her mind, and cared nothing for what anyone else thought. She set the social tone of Bangor. Her face was crosshatched with wrinkles. Everyone said she was upwards of eighty. She admitted to seventy, but she might have been older or younger. Her husband and sons were among the few who had salvaged their fortunes during the embargo. No one was quite sure how.

Mrs. Crosby wore a gown of black silk in the old style. A sheer white gauze fichu lay in precise folds across her broad breast, giving her a resemblance to a pouter pigeon. Her invitations to drink tea with her were understood to be a summons.

Maude stood quietly in Mrs. Crosby's parlor. She had arrived precisely at two o'clock. Mrs. Crosby did not like tardiness.

Maude's gown was new. Mrs. Howard, recognizing the importance of such an invitation, had insisted. It was dark blue calico with a small figure dotted over it. Her hair was parted in the middle, looped loosely over her ears, and caught up behind with a carved shell comb.

Mrs. Crosby's tea parties were known for two things. Her tea service consisted of exquisite blue and white English porcelain cups and saucers, and the other guests invariably were dull. Mrs.

Crosby also liked to make "pronouncements" that commented on the social and moral standards of behavior in the Bangor region. The penalty for disregarding these pronouncements was to become the subject of one at the very next tea party. Mrs. Crosby built and destroyed reputations the way some men built and destroyed businesses.

Anne Stinson, however, was anything but dull. Her curly hair was a hazy shade of yellow. Her eyes were the color of robins' eggs. Her lips were full and red. She was airy and ethereal in a soft, gauzy pink gown. She trailed the deep fringe of her rose silk shawl behind her with an affected disdain for the garment.

"Pleased to meet you," Anne said. She inclined her perfectly modeled head. Little pale yellow ringlets bobbed. Her eyes snapped with restless sparks. She was the daughter of Simeon Stinson of Hampden. Maude remembered going with Eli to tend Mrs. Stinson when she had scalded her hand.

"The same, I'm sure," Maude said.

They smiled their best tea party smiles. Mrs. Crosby excused herself and went to see to the tea.

"Is it true what they say about you and that British officer?" Anne asked. Her voice was low and musical. Her dimples played.

Maude bristled. The story of her defiance of the

British had, in four years, become legendary. She found it extremely embarrassing.

"It most certainly is not!" Maude's chin jutted, offering just a touch of challenge.

"No, I don't suppose it is," Anne replied. She moved restlessly, dragging her shawl behind her. "I so hoped it was. But I knew the minute I saw you. You are not the type to turn the head of an older man. Or ever get into a scrape."

"No, I'm not," Maude said firmly. "Are you?"

Anne poured her shawl into an untidy pile in the corner of the sofa. Her laughter was a quick fluted melody.

"Oh, yes. That's why I'm here, really. I was attending a young ladies academy in Boston. I've been sent home in disgrace. That's why Mother and Father are away. To fix things so my reputation won't be tarnished forever." She sat down on top of the shawl. Maude took a chair with a needlepoint seat.

"What did you do?" Maude asked. Her interest was piqued.

"I shocked the headmistress, straight old stick of a thing. I shinned up the maple tree in the garden. Am I shocking you? No. I think not. I had a note from my older brother, Reuben. He's master of father's ship, the *John Hampden*. I hadn't seen him or been home in an age. I was just sick for the sight of something that reminded me of home. So I climbed the tree. To see if I could catch a glimpse of the ship in the harbor. I got caught."

"You seem very happy about it," Maude said, smiling.

"Oh, I am. But now they have sent me here to benefit my character with Mrs. Crosby's superior wisdom."

The hired woman came in with a tray of tea things, followed by Mrs. Crosby. Anne and Maude assumed proper tea party expressions.

Mrs. Crosby settled heavily into a large wing chair. She planted her little feet on a footstool. The voluminous black silk skirts sighed. The keys hanging from her waist on a chain jingled. Her white mobcap was stiffly starched. It covered her hair completely.

"Anne, dear," Mrs. Crosby said, "bring a chair and sit by me. Shake out your shawl. It's all wrinkled. Have one of these little cakes, Miss Richmond. I understand you leave for your apprenticeship in Orrington next week." Teacups made polite rattles. She handed Maude a cup. Exotic birds strutting in a fairy tale forest of blue decorated it.

"Apprenticed?" Anne asked. "Whatever for?"

"Miss Richmond is to learn the art of midwifery. It is very sensible of her to give herself to such an honorable calling. But it is my duty to warn her." Mrs. Crosby made a significant pause. A pronouncement was imminent. "Sally Robinson is a lady of the utmost respectability. She is wise beyond the wisdom naturally bestowed on women. She is, as I am sure you know, the widow of a physician. When he died, she simply continued his practice as so many doctors' wives do. I have heard, on the best authority, that before her marriage, Mrs. Robinson received mid-wifery training in France. The French entertain some very popish ideas. Mrs. Robinson has been known to attend women of low moral character, if you understand my meaning." The line of Mrs. Crosby's lips was prim.

Anne stared at her knees and fussed with her shawl.

Maude understood perfectly. She had heard the gossip about widows who produced an infant a year after a spouse's death. She knew of women with three or four children and no husband in sight. She attended their ills if they asked her to. So did Eli. She opened her mouth to speak, but Mrs. Crosby interjected.

"Oh, I know the town has a regulation that requires a midwife to attend any who call. But I think it most unwise. One of their own ought to be trained to attend them. These things should not be allowed to filter out to decent women. You are very young, Miss Richmond. You must stay on your guard against the corrupting influences you will encounter. There. I've had my say. Would you have more tea?"

Maude's indignation flared like a bonfire on an October evening. But she said nothing. She and Eli had talked of these things in a general way. To Mrs. Crosby, and most other people, fallen women—those who had lost their virtue—were Eve incarnate. They deserved the punishment of social segregation. But Eli did not share that sentiment. It was one thing, he had counseled, to refuse to condone such behavior in one's self, but quite another to condemn it in someone else. Especially if you knew nothing of the circumstances that compelled those women to behave in such a way in the first place.

"Hasn't the weather been perfect for apple picking," Anne said brightly.

The rest of the tea party passed in similar polite conversation. Maude was relieved when the time came to leave. Mrs. Crosby shifted her bulk and yawned, apparently worn out by her effort to impart wisdom to young ladies.

"Anne, dear, see Miss Richmond to the door. It's time for my nap."

Maude rose to go. Anne followed her to the door.

"I never met anyone of our sex who does such interesting things as you do, Miss Richmond. If I invite you, would you come to a gathering at my home? An assembly, perhaps. My four brothers would dance with you."

"I'd like that very much, Miss Stinson. But I'd

have to receive Mrs. Robinson's permission." Maude put on her bonnet and went home.

That had been a week ago.

The day Maude had dreamed of and dreaded had arrived. It was the day she left for Orrington to begin her apprenticeship. She tied her best bonnet, plaited of yellow straw and trimmed with blue silk ribbons, firmly under her chin. Her gown was an indefinite shade of brown. Neither the bonnet or the gown was fashionable. The decoration was not lavish enough. The waist was not low enough. The skirt was not full enough. Maude seldom thought about how her clothing looked. She was too busy visiting the sick. And when there were no calls, there was the endless round of baking, mending, spinning, preserving, scrubbing, and all the other heavy tasks of housekeeping to do.

In a sense, visiting the sick was simply an extension of the housework Maude was familiar with. On the day Mrs. Howard taught her to darn, she learned to stitch a wound. After she mended a broken chair leg, she splintered a broken bone. The same morning she spent an hour trying to blow cold coals into a blaze, she learned to breathe life back into a half-dead child.

Maude reached for the door latch and glanced fondly around the room that had been hers since her mother's death. The braided rugs were faded and worn, but she cherished them because her mother had made them. The log cabin quilt she and Mrs. Howard had pieced was spread neatly on the bed. The sampler Maude had completed in the twelfth year of her life hung on the gable wall. The letters she had stitched read:

May learning, science, useful art,
Adorn thy life, improve thy heart.
May kind affection, love so dear,
Hereafter bless and guide you here.

It was a cozy room tucked up under the eaves where she could listen to the rain on the roof. In winter she could almost hear snowflakes fall on the shingles. She knew she would miss the way the morning sun slanted through the window and fell in a warm patch on the pine floor.

She went downstairs to find Eli in the small dispensary just off the kitchen ell. He was writing in a big leather ledger, spectacles—a recent acquirement—balanced on the end of his nose. His dark gray jacket was the same one he had worn to the Battle of Hampden. The same button was still hanging loose. It never stayed on no matter how often Maude sewed it.

Maude picked up a cobalt blue bottle and examined it while she waited for Eli to finish.

"I've always loved this color. It looks so pretty when you hold it up to the light."

"Maybe that's why I have such a time keeping

any," Eli grumbled good-naturedly. "You always have them filled with flowers, or stuffed full of dried rose petals." His pen scratched noisily as he made a grand flourish with it. He handed Maude a small piece of paper.

"This is a check for five dollars drawn on the Bangor Bank. You'll need things. Spend it however you like."

Maude thanked him and tucked it into her little leather reticule. Like most of her possessions, it was well worn and out of fashion. Its click, as she snapped it shut, hung loudly in the air. Silence replaced the snap of the reticule. Eli removed his spectacles and made a large business of putting the ledger away.

"Papa," Maude said softly, "I want to go, but I don't want to go." A wail stuck in her throat. She managed to keep at bay the plaintive tone threatening her words.

Eli stood up quickly. He took Maude by the shoulders. She had not grown beyond five feet tall. She would always have to look up at him. She thought of a strong oak and leaned against him.

Eli's mouth worked a moment before any words came. "I know you'd rather live here with me than at Mrs. Robinson's, but you'd miss out on too much if you did that. She is called to all the villages on both sides of the river. From Old Town to Frankfort. Even as far inland as

Dixmont. Don't change your mind now, Maude." He pushed her gently out of his arms, establishing a tangible distance between them.

"It's not that, Papa. I just hate leaving you all by yourself."

"Mrs. Howard will see that I'm taken care of."

"Promise me you'll send for me if the least thing is the matter, if you are ill, or have too much to do . . ." Maude's voice broke.

"Goodbyes still aren't easy for you, are they, Maude?" Eli understood how deeply she had been wounded by her mother's death.

"Maybe it's a mistake . . ." Maude began.

"Go. Now. Young Nathan Thatcher has had his team waiting for a quarter hour. Your trunk is already on the cart." Eli's eyes were over-bright, Maude's stung with unshed tears.

She kissed Eli's cheek and felt a bit of moisture on her lips; her own or his, she couldn't tell.

Her life was at a crossroads. One way was safe and familiar, the terrain easily traveled. The other direction was uncharted, unknown. The feeling she had first encountered at the Thatchers' cabin four years ago stirred. Once again, she sensed herself preparing to bloom in a way few women ever did.

7.

The cart Nathan Thatcher had brought to carry Maude and her trunk to the ferry consisted of a short cargo space, two wheels, and a small seat perched near the front of the vehicle. The oxen hitched to it stood with dumb patience. They slapped their ropey tails at the flies worrying their black haunches.

Nathan had changed dramatically in four years. He was a strapping, tall youth able to do a man's work to earn his keep.

"Good day to you, Nathan," Maude called. Mindful of his recent arrival into manhood, he allowed a small smile and nod to serve as a greeting. He helped Maude climb up onto the seat beside him.

"Gon'ta be a good one, Miss Richmond," Nathan said, his voice deep. His white-blonde hair was still plastered in damp clumps to his head. His shirtsleeves were rolled up. "Sarah John's been actin' up all morning. She ain't happy about you goin' off over to Orrington. Ma says tell you to be sure to wave to Sarah John when we get to the ferry."

"I'll do that, Nathan," Maude said. She folded her hands in her lap. "I'm ready if you are."

Nathan spoke to the oxen and prodded them with his wooden goad. They moved with slow heaviness. The cart lurched and creaked as they swung around and lumbered down the road.

"I will write often," Maude called to Eli and Mrs. Howard, who stood on the door rock. Mrs. Howard waved goodbye with a large white handkerchief and dabbed at her eyes with her other hand. Her smile was brave. Eli lifted his hand more slowly, as if in salute. His gray coat hung a bit crooked from one of his shoulders. It occurred to Maude that nothing would ever be the same again. For a moment she was afraid.

As if he had read her thoughts, Eli squared his shoulders and bowed from the waist to her. The gesture conveyed his pride and confidence in her more than mere words ever could.

At the ferry, Nathan stopped the cart. Maude climbed down to speak to Sarah John. The child stood on a pile of lumber. Her white pinafore, tied over her woolen dress, was rumpled and grass-stained. Her finger was in her mouth. Her hair was pale blonde, almost white. She was very composed. Too composed, Maude thought.

"You ain't never gon'ta come back," she said. Tears welled up in her hazel eyes.

"Of course I'll come back, Sarah John." Maude lifted the child off the lumber pile and sat down with her in her lap. Sarah John buried her face in Maude's neck to hide her misery. "While I'm gone, Sarah John, Mrs. Howard and Papa will need a little girl to look after them. Do you think you could do that?"

Sarah John stirred and regarded Maude with a serious expression. Anything Maude suggested always made sense to her. Her attachment to Maude was absolute. She nodded gravely, yes. Maude set her on her feet.

"I will come to see you when I can. And look, I brought you a hair ribbon." It was bright red. Maude tied it around Sarah John's braids. Sarah John hugged Maude's knees. She let Nathan lift her up onto the back of the oxcart. She stood there and waved as the ferry drew Maude across the Penobscot River to Brewer. Another carter awaited on the other side of the river. He transferred Maude's trunk to his cart and they headed toward Orrington, five miles downriver.

Orrington consisted of a church, a school, a cemetery, and a handful of one- and two-story frame dwellings clustered near a corner where two roads met. One of the roads led west down to a ferry slip directly across from Hampden, the largest town on the Penobscot. The other road led north back to Brewer, or south to Bucksport.

Maude's thoughts wandered as the cart bumped and trundled along. Since the British invasion, Bangor's population had grown to more than a thousand. The Penobscot River still provided the most important source of livelihood. Fishermen caught bushels of salmon and alewives in the spring of the year. The fish were smoked and packed into wooden barrels and shipped to Boston. An increasing number of men cut trees in the vast pine forests north of Bangor. They floated logs downriver to sawmills where the logs were sawn into boards. The boards were in great demand in cities up and down the eastern seaboard.

After the Treaty of Ghent was signed in 1815, officially ending what local inhabitants had dubbed "Mr. Madison's War," the British and Americans maintained peaceful relations. Local politicians turned their attention elsewhere. Wherever she went, Maude heard talk that the District of Maine would separate from Massachusetts and become a state of the Union within two years. There was also a lot of talk about temperance and how the free flow of rum ought to be curbed. Maude was interested in temperance. She had tended, more than once, men, women, and children whose health had been ruined by too much spiritous drink.

The cart bounced and swayed. Maude held onto the side of the seat. Her thoughts went to the apprenticeship she would serve with Sally Robinson. Very few midwives, she knew, had any kind of formal training. Most women learned to be childbirth operators because they were good neighbors helping a friend or relative in need. Most lying-in women stayed in bed for six weeks. It was imperative that friends or family care for older children, wash clothes, milk the cow, tend the fire, and carry on the tasks only female hands were best suited to. These same women also aided with the birth. In this way, the skills of midwifing were handed from woman to woman. The skills of birthing were acquired as easily and naturally as swapping a quilt pattern or memorizing a recipe for blueberry cake. Birthing was just one more aspect of women's work.

But not all women chose to exercise their skill on a regular basis. Those who did choose to call themselves midwife charged a fee. Their good-neighborly work then became their calling, or profession.

Eli had pointed out, Maude remembered, that women midwives were fast disappearing. As more men studied medicine, and women continued to be barred from the same study, man-midwives gained in popularity. The reason for this, Eli believed, was the use of forceps which the man-midwives were trained to use. Female midwives had no experience with forceps. Forceps plucked the infant from the womb quickly, thereby shortening the birth and greatly easing the pangs of travail. This, in Eli's opinion, was a mixed blessing. The employment of a male mid-wife went against nature, violated a woman's right to modesty and chastity. Moreover, forceps in the hands of an ill-trained person, male or female, often caused more damage than good.

Many deaths were associated with their use. Man-midwives with forceps removed from women's hands one of the occupations they were best suited to. Eli had discussed these things with Maude.

The cart rolled up to a modest two-story dwelling on the outskirts of Orrington Village. The house was painted a dull shade of red, the same color many preferred for their barns. Several smaller outbuildings stood behind. There were four small panes of glass over the front door. A kitchen ell was attached to the rear. It was a Cape Cod house very much like Eli's house. For the first time, Maude felt easy about living at Sally Robinson's.

The girl who opened the door was, Maude judged, about sixteen. Her hair was an unremarkable shade of brown. Her features were not striking in any way. She did not speak. She stepped back to let Maude in. She led the way to the kitchen with her hands clasped modestly in front of her—eyes on the floor.

Maude's first impression of the house was one of comfort and neatness. The scent of pine oil and unidentified herbs lingered in the air.

A huge fireplace dominated the kitchen. The mantel boards were painted a soft shade of green. The fire was low. A kettle simmered on the coals. A flax wheel sat in the far corner. The table was polished to a soft sheen. Several baskets of different sizes sat about the floor. One contained a cat and a litter of kittens. Another contained balls of yarn that had not yet been dyed.

A spare-framed woman sat by the fireside puffing gently on a clay pipe. A halo of soft September sun filtered into the room. Motes of transparent dust drifted like a miniature blizzard within the shaft of light. The woman was dressed in the old manner. She wore a rayle which served as a combination shirt, petticoat, and sleeping garment. It had elbow sleeves with modest ruffles. A woolen bodice of deep red was laced over the rayle, flattening her breasts and increasing her royal bearing. Below the bodice, she wore a dark blue skirt with a spotless white apron tied over it. A much-worn and mended pocket hung from her waist. Her head was covered by a curious cap with a wide band which hugged her head at the hairline. It poufed out slightly at the crown. The woman was, Maude guessed, about fifty. Her face was chiseled with a serene expression. Her features were thin and fine, stopping just short of being sharp. She was not handsome, nor was she plain. She did not rise. She indicated a vacant chair. Maude sat.

"I'm Mistress Robinson."

Maude felt as if she'd been ordered to sit by an empress. She straightened her spine, folded hands in her lap, and arranged her feet squarely in front of her as if she were in church. It was an instinctive response. There was no doubt in her mind that Sally Robinson was accustomed to being in command.

"Your father is the only physician in these parts who is opposed to men-midwives. I have great respect for your father. I understand he has trained you in doctoring," Sally said. She puffed a bit on her pipe.

"Yes, ma'am. Since I was very young."

Sally took a long draft on her pipe. She let her gaze wander from Maude's face to her feet. Maude didn't dare fidget. She lifted her chin and met Sally's frank assessment.

"I believe the greatest reason men-midwives are employed is because childbirth operators have not been properly trained. I believe they do not maintain a proper degree of cleanliness."

Maude leaned forward eagerly.

"That's exactly what Papa says."

"It is a canker to me, Miss Richmond, to see men-midwives called to birthing women. Your training with me will be more rigorous than the few months of book-reading these upstart physicians obtain. You will be out at all hours in all kinds of weather. There is the matter of the washing. Records must be kept in exact detail. I go where I am called when I am called. I expect you to do as I say until I decide you are ready to attend births alone. Is that understood?"

The mother cat jumped into Sally's lap. She stroked the cat's back, her hands moving with quiet grace. Her fingernails, Maude noticed, were very clean.

Yes, ma'am," Maude said. Her impulse was to cross her heart and hope to die, but she didn't do it.

Sally set her pipe down.

"I take it you brought clothing more suitable for midwifing than that frivolous gown you are wearing?"

Maude had never thought of her old brown gown as frivolous, but she dared not say so.

"Mrs. Howard saw to it that I packed rayles. I've also brought old sheeting, an oil cloth, some of my father's medicines, and other herbs I thought might come in handy."

Sally nodded.

"Betsy," Sally called softly. The girl who had shown Maude in appeared. "Betsy doesn't speak. She was born that way. A deformity of the tongue. She was left under a bridge to starve when she was three days old. I found her and took her to live with a childless woman down the road. Now she keeps house for me. She will show you to your chamber. Supper time is at four."

For the first time, Sally smiled. The transformation was instantaneous. The angular planes of her face evolved into kind curves. Her eyes softened from icy granite to warm linsey-woolsey.

"We'll get along, you and I, Maude Richmond," Sally said.

8.

The wash house emitted plumes of steam in the brisk late October chill. The sharp odor of vinegar and lye soap made Maude wrinkle her nose in distaste. Every scrap of cloth that touched any of Sally's patients was soaked in the vile concoction. This chore was performed every week—heavy labor, indeed. The night before wash day, every Monday, Maude kindled a fire under the great iron pot. She and Betsy hauled endless buckets of water from the well to fill the pot. In the morning, they ladled the hot water into wooden tubs. Then, Maude scrubbed sheets, bandages, and other linens, rinsed them, rung them out, and returned them to the big pot to simmer. The sound of the hired man's axe seldom stopped. It took a lot of wood to keep the wash house in business.

Babies, Maude had quickly discovered, arrived at the most inconvenient times. Almost immediately she learned why Sally insisted on the old-fashioned rayle, which also served as a night gown, as her professional costume. Dressing in the middle of the night was as simple as dropping a skirt over her head, fastening it, stuffing her feet into her shoes, and grabbing her cloak as she went out the door. It took less than five minutes.

Maude stirred the mass of washing with a

long-handled paddle and fished out the dripping fabric. Wringing out, the part she hated most, was still to come. Her hands, chapped and sore, were relieved only by copious applications of a salve Sally compounded in her kitchen. Once, Maude had dared question Sally about the necessity of such constant cleanliness.

"Women in my care don't die of childbed fever. If you care nothing for the safety of those under your care, I suggest you go home to your father," Sally replied sharply.

Maude closed her mouth quickly and got on with her work. Usually, Sally presided in the wash house, doing her share and making the work less onerous, but on this day she had been called away to visit an aged relative whose life was drawing to a close.

Maude wiped her hands on the back of her wool skirt. She straightened her back wearily. A sharp gust of cool air cut through the warm dampness of the wash house. Eben Wheeldon poked his head cautiously through the door.

For six entire weeks, from the first day Maude had made his acquaintance, Eben had followed her around like a puppy, an adoring look in his cloudy gray eyes. He was the village school-master who boarded at Sally's. A bookish man in his early thirties, he had a homely face and a receding hairline.

"Here, Miss Richmond, let me do that," Eben

said. He lifted a tub of wet washing awkwardly. He was not used to heavy work. He set the tub down twice before he reached the clothesline. Maude thanked him.

"You are much too delicate of stature, Miss Richmond, to carry such a burden. You must call me whenever you feel yourself unable to accomplish such a heavy task. I'm quite willing to be of service to you." Eben smiled, crookedly, warmly.

Too eager, Maude thought, and pitied him for it.

"I rather doubt you'd much appreciate it if I called you away when you are in the middle of conjugating Latin verbs, Mr. Wheeldon."

"Why, no. I was referring, of course, to those times when I am here."

"The only time you are here, Mr. Wheeldon, is after the heavy work is done. Why aren't you at the schoolhouse?"

"I called a recess and left one of the older boys in charge for a few moments while I called on you."

Maude tipped her face up close to Eben's and smiled as sweetly as she knew how.

"Oh," she said, "there's another tub inside, Mr. Wheeldon. I'd be so obliged if you would carry it out." Eben's face registered mild surprise, but he did as he was asked. He breathed a bit heavily as he sat the second tub down, coughed discreetly into his handkerchief, and wiped his brow.

Eben's clothes, Maude observed with distaste, needed washing. His jacket was threadbare at the elbows, his pantaloons bagged at the knees. His boots were nearly worn out and sadly scuffed.

"I was wondering, Miss Richmond, if you plan to attend the gathering at the Severance place?" Eben's eyes were hopeful. For a moment Maude thought he was about to declare himself. She hoped he wouldn't. Even though there was so little about him to admire, she preferred not to have to decline a proposal and hurt his feelings. Certainly, Eben was intelligent and well read, qualities Maude admired in a man, but there was something about Eben's humility, his cringing deference to everyone that put her off. And worse, he craved pity. Once, at a dinner table filled with a sympathetic audience, he had confided that he'd been disappointed in a matter of the heart. He had pledged never to offer his affections to anyone again. He spoke with an odd vulnerability that clung to him like burdocks. This quality had, thus far, enabled Maude to treat him kindly, if not seriously. Unfortunately, she had discovered that while Eben was not inclined to pledge his heart, he was more than willing to wear it on his sleeve.

Maude hesitated before she answered his question, wanting to phrase it in a way that would let her off the hook if Eben forgot himself.

"If Mrs. Robinson and I are not called away, I believe we will attend for short while."

"Then would you deem it an impertinence if I asked you to partner me in a reel?"

"Impertinent of you, Mr. Wheeldon? Why certainly not. But you surely understand that I am in a position where I must look after my reputation. People will talk. Might I suggest, sir, that you dance a few times with Betsy first. That should still any wagging tongues, don't you think?"

"I assure you, Miss Richmond, that I will do my utmost to preserve the honor of your name. How very clever of you to suggest it. Betsy is a dear child. Poor silent creature. I consider it my duty to see that she has a bit of fun."

Maude had seen Betsy's eyes follow Eben. She had noted how Betsy saw to it that the tenderest chicken leg, the largest portions of pudding fell on Eben's plate. She had seen the quiet look of compassion on Betsy's face whenever Eben recited his oft told story of his "disappointment."

"How very kind of you, Mr. Wheeldon. I will put you at the top of my list. And Mr. Wheeldon, as a special kindness to me, would you carry an armful of wood to the kitchen? Good day."

Maude bent to retrieve the empty tubs. Sally came around the corner of the wash house.

"What in the world has got into Eben Wheeldon? He looks like the cat that got the cream," Sally said as she eyed Maude curiously, a hint of laughter in her voice.

"I promised to dance with him tomorrow at the Severances'."

"Don't count on being at the gathering too long. Mr. Stone spoke to me about his wife today. She is nearing her time. And the Fowler children have the quinsy. You've finished, I see. Well, no time to waste. The kitchen needs scrubbing." Sally headed for the house. Her skirts flapped busily in the breeze. Maude sighed and trailed along behind.

9.

Maude's mouth watered. Baked beans, bread, stew, pickles, jellies, and an assortment of cakes and puddings crowded the tables set up just inside the door of the Severances' barn. Everyone had brought something to contribute to the supper. Maude brought gingerbread. Sally brought apple-sauce.

The barn was dim even with sunlight streaming through the open doors. The loft was full of hay. It had been a good year for hay. Leather harnesses hung from wooden pegs. A cow mooed in a stall. Several chickens pecked around the hay strewn over the hard dirt floor.

Mothers left their infants on a pile of hay provided for that purpose, and older children were assigned to mind the smaller ones.

The hard work of harvest was nearly done and

conviviality was the order of the day. An easy buzz of talk filled the barn. Two fiddlers tuned their violins with the tentative scrape of bows on strings. They launched into a lively jig. Couples formed for the first reel.

A good many demijohns of hard cider began to be handed around. The squeak of cork stopples pulled from bottle necks punctuated the rolling strains of music. Maude tapped her foot to the music. She tucked her unlovely hands into the folds of her dark blue, white-figured dress.

Most of the menfolk had adopted the shorter hair cuts made popular by the poet Lord Byron. Some of the elderly gentlemen still wore their hair long, in a queue tied with a black grosgrain ribbon. These men wore knee britches in the old style. The younger men wore the newer-fashioned pantaloons which extended all the way to the ankle. The ladies wore their best gowns of muslin, linen, or wool. The sleeves were wide and skirts were full. The waistline had dropped from just under the breasts to its natural place. Aprons had been left at home. Married women wore ruffled white caps tied under their chins. Unmarried women went bareheaded.

Sally put the food she and Maude had brought on a table.

"Where is Betsy, Maude? I haven't seen her since we got here. Perhaps I shouldn't have let her come on ahead of us," Sally said. She searched the barn's dim interior with her eyes. A note of impatience girdled her voice. Sally liked to keep track of the people entrusted to her care.

"She's dancing, Mrs. Robinson," Maude said, pointing to the center of the barn floor.

Sally, handsome in a dark red wool gown, maneuvered for a better look.

"Dancing? Betsy never dances. There's not a lad on the river that's ever looked twice at her. I was beginning to think she might never have a chance. Who is she dancing with?"

"Eben Wheeldon."

Sally's eyebrows rose in surprised arches. She fixed Maude with a bland stare. "Matchmaking are you, Miss?"

"No, not entirely. I fear Mr. Wheeldon has formed an attachment for me. I do not share it. I hoped to divert him by suggesting he dance with Betsy. She admires him very much."

"Yes, I know. Betsy doesn't speak, but her eyes do. I've seen her watch Eben. She's eighteen. Time for her to start a family of her own. She could do worse than Eben Wheeldon. He's steady enough for all his affected ways."

Betsy's yellow skirt flew and flashed around her ankles. She skipped and swayed through the figures of the dance, face alight with a radiant smile. Eben smiled too, making his plain face more appealing. His jacket, the one he always wore, was brushed and cleaner than Maude had ever seen it. He steered Betsy competently through the dance.

A man in knee breeches came up to Sally. He offered her his elbow. They joined the dance.

People milled about the barn like moths in bright light. Maude stood a little apart and watched. She was not, by nature, a joiner. Observation was as natural to her as breathing. She thought how women's labor had provided the food on the table, and how man's labor had provided the ingredients that went into the food. Why was it, she wondered, that only women cooked and only men planted?

Eben came to claim his dance with Maude. It was, to Maude's dismay, a round dance. It required a great deal of arms around the waist and clasped hands. Eben handled Maude as if she were made of glass. His manners were rigidly correct, but he took every opportunity to press her against his side. He murmured how delightful she danced, how very handsome her dress was. By the end of the last figure, Maude felt as if she'd been mapped, surveyed, and fenced in.

"Perhaps another, Miss Richmond, after you've rested a bit," Eben suggested eagerly. He clung tightly to Maude's hand. She had difficulty drawing it away.

"I'm very fatigued, Mr. Wheeldon. Perhaps you could engage someone else. Betsy is sitting alone. I know she admires your dancing very much."

"Is that so? I never thought of Betsy admiring . . ." Eben said. He paused before he went on. "But you said yourself, Miss Richmond, that one mustn't dance too often with the same person. Talk, you know. I will sit here with you while you get your breath. Speaking of talk, now there's talk for you." Eben inclined his head toward a man dressed in a sober shade of gray. "Edmond Damon. The man-midwife. Delicacy forbids me to say more. I dare say Mrs. Robinson is none too pleased to see him here. I hear he's been called by several women who usually call her. Even Mrs. Severance, I have been given to understand, has lately made use of his service."

Maude stared openly at Edmond Damon. After all she'd heard about men-midwives from Eli and Sally, she expected he would have horns and a forked tail. Instead, Damon was handsome. His eyes were as dark as his curly hair and he carried himself with an assured air. He was the center of attention in a group of giggling young women, none yet married.

Sally strayed across Maude's line of sight, blocking her view of Damon. Sally made beckoning gestures.

"Excuse me, Mr. Wheeldon. Mrs. Robinson is looking for me." As Maude rose to leave, Edmund Damon fastened his dark eyes on her. His glance held her for an instant. She found no warmth, no friendliness in his look. It was like gazing into a frozen pond and seeing no depth. She tripped on the hem of her gown. Eben sprang to her assistance. She shook him off, nettled.

Something about Edmund Damon irritated Maude. She did not know what it was, and it was unreasonable. She made her way to Sally's side.

"I've been called to see a woman by the name of Mollie Smith. She's bad off, I'm told. We must leave now," Sally said.

Maude and Sally made their excuses to Mrs. Severance. Maude was not sorry to leave. She had had about all she wanted of Eben Wheeldon.

There was no time to go home to change into rayles. Maude did not fret about the possibility of her best gown being ruined. She had long since resigned herself to the fact that as long as she tended the sick, her clothing would get soiled with sweat, vomit, urine, and every other bodily fluid imaginable.

It wasn't much more than two miles to the edge of the village where Sally had been told she would find the Smith woman.

The village road wound up and down several steep hills then veered away from the river. The leaves splashed the day with crimson and gold. It was warm for October. Maude slung her gray knitted shawl over one shoulder. Every so often she ran a step or two in order to keep up with Sally's longer strides.

They spoke of some of the lying-in cases they

had recently attended. Sally did not mention Edmund Damon, but Maude broached the subject.

"Eben Wheeldon says there was a man-midwife at the gathering, that he has been in town for several weeks."

Sally kept eyes fixed on the road unfolding before them. A shadow of annoyance sharpened her face.

"Edmund Damon will not be around for long. He will stay just long enough to line his pockets. Then he will head for greener pastures. I've seen his like before. He already has been called to two women who have died from childbed fever." Sally's voice was hard. Childbed fever was the most frequent cause of death to birthing women. Sally's cases rarely contracted the deadly disease. "Two infants he delivered were stillborn. Damon has put it about that others would have died, too, if he hadn't had his forceps to fall back on."

Sally's steps were like small attacks on the road. Dust clung to the hem of her gown. She adjusted the pocket tied at her waist. The pocket contained a few packets of powdered herbs, scissors, a thimble, needles and thread, and a small Testament in case it was necessary to read prayers for the dying.

Maude knit her eyebrows together. What Sally had said troubled her.

"Why do women call a man-midwife if his methods are dangerous?" she asked.

"Some still owe me my fee from the last time I attended them and are embarrassed to call me again. Some just want the rest of the town to know they can afford the man midwife. Some think that because his fees are superior, he possesses superior skills." Sally strode on, then stopped. "Maude, you already know that every two years, as soon as the last babe is weaned, a married woman will be brought to bed with another infant. She gives birth so often she doesn't have time to forget the pain of the last birth. The man midwife promises his forceps will shorten travail and lessen the birth pangs. Women believe this. They believe the old way is no longer the best way."

"Then why not just leave the business of lying-in to men and be done with it?" Maude asked.

Sally's annoyed expression deepened.

"As women, we have little to say about the events that shape our lives, Maude. We cannot vote. We have no voice in how we are governed. When we marry, everything we have, household goods, the clothes on our backs, even our children cease to be ours and become the husband's property. An abused or deserted wife has no recourse in the courts. She cannot divorce her husband. If she wishes to live apart from him, or is widowed, there are few ways for her to earn an honest living."

"She takes in sewing, teaches school, keeps an inn or keeps house for someone," Maude said. She thought of Mrs. Howard.

"Or she practices the art of midwifery," Sally said. "It is the one proud profession women have possessed for centuries. We are the keepers of the mysteries of birth. That belongs to us. Now it is being stolen from us. I have taken you as my apprentice because I am too old for the battles that must be fought to keep our profession in our hands. My duty is to hand on what I know. It must not die with me. Your task is greater than mine, Maude. You must enlighten others. Men as well as women."

Sally's words settled in Maude's head like homing pigeons, nourishing the seeds that had taken root the day she had helped Sarah John Thatcher come into the world.

Sally's footsteps were no longer attacks on the road. She had spoken her piece and relieved her annoyance.

"We are going to see a young woman whom most brand as one of easy virtue," Sally said after a long silence. "She was compelled to sell herself in the streets in order to live. She has been unfortunate enough to get herself with child. She came here from Bucksport. The constable arrested her several times for lewd conduct there, and she was sent off. Orrington doesn't want her either. She has nowhere else to go."

Mollie Smith's dwelling was little more than a hovel, a place most people would hesitate to house animals in, let alone human beings. The roof sagged. The bare boards had weathered to a dull gray. The walls were full of cracks. The windows had no glass. The yard was littered with rusty barrel hoops, rotten staves, a dead chicken, and an old dilapidated trunk. Shards of glass and pottery glittered fiercely in the sun.

Sally and Maude picked their way through the mess to the door, which did not close properly. The floor inside the shack was an uneven mass of hard-packed dirt. There was no fireplace, no well, no comforts or conveniences of any kind. It was the worst place Maude had ever been in.

Mollie Smith lay on a heap of moldy straw covered with a tattered blanket. Her filthy hair hung loose and matted around her face. Her fine-featured face might once have been pretty, but a life of want and hardship had erased whatever beauty she might once have enjoyed. She was, Maude thought, in her twenties. She was big with a child.

"If I ever lay my hands on the bastid who did this to me, I'll knock 'is rotten teeth clear down his filthy throat!" Mollie screamed.

Maude wadded her shawl into a ball and placed it under Mollie's head.

"Simmer down, Miss Smith," Sally said. "Wages of sin are paid in coins of travail, but we are here to help you." She spoke matter-of-factly, and unfluttered.

"Wages of sin my arse. That swine swore we was gon'ta be married."

"How long have you been in travail?" Sally asked. She knelt on the damp floor beside Mollie.

"All night long and all day and I ain't never hurt so hellish bad in all my borned days. The rotten bastid!" Mollie writhed and thrashed. Her face contorted with pain. Maude laid a hand on Mollie's arm. When the pain eased, Mollie lay spent and sweating. The anger had gone out of her.

"That's right, Miss Smith, you just lie there quietly while Mrs. Robinson makes an examination," Maude said soothingly. Fire flashed in Mollie's eyes, seeking a target.

"Who the hell are you to be tellin' me what to do, Miss Priss that butter wouldn't melt in yer mouth? No bastid ever got you knocked up and left yer to fend for yourself, did they?"

Maude ignored Mollie's harsh words. She stroked Mollie's arm slowly.

"Anchor yourself, Miss Smith," Sally said. "We sympathize with your difficulty. We are here to help you. But we cannot if you don't allow us to."

Sally arranged Mollie's knees up so she could

make a visual examination. Midwives did not make internal examinations. Another pain clamped across Mollie's belly. Sally held her hands on Mollie's abdomen to feel the strength of the contraction and assess the position of the infant.

"The child ought to be farther down in the pelvis by this time," Sally said to Maude. Her eyes were troubled.

Mollie's lower lip trembled. "I'm gon'ta die, ain't I?" She was very calm.

"Death is in God's hands, Mollie," Sally said. "Birth is in mine. You can't stay here. I will take you to my house. Maude, go back to the Severances' and borrow a wagon. Don't be long."

10.

Mollie Smith's travail went on for two more days. It was Maude's first encounter with a complicated birth. Nothing had prepared her for the ordeal. She had seen people die. She had sat with the dying, prayed with them, eased their last moments. That had been easy compared to Mollie's suffering.

The household crept through its normal functions, its pace slowed by the abnormal hours Maude and Sally kept. Maude did not sleep more than an hour at a time. Fatigue dulled her senses.

Mollie's screams subsided into strangled gasps

for breath. There was no place in the house that did not harbor the excruciating hiss of air escaping reluctantly from lungs too weak to empty themselves. Maude thought of an animal in the hands of an inexpert slaughterer and shuddered. She wanted to lash out. She wanted to break something.

Maude went to the kitchen to fetch some broth. Eben and Betsy sat at the table peeling apples.

"It's God's will. It's his punishment for sinful ways," Eben said. He alluded to the fact that Mollie was a fallen woman. Maude felt the black presence of her anger engulf her. Frayed nerves, lack of sleep, the utter helplessness of the situation floated upward from a hidden core of her heart. It ignited and exploded in Eben's face.

"God's will? That women should suffer the tortures of the damned to do his bidding? To be fruitful and multiply? All women risk this savagery, Mr. Wheeldon. Not just the fallen. Praise God you were disappointed in love, sir, that no woman will ever suffer to bear your seed!"

The imminence of Mollie's death chilled the air. It soured the regard Eben had for Maude. His face went white, then crimson. He set down the paring knife. His hands balled into fists.

Betsy's eyes melted into an eloquent message of sympathy. Eben turned instinctively to her for comfort.

Maude poured broth into an invalid feeder and went back to the small chamber where Mollie lay.

The chamber jutted out from the main part of the house tucked behind the parlor. Plain white curtains lay across the only window. The bed was narrow, set on blocks of wood to make it high enough to spare Sally's back from too much bending. Mollie's face was like wax. Her hands rested across her belly. She did not move, her eyes were closed.

Strangled breathing lacerated the air. Sally knelt near the window. She read aloud from the small Testament she always carried with her. Her face was tense and haggard from lack of sleep. She was not wearing a cap. Her hair, mostly gray, was braided and bound around her head.

"I sent for Dr. Livermore," Sally said tiredly. She had discussed this possibility with Maude earlier that morning. In difficult cases, it was Sally's practice to send for someone whose skill was greater than her own. "I've told him to bring his crochets."

The crochet was an instrument used to dismember an unborn infant and thereby empty the womb. It was a drastic measure and used only when the life of the mother was despaired of and the chances of survival for the infant were nil.

Maude's courage faded like the leaves that trembled on the maple outside the window. Her knees buckled slightly. She grasped the bed post for support.

"You needn't stay if you don't wish to, Maude," Sally said gently. "It's not a sight anyone ever gets used to. I'll not think less of you."

Maude tipped her head back and took a deep breath. She swallowed hard. She shook her head firmly. "No. I'm a midwife. I'll stay."

Maude knelt on the bare pine floor beside Sally. Her gown cushioned her knees. She felt numb and cold. She could not say the usual prayers. Anger lay heavy as a granite stone around her heart. She had seen death before, young and old alike. Death was as much a part of everyday life as birth. She knit her fingers together tightly. Her knuckles turned white. Please God, she prayed. Nothing else followed. It became a litany. Please God, please God, over and over. The prayer washed over the stony place in her heart and gave no relief. There was no change in Mollie. Her life continued to batter itself away like a bird flown against a window pane.

Dr. Livermore arrived, did his work, and left. Shortly after, with an almost inaudible sigh, like air eased from a bellows, it was over. The house grew unreasonably quiet. The room felt suddenly empty.

Maude reached for the looking glass and held it to Mollie's lips. No vapor clouded it. She reached for the record book Sally had taught her to keep. She wrote: Died this day, Oct 19, 1818, Mollie Smith of South Orrington, 10 morn, in childbed.

Anger clenched Maude's hand around the pen, but it was steady as she wrote. She burned with a glassy heat. It suffused her with a deadly calm. A vicious voice whispered inside her head. It said, only women become victims of the act of love.

Maude had never encountered such an alien idea. It stunned her to think it emanated from her own mind. Mollie Smith had known and accepted it. Sally understood it, too, spent her life confronting the consequences of what the act of love did to women. Women who partook of the pleasures of the flesh risked the tortures of childbirth. All women. Not just fallen women. All women old enough to bear children.

Edmund Damon snaked into Maude's thoughts. Was he privy to this knowledge? Could he have helped Mollie with his forceps, with his secret method, a method unknown to midwives? Would Mollie have died anyway, if not during this lying-in, then in a subsequent one? Did Edmund Damon ever think how the act of love made women its victims? The questions rolled and thundered.

Sally touched Maude's shoulder. Her hand was a reminder that life does not stop. Together, they combed Mollie's hair and tied a blue ribbon in it. They washed her body and dressed her in grave clothes. They arranged her hands in a loose clasp on her chest. They performed the final acts of kindness one woman can do for another.

Maude spent the five dollars Eli had given her on a marking stone for Mollie.

Autumn turned to winter with a bold slice of deeply cold wind. Snow drifted and nearly covered Mollie's marking stone. Her death receded in Maude's memory, but it did not disappear. The heavy weight of anger settled at the core of her being. She carried it close to her heart like a precious gem. It gave her eyes a flinty look. It sharpened the edge of her tongue.

Eben Wheeldon kept his distance. He spent more time with Betsy. At the end of December, he asked for Betsy's hand. They were married at the New Year.

If Sally noticed any change in Maude, she kept it to herself.

In February, a call came from Mrs. Jones. Her fifth child was about to be born. Her previous deliveries had been easy and uncomplicated. Sally told Maude to go, that she was skilled enough for the simple birth Mrs. Jones would present. The specter of Mollie's death formed and troubled Maude for a moment, but her confidence in her own growing skill was stronger. Sally had other cases to see and Maude rode off into the rolling hills of Orrington.

The weather had turned bitterly cold. Maude

rode Sally's gray mare along a snow-packed road near Swett's Pond. She scanned the horizon. A thick pall of dull gray clouds covered the sky. The wind was from the northeast. She knew from the signs that a bad storm was brewing.

Maude rode as far as Mr. Flood's, the Jones' nearest neighbor. She left the mare at his farm. He took her as far as the road that led to the Jones' place. Mr. Jones met them and conducted Maude the last several miles. Snow began to fall heavily.

Mr. Jones left to take his children to their grandmother, saying he would fetch Mrs. Jones' women on the way back.

Mrs. Jones had taken to her bed. She complained that her travail was somehow different than her other births. A small flutter of anxiety twitched at Maude. It gave way as Mrs. Jones pronounced herself perfectly comfortable.

Several hours after Mr. Jones left, a knock came at the door. Edmund Damon stood on the step. Snow covered his hat and shoulders. He was huddled into a heavy black cloak.

"You got here first, I see," Edmund said. He sounded disappointed.

Maude was not surprised to see him. It was the custom for the husband of a lying-in woman to summon three or four midwives at once. The theory was that one out of four would be sure to arrive in time. Every so often, everyone summoned arrived. The case belonged to whoever arrived first.

"Come in," Maude said.

"No need to look so stern. I will be on my way as soon as I dry out a little," Edmund said.

Maude stirred the fire in the kitchen. She added another stick of wood. This gave her time to observe Edmund Damon, to think what she would say to him. She did not like him. She faulted herself for that feeling. She didn't really know very much about him except for what the village grapevine divulged. She had heard that he was most apprehensive of the modesty of his cases. He conducted his examinations by touch alone. He never allowed his eyes to leave those of his patient, thus assuring her that he would not view her private parts and infringe on her delicate sensibilities. Women who had been delivered by Damon swore they would never have anyone else. Others declared they would never let him come near again. There were several disgruntled husbands who did not like the idea of a strange man, midwife or not, touching their wives' bodies.

Maude didn't know what to think. She only knew that being in the same room with him made her uncomfortable.

"The storm has worsened," Maude said politely. She felt small and inept in Edmond's presence. He was very tall and seemed very sure of his right to be there.

"It's a bad one. I don't dare to stay too long. The drifts are a foot deep in some places already. If this keeps up all night, we'll have two feet of snow by morning."

A nibble of uneasiness bit at Maude. She peered out the window.

"Mr. Jones may not be able to get back here with Mrs. Jones' women."

"I wouldn't think so. I had a hard enough time as it was. Will you need my help?" It was a casual question, implying that Maude was not skilled enough to deliver Mrs. Jones.

Edmund lifted his coattails to let the heat dry the seat of his gray wool pantaloons.

"No," Maude replied quickly, coolly. "Mrs. Jones has an easy time of it. Thank you just the same. Could I fix you a hot drink? Tea, perhaps?"

Edmund smiled politely. "I seem to have forgot my manners. Please permit me to introduce myself . . ."

"I know who you are, Mr. Damon."

"And I know who you are, Miss Richmond." Edmund looked out into the storm and paced uneasily. "By the look of those drifts, I'd better not try to get back to town tonight."

"You are quite welcome to stay until the storm is over, Mr. Damon. I will inform Mrs. Jones."

Maude checked on Mrs. Jones' progress, was dissatisfied with it and didn't know precisely why. Mrs. Jones was certain she was having bearing down pains and wanted relief. Maude returned to the kitchen to prepare an infusion of willow bark. Willow bark eased the discomfort of many kinds of pain, including childbirth.

Edmund had removed his cloak. He stood in the reddish light cast by the fire. Evening was drawing in.

"Will Mrs. Robinson have fits when she discovers her prize pupil is in the company of the terrible man midwife?" Edmund's tone was teasing. He, too, partook of the fruits of the village grapevine.

Maude bristled. She was in no mood for teasing. She plunged the willow bark into a mug of hot water and let it steep, like tea.

"Mrs. Robinson is not given to having fits about anything, Mr. Damon. She believes her opinion of you is well founded." Maude took care to speak calmly.

"Local gossip, Miss Richmond, is not the way to form an opinion of one's character or skill."

Little ripples of anger cut across Maude's tongue.

"But it is your cases who die rather steadily, Mr. Damon. Not Mrs. Robinson's."

Edmund's eyes narrowed and grew darker, almost black. His full lips tightened.

"It's no fault of mine if I am not called soon

enough. The Smith woman might have lived had Mrs. Robinson had sense enough to call me at the first sign of trouble."

Anger rumbled in Maude's breast and swelled to huge proportions.

"You are too self-satisfied, sir! You could have done nothing. The Smith woman's child was crosswise and could not be born."

But even in the indignation of her disavowal, the question haunted Maude. It stuck like a burr to a wool stocking. The more she picked at it to make it go away, the more deeply it matted into the fibers of her thoughts. Could Edmund Damon have helped?

Edmund sat down on the settle with his wet feet to the fire. His expression was sullen.

"The storm is much worse. We will be here for days," he complained, ignoring Maude's last remark.

"Mr. Damon, since we are obliged to remain under the same roof until the storm passes, can't we call a truce? Mrs. Jones' time is very near. If you would be so kind to bring some wood and set another kettle to boil . . ."

Edmund rose and made a mocking salute, as if Maude were a general in charge of troops.

"Yes, ma'am," he said. Maude let it pass.

When Edmund returned with an armful of wood, Maude was scrubbing her hands. She wiped them on a linen towel. She dropped her scissors and a length of fine cord into a pot hanging from a crane over the fire.

Edmund put the wood into the wood box with icy clattering. He watched Maude prepare for Mrs. Jones' delivery.

"What are you doing?" he asked.

"Cleanliness, Mr. Damon, is next to Godliness," Maude replied tersely.

"I'm serious, Miss Richmond. I've never seen anyone scrape the skin off their hands or make soup out of twine and scissors as a means of preparing to attend a birth."

"My father is a physician, Mr. Damon. He taught me that infection is spread by contact with unclean things. He, and Mrs. Robinson, believe cleanliness helps prevent childbed fever. We boil everything that may touch the mother and babe."

Maude put another stick of wood on the fire.

Edmund peered into the pot. Skepticism played across his face.

"There was a lot of talk about the connection between unwashed instruments and the spread of disease when I studied in England. Quite a controversy. No one took it too seriously. Waste of time, most thought. I tend to agree."

Maude tied on a clean apron.

"But it is your cases that take childbed fever, Mr. Damon. Not Mrs. Robinson's."

Maude returned to Mrs. Jones' chamber. She

knew immediately, instinctively, something was amiss. The infant's head did not present itself in the usual way. She thought she saw a tiny elbow squashed to the infant's head. She tried to manipulate it into a better position as Sally had taught her to do. It did not help.

For a split second, Maude gave in to panic. She was wrong in her assessment, she told herself. She watched a few more contractions. Nothing changed. The child was lodged in the birth canal as tightly as a cork stopple in last year's vinegar jug.

Outside, the fury of the storm increased. It beat about the corners of the house. There was no hope of sending for Sally or anyone else. There was no one to turn to for help except Edmund Damon.

Maude weighed the idea in her mind. A sound similar to the dying breaths of Mollie Smith oozed into the chamber. It was the wind moaning in the evergreens beside the house. Anger hummed its jagged tune in Maude's heart.

Maude found Edmund dozing by the fire. He had spread his cloak over him to keep out the drafts. The fire had burned down to embers. Maude stirred it and laid more wood on. The sound, as she had hoped, disturbed Edmund and he woke with a start.

"Mrs. Jones is in difficulty. I need your help."

Edmund got to his feet. He flung his cloak aside.

"Are you sure?" he demanded.

"Yes. I'm sure. I've tried manipulation. It didn't help. You will need the forceps." Maude hated to say the last word. But the lash of her anger would not allow her to abandon Mrs. Jones to a fate similar to Mollie Smith's. Edmund reached for his medicine box. He drew out a cloth bag about as long as a man's forearm.

"I assume, Miss Richmond, that you are handing this case over to me." Edmund started for Mrs. Jones' chamber.

"No, sir, I am not," Maude said firmly.

Edmund stopped in his tracks. He fixed his hard, dark eyes on Maude. The logs hissed and crackled. For a moment, Maude thought he would refuse to help.

"A third of the fee goes to me," he said coldly.

"A half, Mr. Damon, if you boil the instrument and scrub your hands." If he refused her demand, Maude was prepared to capitulate and give up the entire fee.

"Now that's a bargain I can't refuse."

Edmund drew the forceps out of the cloth bag. The instrument consisted of two large spoons of metal with wooden handles. There was a slot on one and a button on the other so they could be joined together once they had been inserted into the birth canal. The spoons cupped the infant's head to draw it out. He dropped the instrument into the pot. He took some soap and washed his hands.

By midnight they had finished their work. Maude sat in a straight chair near Mrs. Jones. Edmond sat further away by the chamber door. Except for the application of the forceps and the successful extraction of the infant, Maude had stayed in charge.

She was amazed at how the forceps had eased the birth. But she was equally dismayed by the bruises left on the child's head and the tearing it had caused Mrs. Jones' body. Maude had stitched the tears and soothed Mrs. Jones. She had dressed the infant.

Now had come the time for watching. If Mrs. Jones' condition was to become dangerous and decline into childbed fever, signs would appear before morning.

Mrs. Jones and her infant son slept peacefully. The silence between Maude and Edmund stretched out, cat-like, in the chamber.

Maude folded her red hands in her lap. She tried to sort out the impressions she had received as Edmund Damon wielded the forceps. She had seen, she was convinced, how midwifing would change, for good and for ill. Forceps could be an ally. They had saved the lives of Mrs. Jones and her infant. In order to win the battle to keep midwifery in the hands of women, Maude knew she must learn the new methods or be broken by them.

But forceps were also an enemy. For births that progressed normally, as most did, forceps inflicted more hurt than help. Their indiscriminate use by man midwives overpowered the patient skills of female midwives.

The dilemma, as Maude now understood it, was how to resolve those two points of view. She was certain Edmund Damon, and others like him, would use the instrument in every case, needed or not. She was equally certain that if female midwives learned to use forceps only when it was necessary, they would become more skilled in their work. Lives would be saved. Needless suffering would be averted.

Midwifing, she saw, would change as all things changed. If she did not recognize those changes as they happened, and adapt to them, Sally's prophecy of the demise of female midwives would surely fulfill itself.

Maude made up her mind. She would learn the proper use of forceps. She would ask Eli.

Maude glanced at Edmund Damon. He sat easily with one leg crossed over the other. His dark wavy hair fluffed around his ears. He had made no attempt to ease Mrs. Jones' fears as he applied the forceps. He had laid no understanding hand on hers. It had been the same when Dr. Livermore had come to do his grisly business to Mollie Smith. Even Eli, as kind and caring as he was, left those things to women. That was woman's work.

Edmund caught Maude's glance and smiled. Maude felt no attraction toward him. She did not return his smile.

Mrs. Jones slept quietly. No symptoms of fever troubled her.

The storm raged through the night. Its clamoring was a suitable accompaniment for Maude's thoughts. She stared at her hands as if seeing them for the first time. They were red and ugly from doing useful work. Women's work. They scrubbed and dug and soothed. Sometimes they closed lids on coffins and dressed motherless infants all in the same hour. They were not like the merely functional, mechanical hands of Edmond Damon.

Maude remembered how she had changed Mollie Smith's bedgown as it became soiled with blood and sweat and excrement. She had rubbed Mollie's back for hours. She had even sung to her when nothing else would ease her. These were the things women did for other women because they too had been, or would be, baptized by the blood of childbirth.

Maude turned her palms upward. Her hands were as raw as her heart. For the first time since Mollie's death, tears escaped the citadel of her anger. The granite stones in her throat dissolved and slid away into the blackness of the storm.

11.

When the storm finally blew itself out, the deep drifts held the house in a muffled grip. The wind lifted snow in soft feathery swirls in the fields beyond.

Edmund Damon tended the animals in the barn. He found a pair of snowshoes and set off for town. Mrs. Jones awoke refreshed, with no signs of fever. By evening Mr. Jones returned with Mr. Flood in the sleigh, who conducted Maude safely back to Mrs. Robinson's.

Sally sat in the kitchen, puffed her pipe, and heard Maude's story with her usual calm gravity. The wisdom of her years of experience as a midwife was deep in her eyes.

"Female midwives are barred from receiving training in medicine. We are barred from buying forceps. Those conditions are centuries old, Maude. Some things do not change. Learn to trust your hands. They are your instruments," Sally said. She remained convinced that Edmund Damon and the changes he represented must be avoided. Female midwives, she believed, did not need forceps.

It did not long remain a point of contention between them. In the spring Damon married one of the Brewer girls. They went to Ohio to settle. Eben and Betsy Wheeldon, along with others from the Penobscot region, soon followed.

But for weeks, Maude turned the events at Mrs. Jones' over in her mind. Sally's way of midwifery was centuries old. It was shaped by a tradition of women helping women. It was viewed as an art. Damon's way was new. It was science, the product of a male mind which saw women as mere vessels of birth, a container to be emptied in the most expedient manner possible.

Damon's way, Maude reasoned, inflicted hurt as easily as it gave help. Sally's way also had its drawbacks. When a midwife exhausted her skills, death was the inevitable result. Death, in turn, inflicted a greater hurt. It produced motherless children. The depth of that hurt could not be measured in the size of the bruises on an infant's head or the number of stitches required to close the loin.

Maude walked to the burying ground. It was late March. The sun held a new warmth. She threw back the hood of her dark green cloak. She broke off a bunch of pussy willows, waded through an old drift, and placed them on Mollie Smith's grave.

Maude's anger was gone. It had been replaced by a growing conviction that what Edmund Damon knew, she must learn in order to augment Sally's teachings.

Mollie Smith's life had not been saved because there was nothing else to try. Mrs. Jones' life had been saved because there *was* a new way to try.

The earth was just beginning to tilt its warmth into the season. All around the burying ground were stirrings of new beginnings. It was spring. It was time for sending up new shoots.

Maude walked back to Sally's. She wrote to Eli and asked him to visit her.

Eli arrived the very next week. The roads had broken up, and in some places mud was as deep as a horse's fetlocks. Icy water ran in the ditches in wide, rapid rivulets. Trees hadn't yet budded out. A hazy shadow of palest yellow edged the hillsides. Orrington looked raw and poor. On the north sides of buildings, patches of rotten snow waited for warmer days.

Maude and Eli sat together in the parlor, even though Eli preferred the cozy order of Sally's kitchen. The parlor was used only on important occasions—when the minister came to call, or after weddings and funerals.

Eli looked very fit. He was clear of eye, strong of wind and limb, full of his usual energy. His boots were spattered with mud and a button was missing on his jacket. It was a new jacket of heavy navy blue wool.

Maude's little girl feelings of safety and security settled over her as comfortably as the red shawl wrapped around her shoulders. She had tied a white muslin apron over her old brown gown.

The fire snapped cozily. The room was bright from the light spilling in through the three windows. It was a corner room at the front of the house. It was pleasant despite an arctic nip that still sliced the April weather.

"Won't be long before it will be fiddleheading time," Eli remarked. He greatly relished the tender fiddlehead ferns. He liked to gather them just as they poked their tightly rolled heads through the cool spring earth. Everyone ate them as a tonic after the long winter of dried fruits and smoked meats.

"I don't want to talk about fiddleheads, or make polite conversation," Maude said. She fussed with the fringe on her shawl.

"I gathered from your letter," Eli said, "that you want to talk about forceps." He shifted in his chair near the hearth.

"Yes," Maude said. She rose from the wing chair and paced the floor impatiently. When she had things on her mind, she couldn't settle. She wrapped her arms more closely in the shawl and hugged them to her chest.

"Forceps were invented by Peter Chamberlen in England in the early seventeenth century. If used improperly, by anyone, they can tear the mother's body, or cause fatal hemorrhage. They can crush the infant's head. There are no laws or regulations, that I know of, to govern their use. In my opinion, there is no safe way to use them."

114

"Papa, after what I saw at Mrs. Jones' I'm convinced I must learn how to use them."

"That's a pretty tall order, Maude. I don't know of anyone who would teach you how, even if you could afford to buy a pair. And you need a lot of strength to use forceps. It takes a very strong arm. You know, Maude, physicians have come to believe that they should have a share in the midwife's profession. Forceps get them that share. It's a bad business for everyone. I don't like it and I have stayed away from it. I think you should, too."

"I know, Papa. I know how you feel. But Mrs. Jones would have died if Edmund Damon had not been there."

"Perhaps not, my dear. You are still inexperienced. Mrs. Robinson might have delivered Mrs. Jones without any difficulty whatsoever."

"I know, Papa. But there are other things that troubled me about this. Edmund Damon is not the last man midwife who will come here. You said yourself that physicians are now trained to use forceps. They have an advantage that I do not. How can I ever compete with them? And if I can't, if fewer and fewer women call midwives, if midwifery is a dying art, then there is no point in continuing my apprenticeship."

Maude paused by the hearth. She poked the fire with vicious thrusts of the poker. A shower of sparks flew up the chimney.

Eli balanced his fingertips together. His face was thoughtful.

"What you are learning from Mrs. Robinson goes beyond knowing the signs and symptoms of travail, Maude. Women understand the workings of the internal mysteries of one another better than men do. There's an instinct, a natural empathy, a complicity of feeling men don't know how to employ. Only women know how to give this to one another. It makes the pangs of childbirth endurable. Without you, and others like you, to carry on the art, it will die out all the sooner. Perhaps be lost forever. And womankind will be the worse for it. Perhaps, Maude, you have been chosen. Have a little faith."

"I understand, Papa. I don't want to abandon what is good and right in Mrs. Robinson's teaching. Neither do I want to stand by and watch midwifery die from a lack of new ideas. Or because it fails to adapt to a new idea. It seems to me, Papa, there has to be a meeting of the two philosophies of thought. The use of forceps already has changed the art of midwifery. If I do not adapt to that change, I will be broken by the weight of it. I must learn to use forceps. Will you help me find a way to do that?"

Eli shifted uneasily in his chair. He opened his mouth to speak. He closed it again. He reached for Maude's hand to stay her restless pacing.

"I have complete faith that you intend to use forceps only when all other measures fail, Maude. Make no mistake about that. But first you must be certain that all other measures have failed. It takes longer than six months to learn that. So my answer to your question for now is no. We will discuss the matter again when you leave Mrs. Robinson's teaching."

Maude agreed without any reluctance. She was not disappointed with Eli's answer. She had expected as much. He would think on it. They would talk again.

Eli had other news. Mrs. Howard missed Maude so much that half the time she still set another place at the table. She had had a bad bout with rheumatism, and Eli had hired Mary Thatcher's oldest girl to help with the heavier housekeeping chores. Sarah John was often at the house, too. Mrs. Thatcher's husband had had more ill luck and their finances were very poor. They were talking about Ohio. There was a good possibility they would leave Sarah John behind with Eli and Mrs. Howard. It had not yet been settled. He would let Maude know.

Eli recited other news—who had died, had married, or given birth. Old Hatevil Colson had disappeared and was thought to have drowned in the river. Mrs. Crosby's latest pronouncement condemned those who went to Ohio as disloyal to the United States.

Eli reached inside his jacket and threw out a letter.

"Anne Stinson asked me to carry this to you, my dear. Sprightly little thing she is. Mrs. Howard sent you a supply of pen wipers, a new pincushion and a dozen molasses cookies. And wait until you see what I've brought you."

Eli stepped out of the parlor for a few moments. He returned with a square wooden box. It was finely made with dovetailed joinery. It had brass handles on either side so it could be tied securely to a saddle. It was small enough to be carried easily. Its dark wood was polished to a satin sheen.

"Oh, Papa," Maude said excitedly, "my very own medicine box!"

"Look," Eli said, "there's even a special compartment for your pens and record book." He lifted the lid. Maude exclaimed with delight. Inside, in neatly tied down rows, were a set of various sized pill bottles in the deep cobalt blue Maude admired so much.

"I had Perez Hamlin over in Hampden make it just for you. I took care of a bad wound on his arm and took this in trade as my fee."

"Thank you, Papa. I don't know what else to say," Maude said. She stroked the glossy wood with her fingers.

"The happy look on your face is thanks enough, daughter. It's a rare man who is fortunate enough to have a child such as you."

12.

Maude read Anne Stinson's letter as soon as Eli left.

April 2, 1819
Hampden

Dear Miss Richmond,
It has seemed to me somewhat Ridiculous that we should be separated by a Mere ripple of water and not have had the Pleasure of one another's company since we first met at Mrs. Crosby's. I consulted your father about coming to Call, but he advised Restraint on my Part lest, I suppose, I distract you from your Duties with Mrs. Robinson. Thus I have done as he asked. Do you remember that I told you I had been sent Home from School in Disgrace? Father has smoothed that over Nicely. He is such a dear. But Mother has spent the Winter lecturing on my duties— horrid word—as a Respectable young lady about to be Married. She has led me through the Intricacies of preparing a Trousseau against the day Mr. Crosby

and I are married. I have begged her Constantly to let me have a few Ready-made gowns from Boston, but she insists dressmakers are far too Dear and it is to my Benefit to ply by Needle with Industry, the one Virtue sure to impress old lady Crosby. Since I have bowed to Mother's bidding with as much Grace as I am capable of, she has decided to Reward me with a Quilting party. And it is for this reason that I write. I have set the date for May 2—a bit Distant, to be sure, but given your singular Duties, I thought it Wise to warn you in plenty of Time. We will be a large Party—30 or so—the Gentlemen will join us in the evening. I expect you to remain the Night with me. The Mud should be most dried up by then, don't you think? Do write immediately and say you will join the Party. If you won't I shall call it off as No One there will be nearly so Interesting as yourself. I have told all my Brothers that you will be here and they have agreed to Partner you for every Dance. They are fine dancers.

With sincere Felicitations and Fond Remembrances of our first Meeting, I remain your Friend,

Anne Stinson

Maude received Sally's permission to make the visit and wrote to accept the invitation.

April 4, 1819
So. Orrington

Dear Miss Stinson,

Mrs. Robinson has kindly Agreed to your Proposal for the 2nd of May and I will take Mr. Brazier's ferry across the River, arriving at 10 in the morning of your quilting. There is no need to send a conveyance as my baggage is Small. My hands are in Poor condition for wielding a Needle, but I shall do my Best to be agreeable company. In the meantime, I shall be Diligent in applying the salve my father left for me. I have often thought of our Afternoon with Mrs. Crosby and am delighted at the prospect of enjoying your Company once again.

With sincere Thanks for your Kind invitation, I remain your friend,
Maude Richmond

Anne was waiting when Maude stepped off Mr. Brazier's ferry. Her doll-like face was lit with smiling. She wore a cloak in a soft shade of blue and gloves of soft gray leather. She sat in a handsome little cart behind a dapple gray pony the very color of the ribbons on her smart bonnet. The pony shook his head and nickered softly. His harness jingled. Anne held the reins firmly.

"Call me Anne," she said. Little blonde ringlets danced around her face.

"Call me Maude." Maude pushed back several strands of hair escaping from beneath her red hood. She adjusted her black cape around her shoulders. She set her valise in the cart and climbed up beside Anne.

"Is it true the man midwife left town because of you? I heard it whispered everywhere that you and he got snowed in at Mrs. Jones'. I heard you spent the night there together and he was obliged to leave town so as not to dishonor your good name," Anne said with her customary directness. Her words were bright arrows with no sharpness.

Maude had not heard that particular version of the events concerning Edmund Damon and herself.

"No, it is not true," Maude said firmly.

"I thought not. Pity. I was so hoping for a bit of

good gossip. Nothing scandalous has happened for such a long time."

Anne spoke to the pony. He picked up his feet with slow daintiness and drew the cart up the hill from the ferry slip to the road to the Lower Corner of Hampden. They turned right and rode past the homes of Judge Kinsley, Mr. Patten, and Mr. Emery. They crossed Reed's Brook where the British had come ashore in 1814. They went past the academy where scholars from the surrounding towns ciphered and translated Homer and Virgil from the Greek and Latin.

Presently, they pulled up at a large brick dwelling. This part of town was known as the Upper Corner. The house sat very near the road. A fanlight with graceful leading ornamented the front door. A forsythia bush bloomed by the door.

"Here we are," Anne said. A hired man came to hold the pony as Maude and Anne climbed down from the cart.

"That's where John lives, across the road." Anne pointed to a large three-story frame house with a barn almost as large as the house attached to the rear. "I see John every day. Just like when we were children."

The center hallway of the Stinson house was adorned with white wainscotting. Carpets from England lay on the floors. A staircase rose gracefully in a slender curve to the second story.

Anne and Maude found Mrs. Stinson in the

dining room calmly sorting out the details of arranging Anne's party. She was much like Anne, but in a faded, less spirited way, and dressed in a morning gown of green plaid calico. Her hair was the color of dried weeds, her hands covered by little black lace mitts.

Anne introduced Maude.

"Eli Richmond's girl," Mrs. Stinson said. "So good of you to come, Maude. Anne has not stopped talking of you since she met you. I remember your dear mother, rest her soul. Lydia. She was known for her good works to the poor. Anne, dear, ask the hired girl to put out another tea table in the north parlor. And will two quilting frames in each parlor be enough? That is ample space for sixteen. We could squeeze in one more table and make room for twenty." Mrs. Stinson sorted napkins as she spoke.

"I'll see to it, Mother," Anne said. "You go tend to the cakes and pies."

Mrs. Stinson smiled vaguely and went into the kitchen. Anne took Maude into the room Anne referred to as the library, which contained ceiling-to-floor shelves full of books. They laid their outer garments on a leather chair.

"Your mother is very busy with your party, Anne. How fortunate you are."

"Mother is enjoying this more than I am. I'm the only girl, and the youngest. Mother wants to do this with all the proper fanfare. She won't get to do it again. I'm certainly enjoying all this attention. But I do confess to a certain sense of being taken over and left out of deciding what should be done. Mother says I am altogether too missish and spoiled. Perhaps I will have a fit of the vapors and refuse to appear this evening," Anne said a trifle peevishly. The tenseness in her expression did not blend with the more joyous feelings the party was intended to elicit.

"Please don't," Maude said with mock seriousness. "I left my smelling salts at home. Should I send to my father for an emetic or purgative? Surely, there is some remedy that will restore you to the proper state of excitation."

Anne wrinkled her lovely, straight nose in disgust at the mention of taking medicine.

"What we need is a romp," she said.

Anne took Maude's hand. They ran out into the hallway and up the stairs two at a time. Anne ignored the sound of a torn hem.

"I'll go first," she said. She straddled the banister in a most unladylike way and slid all the way to the bottom. She dismounted just before she came up against the newel post and landed gracefully on her feet, her soft-soled shoes making no noise. The trick obviously was the result of years of practice.

"Your turn, Maude," Anne called up the stairwell. Maude hesitated. There was something desperate in Anne's playfulness. Maude did not quite understand it. She walked slowly back down the steps. She sat down on the lower one.

"Are you always like this?" Maude asked quietly. She sensed conflict in Anne.

Anne ignored the question. She sighed deeply and sat down beside Maude.

"You are much too serious, Maude," she admonished playfully.

"And you, Anne Stinson, are a romp," Maude said.

Anne's good humor bubbled out again. It seemed genuine this time.

"Oh, how true! But once I marry John, I will become properly sedate. I will give birth to a child every two years. I will pour endless cups of tea for the old ladies. I will wear little white caps with ruffles."

Maude sensed something unstated and prickly lurking beneath Anne's words.

"Perhaps you are not yet ready for the duties of marriage," Maude said.

"Oh, of course I am! I admire John so much. I've known him since we were in walking strings. Everyone says how perfectly matched we are. Father has hoped we would marry one day. He always has wanted a connection with the Crosbys. If you can't be one, marry one. That's what he says. John is very good to me. So attentive. And so affectionate." She inserted a sigh into a pause. A line of seriousness appeared in her eyes and remained. "Marriage is for such a long time."

"I've never given it much thought. At least for myself. I want to be a midwife. Not a wife. Papa seems to think I will want a husband someday, though."

"Everyone marries. And women must if they are ever to have a home of their own, something that belongs to them. You could have one of my brothers and live near John and me. We would be sisters. Charles is the handsomest, but Reuben will be the wealthiest. He is already a master mariner and barely twenty. Isaiah is the most fun, but father doesn't think he will amount to much. George is very intelligent but tends to be a bit dull. You will meet them this evening."

Anne stood up. Her odd mood seemed to have disappeared.

"I am looking forward to their company," Maude said.

"Let's go look at your gown. If it is as demure as that one you are wearing, *something* will have to be done!"

13.

The Stinson house overflowed with the light laughter and soft chatter of female voices. Each woman at the quilting had brought a scrap bag. They traded treasured bits of fabric

127

with one another. They shared news of local happenings. While they talked, intricate patterns sprang from their fingers and flowed into the quilts. The day was darned with the invisible filaments of women's work. Every woman in the room manufactured a strand of it. They were women among women doing women's work.

Maude stabbed her needle in and out of the log cabin quilt in the frame. She looked around the room. The Misses Herrick and the Misses Patten, the Misses Emery and the Misses Crosby, chattered and laughed and drank innumerable cups of tea. They will all have need of me sooner or later, Maude thought. They are all made equal in childbed. Maude misjudged the position of her needle and pricked her finger. A bright drop of blood oozed from the tip. Women, she thought, are bound together by the blood they shed doing women's work.

Anne nudged Maude sharply.

"Maude, you are looking much too serious and faraway," Anne admonished.

"I was thinking about women's work," Maude said.

"Well, stop it at once. Here, let me thread your needle."

Precisely at four, Mrs. Stinson rose. The ladies, as if on cue, put away their quilting and went home to rest and change into their evening clothes.

Upstairs, Anne and Maude helped one another dress. Anne fussed with Maude's hair. She arranged it into an ornate coil and applied a curling iron to the little tendrils escaping around Maude's ears. She sprinkled sugar water on the curls so they wouldn't droop later on.

Maude's cheeks grew bright with excitement. The fluff of dark hair around her face softened the broad lines of her cheekbones, making her look almost pretty.

Anne settled a silk gauze shawl, the color of moonbeams, fine as a spider web, around Maude's shoulders. Maude's pale pink dress was not silk. It was finely woven cotton, simply made with puffed sleeves and a wide, low neckline.

The rattle of carriages and chaises signaled the return of the guests. Anne and Maude went downstairs to greet them.

The sedate conversation of the afternoon rose to a higher pitch, laced with the heavier baritones of the gentlemen. Gowns shimmered in the light of a hundred candles. Young ladies favored silks of blue, yellow, green, and pink. Older ladies preferred deeper blues, browns, and rusts. The rougher textures of the men's short-waisted jackets lay darkly against the extravagant embroidery of their waistcoats.

The evening progressed with music and dancing. Maude was never without a Stinson brother at her side. She laughed and flirted and conversed. She forgot about her chapped, red hands. She forgot about man midwives, and forceps. Time passed very agreeably.

It was after midnight when the party ended. Maude and Anne retired to Anne's chamber and changed into night clothes. It was a frilly room, the bed curtains edged with knitted lace, the sheets edged with delicate cutwork. The counterpane was embroidered white on white. Anne sat on a stool near the hearth. The fire snapped cozily. The only light in the room came from the fire. Shadows hovered in the corners. They pressed down from the ceiling—hemming Maude and Anne in the circle of firelight. Maude brushed Anne's hair with slow, careful strokes.

"I think Charles was quite taken with you, Maude," Anne said dreamily. Charles had been the most attentive of the four brothers. He was extremely handsome, and Maude had found him amusing.

"He was only being polite because you asked him to," Maude said. She had been very flattered by his attentions. But she knew that Charles Stinson's interest did not go beyond social civility.

"Well, Reuben was certainly being more than polite. I saw him keep your hand longer than was necessary when we said good night. He's not handsome like Charles, but he's very nice to be with. Mariners usually are for some reason."

Anne hugged her knees and gazed into the fire. It was impossible to tell where her thoughts were. Maude tied Anne's hair back with a blue ribbon.

"Reuben was less interested in me than in making the Herrick girls jealous, Caroline, in particular, I suspect," Maude said. The four pretty Herrick sisters had been the center of attention all evening. Maude had been impressed with their flair for socializing.

"Yes that's true. They are as gauzy as the shawl I let you wear. I hate to say it, because Reuben is my favorite brother, but he doesn't have a chance of escaping one of the Herrick girls. But you needn't despair, Maude. George danced more than one dance with you. And I noticed Isaiah made it a point to lead you into supper."

"I'm not in despair, Anne. And you know it. I like your brothers very much, but I am not yet ready to look upon them, or anyone else, as a candidate for a husband." Maude gave Anne's hair a playful jerk. Anne yelped, overdoing her reaction. She darted to the bed. She grabbed a pillow and smacked Maude on the backside with it. Maude grabbed the other pillow and smacked her back. The pillow fight was over quickly. It was late and they were tired. They collapsed into the middle of the bed. The feather tick rose up around them in a heavy billow.

Maude lay on her back with her hands relaxed across her belly. Anne lay beside her with her arms flung above her head. A vast expanse of dark and light hair flowed and spread beneath their heads.

The firelight flickered. Shadows leaped suddenly closer.

"Maude," Anne whispered in a tearful voice. Maude's instincts flared. She had sensed an edge in Anne's mood all day. "You are so much wiser than I am. So very sensible. I knew I could talk to you about anything from the very first day we met."

Maude reached for Anne's hand. It was tense, like that of a lying-in woman in the midst of a bearing down pain.

"I'm listening, Anne," Maude said gently, soothingly.

There was a long silence, but Maude did not prompt. She was accustomed to waiting for the inner workings of human nature.

"Last year, right after I was engaged to John, Mother had a talk with me. I had planned to marry right away. But after what Mother said, I changed my mind. I've been putting the wedding off ever since. Now I've agreed to marry early in June, but I want to put it off again." Anne's voice was so small, Maude strained to hear.

"What your mother told you must have been very serious," Maude said. She lay her head very near Anne's in a gesture of comfort.

"Mother told me that men, even dear John, are

possessed by certain animal passions that women do not share. She said that John, after we are married, because he is my husband, will have the right to . . . use my body, to be physically intimate anytime, in any way he chooses. She said that as his wife I cannot refuse, that it is my duty to please him. She said the . . . the unpleasant aspects of this are compensated by the joys of mothering the children that will result."

Maude was not surprised by Anne's fear and misinformation. She often had encountered the ignorance of women concerning the workings of their bodies and the act of love. Women frequently did not understand that the husband's seed was the source of their constant state of childbearing. Nor did they perceive that they had any choice in the matter of coupling.

Sally Robinson did what she could to enlighten her lying-in cases about the basic workings of their monthly cycles, conception, and childbirth. She had taught Maude to do the same. It was not an easy task. The workings of a woman's body were not well understood. No one knew how conception actually transpired. Or at what point in the lunar cycle a woman was most likely, or least likely, to conceive. And once conception occurred, there was no certain way to be sure of it until the woman was four or five months gone with the child. As for the act of coupling, men were assumed to have a greater capacity for passion and pleasure than women. It was widely believed that God had intended women to be vessels for man's seed, the means for man's pleasure. Women were expected to submit without complaint.

The act of childbirth was as intimate as the act of love, Maude believed. Women spoke of these things to one another. She had gleaned a great deal of information listening to her lying-in cases talk. She knew the most important thing for Anne to do was rid herself of the fear her ignorance caused.

Maude sat up and reached for the pillow Anne had smacked her with. She folded it in two as Sally once had instructed her.

"I can help you understand the workings of men's and women's bodies, Anne," Maude said.

Anne rolled over on her side to watch. She wiped her cheeks with the back of her hand.

"This," Maude went on, indicating the folded pillow, "is something like how a woman's exterior parts are shaped. Up here, where the pillow doubles, is an opening. It is very small. Urine flows out of it. Down here is another opening. For the bowel. Between these two there's a third opening. Where the monthly blood flows from. This is the opening that is important to the physical union of marriage."

Anne's eyes widened in surprise. Her face opened into an expression of curiosity.

"I had no idea," she murmured.

"If the monthly flow ceases after a woman has coupled with her husband, then it is likely that she is with a child."

Maude reached for the unlit candle in the holder by the bed. "Surely, you have seen little boys without their diapers and know what the male member looks like?"

Anne nodded her head, yes.

"When a man is desirous of sexual pleasure, his member becomes firm, like this candle. And woman, desiring the intimate attention of her husband, becomes moist and willing to receive him. Like this." Maude inserted the candle between the folds of the pillow to illustrate. "I am told that if the husband and wife are patient and tender with one another, it is a very pleasurable sensation for both. Of course, children are the inevitable result of such a union."

"But what if it isn't pleasant, and I don't like it?" Anne asked. She sat and drew her knees to her chest. She folded her bedgown down around her feet.

"Then it must be as your mother says. A duty to be performed."

"Duty." Anne's hair spilled around her in a tumble of blonde. "And part of my duty is to bear a child every two years. I will lose my looks and ruin my health. John will not love me anymore if that happens."

It was a reasonable fear. For many women, the act of love was fraught with humiliation, pain, and even death. Wombs fell from the strain of being occupied by infants so frequently. This condition caused difficulty with urination, painful back aches, and variety of unpleasant infections for which there was little, if any, relief. Waists thickened. Veins in legs bulged. Teeth fell out.

Few ways existed to delay or avoid child-bearing. Abstinence from the marriage act was the only certain way. But men seldom agreed to that, and women, too, found it disagreeable. Abstaining women complained of melancholy.

"There are certain things you can do, Anne, that might prove helpful in keeping your health," Maude said. "The female opening leads to the womb where the infant grows until it is born. The womb, in turn, has a tiny opening where the male seed is taken in. If the seed can be prevented from entering the womb, a woman will not conceive. Mrs. Robinson advises a pesssary of lamb's wool soaked in olive oil, if it can be obtained. Melted candle wax if the olive oil can't be had. The pessary is then inserted all the way to the opening of the womb to block it so nothing can enter."

Maude searched about the room for materials to illustrate. She retrieved Anne's sewing basket and removed a ball of yarn about the size of the large marbles boys played games with. She undid

136

the yarn so that a strand was left unwound. She inserted it between the folds of the pillow in the place where she had inserted the candle. The end of the strand of yarn remained visible.

"See?" Maude said. "The end of the yarn makes the pessary easy to remove. All you do is pull. Carefully. You must use a pesssary each time you desire a connection with your husband and allow it to remain until morning."

Many women used Sally's pessaries. Some even managed to avoid conception for three or four years. But nothing was completely reliable. Inevitably, pregnancy succeeded pregnancy until the monthly flow dried up completely when a woman reached her fifties.

The tenseness left Anne's face. Maude smoothed out the pillow and replaced the candle and yarn.

"I love John very much," Anne said quietly, her words muffled against the counterpane. "But I dreaded the thought of becoming his possession, as if I were a chair to be sat in, or a pet dog to be tied up on a leash. It seemed to me that if he had the right to make such demands, as Mother said, than I was little better than a slave."

"But now you are enlightened, Anne. You can speak to John of your fears and tell him what I have told you. If he truly loves you, he will not wish to ask, or demand, anything that gives you hurt. A woman's body should not be a prison.

It should be a fountain from which flow the generations of mankind, not as man demands, but as woman desires."

They tucked themselves under the counterpane. Anne lay quiet and relaxed.

It occurred to Maude again how inextricably women were bound together by the work of their hands and the workings of their bodies.

The fire's dying flickers danced on one spot on the ceiling. Shadows settled like a gauze shawl into the room and troubled no one's sleep.

14.

The strands of social connection Maude darned into her life at Anne Stinson's quilting were sturdy ones. That summer she witnessed Anne's marriage to John Crosby Jr. Maude's private gift to Anne was several dozen lamb's wool pessaries with instructions for making them. Anne did not conceive on her wedding journey as brides often did. John, Anne had confided, was more ignorant than herself about the act of love. Maude's information had greatly eased their awkwardness with one another. The entire proceeding had, Anne said, been rather pleasant.

The days spent on rare visits with Anne were interspersed with days in the wash house and long nights sitting in kitchens waiting for infants to burrow their way into the world.

Eighteen-nineteen was a busy year of comings and goings—to mean hovel and grand house, to married lady and woman of easy ways. In childbirth, all women needed Maude equally.

There was a certain sameness to the lying-in cases Maude visited, but it was not the kind of predictability that inspired boredom or caused her to wish for other employment. Women about to give birth, Maude observed, turned inward, centered their very spirits on the life about to leave their bodies. Maude could put no name to that stillness. But it was there. It manifested itself in the early stages of travail. Those most turned in on themselves, most attuned to the workings of their bodies, often had shorter, easier travail. It always mystified Maude how the women in her care were able to lay aside their fears of pain, of deformed infants, of stillbirths, of death, and endure the time of travail. She wondered why women did not rise up and cry in one voice, "No more!" But they did not. Year after year they did their duty. They bore children. They fulfilled their destiny as women.

Yet, Maude observed, if a woman was lying-in for the fifth or sixth or tenth or twelfth time, despair and melancholy often set in immediately after the birth of the child. It was a difficult affliction to address. Even Sally was baffled by it. Maude suspected that not every birth was

139

considered a gift or a joy as women had been taught to believe. Sometimes, women in a state of melancholy refused to nurse their infants. In extreme cases, women abandoned their babes, left them under bridges or in ditches. But more often, melancholic women simply refused to recover from lying-in. They spent the rest of their lives as invalids. In such cases, little could be done. Maude observed, however, that those women taught to make Sally's lamb's wool pessaries often had a lift in spirits and resumed their normal wifely functions.

The time Maude did not spend in the wash house or visiting the sick was taken up with long talks of instruction with Sally.

Eighteen-nineteen also was a time of great political change. Much of the talk Maude heard on her visits to the sick was about the impending event of statehood, and the following year, 1820, on the 15th of March, Maine separated from Massachusetts and became a state. Church bells rang all day. Taverns filled with revelers bent on lifting their mugs in endless salutes to the brand new state of Maine. Bonfires were lit, and General Jeremiah Herrick of Hampden decided to hold a gathering to celebrate the occasion. Maude and Eli were invited, but Maude did not want to go.

Maude went upstairs to Eli's chamber to give him his newly brushed jacket. The room was filled with the clutter of the doctoring profession, as if the contents of Eli's mind had spilled over and taken up residence. A book about botanicals lay open on the bed. A chart depicting the circulation of blood was tacked to the wall. A well-worn anatomy book lay on a chair. It was a comforting place to be and that was why Maude wanted to be there.

Dark circles smudged Maude's eyes. Her expression was tense in an effort to express what she felt without letting the weight of it rule her life. She leaned against the door frame as if her body had become too heavy for her spine to support. As usual she had on her old brown gown. It had been refurbished with a new collar and a set of plain lace cuffs.

"It will do you good, Maude," Eli insisted. "A change of scene will help you take your mind off Sally's accident. For a little while anyway. Then you will be able to think about it more easily. And it won't hurt quite so much."

Eli shook the wrinkles out of the maroon silk cravat he always wore to social gatherings. His face, too, bore the marks of the strain of the past few weeks. The lines in his forehead, it seemed to Maude, were deeper.

Three weeks ago Sally had been crossing the ice on Swett's Pond. People often used the ice as a shortcut during the winter months. But a thaw at the end of February had weakened the ice in spots and Sally had fallen through. Ice fishermen found her with her fingers frozen into the edge of the ice, frozen to death. She had waited for death as she had waited for life. Maude had received the news with a shock of horror and disbelief. For days, she had felt as if she, too, were on thin ice and about to go down into the awful icy dark. But Eli had heard and he had come to bring Maude home. Gradually, the horror of Sally's death had subsided, but she still dreaded going to a gathering where the conversation might turn to talk of what had happened to Sally.

Eli folded his cravat around his neck. He tied it with the quick, deft movements that made his surgery successful.

"I think talk about Sally's accident has pretty well died down. All anyone will want to talk about tonight is statehood and the Missouri Compromise. Anne and John Crosby will be there. I spoke to her father just this morning down at the wharf. She's just back from Boston visiting relatives. You haven't seen Anne for months."

Maude's eyes could not meet Eli's. Her head drooped like that of a tired horse. She stirred as she became aware he was waiting for her answer.

"Perhaps you're right, Papa. I would like to see Anne. She always has some outrageous tale to tell that makes me laugh. It would be nice to laugh again after so much sadness."

Eli put on his stern father face. In a playfully

gruff voice he said, "If you don't go, daughter, I will declare you possessed of the melancholy and put you to bed with one of my nastiest tonics."

Maude smiled a small smile.

"Perhaps you are right, Papa. Moping is of no use to anyone. It might do me good to get away from my frets for awhile."

Maude's biggest fret was the void Sally's death had left. The other midwives in the region did not subscribe to what they referred to as Sally's Frenchified methods. They were of an older generation, cowed by what they believed to be the superior education of the physicians in the region. They were only marginally upset when they were not called to attend a birth. They grumbled some about the loss of their fees to physicians, but they did nothing to improve their ways. They weren't ones to give any thought to what would happen to their calling once they were dead and gone. And that was at the heart of Maude's grief. The hungry depth of Swett's Pond had swallowed not only a human life, but the irreplaceable intelligence it contained.

"Sally was a good woman," Eli murmured, deliberately understating Maude's feelings. He buttoned his vest and brushed his gray hair away from his temples.

At one time, Maude entertained hopes that Eli and Sally might look favorably on one another and consider matrimony. But they had not.

"And a good teacher," Maude said. She let silence stretch out into the room. Eli removed the anatomy book from the chair. He sat down to pull on his boots. Maude moved from the door and sat down on the bed opposite Eli.

"Even without the rest of the time you were supposed to spend with Sally, you are the best midwife you can be, Maude."

"She told me that the night before her accident. As if she knew what was going to happen and she would never have another chance to say so. I've learned to use my hands as instruments just as you said I would, Papa. Sally showed me how to trust them. Of course, I still make it my business to know which physicians have forceps and are most skilled at applying them. Just in case. Sally didn't mind me doing that. But she would never have done so herself. It just wasn't her way."

The matter of forceps had lost its urgency as Maude came to rely more and more on the skill of her hands and the intuition of her touch. She and Eli had several conversations about the matter. Each time Eli had counseled patience. Maude had complied, but she still believed she must acquire the skill to use forceps. Eli could not teach her. He had never used the instrument. And none of the other physicians would trust a mere midwife with knowledge of the very device that got them called to lying-in cases in the first place.

Eli sat back in a chair and thought a minute.

"You only know for sure something has changed after it actually has been transformed into something different. Sally knew that. Most changes are random, not predictable. I think that's part of the reason she took you on. She wanted to influence, in some small way, how the changes in midwifery would happen. She didn't want the art of midwifery to remain unchanged. She had great faith in you, Maude, and in your ability to bend in unusual ways. I think that's why she didn't put up any fuss about you calling in a physician with forceps if you believed there was a need."

Some of the tension left Maude's face. Her shoulders relaxed a bit. "Losing Sally was like losing a part of myself," she said quietly. She hadn't thought of it quite like that before. It felt like an elemental truth. Until she discovered someone else who could replace that loss, she would never be quite complete. In a sense, Maude thought, Sally had created a new entity: Maude Richmond, Midwife. And in doing so Sally had fused a part of her spirit into her creation. Perhaps, Maude thought, it was a kind of birth, being made a part of someone else, then separated by a very painful event and having to learn to be yourself.

The icy place of Sally's death began to melt just a little.

Eli laid his hand on Maude's.

"Goodbyes won't ever be easy for you, Maude.

Your caring heart will hang on until it's certain there's nothing left to be done but let go. Sally knew you were the right one to carry on her ideas."

Eli rose and handed his jacket to Maude. She held it as he slipped his arms into the sleeves. Eli understood how familiar, ordinary tasks soothed the spirit.

Eli enjoyed gatherings. He was, by nature, an outgoing man. Maude knew he would worry if she stayed at home brooding. She knew it would cloud his pleasure, so she capitulated and took his prescription.

"All right," she said. "I will go. Sarah John can help me get dressed."

The previous fall, the Thatchers had finally gone off to Ohio to try their fortunes there. Sarah John had several tantrums about the impending move, and Mrs. Thatcher asked Eli for advice. As a result, a satisfactory arrangement had been worked out for all concerned. Sarah John now helped Mrs. Howard with the housekeeping in return for room and board for a year. But they all knew that after the year was up, there would be another, and another. Sarah John was in the Richmond household to stay. Even at six, Sarah John had great patience for keeping things well ordered. She already was indispensable.

"I will have the sleigh ready in fifteen minutes," Eli said.

Maude stood near the windows in General Herrick's parlor, tall, narrow windows draped in dark gold velvet. The room occupied one corner of the front of the house situated on Kennebec Road. The doorways between the rooms arched gracefully. The woodwork and wainscoting were painted a pale shade of gold. Several sofas and chairs upholstered in dark brown stuff were placed about the perimeter of a carpet with a geometric design in turkey-red and dark, dark green.

Maude had paid her respects to the Herrick girls. Then she retreated, as inconspicuously as possible, from their innocuous chatter. Anne had not yet arrived.

Maude's pink gown was the same one she had worn to Anne's gathering more than a year ago. She carried a painted paper fan with carved wood ends.

It was early evening, the sun just setting. Mauve and pink shadows fell across the snow in the general's yard. Bits of conversation floated to Maude, but she only half heard.

"Hasn't this been a long winter? Did you hear . . ."

"Betsy Patten's been in Boston all winter, and she says the latest gowns have much lower waistlines this season. And shorter skirts . . ."

"Good lambing this season, Mr. Emery. The older ewe of mine . . ."

"I heard they caught some rum smugglers hauling two, three hogsheads of rum on a big sled. All the way from Canada in the dead of winter . . ."

"A woman from Hermon was seen riding astride! And wearing leggings like a common Indian!"

Maude was so deep in her effort to avoid the frivolous chatter, she did not notice anyone approach. It startled her when a male voice spoke her name.

"I presume you are Maude Richmond, the heroine of the infamous British invasion of Bangor."

Maude faced the intruder. She expected an ill-mannered boor she could dispatch with the sharp edge of her tongue. But the man who stood before her was not much taller than she. He was by far the shortest man in a room. He was, she judged, in his mid-twenties. His eyes dominated his face and were the color of blueberries. Sweet blue eyes. His nose was finely made above a wide, handsome mouth. His lips hovered near a smile. His hair was the color of an autumn leaf—gold and bronze—thick with just a hint of a wave and brushed neatly back at the ears. Rebellious little wisps fell across his brow. His face was deeply tanned, as if he spent much time outdoors in all seasons. There was a boyish quality about him.

Maude decided the man was too ill-mannered to be taken seriously. She drew aside her pink skirts and opened her fan with a loud, authoritative snap.

"I don't believe we've been introduced. Please excuse me," Maude said brusquely. She tried to step around the man. To her surprise, he did not move, blocking her retreat.

"Quite right, Miss Richmond, but if my cousin Anne Crosby were here, she would remedy that in an instant. I'm Samuel Webber. Anne sent me in her place. She caught a chill and I advised her not to stir from her bed. She asked me to look after you." His eyes were warm with a light that reminded Maude of the blue haze that hung over the hills of Orrington on a fine June afternoon.

"I can look out for myself, Mr. Webber," Maude said. She closed her fan with another sharp snap. The smile playing on Sam's lips relaxed into an engaging grin. It increased his resemblance to a ten-year-old boy.

"So I have heard, Miss Richmond." There was unmistakable admiration in Sam's voice. His tone matched the message in his eyes.

Maude no longer wanted to move away from him.

Sam extended his right hand instead of bowing as was the proper custom at social gatherings.

Maude took his hand—small, not much larger than her own, a little rough on the palm. His fingers were tapered, his grasp firm, yet gentle, as if he understood how to handle fragile things.

"How do you do," Maude said in her best formal manner. She kept her tone cool. His reference to her actions when the British invaded Bangor had ruffled her. The story of her encounter with Captain Barrie and Colonel John had been embellished to such a degree that half the town believed the captain had sworn to shoot her on sight and the other half believed the colonel had pledged undying affection and had died of a broken heart. In fact, so far as Maude knew, the British had simply left the Penobscot region and returned to England.

Sam laughed softly.

"Anne said you would bristle like a raspberry thicket if I dared mention the British. Please forgive me. I couldn't think of another way to engage you in conversation without going through the dreary formality of asking one of the Herrick girls to introduce me. If I had done that, you would have been the topic of tomorrow's tea party gossip, or worse, the subject of one of old Mrs. Crosby's pronouncements. I was sure you would forgive me less quickly for that than for a breach of good manners. Anne has told me so much about you. I wanted very much to make your acquaintance while I am visiting with her and John. Besides, you are the only woman in the room shorter than I am." Sam smiled and the blue field of his eyes deepened in intensity to an expression of kindness and concern.

Maude's ruffled feathers smoothed out. Despite her effort not to, she found Sam Webber endearing.

Maude tilted her head to one side and regarded Sam thoughtfully.

"Perhaps, Mr. Webber, you are like cheese and improve with time. If you can assure me your conversation is even the smallest bit better than your manners, then I won't mind making your acquaintance." Maude observed Sam to gauge the effect of her words.

Sam's eyes crinkled at the corners. He laughed the same soft laugh. His eyes left her face for an instant, and it was as if she were without a shawl on a chill evening.

"You have my word on it," Sam said. He offered his arm. They joined a small group near the punch bowl. The group included the general.

General Jeremiah Herrick was a bit younger than Eli, in his mid-fifties, very tall, and he used his height to either condescend to his listeners or intimidate them. He owned the store at the Lower Corner, a stone's throw from his house, and held a controlling interest in several schooners engaged in various trades. He was a member of the militia, though his title was purely ceremonial. He had been noticeably absent from town in 1814 during the British invasion. He was thought to be a cultured man because he had introduced to Sunday meeting the playing of religious music on the bass viol.

"My dear, Miss Richmond," the general said, "I am so pleased you joined us to celebrate the happy occasion of acquiring statehood. It has been a long time in the making. It is indeed an accomplishment to be proud of." The general had been a delegate to the various conventions which had lobbied for separation from Massachusetts. He inclined his shoulders, deferentially, toward Maude. She had heard that he had hoped for the governorship of the new state of Maine. That honor, however, had gone to William King despite a lot of talk about how King had traded with the British during the embargo. King had registered his ships under the flag of a neutral country. This had sat ill with those who had obeyed the Embargo Act and had gone bankrupt as a result.

The question of statehood, bound up as it was with the issue of slavery, had been hotly debated in every kitchen Maude had sat in the past year. She had listened to the talk, read newspapers when she could get them, and had long discussions with Sally on that subject. She was completely opposed to slavery. She did not stop to consider her words as she replied to the general.

"I should think the slaves in Missouri are wondering what all the celebration is about." As soon as the words left her mouth, Maude regretted them. It was one thing to discuss political questions in kitchens with other women, but quite another to cast them out into the gurgling waters of social conversation with gentlemen present. Politics was the sphere of men. It was too vulgar a subject for the delicate sensibilities of women. Anne had told Maude repeatedly that men did not admire women with opinions, especially political ones.

The general pulled himself up to his full height. Conversations stopped. Amos Patten cleared his throat several times as if a sentence had stuck in his craw. One of the Herrick girls inquired brightly if anyone cared for more punch. Sam Webber's lips curled into a small smile. His face registered an oh-you've-done-it-now expression which neither condoned nor condemned.

"How like you, Miss Richmond, given your noble calling, to concern yourself with the welfare of those God has seen fit to make less fortunate than others," the general said. His shoulders drooped again.

Maude measured her response. She had never learned the niceties of meaningless social chatter despite Anne's best attempt to teach her. If she ignored the general's remark, it would imply tacit agreement with a concept she was opposed to. But Anne had made it clear that gentlemen, such as Sam, did not admire ladies with opinions. Maude wanted Sam Webber's admiration very much, but she wanted to be true to herself even more.

"I find your views on the Missouri question very interesting, Miss Richmond," Sam said, as if he had read her mind. There was safe mooring in his words.

"Statehood is too dear when the price of purchase is slavery," Maude said.

General Herrick raised his eyebrows and squared his shoulders. Maude thought of the Thatchers' huge ox team plodding steadily on, capable of trampling anything in its path.

"Perhaps," he said, "you don't comprehend the broader aspects of the issue, my dear. The Missouri question was resolved by great statesmen. It was a long and careful process." Clearly, the general was annoyed.

Only Maude, Sam, and the general remained by the punch bowl. The others had drifted to other, safer groups in the room. Maude was very aware of Sam being aware of her. She glanced at him, liking what she saw. He stood quietly, hands clasped behind his back, feet planted a little apart, like a mariner, able to ride out any tempest.

"I am perfectly aware that Maine came into

the Union as a free state and Missouri as a slave state to preserve the balance of power in government," Maude said. She also knew that Maine's separation from Massachusetts had caused ill-feeling between Federalist and Republican factions about whether or not separation would injure the coasting trade. She commented on it.

"How very clever of you to have comprehended such a complex subject, Miss Richmond," the general said. A lance of fury pierced Maude. She tightened her grip on her fan. She wanted to rap him with it.

"If Maine is worthy of statehood, sir, she deserves to come into the Union on her own merits instead of being yoked to Missouri with an issue that debases both." The merits for statehood, Maude knew, were many. Maine tended toward Republicanism; Massachusetts toward Federalism. The population of Maine was growing faster than that of Massachusetts. The Federalists feared Maine's faster increase in population would, in time, shift the balance of power in favor of the Republicans. Added to that was the fact that Maine was very far from the seat of government at Boston. Separation would simplify any number of governmental matters and, some felt, free Maine from a government on the path to corruption and ruin. Maude said as much.

"You are very outspoken, Miss Richmond,"

the general said. "I suppose next you will be advocating suffrage for the ladies." The hearty attempt at humor in his voice did not cover a note of alarm. He took a small step backward. The general was a Federalist. That party's numbers were composed of persons of social position—merchants, lawyers, Congregational church ministers. He never knowingly invited a Republican into his home. The Republicans were mostly farmers, physicians, and the poorer, discontented elements of society.

It nettled Maude to have her opinion so completely disregarded. It nettled her even more to think that Anne, and indeed every woman at the general's gathering, had been trained to believe politics did not affect their lives and was a subject better left to the gentlemen.

"The thought of woman's suffrage had occurred to me, sir," Maude replied. She wished for a magic spell to transform the general into a female.

The general allowed himself to be distracted by a conversation about highways and bridges going on just behind him. He excused himself with a tight little smile and joined the other group.

Maude's stomach was in knots. It was not the first time she had encountered condescension, but it was the first time she had felt shackled by it. There were, she thought, many kinds of slavery for women. Childbirth was only the beginning. Her fury fought for expression.

"If you say one word, Mr. Webber, I shall forget my manners entirely," Maude said. She snapped her fan open and closed, open and closed.

"Under the circumstances, Miss Richmond, I should say you were entitled to."

Maude allowed Sam to take her hand and draw it through the bend of his elbow. He propelled her toward an empty sofa at the far end of the room near the windows where she had stood earlier. It was fully dark now, but a new moon had risen. The snow in the yard gleamed silver like the scales of an Atlantic salmon.

"I suspect, Miss Richmond, you will be the subject of tomorrow's tea party gossip for reasons other than the fact that you and I are sitting alone together on this sofa. I can just hear old Mrs. Crosby's pronouncement. 'Midwives with opinions give birth to anarchy,' " Sam said. His eyes folded into the beginnings of laughter. Maude gave in and laughed with him.

"Alas, Mr. Webber, you are quite right. I fear I will never learn to govern my tongue. Anne despairs of me."

"But I do not, Miss Richmond. I am most interested in your views on separation and the coasting trade. I've been engaged in coasting these past several years."

Ships engaged in coasting sailed the waters of the Atlantic from the St. Croix River to Florida and back, trading at various ports along the way including Portland, Boston, New York, Baltimore, and Charleston. They carried smoked fish, lumber, leather, and textiles from northern cities to the south where they picked up cotton, tobacco, indigo, and other goods. Massachusetts had recently enacted a law that allowed coasters access to its harbors without entering or clearing customs.

The crews of the coasters were seldom the same from port to port. They came and went with the regularity of the tides. Most of them were rough and liked their grog. They were frequently in brawls of one kind or another.

"Then you are a mariner," Maude said.

"Yes and no. I'm a physician by trade, but I sail as ship's surgeon on the Stetson lines of Portland."

"I have never heard of such a thing, unless it was in the navy. A ship's surgeon. How did you come to that, Mr. Webber?"

"It's something of a long story."

"Since I am obviously welcome nowhere else unless I keep my own opinions to myself, the rest of the evening is at your disposal."

Sam crossed his legs comfortably and settled himself into the corner of the sofa. His eyes lingered on Maude's face, slid quickly to her feet and back to her face. It was an appraisal. Maude was not discomforted by it. His manner contained more that was curious and admiring and little that was conquest.

"Maybe you remember my father, Moses Webber?"

Maude did, but vaguely.

"Your father tended him years ago when he broke his leg. My father was a mariner in his younger years, and I always thought I'd follow in his path, me being the only boy. Well, Father had other ideas, wanted something better for me than he had, so he pressed me to try my hand at something else. I remembered how interested I was in bones and muscles and how they worked and how your father explained those things to me when he tended Father's leg. So I thought I'd give doctoring a try. Old Dr. Livermore apprenticed me about five years back. I stayed with him a couple of years, then I read medicine at Harvard for another year."

"My father read medicine there just before the War for Independence."

"There have been some changes since then. Men-midwives. Controversy over venesection and questions about just how effective bleeding is as a cure for certain ills. A lot of talk about antisepsis. There's even a whole new field of study pertaining to childbirth called obstetrics. I studied it for several months. Got to be pretty good with a pair of forceps. But I just couldn't reconcile myself to the fact we were being taught that forceps were a necessity in all the lying-in cases I saw. I knew perfectly well the ladies handled the event more naturally and easily when left in the hands of a competent midwife."

Maude felt herself warming to Sam Webber. She certainly approved of his views.

"What has all this to do with your work as a ship's surgeon?"

"While I was at Harvard, I made the acquaintance of another student by the name of Joshua Stetson. He studied law. Wild as a hawk. But for some reason, we took to one another. We had a speaking acquaintance. Apparently he and his father didn't see eye to eye on the matter of his allowance or the company he kept. I never did learn all the ins and outs of it, but I did find out his father was Phineas Stetson, the owner of the Stetson Lines. I liked what young Stetson had to say about Portland, so I hung out my shingle there when I finished my studies. But I kept finding myself thinking more about the sea than curing croup and quinsy. On a whim, I shipped out as a common seamen. The sea is in my veins like Father's, I suppose. The master of the vessel was a brute, and the crew were the dregs. I got plenty of practice setting bones and stitching knife wounds. Found I liked it better than any other kind of doctoring."

Sam paused in his recitation. He asked if he were tiring her. Maude shook her head no. She indicated he should continue.

"When we made the Indies, I looked for

another berth. And wouldn't you know it, there was a Stetson Line ship in port. With Phineas Stetson aboard as master. He had a severe case of gout and had delayed sailing because of it. Didn't trust the mate with command. Had a cargo to deliver. I proposed signing on as Stetson's personal physician and guaranteed to keep him fit enough to see the vessel home safe to Portland. And that's what I've been doing ever since. Now, Stetson confines his business to the coasting trade. He goes to sea less and less often. I half expected Joshua, the son, to take over the duties of master, but he hasn't yet. Still wild as a hawk. Anyway, Phineas Stetson was quick to see that having me aboard attracted and kept decent seamen. Oh, I stitch more gashes than I care to sometimes, and there's nothing like having a man fall from a rat line and crack his skull to take a few years off your life, but I like what I do and I plan to stick with it."

Sam paused again. A little silence grew between them, but his eyes still spoke. Maude's eyes spoke back.

"And what of you, Miss Richmond? Anne has acquainted me with your history. She says you are an accomplished midwife."

"All I try to accomplish, Mr. Webber, is to alleviate the travail of my cases as best I can. The general's view notwithstanding, there's nothing noble in my calling. It is the means to earn my

161

living. I chose it because, like you," the thought delighted her, "I wish to follow my father's example and employ myself with the love of the art of healing which he taught me."

She had not intended to reveal that important part of herself—but Sam Webber was so calm and easy, so uninvasive in his manner—she simply forgot herself. Talking with him was very much like talking with Sally Robinson.

"There is a Miss Herrick headed our way," Sam said. "She intends to make us circulate. But before we are forced to attend to social duty, Miss Richmond, I wonder if I might receive your permission to call while I am here visiting with the Stinsons." His eyes enveloped Maude in deep blue. Again, she was acutely aware of him being aware of her.

"If you had not asked me, Mr. Webber, I would have asked you."

"And I would have said, yes, Miss Richmond."

"And so I do, Mr. Webber."

Sam flashed a smile of triumph and delight.

The gathering progressed from conversation to dancing to a late supper. Maude danced once with each gentleman who asked her, including Sam Webber. She would have liked another with Sam, but the specter of tea party gossip prevented her. The general did not engage her in conversation again except to say good evening.

Maude and Eli arrived home at midnight, and

Maude went up to her chamber and lit the candle. She was more happy and elated than the day Eli had hung out the sign that said, ELI RICHMOND AND DAUGHTER, PHYSICIANS.

She wished for Sarah John's nimble fingers to help with the lacings of her dress, but the child was fast asleep on her cot in the kitchen. Maude yanked impatiently at the fastenings. So much in a woman's life, she thought, was cumbersome and confining. The weight of yards of material and skirts and petticoats hampered movement. Corsets restricted breathing and deformed bodies. Laws were made by men for men. A political opinion from a female mouth was disregarded. And yet, there was Sam Webber. And her father.

Maude undid her hair. It fell only to her shoulders instead of to her hips as most women's did. She now kept her hair trimmed to that length to make it less time-consuming to comb and care for. She did not braid her hair at night and she did not wear a cap to bed. Mrs. Howard would have been horrified had she known. In summer, when the chamber was unbearably hot, Maude abandoned her bedgown and slept naked. Whenever she could, she made a conscious effort to loosen some of the strictures enclosing her life. But some of those strictures, she knew, were less tangible. Some were deeply embedded in everyday attitudes and perceptions of the spheres in which men and women were expected to move. They might never be loosened without some drastic measure to make those attitudes and perceptions change. The slaves of Missouri and women, Maude thought, had a few things in common.

Maude did not know if she would live to see attitudes toward women change. She did not know how to make the changes begin, but she thought that not wearing bed caps and unbraided hair in her own life were a very good place to start.

She reached for the pine-framed hand mirror. It had been her mother's. She stared hard at her reflection. She thought of Sam Webber's blueberry-colored eyes lingering on her face. Did he see her as she saw herself? The face in the glass was her adult face. She still resembled her father too much to be called beautiful. Yet she was not plain. Her cheeks glowed with health. Her eyes were clear and bright, and deep with caring. Her nose was short, her chin strong and determined. Her mouth was shaped like a bow. It turned up slightly at the corners. She always appeared to be smiling slightly. A good face, she thought. That was it—she had a good face. Not so beautiful as to cause women to mistrust her and not so plain as to repel men. She was certain Sam Webber did not think her plain. She believed he had seen beyond the contours of her body and already was acquainted with the more complex vistas of her heart. The thought pleased her. She smiled into the mirror and laid it aside.

She pinched out the candle and lay awake a long time. She heard the horse stamping in the stall. She heard Eli's bed ropes creak as he settled himself for what was left of the night. She fell asleep remembering the strong, hard feel of Sam Webber's arm, firm as an anchor under her hand.

16.

Maude, up to her elbows in soap suds and soiled linens, let her attention wander from her tasks inside the steamy wash house to the line of maples edging the field just beyond the open window. It was late May when trees appear to leaf out overnight. Everything was green and blossoming. The fields and farms along both sides of the Penobscot were suspended in the timeless ritual of renewal.

In the weeks since General Herrick's gathering to celebrate statehood, Maude had become aware of a soft haze of happiness misting the branches of her soul whenever Sam Webber was near. The feeling grew and kept pace with the leisurely greening of the Bangor countryside. Her heart raced and sang like a brook freeing itself from winter ice.

Maude hummed a few bars of "Greensleeves." She wrung out the last sheet and put it in the willow basket. She wiped her water-puckered hands on the hem of her gown, patched and faded to pale blue. The skirt was soggy with slopped water from knees to hem.

"Sarah John," Maude called. She pushed several strands of straying hair away from her face.

Sarah John came into the wash house with a cautious creak of the door. Two long, white-blonde braids hung down her back. Her narrow, pale face held no expression, except mild curiosity. Her gown had grass stains at the knees. She stood very still with her hands behind her back. It was an uncharacteristic pose for the child. Usually, she was in motion. She liked hanging the wash to dry on bushes behind the barn. It wasn't like her to be unenthusiastic.

"Are you going to help me, Sarah John?" Maude asked. She pushed her sleeves, impatiently, above her elbows.

Sarah John grinned and said nothing. Maude couldn't imagine what had gotten into the child.

"Got somethin' for ya," Sarah John said. She thrust a bouquet of violets and mayflowers into Maude's hands. "Mr. Webber said bring these to surprise you."

In an instant the wash was forgotten.

"Sam? Mr. Webber? Mr. Webber is here?" Maude had not expected him. His visit with the Stinsons had come to an end. She thought he had shipped out and would be away for six or eight weeks.

Sarah John nodded her head, yes. Her braids bounced and her face lit up with a happy grin.

Maude gave no thought to the work at hand, no thought to her appearance. Nothing in her reaction to Sam ever had anything to do with thought. The very mention of his name precluded rational thinking. She flew out into the yard.

Sam sat on a horse he had hired from Hatch's stable. Maude looked him over carefully, making certain nothing about him was different, that the warm message in his eyes, his smile, had not altered or disappeared. He wore no hat, his hair still the color of autumn leaves. Was there a bit more gold in it than she remembered? Was his face a bit thinner?

Sam dismounted awkwardly, unused to sitting on a horse. Maude found his clumsiness endearing. It aroused tenderness in her—inspired a need to shelter him. He reached into his pocket and withdrew a few dried currants. He fed them to the horse. The kindness of the gesture pulled at Maude's heart and endeared him to her all over again. She thanked him for the bouquet.

"I thought you had gone until the end of July," Maude said. She tried to keep relief out of her face. She did not wish to be a millstone around his neck and prevent him from coming and going as he wished.

"When I got to Portland, I had word there would be a delay for another two weeks. So I made a short journey to Boston and came straight back here."

Sam stood with one arm flung up across the saddle. Maude leaned against the horse's thick, warm neck. She stroked its smooth shoulder. The horse's big body afforded them a kind of privacy, shielded them from the windows of the house where, Maude suspected, Mrs. Howard hovered. Sarah John undoubtedly kept watch through a crack in the wash house door.

"I am very glad to see you, Sam," Maude said. She recognized shyness in her manner. But it was not because she knew Mrs. Howard and Sarah John were observing them. The intensity of her caring for Sam engulfed her in a flowering of feeling that left her amazed.

Maude remembered telling Eli after the British invasion how she did not want a husband. That was no longer true. More and more it seemed to her that what she *thought* that she wanted was less reliable than what she *felt* about what she wanted.

She had a magnificent regard for Sam Webber. She had even tried on his name. Maude Richmond Webber. Maude Webber. She liked the sound of it. She liked the feel of it. But other, conflicting feelings also beset her. As much as she craved Sam's presence in her life, she did not like the idea of annexing herself to him in such a way that she lost herself in the process. It was very confusing to feel one way and think another.

Sam reached for Maude's hand. He laid it against his cheek for a moment, his skin the texture of a cat's tongue, smooth and rough at the same time.

"I couldn't wait to get back to you, Maude," he said quietly, his eyes bluer than blueberries and deep with emotion. Such sweet safety dwelled there, such hints of other depths Maude dared not dream of yet, such messages of ardor of an intensity that mesmerized her. Sam transformed the flow of her thinking into a river of emotion as deep and wide as the Penobscot.

"Sam," Maude said, a summing up of the time since she last saw him. "Sam."

The horse shifted his stance and broke the silent interplay between them. Maude tucked her hand into the crook of Sam's elbow. They walked to the shade of an elm near the barn and sat down on the grass. Maude laid the bouquet aside. The fluted melody of an oriole filtered down from the highest branches. A breeze ruffled the new leaves.

"I brought you a present from Boston," Sam said. He reached inside his jacket and drew out a metal tube-shaped object. It had a wide flair on one end, like a trumpet, and a smaller flair at the other end.

"What is it?" Maude asked, mystified. She turned it over in her hand and hefted it. It was not heavy. It reminded her of a toy horn, but she was certain it was not a toy.

"It's a new invention. Something a French physician dreamed up last year. I read about it in a medical journal last fall. I never thought I'd get my hands on one this soon. It's a stethoscope. For listening to the heartbeat. The inventor claims that heart sounds are useful in diagnosing certain illnesses. You can hear lung sounds with it, too. Ought to be useful in cases of consumption or croup. Maybe you can find a way to apply its use to midwifery."

"But you must keep it for yourself," Maude protested.

"Oh, I'll find another. I don't really need anything like it for stitching wounds and setting bones. I bought it for you. To experiment with. Here. Let me have it. You lie down. I'll show you how it works."

Maude gave no thought to what Mrs. Howard must be thinking. She lay down on the grass under the tree, as close as an embrace to Sam. All thought had flown completely away.

Sam pressed the stethoscope's wide end against her chest and lowered his ear to the narrow end.

"Tick-tick. Tick-tick. Tick-tick," he said. "Steady as a clock. Now if your heart sounded irregular, like a lad with a new drum, I'd have been worried. Now breathe in deep and let it out. Whoosh. Clear as the sound of the breeze up there in the elm. Just like it's supposed to be. Here, you try it."

They changed places. Sam pillowed his hands comfortably behind his head with ease, comfort, and trust in his manner. It was precisely how Maude felt about being near him.

Maude laid the stethoscope's wide end on Sam's chest. She lowered her ear to the narrow opening. The heart was the seat of the emotions, the center of all that was fierce and warm, sad and joyous. His heart held all things good and right and spoke them with his eyes. What else would she hear? She heard lub-lub, lub-lub, a deep, steady, predictable sound, something you could depend on.

Sam breathed deeply and blew air out. His lungs whooshed just as he had described.

Maude removed the stethoscope and laid her hands where it had been. Her fingers absorbcd the steady beat of him. The little wisp of air he breathed in and out grazed her fingers. He took her hands and kissed each knuckle, one by one.

"Maude," Sam said softly, "I know we've known one another only a short time, but I must speak . . ."

Maude placed her fingers against his lips to stop his words. She knew what he wanted to say. She was not ready to hear it. Not yet. She was relieved when the door slammed and Eli came striding across the yard toward them.

Sam scrambled to his feet and shook hands with Eli. Maude retrieved her bouquet.

"Come in, come in, Sam. Mrs. Howard says she's planning on you for supper," Eli said.

They settled in the parlor to talk. The windows were open and the cream colored muslin curtains shivered in the breeze. Mrs. Howard had fitted the fireboard into the fireplace opening only that morning, a sure sign that a new season was at hand. Many years ago, Maude's mother had stenciled the pasture scene on the fireboard.

Eli sat in a Windsor chair by the window. Maude chose the rocker. Sam pulled up a stool near Maude.

Maude showed Eli the stethoscope and explained its use.

"Now that's the most useful thing I've seen in all the years I've been doctoring ills. What do you make of it, Maude?"

Now that she was inside the safety of the house, Maude's mind began to work again. She felt much less at the mercy of her feelings for Sam.

"I'm very pleased with it, Papa. I wonder if it could detect the heartbeat of an unborn babe?"

"Now that's a wonderful idea," Sam said. He leaned toward Maude with an eagerness that set her heart bouncing again.

"I'm not sure what you mean, Maude," Eli said.

"There are many instances when I am uncertain whether or not the unborn babe is alive. Sometimes a babe will not move for weeks before birth. If I could detect a heartbeat, then I would know there was no cause for alarm. If I didn't hear one, I'd know the birth might be a complicated one. And twins. If I heard two heartbeats, I'd be better prepared."

"I think you have really hit on something useful, Maude," Sam said. "If it works, it could take some of the guesswork out of delivery."

"I thought I might ask Anne to let me listen to her unborn babe," Maude said. The "chill" that had prevented Anne from attending the general's gathering had proved to be the nausea associated with the early months of being with child. Anne had stopped using the pessaries and had conceived immediately. Maude expected that Anne's lying-in would take place in late August.

"I've brought you the latest medical journal, sir," Sam said, pulling the volume from a pocket inside his jacket and handing it to Eli.

"Why, thank you, Sam. I'll certainly enjoy that. Maybe someday Maude will write about her experiments with the stethoscope as a tool for the midwife."

"Perhaps I will, Papa. But no medical journal would ever print it," Maude said.

Mrs. Howard appeared in the doorway. She set

on a table a vase containing the bouquet Sam had given Maude.

"You've been called, Mr. Richmond. There's a man over toward Brewer who missed a stick of wood he was splitting. Split his ankle wide open instead." Mrs. Howard handed Eli a slip of paper with directions on it for finding the injured man.

After Eli left, Sam closed the parlor door. Before he could speak, Maude turned his question gently aside.

"Don't ask me yet, Sam," she said. "Not just yet."

Sam drew Maude into his arms. All thought fled. The heady perfume of mayflowers filled her senses. She almost changed her mind.

17.

Maude walked slowly beside Sam along the river's edge in the horse pasture behind the house. The horse nickered to them from a distance, and settled herself to graze. It was September. Sam had just returned from Portland. He had come in haste. He still wore his seaman's visored cap and a navy blue jacket with silver buttons. The cap shadowed his eyes. He did not look like a ten-year-old boy. He looked like a mature man determined to get what he wanted. While he was away, he had written and asked Maude to marry him. She had not replied to his question directly. She had written him that she would give her answer when his voyage had finished and he returned to Bangor.

Maude had thought a long time about what she would say to Sam, had laid awake nights thinking of it, had wrestled with the in and outs of it. If she listened to her head, her heart became outraged. If she listened to her heart, her head told her she would have to give up her calling. She knew how the cares of keeping house and childbearing limited a woman's life. She loved Sam, but did not want to be limited. She did not know how to tell him so without causing him pain. She decided to be as forthright as possible.

The skirt of her russet wool gown snagged on a dried weed. She yanked at it. Sam bent and untangled the fabric.

"When I determined to be a midwife, Sam, I decided I would never want to marry," Maude said gently. She did not look at him. He was too near—too essential to her idea of how a woman and man could love and care for and nurture one another. She was too much of a coward to witness the pain she knew would dull his eyes.

To Maude's surprise, Sam grasped her gently by the shoulders. He turned her so she faced him.

"That, Maude Richmond," Sam said softly, "is a bald-faced lie." There was no anger in his voice or manner. It was one of the things Maude loved best about him. He was always levelheaded and reasonable.

"Oh, Sam. I didn't mean to be dishonest, to let you believe I entertained hopes of being your wife. I'm not like Anne . . ."

"Of course you are not like Anne, thank God," Sam broke in. "I love you, Maude, because you are not content to sit in a big house, waited on hand and foot by the hired girl, with nothing more important to do but drink tea and brag about the new baby."

Anne had been delivered successfully of a son the week before. Before its birth, Maude had detected the babe's heartbeat with her stethoscope. She had written Sam of it.

"That's not fair, Sam," Maude said coming to Anne's defense.

"Yes, it's fair, Maude. It's fair because I knew the minute I laid eyes on you that you would never settle for a life of idleness like Anne has . . . no matter how much you groan about lost sleep and the labor of the wash house. If you had wanted that kind of life, you could have set your cap for one of Anne's brothers."

Maude made no denial. Sam took her hand and kissed it lightly. She did not draw her hand away. The distressed expression on Sam's face dissolved into a crooked little smile.

"All I want, Maude," Sam went on, "is to be

your ballast, not your anchor. How do I make you understand that?"

Sam released Maude's hand. She walked a little distance away and sat down on the grass. She gazed out across the river. Seagulls bobbed like cork stopples. They floated on the current without a care where it took them. Why, Maude thought, couldn't she be like a gull and let the currents of life carry her wherever they went?

"I understand, Sam. But marriage isn't in practice the way we dream it to be."

"But it can be, Maude," Sam persisted. He removed his cap and sat down beside her.

Maude watched the seagulls wheel aimlessly on the whim of random air currents. They settled heavily onto the surface of the river. How, she thought, could she make Sam understand that she feared the burden of women's work marriage imposed? Not that she wouldn't willingly do the work if she chose such a course. She was not afraid of work. She was afraid of giving up too much of herself in return for the comfort and safety of a man's love and caring.

"Because of childbearing, Sam," Maude said at last. "And the work of caring for children. Ruining my health from it. Dying . . ." She trailed off, not quite sure how to say what she felt. She remembered her dream about Mollie Smith earlier in the week. In the dream, Mollie's infant, its skin blue, instead of refusing birth, lay with its head and shoulders out of the womb. Its tiny face contorted into some unknown emotion. Mollie writhed and moaned in agony. The child refused to be born any further. Then slowly, Mollie's face faded away and became Maude's face. The infant stirred and tried to claw its way back into the womb. Maude had woken with sweat running down her face, her hair matted against her head. Her knees were drawn up in the birthing position as if she really had been in travail.

She told Sam about the dream.

"Are you afraid of death?" Sam asked carefully. Concern and empathy whirled in his blueberry eyes.

"Not death, Sam. Not the end of life. The end of Maude Richmond, midwife." Maude rested her hand on Sam's arm. She comforted herself with his nearness. "I'm plagued by the notion that my affection for you is not deep enough to give up a part of myself for you." She spoke simply, quietly, almost apologetically. She waited for pain to mark his face, waited for his anger at being rejected, waited for him to reveal a side of himself she could not love.

"Dearest, Maude, I don't want you to give up any part of yourself for me. Those things you want for yourself are the things I love in you. While it is true marrying me will mean leaving Bangor and your friends and family, it is also true that what you leave behind here you can put into practice in Portland. We will be much closer to Boston. I have access to medical libraries there. I can bring you books and ideas. You can keep learning all there is to know about birthing. And I will keep coasting. The work suits me . . . patching up cracked heads and bruised knuckles. With what I earn and your fees, we will have enough to rent a small house and hire a housekeeper. We could take Sarah John with us, if you'd like. With me gone two months at a time, you would be free to come and go as you please. I don't want you with barnacles on your beam, my love. I want you in full sail. I'd be lying if I said I didn't want to share your bed. But you know the use of lamb's wool and olive oil. And the French, bless them, have devised something called a French letter. It is designed to prevent disease, but it also captures the male sperm before it can do any harm. For pity's sake, Maude, we're both familiar enough with the workings of human anatomy to figure out a way to prevent childbearing until we decide it's time."

Maude did not know what to say. Her need for Sam shrieked and clamored like the seagulls overhead whose cries hung in the air like kites. She watched their idle circles. They were greedy, boisterous birds. She had never admired them very much. No, she thought, she wouldn't make a very good seagull. She was not content to drift along on capricious currents. She was a woman of reason, of action, of deep caring, things she knew and admired in herself. She turned to Sam and took his face in her hands. She kissed him. She parted her lips and touched her tongue to his. Sam drew a little away and regarded her curiously. Her kisses usually were chaste and fleeting. She kissed him again, more deeply. Whatever womanhood held in store for her, she felt ready to meet it. Sam was her friend, her ally. She loved him with every fiber of her heart.

Maude lay back in the brown September grass amid the dried weeds, unmindful of stains and damp. She gave herself up to the non-thinking tides of emotion lapping at her very foundations.

Sam settled himself beside her. A happy grin lit his face, warmed the blue of his eyes. She was very aware of his body—how neatly made it was: narrow of hip, small and compact, well-muscled from heaving-to with the crew of the Stetson ship. Her special woman's place grew soft and moist with want and longing.

Maude interrupted their kissing and murmured, "Do you own forceps?"

"Yes," Sam whispered back, his expression puzzled.

"Will you teach me to use them?"

"Of course I will. I'd planned to give them to you as a wedding present."

"Then I guess I'd better marry you, dearest Sam."

Maude wrapped her arms around Sam's strong back. The rough texture of his jacket was scratchy beneath her fingertips.

Sam crushed her to him with a little yelp of joy.

The tide had receded to its lowest ebb and the seagulls had disappeared from the sky when they went to tell Eli.

Part Two: Fanny

1.

Fanny Abbott walked carefully down the narrow track along the pasture rock wall that led from the house to the wharf at the edge of the Penobscot River. She shivered beneath the folds of her green kinsale cloak, not so much from the chill as from the excitement of the whole thing. She strained to see across the river. Everything was dark except for small twinkles of candlelight that marked a homestead on the far shore. There was no moon, no stars.

The hood of the cloak covered Fanny's auburn hair. At sixteen, she was as tall and slender as a young willow. She moved with grace. Her face reflected her determination to do as she pleased. The gaze of her amber eyes was direct and uncomplicated. Her mouth was deceptively soft, a definite firm line to her lips. She held her head high, slightly inclined to one side. When she went to town, men's heads turned to watch her.

Presently she heard the splash of water and turned toward it, trying to determine if it was just the river current lapping at the wharf, or the sound of oars dipping rhythmically in the water.

Yes! It was oars! Her heart leaped. Robert had come for her just as he said he would.

Fanny snatched up the small bundle she had brought with her. It contained her best shawl, an extra dress, and some bread and cheese. Oh, wouldn't her older sister, Mercy, be aghast when she read the hastily scribbled note she had left on the kitchen table. But Mercy would forgive her once she knew about the wedding. As for Pa, well, she'd rather not think about what he would say. Not that it mattered. It was 1830, not the olden days like Pa was always harping about. Pa would see it her way in time, once she was married to Robert Snow.

The thought of spending the rest of her life with Robert gave her courage, made her so pleased with their adventure, that she hugged herself with delight. She remembered every detail of the day Robert Snow had first appeared at the farm last spring. She had seen him from the window in the kitchen. It was an important event because handsome young men did not often come to the house. Fanny's father, Simon Abbott, conservative in all things, did not sanction social contact with the young people of Fort Point Village. He wanted his girls kept pure, he said.

Fanny had stepped into the back bedroom she shared with Mercy, and repinned her hair. She took off her soiled apron and tied on her company one. The water bucket was nearly empty and gave her the perfect excuse to go out in the yard to get a better look at the visitor. She lingered at the well and eavesdropped on the conversation between the man and her father.

She heard Robert say he had come to town to visit his aunt, his mother's sister. He was from Portland and unfamiliar with the Penobscot country. No one from the village knew anything about his aunt, he said. He had been directed to a country lane, lost his way, and ended up at the Abbott place to ask directions.

Simon scratched his beard, iced with gray, and thought a minute. He was a burly man, broad as a workhorse. The vague expression that had come over his brown eyes since his wife's death played on his face. Fanny remembered how he shook his head, as if "no" was the most important word he knew. Simon had never heard of Robert Snow's aunt.

It was supper time and would soon be dark. Simon recognized the opportunity to make a little cash money and offered Robert room and board for the night. Fanny had been surprised and pleased by her father's suggestion. She was tired of living like a prisoner on the farm and never having any fun with people her own age.

Mercy responded to the situation with her usual competence. She set the table with the best dishes. She fixed dandelion greens, alewives from the river, corn bread, and pudding. She, too, responded to the rarity of the occasion. Her small, brown eyes sparkled with a vitality they usually lacked. Her plain brown hair, parted in the middle, was combed smoothly over her ears and tucked into a tidy knot at the base of her skull. Her narrow face was unremarkable, but what she lacked in looks, she made up for in kindness and competence. Fanny knew how attracted Mercy was to Robert's easy talk and dark good looks.

During supper, a current of tension crackled in the air between Fanny and Robert Snow. Simon ate and appeared not to notice.

That night, Fanny and Mercy lay together in the big bed they shared.

"Mr. Snow is so handsome. Such a gentleman. Don't you think so, Mercy?" Fanny whispered.

Mercy pressed her lips together primly. At twenty-one, she had never walked out with a man. Fanny knew she resented it.

"Handsome is as handsome does. You'd be better off to settle yourself to learning the dressmaking I've been trying to teach you. Heaven knows we could use the extra money you'd earn by taking in sewing."

"I'd rather be married and have a house of my own," Fanny said sharply, "so I wouldn't have you and Pa always telling me what to do!"

"Then you'd have a husband telling you what to do!" Mercy retorted.

"Which is more than you'll ever have, Mercy Abbott!"

The following Sunday, Robert showed up in meeting. He asked Simon if he could walk home with Fanny.

"Might's well," Simon grunted, to everyone's surprise. Fanny shot a triumphant look at Mercy, gratified to see that Mercy was not pleased. Fanny fell in step with Robert. Pa and Mercy walked on ahead, ears tuned, Fanny knew, to everything she and Robert said. But there wasn't much of anything to hear. They hadn't talked much on the two-mile walk back to the farm. Robert picked a few bluets and handed them to Fanny. As he did so, his fingers brushed hers ever so lightly. Just like a summer butterfly, Fanny remembered thinking. Robert smiled, and she liked the way his teeth were white and even, not one of them missing or decayed, an uncommon occurrence in a seaman.

Robert said he was staying at an inn in the village. He would remain there until his vessel, berthed at Portland, had been scraped and caulked and made ready for the next voyage. He wasn't sure how long that would be. Six or eight weeks perhaps. He had learned that his aunt had gone out to Ohio to live with her daughter. He had no further obligations. In the meantime, perhaps Fanny would permit him to call. His ice-blue eyes caught Fanny's amber ones and held.

She read something glittery and adventurous there. Red-brown lights glinted in his hair. He was the most elegant looking man she had seen in all her sixteen years.

June turned into July and heavy heat settled over the farm in a haze of scorching blue. Robert came to the house frequently and Simon, inexplicably, tolerated the visits. Robert took care to make himself useful. He came to help with the haying and was at the house every day for a month. Fanny fought with Mercy over who would do the cooking, won out, and pretended that Robert was her husband coming home every noon to be fed.

Whenever Fanny could slip away from Mercy's watchful eyes and the hated dressmaking, she sneaked down to the meadow to gaze at Robert's well-muscled arms glistening with sweat. She liked the slick sheen of him, the bronze triangle of his tanned back, the woolly mat of hair that lay like a shadow on his chest.

Simon accepted Robert's help without comment. He remained oddly detached from conversations and took no interest in anything except the farm work.

On Sunday evening, after Simon finished reading aloud from the Bible, Mercy allowed Fanny a few minutes alone with Robert. She had decided that Robert wasn't quite the catch Fanny considered him to be, and if Fanny wanted to waste her time with him, that was up to her.

Sometimes Fanny walked with Robert down the pasture track to the wharf. Once, they sat on the doorstep very close to one another to watch the moon rise. Fanny rested her head on Robert's arm, his linen shirt soft against her cheek. She liked the sunny warm smell of him. Robert groaned and Fanny drew her head away.

"What is it, Robert?" she asked, fearing that she had irritated his sunburned arm. In reply, he kissed her lightly on the lips. From then on, everything changed. Fanny felt it most as she lay beside Mercy trying not to toss and turn, but burning with a heat that had little to do with the humid, still air that clogged the room. But worst of all, Pa had seen the embrace and had forbidden Robert to set foot on the farm again.

"Shifty," Simon said tersely, not explaining further. Fanny begged and pleaded.

"If Ma were alive, she'd let Robert come here!" she complained. That outburst had made Simon more adamant than ever. But his eyes grew moist and Fanny knew the mention of her mother had hurt him. She didn't care. That night she saw him place flowers on her mother's grave in the little family cemetery in the grove in the home pasture. She remained unmoved. She wanted Robert.

One day in late August, Simon went to help a neighbor get in some hay from a field on the far

189

side of the village. Mercy went the opposite way, glad, she said, to be relieved of her responsibility as Fanny's chaperone. She was going to sit with an aged relative whose wasting illness was in the final stages. Fanny was glad to be home alone, free of Simon's moroseness and irrationality, and Mercy's constant lecturing.

In the barn was a calf whose mother would not nurse it. Fanny knelt in the pen and held an invalid feeder while the calf sucked from it. She did not hear Robert approach, but she sensed his intense presence and knew that he was there in the barn with her. Wishes, she thought with joy, do come true.

Robert looked down at her with his unusual ice-blue eyes. He said nothing, simply held out his hand. Fanny took it, not fully understanding what he wanted, but aware that it had something to do with the ache in her middle that kept her awake at night longing for him. She knew she felt something wonderful for Robert Snow. She thought it was love.

They climbed to the loft where the new hay had been spread and piled. The air was heavy with the scent of dried grass, the pungent odors of sheep, cattle, and horses. Chickens gabbled and clucked out in the yard.

Fanny was not afraid. She was curious. She had seen farm animals mate and reproduce and understood the role of male and female. Robert

190

kissed her hands, her neck. "You are the most beautiful creature I've ever known," he murmured. "I adore you. Fanny, you drive me wild with desire."

She had never heard such sweet words. Like honey, they were that golden, that delicious. She helped him unpin her hair, and long auburn strands fluffed in the soft breeze that filtered through the hay. She was speechless with the delight of his attention.

Robert unbuttoned his trousers. He pushed Fanny's skirt high up around her soft white thighs. In summer she did not wear underdrawers. She arched toward him and took him into her body without coherent thought for the Bible lesson about Mary Magdalene Simon had read the evening before.

Later, they leaned against the well and drew up a bucket of cold, sweet water and drank. She waited for Robert to ask her to marry him. He did not, but he swore undying love to her and arranged for them to meet each evening in the dense pine grove a mile downriver.

Early in September, Robert said, and Fanny remembered his exact words, "I have been called back to Portland. We can be married there."

And now he had come for her just as he had promised.

2.

Two days later, they were in a small sailors' rooming house on Fore Street, close to Portland Harbor. Fanny settled in with a blissful feeling of release from the drudgery and restrictions of life on the farm. Robert said he would buy a little house for her, and she would wait there while he was away at sea. She would write him passionate letters, and make him a shirt and a quilted robe, and embroider him a pair of slippers. But things did not go as Fanny imagined. Robert was much occupied with the loading and impending departure of the vessel he was to sail with—or so he said. Fanny was left alone much of the time with little to do. She was not used to being idle. She passed the time with a serving girl, Nancy, at the Fore Street Inn where she took her meals.

"Everyone calls me Nance," she said. Nance was buxom with pale hair and a quick smile. "You're new around here." She set a plate of beans on the table and wiped her hands on her apron.

"Yes, I am," Fanny confided. "I've come here to be married. Then my husband goes on a voyage to South America."

"That's what they all say, Miss. They will promise you anything. You want to hang right onto him and get him to the altar quick. Them sailor men got a girl in every port. What vessel he on?"

"The bark *Lady Ellen*." Fanny nibbled her food. She wasn't hungry. More and more she worried about Robert's intentions.

"That's one of the old Phineas Stetson's vessels. Oh lord, the stories I can tell you about that old codger. The *Lady Ellen*, la-di-da. Named for his second wife and she's no lady. Ellen Brackett, she was. Got her start right here in the inn. I was just a young one with a job scrubbing pots. But I kept my eye on what went on out front. Old Phineas, he always had an eye for a neat waist and a trim ankle. And Ellen, she sure had that and then some. She did a whole lot more than serve a round or two of ale, now let me tell you. Then Phineas took a fancy to her and she hooked up with him. He must have been close to fifty, then . . . this was fifteen years ago or so. And she barely twenty. Well, I guess Phineas was either right over the moon about her or she knew how to cast her bread upon the water, because he up and married her, and wasn't that the wonder of the day. Then there was all the talk about Phineas's son, Joshua. Joshua comes in here some. Well, the story is, he didn't take much to Ellen as a stepmother. It was told around that she abused him some. But I don't see how that could be. He was about sixteen when Phineas married her. Seems more likely, and I heard this from a girl who worked up at Phineas' house, that Ellen and Joshua took a fancy to each other and Phineas caught them in the act. Wild as a hawk, he is, that Joshua. And old Phineas, he keeps his hand on the purse strings tight as a new-strung bed rope and don't give Joshua a penny. As for Ellen, well, I'd say she has ways to get what she wants out of old Phineas. But I'd bet poor Joshua don't like it a'tall." Nance grinned, pleased with herself for initiating a newcomer into the local gossip.

The story fascinated Fanny. She had lived a sheltered life, had read no novels, had heard little gossip aside from who had been born, died, got married, or injured. Nance's talk was entertaining. It passed the time while she waited for Robert to set the wedding day and find a house. But Robert put it off again and again.

Fanny bided her time until she was certain. Then she told Robert about the child she was carrying. That night Robert caught the first vessel sailing with the tide.

For days, Fanny stayed in her room and wept. If only she had listened to Mercy. If only she had taken Nance's advice and made Robert keep his promises. Twice she packed her belongings. Twice, the thought of a long winter of Mercy's disapproval and Pa's terrible judgment made her unpack again. She had no money. She was too ashamed to ask Nance what to do. She lay on the bed in her room trying to think of an easy way out of her predicament. The only thing to do was to go home to Pa and Mercy. But she was too ashamed to let them see how wrong she had been. She fell asleep with her arms around the pillow where Robert had laid his beautiful head.

By evening of the next day she knew what she had to do. She borrowed sewing tools from Nance and spent the day letting out the seams of her other dress so it would conceal the roundness of her belly. The material was too thin for early November, but it clung to her figure and revealed the parts she wanted revealed. She cut down the high collar so the little crevice where her breasts cleaved together was exposed just a tiny bit. She rummaged through her cache of laces, ribbons, and feathers and found enough to re-trim her straw bonnet.

When it was twilight, she dressed herself and did her hair so that it swept away from her ears and fell in a long, bushy mane down her back. She pinched her cheeks hard to give them color and went out into the street. Surely, there were other men with more means than Robert, who would find her attractive and wish to take care of her.

She chose the corner of Fore and Union streets where pedestrian traffic was busy. It was not far from her lodging and near the well-frequented lanes that led to Union Wharf.

195

Two mariners came by and eyed her up and down.

"Look at the prow on that one, mate. How'd you like to find that between the sheets tomorrow morning?" one man said.

Fanny's stomach did a flip-flop and she began to wonder if she had made a terrible mistake. This was not what she had expected.

"Aw, yer in yer cups too much to get it aloft even," the other man said. He stumbled drunkenly.

Fanny pulled her shawl across her chest to conceal the cut of her dress. Her courage waned. She was frightened. The men lurched away down the street and relief calmed the nausea in her stomach. She renewed her resolve. She would wait until a more respectable man happened along and she would ask his help. But when a man in an evening cape came in sight, she stood frozen in the street, too tongue-tied to speak. She couldn't do it. She couldn't sell herself.

Fanny hung her head and hot tears of shame and despair dripped down her cheeks. She knew she would have to go home after all.

"Are you ill?" A pair of eyes, neither brown nor blue, peered out of the fading light. Fanny had not dreamed the man in the evening cape would approach. He was too grand for her. She began to tremble, her tears multiplied, and she could only shake her head, no. Suddenly, she was on the verge of hysteria and sobbed uncontrollably. The man guided her to a nearby set of steps in front of a store and pushed her gently to sit.

Fanny saw him a little more easily now that he was closer. He was slight of frame and only a little taller than she was. He was neatly dressed in a finely tailored black suit with a white cravat tied perfectly under his chin. He was beardless and smelled of freshly ironed linen and scented shaving soap. She had seen him before, she realized with a start. Nance had pointed him out one day. It was Joshua Stetson.

"I know you. I've seen you at the inn. I heard Nance call you Fanny," Joshua said.

Fanny wiped her face with the back of her hand and fished for the handkerchief tucked into the wrist band of her dress. Her teeth clattered and she could not answer.

Joshua helped her to her feet. "Better come with me," he said. With his arm supporting her, he guided Fanny to a rooming house on Cross Street, a stone's throw away.

Fanny did not resist. Her mind had stopped functioning. She felt his kindness and responded blindly to it. She had nowhere else to go. The landlady had threatened to evict her that very day.

Joshua's room was modest in size, but pleasantly furnished with a large bed, a linen press, and a pine commode. Two overstuffed chairs were drawn up to the hearth. Fanny allowed Joshua to settle her in one of the chairs near the fire. He handed her a glass.

"Here," he said, "drink this." Fanny drank and choked on the Barbados rum the glass contained. The liquor revived her enough so she could speak.

"I can't stay," she stammered. Being in his room alone with him was a terrible mistake. Another terrible mistake. She had to go home.

"You don't make a very good doxy, Fanny-whatever-your-name-is. Too much pride. No experience. I suggest you give it up."

Joshua's words struck like a slap in the face and Fanny felt herself blushing. Her mind cleared and she stopped crying. An odd calm settled over her.

"I intend to, Mr. Stetson."

"Ah." Joshua lifted his glass in a mock salute. "My reputation has preceded me, I see. Never fails." He refilled Fanny's glass. She shook her head, no.

"Drink it," he commanded. She refused, pushing the glass away.

Joshua lounged easily against the mantelpiece, regarding her with an air of detachment, as if she were an insect on a blade of grass, too ordinary to take much notice of.

He was, Fanny supposed, about thirty, not handsome, though he had a pleasant face. He did not smile and she wished he would.

"Now that you have thawed out some," Joshua said, "I will take you back to your lodging."

Fanny stood up quickly. "I have troubled you enough, Mr. Stetson. I thank you for your kindness. I know my way back to Fore Street." She did not want him to know she had no place to go.

"Will the landlady be pleased to see you, I wonder?"

Joshua had not taken his eyes from her face and Fanny stirred uneasily. She clutched her shawl tightly around her. She felt as if he had the power to probe her mind, to strip her of her facade and reduce her to the nakedness of her folly. She avoided his eyes. He tipped her chin up with one finger so she had to look directly at him. If she said anything but the truth, he would know.

"The landlady will let me stay one last night and in the morning I will borrow some money from Nance and go home to my father and sister," she said meekly, miserably. Tears trailed down her cheeks again. He had been kind. Perhaps he also would be compassionate.

Joshua eyes roamed Fanny's body and came to rest on her bulky midsection. She blushed to the roots of her hair.

"So that's it," Joshua said softly. "You are in circumstances of, shall we say, a rather delicate nature." He reached for Fanny's left hand. "No narrow gold band. No money to pay the landlady.

And no prospects in sight." He seemed pleased at the idea.

"Thank you for your kindness," Fanny said stiffly and turned to go.

Joshua moved around her and leaned against the door so Fanny could not open it. His brown-blue eyes darkened with an expression she could not fathom. It came to her that she ought to be frightened, but it was not fear that she felt. It was fascination. And something more, something deeper that responded to his impulsiveness and roused similar feelings in her.

"Stay here. The rent is paid. It's warm. And safe."

Fanny did not feel safe. Wild, Nance had called him. She felt the wildness in him, an untamed spirit that reawakened the sense of adventure she thought she had lost when Robert had gone away.

"I don't work for nothing, Mr. Stetson." Fanny tossed her head and made her hair fly to let him know there was wildness in her, too, and even though she was vulnerable, she still had fight left.

Joshua's face collapsed into a grin and he laughed. The smile transformed his wildness into playfulness.

"Oh, I like your spirit, Fanny," he declared. He took a long drink from his glass and his face clouded again. "My dear Fanny, don't you know what's out there?" He swung his arms out in an expansive gesture. "There are mariners out there who would think nothing of dragging you into an alley with no intention of paying you for the convenience. There are men who would abduct you and force you to sell yourself forty times a day and pocket the money they earned from it. There are even women, lovely Fanny, who would strip you naked just so they could sell your clothes for what little they would bring. Stay here. You can decide what to do in the morning."

Joshua put on his stovepipe hat, swung his evening cape around his shoulders, bowed formally from the waist, and left.

Fanny stared, dumbfounded, at the door as it latched behind him. She sat back in the chair, feeling suddenly weak and nauseous. The warmth from the fire lulled her. The chair was very comfortable. It wouldn't hurt to stay just this one night. She gave in to the fatigue that had crept into her body. The rum she had drunk made her sleepy.

When she woke the next morning, she found Joshua Stetson's evening cape tucked around her knees.

3.

The clock on the mantel said 9 a.m. Alarmed that she had slept so long, Fanny kicked aside the cape and searched frantically for her shawl, finding it laid neatly on the bed. She wrapped its familiar folds around her shoulders. Her hand was on the door latch when Joshua eased into the room with his arms full of brown paper parcels and bandboxes. He was dressed as finely as before, but in ordinary clothing—a gray tweed jacket, a modest white neckcloth.

"For you," he said breezily, laying out lengths of woolen and cotton stuff, gloves, two bonnets, lace, ribbons, and sewing supplies. "Do you know how to sew?"

Fanny nodded dumbly. She recognized the impulsiveness of his gifts, but sensed calculation in his action. She knew from what Nance had told her, that Joshua Stetson never did anything for nothing.

"Good. Make yourself something that fits." He indicated the yard goods he had brought.

"Mr. Stetson," Fanny said carefully, "I can't take your presents. I—I have to go." A plan began to form in her head. She could accept his presents and after he had gone she could sell everything.

"Where, Fanny? Home to Papa?" Joshua's words were mocking and full of needles. "Out into the street into the clutches of the first drunken sailor who comes along?"

"No!" Fanny cried. "I will never do that again. I must go home." Her lips trembled as they shaped the word "home." She was on the verge of tears. Her back ached and she was hungry.

And this perverse man apparently took pleasure in tormenting her. She abandoned her half-made plan to accept his gifts. She held out her hand. The adventure was over.

"Goodbye, Mr. Stetson. I'm grateful for your kindness."

Joshua ignored her hand. He did not try to block her from leaving. He clasped his hands behind his back and stared morosely at the cold ashes on the hearth. He might have been the minister come to Sunday dinner or a little boy whose favorite plaything had been put away.

"You could stay here." It was a request, a suggestion, not a command. There was no wildness, no playfulness in his voice or manner. She could not define what it was about him him that kept her from opening the door and leaving.

"It won't be easy at home, you know," Joshua said softly.

That was true. If Fanny went back to Fort Point, her life would be that of a spinster with a bastard child to raise. She would be invited nowhere, not even welcome at church. And worse, her child would suffer from the pointed fingers and remarks whispered behind the backs of hands. Nor would Pa ever let her forget her sin. Mercy would be kind, but would take Pa's part to keep peace.

Fanny looked around Joshua's room. It was spacious, airy, and full of light. The furniture was comfortable and the floors were clean. It was much nicer, by far, than the room she had lived in at Fore Street. She felt a sliver of temptation creep into her. It communicated itself to Joshua. He turned and fastened her with a speculative look, waiting for her reply.

"If I stay, Mr. Stetson, then surely you will expect something from me in return." Fanny removed her hand from the latch. No harm in testing the waters a bit.

"Nothing you won't be willing to give, when the time comes, Fanny-whatever-your-name-is." Wildness edged his words and Fanny thought perhaps adventure had not gone to sea with Robert after all.

"Hogan. My name is Fanny . . . Hogan." She lied to protect Pa and Mercy, and to show she retained a small shred of decency.

"You have nothing to lose if you stay, Fanny. All any woman has of value is her virtue. Obviously, you've already lost that." Joshua's words robbed her of what small sense of decency remained to her. Shame bit her face. She drew her shawl closely around her. For the first time, she felt like a fallen woman.

And so, Fanny settled in.

The days passed in a haze of unreality marked by Joshua's erratic comings and goings. She expected Joshua to assert his right to share her bed, but he did not. Mrs. Winship, the landlady, brought meals three times a day, and Betty, the hired girl, came once a week to clean. Fanny did little but sew and sleep and watch her abdomen round out until she no longer could fasten her old dresses around her.

Other packages arrived. Perfumed soaps. A music box that played a tinkling tune. A length of rust-colored silk that made Fanny gasp with pleasure. All her life she had longed for gaiety and pretty things, but Simon had not approved of the pleasure she yearned for. There was no money for fripperies. She and Mercy had spun or sewed or baked everything they had. Thus, each present Joshua sent took on fairytale proportions. It was a dream that wrapped around her like a spider's silken web. She was caught and she did not care. She took whatever Joshua gave. It did not trouble her that she was in his debt. He had promised to take care of her until mid-May when the child would be born. This was her adventure and she made up her mind to enjoy it.

It was mid-December and uncommonly mild. It had rained every other day, keeping the streets full of churning mud. Fanny no longer went to the inn to talk with Nance. There was a new serving girl now. Nance had gone to get married.

The harbor was nowhere near freezing. Shipping, and the bustling life along the waterfront, went on. It was unheard of not to have had cold weather by now.

Fanny's pregnancy was in its fourth month. She no longer wanted to sleep all the time and the nausea of the early months had passed.

She heard the tap of Joshua's boots outside her room and a little ripple of pleasure gilded her being.

"Get dressed, Fanny," Joshua called through the door. "I'll come for you in an hour. Be ready."

When he returned, he raised his eyebrows in admiration and Fanny felt herself glow under his approval. She wore a high-waisted gown made from the rust-colored silk. She had looked in the mirror and knew it set off her auburn hair and fair skin. The dress fit snugly under her breasts, now rounded like plump fruit from her pregnancy, and fell in soft folds to the top of her slippers. The neckline was modestly filled in with lace and ruching. The sleeves fit snugly at the wrist and puffed at the elbow. She had learned more about dressmaking from Mercy than she had realized. She had never owned such a magnificent dress.

"Is it all right?" she asked, craving his admiration.

"My dear, Fanny, you look like a queen." Joshua's words were like cream to a cat. He was not too often inclined to such compliments, but when they came she reveled in them.

The rain had stopped. The mild weather held.

Joshua handed Fanny into a hired conveyance.

They rode in silence with only the sound of horses' hooves to disturb them. Predictably, Joshua's mood had swung and he seemed pre-occupied with his own thoughts. Fanny did not intrude. She went out of her way not to offend him. No sense in killing the goose that brought the golden eggs. Presently, Joshua rapped on the carriage roof with his walking stick and leaned out the window to speak to the driver. The carriage slowed and stopped.

"We are on State Street, Fanny. No mud here. Proper cobblestones. Everyone who lives here has earned the right to." Fanny nodded and smiled. "I'm not talking about good deeds, Fanny. I'm talking about money. Money is rarely earned doing good deeds, Fanny. You see that house? That's my father's house." Joshua indicated a large brick dwelling with numerous chimneys and a wide curving drive. Wildness played in his eyes. "If it weren't for my stepmother, it would be mine some day, all of it. Everything. But Ellen . . . The future lies up the coast, on the Penobscot River, at Bangor. This country is growing, Fanny. And the one thing that is going to make it grow is lumber. Lumber for houses and mills, for fine furniture, and ships, and wharfage, and boxes and barrels for shipping goods around the world. Bangor is where the lumber is, Fanny. Hundreds of thousands of acres. Entire town-ships are going up for sale by money-hungry proprietors who haven't the imagination to see how lumber can make wealthier men than State Street ever dreamed of." Joshua's eyes glittered with a light that burned hot enough to set his father's house afire.

Fanny thought of Nance's gossip about the Stetsons. It had a core of truth. Ellen Stetson had somehow deprived Joshua of his eventual inheritance from his father. It did not seem an important piece of information to Fanny. Step-mothers, and the havoc they created in families, were as common as the day was long. What disturbed her more was the talk of Bangor.

"Drive on," Joshua said to the coachman. They moved slowly down State Street, onto Danforth, and finally back to Fore Street and on to a part of the waterfront Fanny had never seen. Here, they stopped again. A rickety wooden building, with a sign hung at a crazy angle, rose out of a tangle of grogshops, tenement dwellings, and stables. The sign said, ROOMS. A band of ragged children, without shoes, fought over a loaf of bread. A drunkard slumped in the doorway forcing pedestrians to step over him. Women plodded slowly by, dressed in drooping feathers and faded satin ribbons, their pinched faces devoid of expression.

"Why are we here, Mr. Stetson?" Fanny stirred up easily, searched for the wildness in Joshua's eyes and found none.

"Don't alarm yourself, Fanny," Joshua purred. "I thought it might amuse you to see what you gave up when you decided to accept my good works. This, my dear, is a brothel. It's where fallen women, like yourself, go when they have nowhere else to go." A glint of sardonic humor flashed in Joshua's expression. But Fanny was not amused.

The air smelled of rotting fish and human filth. It made Fanny queasy. She had not known that such squalor and degradation existed. It appalled her to think how easily she might have ended up in a place like that. She owed Joshua so much, much more than she could ever repay.

"Please, Joshua," Fanny whispered, using his Christian name for the first time, "Let's go home."

Joshua took her gloved hand and pressed it lightly to his lips. The gesture enchanted Fanny. It was the first time he had touched her since the night he had rescued her from the terrors of the street. He held her hand all the way back to Cross Street. Perhaps, Fanny thought excitedly, he would come around and want to marry her. After the baby was born.

When they arrived at the rooming house, Joshua said, "I'm leaving for Bangor tomorrow. This weather won't hold much longer, and I want to get there before the Penobscot River freezes in for the winter. I've bought an interest in a lumber schooner and I won't be back. I've spoken to Mrs. Winship. I've paid her to see to your needs until after your confinement. I want you to join me once the child is born. You can be of use to me in Bangor. Send a message to Hatch's Tavern. But come without a child at your breast, Fanny. You will be of no use to me with a babe in your arms."

He kissed her lightly, impulsively, on the lips and left.

4.

The walls of Fanny's room closed in around her after Joshua left. It was her nest. She feathered it with the small housekeeping tasks Betty, the hired girl, did not do. Fanny shook rugs out the window, made her bed, kept things neat. She began to stitch a set of childbed linens, the small garments, blankets, and diapers the babe would need. Time passed, if not quickly, then tolerably.

Fanny did not anticipate the infant's arrival with pleasure. The birth would free her body of its burden, but birth simply shifted the burden from within to without. She brooded about whether or not she would survive lying-in. Many women, she knew, did not.

Fanny's mother always had made extensive visits to the minister to ensure that her spiritual life was in order as childbirth approached. It was well she had. She died after giving birth to yet another stillborn son the year Fanny was thirteen.

The bigger Fanny's belly got, the more active the unborn infant became, the more Fanny brooded. Her isolation increased with her size.

There was no word from Joshua. She missed him. She chided herself for the folly of thinking her arrangement with Joshua was adventurous. Nor could the impending ordeal of birth, she concluded, be construed as an adventure.

A cold spell at the end of December froze everything, then gave way to unusually warm days. By New Year of 1831, the ice left the harbor and did not return. Fanny eased her growing sense of doom and loneliness, her self-loathing for the fix she had got herself in, and her resentment at how the unborn child had taken over her entire being, with daily walks up Cross Street.

Cross Street, despite its nearness to the seamy elements of waterfront life, housed a somewhat more genteel class of people. Yards were tended and pigs were kept properly penned. The rooming houses, of which there were many, catered to visiting relatives, indigenous spinsters of respectable reputation, and an odd assortment of traveling merchants, itinerant preachers, and nomadic seamstresses.

The landladies of Cross Street tended to put

on airs and were decidedly inclined to appoint themselves the keepers of the public morals. They snubbed Fanny whenever she chanced to encounter them on her daily walk. Fanny was mortified at the way they drew aside the hems of their skirts and refused to acknowledge her presence by even the smallest nod. Fanny had seen her landlady, Mrs. Winship, hobnobbing over back fences and knew perfectly well that lady's loose-hinged tongue had spread the tale of her predicament.

It dismayed Fanny, but did not surprise her, when Mrs. Winship asked to see her on a matter of the utmost delicacy.

Mrs. Winship stood as close to the door of Fanny's room as she could, as if fearing she would be contaminated by Fanny's illegitimate pregnancy. She clasped her hands rigidly over her apron. Her faded hair was tucked severely under a white cap tied primly under her chin.

"I've been to see the Reverend Mr. Dow," Mrs. Winship said nervously, "and he fully agrees with me, as do all my near neighbors, that something must be done. You don't fool us with a Mrs. in front of your name. Why the very idea! I've never had such goings on under my roof. If it wasn't for Mr. Stetson being so generous about your keep and me in need of what he sends, I'd have turned you out long ago and sent you packing off to where you belong." Her eyes glittered hard and mean. Fanny thought of a weasel she had once chased from her father's chicken house.

"The ladies of the church, and the Reverend Mr. Dow, have held a meeting, and we've decided that the least we can do, as Christians, is point out the error of your ways and exhort you to pray for forgiveness. Since you are not fit to raise a young one, there are several God-fearing women in the church who can offer your child a decent home. The Reverend Mr. Dow begs you to allow him to call on you so he can pray with you. And I would be greatly obliged if you would find other lodgings as soon as your confinement is over." Mrs. Winship pursed her lips and looked down her nose.

Mrs. Winship's words coiled around Fanny's heart and squeezed. How could she be as evil as Mrs. Winship made her out to be? She had loved Robert Snow, had truly believed they would marry and make a happy life together. What had she done wrong? Certainly, she had disobeyed her father. Wasn't that her only sin?

Deep down she knew it wasn't. She was bad, a bad woman, the kind of woman men made sniggering jokes about and decent women only spoke about in whispers. Nothing could change that, not prayer, or churching, or the exhortations of the Reverend Mr. Dow. She had made her bed, now she must lie in it. The thought enraged her.

"Get out! Get out! Get out!" Fanny screamed. Mrs. Winship did not move fast enough, and Fanny picked up a book and threw it at the lady's head. It missed and bounced off the door frame. Mrs. Winship fled, leaving the door open behind her.

5.

Late in February, Fanny at last received a letter from Joshua Stetson.

February 26, 1831
My dear Fanny,

I arrived at Bangor the day before the Penobscot River froze after an easy Journey of three days. At present all the local Sages are prophesying the Imminent end of the World because of this most unusual warming we have lately enjoyed. Indeed, a farmer hereabouts actually plowed his Fields this week.

I am told there are nearly 3,000 Inhabitants in Bangor, 16 of Them lawyers, which will give you some Clue to the demand for their Service as land changes hands here as often as a Woman changes her mind. I have been most Fortunate to arrange an Introduction to Mr. Rufus Dwinel and Mr. Samuel Veazie, who operate extensive lumber businesses. Without contracts from them to ship their Boards and Shingles downriver, one has little Chance of large success. These two Gentlemen are generally not on speaking terms and are constantly Suing one another for the most Petty infractions of the Law. That is how they accumulate various Properties which they in turn sell for a goodly Profit, and is, in fact, a very sound way of building one's Finances, as I have quickly learned.

I have lately received a most hysterical communication from Mrs. Winship, who complains of being Ungratefully treated and not Deserving of a book thrown at her head. I assume she refers to a Display of your defiant Spirit of which I was once the Unfortunate witness. I have written to Mrs. Winship to soothe her ruffled feathers and you may be Assured she will not turn you out on the street where the neighbor Ladies would surely point their Fingers at you and shout Shame, Shame, in your face. Perhaps, my Dear Fanny, your warring Spirit might be a boon to the female scholars at Atkinson, not far from here, who have started a project calling for the Reform of ladies' fashion. Any person who joins them pledges herself to refrain entirely from wearing Busks, Boards, Stays, Cushions, Pillows, Bolsters, or any kind of furnishing which is likely to cause consumption or endanger life. Life in this Wilderness appears to bring out the Wildest ideas in the Ladies and I am Convinced you would find yourself quite at Home here.

I assume you are unacquainted with any Ladies who possess the Skills you will soon require. The day I sailed for Bangor, I had a chance encounter with Samuel Webber, a physician, with whom I was briefly acquainted at Harvard College and who now is ship's surgeon on my father's line. Webber's wife is living at Portland on York Street. Mrs. Webber is, according to her husband, a midwife of some Skill. He says you may send to her at any Time of day or night and she will assist you when the day of Confinement arrives.

Bangor boasts of any number of educated and genteel Ladies and Gentlemen who attend lectures at the Lyceum. Many of these Lectures are printed in the *Whig and Courier*, the local newspaper. I shall send you copies. The lectures often devolve on the Question of Temperance and the Impropriety of selling spirituous liquors; in my Opinion a waste of breath, and clearly a means for the Rum smugglers to become Wealthy. Prosperity, my Dear Fanny, depends entirely on the wages of Sin. Would you not agree?

Until Future and as yet Unknown circumstances dictate that our Paths should cross again, I remain your most humble and ob'dt servant,

J. Stetson

Joshua's letter infuriated Fanny, but also gave her a sense of relief. She read it through several times before she replied.

Portland
February 28, 1831
Dear Sir,

I am most Grateful to receive your Kind suggestion that Mrs. Webber might be called to Aid me when my Time arrives. As for Mrs. Winship, that Woman has taken great Pains to avoid the sight of me, but does, I confess, continue to see that my Meals are sent, and what few small Wants I have are met. The days have passed slowly and Unhappily, for the most part, and I often wonder if I did the Right thing in remaining here. Perhaps it would have been better if I had ended up in that dreadful House you so Unkindly pointed out to me. At least then I might be Dead and released from these days of Discomfort and Isolation. I am reading the books and newspapers you have so Thoughtfully sent and I thank you for it. My Education, while adequate for most females of my class, did not cover the works of Milton. Mrs. Winship has slid any number of Religious tracts under my door, which I have used for kindling. She is a Baptist, a religious Sentiment which sits ill with the Congregationalist teachings of my late mother. I have received the dear Gold Locket so nicely engraved with a letter 'F' and wear it Always as a token against the Days that are past and Those that are to follow. As for your Sanguine comment that 'prosperity depends on the wages of Sin', I have only to consider my current circumstances and the Bountiful rewards you have heaped on me, and agree; provided you also Understand that I am also Rich in Guilt, Shame, and Lost

Honor. I remain your respectful and ob'dt servant,

Mrs. Fanny Hogan

Fanny blotted the ink, dusted it with fine sand, and left it on a table outside her door for Betty to take to the post office.

April, the last month of Fanny's time of being with child, left her lethargic and uncomfortable. Her ankles and hands had swollen some and she hadn't the energy to carry on her ritual of dusting, sweeping the hearth, making her bed, and shaking the rugs. The loss of the comfort of that predictable routine deepened her gloom.

She thought often of her mother, and the short intervals when her mother was not carrying a child. She and Mercy and Ma had picked field strawberries every summer and made pots of jam. She remembered when the three of them had scrubbed fleeces clean after Pa had sheared sheep. Ma had used the tag ends to stuff the bodies of two identical rag dolls she had made. Fanny thought longingly of those days, and others like them, knowing full well they were gone forever. She cried herself to sleep at night, gritted her teeth the next morning, and waited. She cursed Joshua Stetson part of the time and thanked God for him the rest. She wondered more than once if it would be easier to be punished for her sin than rewarded for it.

Fanny's travail began early in the morning of the second week of May. At first she thought it was indigestion, but the discomfort clutched the small of her back and eased around the sides of her swollen belly in slow, rhythmic intervals. She remembered her mother saying travail was like a strong hand clenching and unclenching its fist. Women from nearby farms always had come to take care of Fanny and Mercy, and to run the household while her mother was confined in childbirth. They had supported her mother in the birthing position, had rubbed her back and soothed her with quiet words. They had included Fanny in those ministrations, allowing her to hold cool drinks for her mother to sip. But for Fanny, there were no helpful women wise of the ways of being female to call, except the midwife, Mrs. Webber.

Fanny eased herself out of bed and fumbled for the candle. The simple act of lighting it, of doing something ordinary in the face of the extraordinary thing that was soon to happen, calmed her. She caught a glimpse of herself in the mirror, was arrested by what she saw. Her face was haggard, thinner than it had been. She fingered the gold locket and wondered for the hundredth time if Joshua was fond of her, and if she could get him to think about marrying her. She pushed her hair away from her face. Long strands spilled down her back in a thick tangle. Her belly protruded beyond her breasts. I look like a fat squash, she thought, and almost laughed, almost cried. She wanted her mother, she wanted her sister Mercy.

Fanny knew enough about birthing to know that infants did not hurry from the womb. She went back to bed and waited until she heard Betty stir, then sent her to York Street for Mrs. Webber.

6.

The clock on the mantel struck seven. It had ticked away the hours and days and months to this moment. Fanny lay in bed on her side, knees drawn up nearly to her chin, listening to the clock's steady tick. It was her life ticking away. On this day, she would begin another life, that of a mother to a child.

The midwife's appearance was youthful, her age difficult to determine. Thirty, perhaps, or less, Fanny thought. Mrs. Webber was small and quick, her figure was as rounded as a well-fed winter chickadee. She wore no bonnet, a gesture that aroused Fanny's mild curiosity. Women wore bonnets when they went outside. But the midwife did not. Her hair was dark and straight, and wisps escaped from a simple coil at the nape of her neck. She was not beautiful, nor was she

221

plain. Fanny had the quick impression of warmth and concern. The midwife carried a scarred pine medicine chest under one arm. She set it on the floor near Fanny's bed, pulled off her jacket, which did not match her gray wool skirt, and dropped it unceremoniously in the nearest chair. She smiled and held out her right hand.

"I'm Maude Webber." Fanny took Maude's hand, noting its small, tapered fingers.

"I'm Fanny . . . Hogan." She still hesitated whenever she lied about her name. The midwife did not seem to notice nor to care that no women had come to assist, no anxious husband hovering outside her door.

"I understand from Betty that your child has decided to arrive today." Maude's voice was as softly padded as the rest of her, as calming as the whir of the spinning wheel.

Maude moved around the room in a brisk way. She inspected the ewer and basin, the chamber pot, fingered the childbed linens and poked at the fire. Fanny knew at once she was in capable hands.

"The air is very stale in here," Maude commented. She opened the window and the cheerio of robins drifted in. "You will be needing great breaths of air during your illness. When did it begin?"

"About four this morning. I thought . . . does it always feel like this, Mrs. Webber? I expected it to hurt more." Fanny wanted the child's birth to hurt, wanted it to hurt a lot—to remind her of her sin, punishment for what she had done.

Maude smiled, a pleasant smile that held no mirth. "I've never birthed a babe of my own, Mrs. Hogan, so I cannot give you the benefit of my personal experience. However, you are a very long way from delivery and that accounts for the lack of severity of your illness. But you must not worry. I will teach you how to use each pain to aid in expelling the infant from your womb when the time comes. You will find it pretty hard work, a labor, indeed, but not so hurtful as you fear. You must get up, Mrs. Hogan. Your fingers are a bit swollen, I see, and your feet, too. I'll soak them in cool water."

A rap sounded at the door. Betty appeared with a large jug of hot water in one hand and a pail of cold water in the other.

"Thank you, Betty. Put the hot water on the hearth," Maude directed. "I'll call you if I need something else."

Maude mixed some of the hot water with the cold and poured it into the basin. She placed Fanny's feet in the water.

"You will find this very soothing, Mrs. Hogan."

Fanny pushed a tangle of hair away from her ears. She liked the comfort of having the midwife in charge, of being taken care of.

"My mother used to wash my feet like this

when I was a little girl and had been out all day with bare feet. She never let me go to bed with dirty feet," Fanny said.

"This will relax you. Relaxed muscles make for a much easier birth," Maude said as she bent over the hearth. "I'm making an infusion of willow bark," she continued. She rummaged through her medicine chest and drew out several small cloth bags containing dried herbs. Everything in the medicine chest, Fanny noticed, was perfectly ordered. "A willow bark infusion will ease your discomfort later on."

Fanny's pains had been coming every twenty minutes or so. She bent forward as another curved around her lower back. In an instant, Maude was at her side. She rubbed Fanny's back in slow circular motions until the pain eased. She removed Fanny's feet from the basin and dried them. Fanny thought she was to lie down again.

"Oh, no, Mrs. Hogan," Maude said. She took Fanny firmly by the elbow. "You must walk a while. Come to the window. It's nearly summer outside although it's only May. See how green the grass is, hear the birds. And breathe some fresh air."

Fanny spent the next hour pacing and breathing. Her white bedgown billowed softly around her heavy body. She rubbed her stomach as she paced and was only mildly uncomfortable.

Perhaps, she thought, a terrible birth was not to be her punishment, after all.

Maude stripped away the bedclothes and tightened the rope webbing that held the feathered tick. She shook the bedding out the window to air it. She smoothed the tick onto the rope webbing. Then she covered the tick with a large oilcloth to protect it from birth fluids. She drew a clean sheet from a parcel she had brought with her and spread it over the oilcloth. She drew out another sheet and spread it, folded double, across the middle section of the bed.

Fanny did not recall any such elaborate preparations at her mother's lying-in, but she liked the idea of order and cleanliness, longed for it.

Maude finished preparing the bed and stirred the willow bark brewing in a pottery teapot by the fire.

"It's time to rest awhile, Mrs. Hogan. And I must make an examination."

Fanny obeyed willingly—there was such comfort in Maude's manner. It felt good to give herself up into the care of a kind person after the meanness she had received from Mrs. Winship and the ladies of Cross Street.

Maude pulled a straight chair near the bed and sat close to Fanny. Maude, Fanny noted, smelled of clean fabric and fresh air.

Maude placed her hands on Fanny's belly.

Her hands left a scent of peppermint in the air.

The sensation of Maude's hands lying so familiarly on her belly struck Fanny as oddly incongruent. For nine months only she had mapped the contours of her bulging middle; no one else had witnessed the sharp kicks and rolling motions of the unborn infant. A small pang of resentment at such intimacy crept into her mind, but another pain spiked across her back and all her concentration turned to breathing in slow, easy, instinctual puffs.

Maude nodded approvingly.

"You're making excellent progress. The womb is tightening strongly, as it should. The infant's head is in the proper position," Maude said. She produced a horn-shaped instrument and applied it to Fanny's belly. Maude nodded her head in satisfaction. "The infant has a strong heartbeat," she said.

Maude rose and went to scrub her hands with the lye soap she had requested from Betty. She drew spotless white sleeve protectors over her arms.

"There's no modest way to give birth, Mrs. Hogan. There are a great many doctors, and indeed, midwives, who perform the delivery of infants under draperies. They never view what is going on with the mother. In other words, they rely solely on touch to determine how the birth is progressing. I believe this is a most dangerous practice. It's not my way, not the way I was trained. In order for me to understand the changes your body undergoes as the birth progresses, it is absolutely necessary for you to allow me to view the opening where the infant's head will emerge. And you must allow me to touch the area."

Maude plumped the pillows and arranged them comfortably behind Fanny. She showed Fanny how to sit in a half-reclining position with her knees drawn up.

Fanny cooperated, but her cheeks colored hotly at the thought of Maude inspecting her private parts. It wasn't decent. No one but Robert had ever seen her naked, and then only under the quilts. When she had begun her monthly bleeding, she had not allowed Mercy to see more than her thighs, and only to let Mercy show her how to tie a pad of rags and cotton wool between her legs to collect the flow. But this was different, she told itself. This was a dangerous time. Her infant's birth could not be accomplished in safety without causing some embarrassment. Perhaps that was the beginning of her punishment; the price she would pay for getting herself into such a fix.

Fanny drew her bedgown up over her belly to indicate her cooperation, revealing the thin, pigmented line that ran along the contour of her belly. She screwed her eyes shut and held her breath. She expected discomfort, but Maude's fingers probed gently, explored and learned without invading. Fanny let out a great whoosh of air when Maude finished the examination.

"Do that again," Maude encouraged, "breathe in very deeply, hold it, and use your belly muscles to push the air out." Fanny complied. "As the pains get closer together, Mrs. Hogan, they will become more intense. During each pain you must breathe as I have just instructed you. It will aid the infant's journey as well as ease your travail. It will be some hours yet. You must walk some more. I'm going to find Betty and ask her to bring you some broth. Please avail yourself of the chamber pot if you feel the need."

Fanny lay against the pillows. She had expected childbirth to punish and cleanse and purify her soul. Instead, she found herself almost enjoying it. She smiled ruefully. But what about after the child was born, after Mrs. Webber had done her work and gone? How could she take care of an infant without money or friends to help her? She thought of the sign that said ROOMS and shuddered. She could go to Joshua. He wanted her, she knew he did. But he had said not to come with the child. Perhaps Mrs. Winship was right. Perhaps she should give her infant to some good family to raise. Another pain clutched her back and canceled her thinking. A strong one. When it eased, she drew up her bedgown and inspected the place between her legs where the infant

228

would emerge. She had never been present at the moment of birth of any of her dead little brothers, but she had seen farm animals born. Her father considered it a tedious, messy business. She had thought it miraculous, and now that miracle, in spite of the evil things she had done, was happening to her. It made no sense at all.

Fanny rose and eased herself heavily onto the chamber pot. It was awkward to sit so low to the floor. She emptied her bladder and tried to heave herself up to a standing position. She could not. She tried again and succeeded only in rocking herself from side to side, putting herself in danger of oversetting the pot. The rim bit painfully into her bottom. She shifted her weight and giggled at the foolishness of her predicament, the absurdity of her entire situation.

"I can't get up," Fanny said when Maude returned a few minutes later. Fanny's knees were scrunched up under her chin, her big belly sagging between them.

Maude broke into a broad smile. She took Fanny's hands and helped her carefully off the pot. Fanny linked her arm through Maude's and they strolled about the room. She sipped the broth Maude gave her. She confided some of the recent events which had brought her to Portland.

"I had a letter from Joshua Stetson, Mrs. Webber. It was he who recommended you to me. He says he's acquainted with your husband."

"Oh, yes. Mr. Stetson was at Harvard College when Mr. Webber studied medicine there back in 1818, I think it was. I believe Mr. Stetson studied law, but did not stay long enough to take his examinations. My husband said Mr. Stetson's behavior was often wild and unconventional."

"I heard his father disowned him." Fanny repeated Nance's story. Talking to Maude Webber was as easy and as comfortable as an old pair of shoes. They might have been sisters instead of midwife and lying-in woman.

"I believe there's some truth to that story. I've heard a number of variations of the same one. Phineas Stetson does have a very young wife. And she is known to be the apple of his eye. And it is true that Mr. Stetson never sees his son. My husband is under orders to notify Mr. Stetson at once if Joshua so much as sets foot on the Stetson wharf."

So he is an outcast too, Fanny thought, like me. The idea wrapped around her snugly. Joshua was wild and no one wanted him.

"Joshua has been very kind to me." Fanny wanted Maude to know that. He was not just wild, he was kind. She loved him for being kind.

Fanny stopped in mid-stride. She did not like the implications of Joshua and his stepmother . . . she turned from the thought and changed the subject.

7.

Sweat stood out on Fanny's face, washed her in a slick stickiness that Maude's dabbing with a damp cloth could not wipe completely away. She took deep breaths and pushed and panted according to Maude's instruction. They had dropped all pretense of formality and called one another by their given names. They were Maude and Fanny, two women engaged in woman's most elemental experience, giving birth.

The thin angry cry of the babe trailed into the room. Fanny held her breath and listened. The burden of the last nine months was separate from her body. Relief kneaded her muscles, and she relaxed, she realized, for the first time in months.

"You have a fine girl, Fanny," Maude called softly. She cut the cord and tied it. Fanny could feel these things happening, she could see them. She did not yet comprehend them. Her abdomen, where Maude placed the wet, squirming child, looked like bread dough that had just been punched down.

"You two get acquainted while I finish on this end. The afterbirth will emerge in a few minutes, and I'll bathe you and the child, then you can sleep for as long as you want," Maude said. Her sleeve protectors were stained with blood.

Her hair slipped from its knot in unruly wisps. She hummed a few bars of "Greensleeves," and didn't seem to care in the least how she looked.

The infant waved her tiny arms and legs in jerky, spasmodic circles. She had stopped crying and was oddly silent. Her little pink mouth opened and closed with soft sucking sounds.

"Like a bird," Fanny whispered. "Just like a baby bird in the nest looking for its first meal. A perfect little birdie. Hello, Birdie." Nothing had prepared her for the elation she felt as she stared at her newborn daughter. Here, lying outside her belly was what had lain inside all those unhappy months. A moment ago, she had been just Fanny, one person, and now there were two, and that little pink birdie was a part of her, a part of Robert. She thought of her mother and wondered if she had felt like this after giving birth to her daughters. But even in the midst of her elation, the wonder of it, a part of her did not want to get too close to the infant.

"Have you thought of a name for the babe?" Maude asked.

"No," Fanny replied. She hadn't thought of any names, hadn't considered until this moment that the child must, of course, have a name. "I will call her Birdie until I think of one."

Birdie opened her eyes at the sound of Fanny's voice and searched for the source of the sound.

Her eyes found Fanny's and even though Fanny knew that newborn babes did not see well, she felt certain Birdie saw her.

Birdie's dark hair was wet to the touch, yet downy, like a new chick. Fanny stroked Birdie's cheek with her finger and the infant turned her head to follow the touch. She found Fanny's finger and sucked. Fanny allowed a little bubble of laughter to break the quiet. Maude looked up and smiled. She finished her work.

"A little less humor, if you please, Fanny," Maude said with mock severity. "This is not a laughing matter." She showed Fanny how to hold Birdie to her breast. Birdie found the nipple, latched on, and sucked greedily and Fanny felt herself flow through the milk in her breast into her newborn child. She felt as if Birdie had somehow snared her in an invisible web, a web so strong she never wanted to free herself from it.

Maude gave the baths she had promised, made the bed up clean, and gave the news to Mrs. Winship and Betty. Fanny lay back in the pillows with Birdie in her arms and slept.

Later that week, Fanny wrote to Joshua.

May 18, 1831
Dear Sir,
Four days ago I was delivered a Fine

Girl by Mrs. Maude Webber, the same Lady you so kindly recommended to me. Mrs. Webber has stayed here with me since then, sleeping on the floor on a pallet quite grudgingly provided by Mrs. Winship. Mrs. Webber leaves of this Day, but will call to see me each day for the next several weeks. Her service has been most invaluable to me. Her fee is five dollars Silver Money. I am Most desirous that you send that amount to her at her lodging on York street. I had thought, also, to give her my Locket, the one you sent that is so dear to me, but she would not have it. Thank you, Sir, for your kind treatment of me in this very melancholy time. I remain forever in your Debt, Sir, and your most humble and ob'dt servant,

Fanny Hogan

Fanny gave the letter to Maude to take to the post office. Maude read the address and weighed the letter in her hand.

"You will be going to Bangor when you are able to travel." It was a statement, not a question.

Fanny avoided Maude's eyes, avoided a direct reply. She did not know what she would do.

"I owe him more than I can ever repay," she said.

"What about your father and sister? Will you write them about Birdie's birth?" Maude's eyes held no judgment, no censure. She knew Fanny's story and cared only that Fanny and the child would not suffer any deprivation.

Fanny shook her head, no. She couldn't tell Pa and Mercy. But she wanted to.

"What will you do, then? Once Joshua gets this letter, his support will end."

"I know, Maude. I'll manage. Somehow." Fanny fingered the material of the dress she wore, thought of the beautiful rust-colored silk gown she had made. There was no way she could ever provide for herself and Birdie to match the splendor of the things Joshua had given.

"I see. But even if Joshua changes his mind and wishes to continue his support, you must consider Birdie. If you accept the financial aid of a man who is not your husband, Birdie's chance for a normal life will be compromised."

Fanny had not thought of that. She reached instinctively for her child as if to protect her from the judgments of society at large. The bond that had formed between them stunned Fanny with its strength. She rubbed Birdie's narrow back. Birdie drew up her legs and nestled into Fanny's neck. Fanny had not counted on this bond between them.

"Go home, my dear," Maude said gently. "Your father won't cast you off. You can say that you are a widow."

"You don't know Pa, Maude. He would never believe me. Pa is very changeable. He wants people to think very highly of him. He won't stand for anything that makes him look bad." Her words lacked conviction and she knew it. Perhaps, Maude was right.

"Surely, your father and sister are heartsick at not knowing where you are, or what has become of you. I will mail your letter. Get plenty of rest and stay off your feet."

Fanny watched Maude's tweedy figure recede up the road toward York Street with a sense of wrenching loss. Home. She wanted to go home.

8.

It was nearly evening when the coach pulled into the yard outside Lane's store in Fort Point. The coach had rocked and swayed all the way from Belfast until Fanny's teeth shook. Birdie, wrapped in a thick shawl, resembled a bundle of clothing. She had slept through it all. Fanny did not recognize any of the other passengers and spent the entire trip ignoring them.

The moment Fanny had dreaded was upon her. The coach rattled to a bumpy stop, and she stepped awkwardly out into the yard, pretending she did not see old lady Twining's eyebrows disappear into her ruffled cap. She eased around the far side of the coach out of sight of the village layabouts who always gathered to watch the coach arrive. She saw Caleb Adams whisper something behind his hand to one of his cronies. The men slapped their thighs and laughed so loudly they startled a flock of starlings. Fanny's face burned with shame, convinced the men were making sport of her. She shifted Birdie to her other arm, hefted her bandbox, and started off up the main road toward home.

The dust on the road sifted across the toes of Fanny's walking boots, marring the shine she had so carefully given them. She had dressed herself modestly, choosing a dark dress and simple hat to achieve the look of quiet respectability Pa expected from his girls. As usual, she could do little about her hair, which escaped in orange-brown puffs from beneath her bonnet. Her hair refused to be harnessed into any of the sleekly composed fashions of hairdressing, and she fretted about it.

The road curved and dipped, crossed Butler Brook, then skirted John Nason's woodlot. The trees had leafed out into their summer shade, and wildflowers dotted the side of the road.

Fanny stopped to rest. She had been almost seventeen when she had left. Now, she was nearly eighteen. Had it been only a year? She picked the petals off a daisy and thought of the ones Robert Snow had given her. He loves me, he loves me not . . . How could she have been so innocent? She scuffed the dust off her boots with her handkerchief. Birdie stirred and slept on.

Soon, Fanny came in sight of the long hayfield that marked the beginning of Pa's property. The road ribboned out, giving a clear view of the Penobscot River in the distance to the right. The early evening air was alive with birdsong and fragrances Fanny had forgotten existed. The summer odors of damp earth, the slight tang of salt in the breeze, the unmistakable scent of manure set Fanny's heart racing with an exhilaration she had never expected to feel again. She quickened her step, was tempted to drop her bandbox and run. Her arm ached from carrying Birdie, and for one brief second she considered dropping the child, too, and running the rest of the way home.

She shifted Birdie to her shoulder and kept up her steady pace.

The farmhouse sat, just as she had left it, on a gently rising knoll a ways back from the road. Its silvery gray clapboards shone in the fading light. Stone walls girdled the fields in sturdy dark bands just as she had left them a year ago. The fence around the front yard sagged a little more than it had, but Mercy's bed of perennials had come up and some were about to bloom. Grandfather

Abbott had come from Easton, Massachusetts, way back in 1795, built the house, and settled his young bride there. Fanny was the second generation to have been born on the farm, in Grandmother Abbott's wide tester bed. The farm was not just home, it was as central to Fanny's being as the air she breathed.

The windows on the north side of the house were open to allow cool evening air to circulate through the rooms. There was no one about, but a soft circle of lamplight drifted through the kitchen window.

Fanny found Mercy in the kitchen stirring a pot of pea soup. The aroma twisted Fanny's stomach into lumpy knots, reminding her that she had not eaten since morning.

"Mercy," Fanny called through the open door, "I'm home."

Mercy whirled around, her plain face stamped with disbelief. She dropped her wooden spoon with a clatter.

"Fanny! In the name of heaven what are you doing here?" Mercy pulled her calico skirt away from her feet and hurried to close the door that separated the kitchen from the rest of the house. She drew Fanny inside and closed that door, too.

"I've come home, Mercy. I know I've done wrong, but I thought Pa and you and I could overlook the past and . . ." Fanny trailed off, stunned by the stoniness in Mercy's eyes.

"Overlook the past! Fanny, Pa has been like a madman ever since you ran off. He has been to Belfast, to the docks, every week, *every week,* since you left. He has talked to every mariner he crossed paths with trying to find out what had become of you. And what he heard didn't please him much, I can tell you!"

Just as Fanny had feared, the story of widowhood would not work.

"Mercy, it wasn't like that. Robert said he would marry me. But he didn't. He left me."

"And why wouldn't he, with you acting like a common trollop?" Mercy turned back to her cooking. "Pa won't put up with your being here."

Birdie stirred and whimpered. Fanny tried to hush her, but knew from the fullness of her breasts that Birdie was hungry.

Mercy rattled dishes in the cupboard and clashed pot lids. Birdie let out a sharp cry and Mercy dropped a saucer. She sank slowly into a chair at the table.

"Fanny, it's bad enough having the whole village know my sister is a fallen woman, but a child! I never thought . . ." Mercy's face had gone pale. "Fanny, you can't stay here. Pa will be fit to be tied. I don't know what he will do, seeing you so sudden. He's acted real odd for months now, more so than before."

Tears rolled down Fanny's cheeks. "I'm so tired, Mercy. Can't I just go upstairs to the spare chamber and rest? I'm so tired." Her tone was childish, almost peevish.

"I can see that," Mercy said softly. She lifted the edge of the shawl. Birdie's ice-blue eyes fastened on Mercy's face.

"Does the babe have a name?"

"I've called her Birdie since she was born," Fanny replied.

"Oh, Fanny, why is it you never think about anything before you do it? Birdie isn't a Christian name!" Tears trickled down Mercy's cheeks. "I've worried so much about you, Fanny. I tried to think if it was something Pa or I did or if you really were just plain foolish like Pa said." She took Fanny's hand. "You go up the back stairs. We will decide what to do tomorrow. I've got to figure out a way to tell Pa you're here and get him calmed down enough to talk to you."

The chamber room was unfinished except for the wide pine floorboards which were painted brownish-red. The rafters still had bark on them. They had been hand-hewn by Grandfather Abbott. The room was furnished with some of Grandmother Abbott's things—a big bed, a blanket chest, even the cradle that had rocked Pa, Mercy and herself. It was cozy under the slanting roof. For the first time since she'd arrived, with Birdie settled comfortably in the cradle, Fanny felt as if she were home.

Later on, Fanny heard her father come in, heard

his boots hit the kitchen floor with two loud clunks. His voice rumbled, but Fanny could not make out his words. The soft murmur of Mercy's voice blended with the rattle of cups and plates. Outside, a sheep bleated.

Fanny cowered in the chamber room, torn between a desire to run downstairs, confront her father, and get it over with, and the need to hide from his disapproval. Her father was not a cruel man, but he was proud, fiercely proud, and he required that his name be above reproach. He paid his bills on time, provided as well as he could for his family, and went to church every Sunday. He was respected by his neighbors. His forgiveness, if it ever came, would not come easily.

Birdie's loud wail woke Fanny some hours later. She did not know how long the baby had been crying. Panic stricken that Birdie's cries would waken her father, Fanny sprung from the bed and lurched against the commode. A china cup crashed to the floor. Feet clattered on the stairs and the door flew open. Fanny cringed against the wall. Birdie lay in the cradle, wailing loud enough to wake the dead.

Simon Abbott's nightshirt was tucked hastily into his pants. He was barefoot, his gray hair all awry, his beard scraggly in the light of the lamp he held aloft. His eyes burned with a glow Fanny didn't recognize. He looked like the picture of an

Old Testament prophet Fanny once had seen.

For a long minute, the air between them lay dead and stale. Only the bleat of Birdie's crying and the strange inhuman fire in Simon's eyes disturbed the room. Fanny dug her fingernails into the beam behind her back.

"Jezebel! Daughter of Hell! Get out of my house!" Simon hissed. He did not move. His contorted face held the most ugly expression Fanny had ever seen. She hardly dared breathe.

Mercy eased her way through the door and stood between Simon and Fanny. Her face was whiter than goose down in the flickering light.

"Fanny will be gone in the morning, Pa. She just came to say she's sorry, Pa, to ask your forgiveness. Pray with her, Pa."

Simon Abbott glared at his elder daughter. "Go back to bed, Mercy. Tell this whore to leave my house." Simon moved as if he were made of wood. His eyes focused on the beam beyond Fanny's head. She tried to intercept his gaze.

"Pa," Fanny whispered. "Please let me stay until morning." Simon seemed himself again, but it was fleeting. Birdie's wail increased in volume, and Simon turned to Mercy.

"I believe your dear mother has given me a son at last," Simon said pleasantly. "Hear him crying? Bring him downstairs, Mercy. Your poor mother needs her rest." The sound of his footsteps retreated down the stairs.

Fanny dissolved into a sobbing heap on the bed. Mercy sat down beside her and stroked her hair.

"I've never seen him this bad, Fanny. He hasn't been right for months. Sort of faraway. Sometimes he thinks I'm Ma."

Fanny beat the pillow with her fists for one furious moment. "I know someone in Bangor who will take me in, Mercy. But I can't take Birdie. Not at first. I'll have to leave her with you."

"Leave Birdie with me! Fanny, you're as confused as Pa is! I don't know how to take care of an infant. And who would feed her?"

Fanny's thoughts were racing. For first time, she began to see an end to her burdens.

"Listen, Mercy, Pa thinks Birdie is his child. You could let him keep thinking that. It wouldn't be for long. A month or two at most, just until I can get settled in Bangor. It's not hard to take care of a child. No worse than taking care of motherless lambs. There must be someone around who has just lost a child and has plenty of milk and would hire out as a wet nurse."

"Why, yes, I believe Sarah Smith just lost a babe. But we'd need money."

Fanny fumbled in her bandbox for some of the money Joshua had sent her. "I've got five dollars. And this locket. It's gold. You can sell it." Fanny unclasped it and handed it to Mercy. Mercy would not take it.

"I can't take your locket, Fanny," Mercy protested.

Fanny fastened the locket around Birdie's neck. "There," she said, "I've given it to Birdie. If you ever need money while I'm gone, you can sell it. Oh, Mercy, you've got to do this for me! There isn't any other way except for an orphans' home or finding a family to adopt Birdie and I can't do that. Here with you, she's with her family, her grandfather and her aunt. She's *home*." Fanny wiped tears away from her face with a flat of her hand. Mercy, too, was visibly moved.

"All right, Fanny. I'll do it. But just for a month or two. And if Pa gets right again before you send for Birdie, I'll write to you to come and get her." Mercy held out her arms for Birdie and Fanny deposited the child into them.

"Would you give her a name, Mercy? Something pretty and dignified. Not right this minute. You can surprise me when I come back to get her."

Mercy went back to her room taking Birdie with her. Fanny lay awake thinking about what she had done. The thought of leaving Birdie, even for a few weeks, cut across her heart like scalded milk. She did not know how she would endure the separation. But she knew she must.

And when she got to Bangor, she must convince Joshua Stetson to marry her. She would do anything, anything to make life easier for Birdie.

9.

Fanny stood alone and uncertain on the wharf at Bangor. Sail lofts, shipbuilding, grogshops, and establishments of dubious reputation crowded the water's edge. A few mariners eyed her curiously and she shuddered, remembering her experience in Portland and how easily she might have ended up in the house with a sign that said ROOMS.

She trudged up the road to what she hoped was the center of town in search of Hatch's Tavern where Joshua had said to look for him. Carts and drays, hand barrows and chaises rumbled around her in a bustle of commerce that attested to Bangor's determination to transform itself from an uncivilized frontier town to a gracious city that might someday rival Portland.

The road was damp and oozy, and the hem of Fanny's skirt dragged in the mud. Her breasts, tightly bound to cause them to stop producing milk, ached and she longed for her babe to relieve them. She put her discomfort out of her mind. She had to find Joshua. The thought had goaded her all the way up the river, and she had despaired of the wind ever blowing fresh enough to push the schooner she traveled on faster than a crawl. Now, she couldn't make her feet walk fast enough. She passed a few frame dwellings, a distillery, and several shops. She came to a corner and was unsure which way to turn. A small boy ran out of a yard bowling his hoop. Fanny stopped him and asked directions. He pointed the way.

Impatience bit at Fanny's heels, and she almost ran the last few hundred yards. She had to find Joshua, find out how quickly they could marry, and how quickly she could send for Birdie. But not Birdie anymore. By now Mercy would have found a proper name for the babe. Something pretty, something dignified.

The tavern keeper was civil and polite.

"Joshua Stetson. Now let me think," the man said. He scratched his head and took such a long time thinking that Fanny wanted to shake him into action. "Seems as though I've heard that name somewhere. There's so many people from away gettin' off the boats these days it's hard to keep track. You never saw so many men comin' up here to speculate in the wild lands. Gamblers, that's what they all are. Lookin' to make some quick money. Some do, but most don't, now let me tell you. Joshua Stetson, you say? Let me ask one of the hired girls. And the cook. Those women, they always know what's goin' on."

The man was smiling when he returned and Fanny felt a wave of relief wash over her.

"Well, they say the man you're lookin' for has a place over on Summer Street. Nice place. Just been built. Been cuttin' quite a swath, they say. I wouldn't go over there if t'was me. There's been a lot of fever here lately. They say they heard this Stetson is sick of it and his life is not expected."

Relief turned to anxiety with a sickening lurch of Fanny's stomach. She did not worry about going somewhere there was fever. All she understood was that Joshua needed her, he was sick and needed her care.

"How do I get there?" she demanded.

The man hesitated in the most maddening way.

"You a relative?" he asked.

"Cousin. I'm a cousin. Lately widowed," Fanny said. The words rolled effortlessly off her lips. Joshua was sick. He needed her. This slow-witted man knew where Joshua was. She would have confessed to being Queen of England to get him to say where Joshua could be found.

"Go back the way you came to Union Street. Then take the second road on your left. That's Summer Street. The only place there is the one you want. Big white columns on the front."

Fanny dashed out the door without so much as a thank you.

"Hey," the man called after her, "I do a little undertakin' if you find out you need one."

Fanny ran. Undertaker. Find Joshua. The fever. The words nipped at her, made her feet travel the distance more quickly than she had thought possible.

The house looked like one Joshua would choose for himself—an elegant house, a house with style and grace. Four large white columns rose the height of the two stories. They supported the gable end, which fronted the street, forming a narrow veranda. Two tall chimneys jutted out of the easy pitch of the roof. The earth around the house was still raw from the trampling of the builders' boots. There was no grass, none of the shrubs and perennial plants Fanny associated with home.

The house, she knew instinctively, was not a home in the sense she understood the word. But Joshua was in there somewhere, and he was sick and needed her to take care of him. Taking care of people made a house a home. The house had room enough for a child, too. Her thoughts flew wildly, like a flock of birds startled into flight.

Fanny lifted the brass knocker, shaped like a man's clenched fist, and let it fall. She waited. No one came to the door. She tried the latch and the door swung open into a long hallway with a graceful stair rising to the floor above. She made her way down the hallway, calling to Joshua as she went. Her voice echoed back from high ceilings, lost in the formal proportions of the rooms. She had never seen so much space for one person. Her father's house would have fit easily into the downstairs rooms. She was awed by it, almost afraid of its splendor, but it drew her and she pictured herself as mistress of all this space and grandeur.

The rooms were sparsely furnished, as if the bulk of its expense had gone into its building. But what little furniture there was, was beautifully made. The floors were covered with lovely rugs of intricate design. She caught glimpses of tiled hearths, the flash of crystal, the sheen of polished metal, the dignified fold of velvet. If she could get Joshua to marry her, she thought, all this would be hers. Excitement at the idea nearly canceled her anxiety and a quick nibble of guilt put her back to her purpose. Joshua was sick. She had to find Joshua.

Fanny called his name again. There was no answer, but she thought she heard a muffled sound upstairs, like a cough or moan. She made her way up the stairs and listened again. She pushed open the nearest door and gasped at what she saw. She hurried to the figure lying in a tangle of blankets and sheets on the bed.

Joshua's face, what Fanny could see of it, was ashen and looked as if it hadn't seen a razor for days. His lips were dry. His nightshirt was soiled with vomit. There was no wildness in him.

The room was vile with the odor of an unemptied slop jar.

Fanny threw open the window and peeled the filthy covers away from Joshua's body. He did not move or respond to her action. Asleep or unconscious, she did not know—could not tell.

"Joshua," she said softly, "It's Fanny. I've come to take care of you." He lay quiet and unmoving. Fanny removed her bonnet, flung it aside, and rolled up her sleeves. She found her way back down the stairs to the kitchen and brought back a basin of cool water and a towel. Cleanliness, that was what Maude Webber had said, the proper degree of cleanliness helped people get well and stay well. She bathed Joshua's face and washed his entire body, as if he were an infant. He felt cooler to her touch when she finished. She found a clean night shirt to put on him. Then she changed the filthy sheets, scrubbed the floor, and set the room to rights.

She went back to the kitchen, found some wood, and started a fire on the hearth. She made oatmeal gruel and tried to spoon it into Joshua's mouth. He made no effort to swallow so she set it aside. She pulled a chair close to the bed and sat down wearily to watch. So much of a woman's life was spent waiting, she thought.

It was dusk. She had been up since dawn. Her eyelids drooped. Her breasts ached and milk seeped from them and wet the front of her dress. She was too tired to care. All that mattered was that she had found Joshua. She would find a way to make him well. And he would love her for it and want to marry her, and she'd have a home for her child.

When Fanny woke, the house was filled with dark—filled with the heavy velvet silence of it. There were no sounds from the street, no glimmer of lamps or candles anywhere. She groped her way down to the kitchen and used a coal from the dying fire to light a candle. She went back to Joshua's room and bathed his face and arms again with cool water. She leaned close to his ear and spoke his name. His eyelids fluttered, but if he saw her and knew her, he gave no indication. He breathed deeply, almost a sigh, and lapsed back into the deep, sleep-like state he had been in all day.

The next day he was delirious. Fanny tried to prevent him from thrashing, but could not. He muttered and rambled, and she listened with a mixture of horrified fascination and undisguised curiosity.

"No, no, no, Ellen!" Joshua ranted. "You can't. Ellen, no!" And moments later, in a harsh cry, "You're old enough to be her father!" His facial expressions registered rage, despair, pain. Fanny stroked his brow and spoke to him in a wordless kind of cooing women use instinctively to soothe a fretful infant. He calmed and seemed to sleep. Then he began again, over and over, repeating himself.

"No more, Ellen. He'll find out. Not another penny. I'll leave. Go to Bangor." Joshua's face contorted. "You filthy swine. You can't do that

252

to me. No, Ellen, no!" Joshua's voice dropped to a broken whisper and a tear trickled out from beneath one eyelid.

Fanny pieced Joshua's ramblings together with what she had heard from Nance and Maude and began to understand.

Apparently, the gossip was quite accurate. Ellen had been no better than she ought to be when she married Phineas Stetson. But her hold on the old man was so great, she got him to change his will to make her his sole heir. Then, Ellen had grown tired of Phineas and took to amusing herself with Joshua. She told Joshua about the will and said if he was nice to her, she'd see that he was taken care of. And, Fanny surmised, Ellen had taken care of Joshua in more ways than one. And the attraction had been a mutual one. Phineas had caught them together one night when Joshua was home from Harvard. Ellen let Joshua take all the blame. Phineas disowned him. But Ellen saw to it that Joshua was kept in funds.

Fanny heard and understood and her heart ached for Joshua. He had been used so badly. No wonder he was so wild and difficult. Outcasts. He and she were outcasts—a bond between them.

Two more days passed. Fanny grew exhausted from lack of sleep and worry. She had not left Joshua's side except to bake bread so she would have something to eat.

It was Sunday. In the distance, a church bell tolled its urgent call. A breeze blew in the open window and fluttered the lace curtains. The sun was warm in Fanny's lap. She dozed. When she woke, Joshua's eyes were open and he looked right at her.

"Fanny," he said in a thin voice. "Don't leave. You can stay here."

She knew then he would recover.

10.

Joshua recovered slowly. Fanny wrote Mercy to say she'd be unable to come for Birdie as quickly as she had hoped, and would Mercy keep the babe a little while longer. She sent Mercy part of the money Joshua had given her for food. There was no reply.

Fanny installed herself in one of the other bedrooms and ran Joshua's household as if she were his wife. She liked to pretend she was.

When Joshua fully recovered, whatever notions Fanny had left about coaxing him into a discreet wedding ceremony were quickly lost in the swirl of attention he lavished on her. He sent for dresses and bonnets from the best Boston dressmakers and selected a small library of books which he insisted she read. He employed a dancing master and a music teacher, and Fanny discovered she had a certain skill for singing.

The days passed in a haze of cultivated activity.

"You're good to have around, Fanny," Joshua said. He expressed no gratitude that she had nursed him back to health. And as his strength returned, so did his wildness. Once again, Fanny was caught up in the adventure of never knowing what Joshua would say or do next.

Fanny wrote Mercy twice more; once to send money and to say she had been taken in by an "old friend" who "urged her to stay another week or so." The second time was to ask Mercy to be patient a while longer, that she would come to get Birdie in a month or two. When there was no reply, Fanny assumed Mercy had no objection to the arrangement. Her twinges of guilt receded and vanished. Her milk dried up, her figure slimmed out, and Joshua made the days as easy and soft as a featherbed.

It was curious, but nevertheless a fact, Fanny soon discovered, that no one in Bangor knew anyone else; no one inquired too closely into one's family connections or social background. The newcomers, adventurers, and opportunists who flocked to the infant town on the edge of the vast northern wilderness speculated in land, established businesses, or worked as woodsmen, sailors, seamstresses, washerwomen, or innkeepers. They didn't care two cents about anyone's personal pedigree. What counted was how quickly one became affluent enough to build a house like the elegant mansions already entrenched on Broadway.

Bangor produced a surprising number of wealthy men and women in a very short amount of time—that this often was accomplished in less than legal ways didn't bother anyone much at all.

A few local washerwomen quickly realized there was more to be wrung from a man's pockets than dirty wash water. They adjusted their priorities and set up rival establishments to cater to the more urgent needs of the woodsmen who emerged from the lumber camps in mid-spring after a long winter deprived of female company.

Rumrunners and grogshops prospered too, despite the outcry of the local clergy, whom few took very seriously anyway. Sailors arrived almost hourly from ports all over the world looking for a good mug of rum to oil parched throats. Business was brisk.

To be sure, there were plenty of men, like Joshua Stetson, who could boast a Harvard education, but didn't, and a fair sprinkling of polished daughters fresh from Boston finishing schools. These young ladies were in much demand as wives. Such women added tone to the raw community and made their otherwise uncultured husbands appear more refined.

There was, also, a small core of native sons and daughters, as they liked to think of themselves, descendants of the men and women who had settled Bangor in the 1770s when the region was still called Sunkhaze. But even these select few preferred to steer conversations away from their antecedents, because everyone knew perfectly well that someone's grandfather had jumped off a British or French ship in Boston back in 1772, stolen a horse from a penniless widow, and headed north for the anonymity of the Penobscot settlements. And each of these select families had at least one female connection who was never mentioned for reasons best left alone. By tacit agreement, everyone simply ignored the whole distressing issue of personal pedigree.

It was, Fanny was quick to notice, much easier to determine one's position in the odd pecking order of Bangor's social strata by the amount of money one had amassed. That amount determined where one lived. If you had a lot of money, you went to the top of the roost over on Broadway. If you didn't have any at all, you ended up in the mire under the roost in Joppa—down in the roughest part of the waterfront where the riff-raff congregated.

It didn't take Fanny long to figure out where she belonged. Without Joshua Stetson, she had no place; with him she was safe, taken care of, and protected from the harsher realities of life.

Fanny's twentieth birthday came and went, and she had two small diamonds in her ears to commemorate the event, a gift from Joshua. Under Joshua's guidance, Fanny evolved quickly from a self-conscious farm girl into an accomplished young woman capable of planning and executing a dinner for twenty, managing the hired girls who did the domestic tasks, and conversing intelligently and wittily on the political questions of the day. She could charm a room full of men with her artful rendition of "All Through the Night."

The businessmen, the lumber barons, the politically powerful whom Joshua brought to his house were, Fanny knew, deliberately wined, dined, and dazzled by her orange-brown beauty. Joshua introduced her as, "My dear cousin Mrs. Hogan, lately widowed," but no one was fooled.

Joshua was invited frequently to the Broadway mansions, but Fanny was not. And Joshua, in his perverse way, did not seek to impose her on his influential connections. It nettled Fanny to be left out. But she had to accept the snub. She was a fallen woman. And while her status as Joshua's lady friend prevented her from being included on Broadway, it did not prevent the Broadway gentlemen from enjoying her company on Summer Street. Because of her efforts, Joshua always got the political favors he sought. He prospered magnificently and, amused at Fanny's complaints about the snubs from the Broadway ladies, decided to indulge her. He built her a house, more sumptuous and elegant than any Bangor had ever seen, on a parcel of land on Oak Street, directly adjacent to Broadway, as close as you could get without actually being there. In the summer of 1835, Joshua installed Fanny there, much to the consternation of Mrs. Veazie who immediately relayed the news to all her acquaintances. Mr. Veazie raised no objections since he had enjoyed Fanny's singing very much on several occasions, but Mrs. Veazie made his life so miserable that he gave in, removed upriver to his mill site, founded a town he named after himself, and blamed the whole thing on Rufus Dwinel who had sold the land to Joshua in the first place. It kept him happily involved in litigation against Dwinel for years. Mrs. Veazie was mollified. The other Broadway ladies had to content themselves with refusing to nod whenever their carriages chanced to pass Fanny's.

A note from Mercy marred Fanny's delight and enjoyment of the new house. The note arrived dog-eared and bedraggled, as if Mercy had carried it around awhile before mailing it. The note said that Simon Abbott had died suddenly, that Birdie had been ill with croup, was now well but still weak, and Mercy hoped Fanny wouldn't think of sending for Birdie right away as the house was pretty empty with Pa gone.

Guilt pricked at Fanny's heart as she read the note. She ought to go home. That was the decent thing to do. But if she went home, she'd have to tell Mercy about the way she lived and she would bring shame on Birdie. All of Fort Point would be able to tell, just by looking at her, that she wasn't respectable. She couldn't do that to Birdie, or Mercy. She had to protect them. She sent money instead, and that went a long way toward soothing her conscience.

Soon, there were other matters to take Fanny's mind off Mercy and Birdie.

Fanny paced the library of her new house, oblivious to the exquisite inlaid furniture which had arrived on one of Joshua's ships. She was furious, so furious she had thought about driving down to Mercantile Row herself, then dismissed the idea, knowing full well Joshua would tolerate her temper in private, but would never allow a public display. Instead, she sent the housekeeper, Mrs. McGuire, with a discreet note requesting his presence at four in the afternoon.

Joshua came through the door as the little French clock on the mantel struck the hour. He fixed his eyes on Fanny and eased into the small, sardonic smile she had come to know so well. Joshua had fleshed out a little since his illness, but he still retained slimness and slightness of stature that inclined other men to misjudge his business acumen. He appeared to give the other party the advantage, but in reality, most of the profit from his business dealings went into the

Stetson counting house. Fanny had learned to recognize his subtle manipulations.

"Joshua," Fanny said evenly, "I know what you're trying to do and I want no part of it. They have to go, both of them! Today! I won't let you do this. I won't have it!" She glared at Joshua.

Joshua leaned against the mantel and lit a cigar, filling the room with acrid, blue smoke. He puffed a moment.

"Surely, Fanny, you aren't jealous."

"No, I'm not jealous," Fanny denied quickly, too quickly.

"Then what's troubling you, Fanny. Tell me, my dear, so I can make it right." Joshua's eyes glinted with mischief. Fanny knew the signs. He was playing with her.

"You know what I mean. It's those . . . women. Violet and Flora. They arrived this morning and said you had employed them to entertain your business partners."

"And how is this distressing you, Fanny?"

"Because they aren't respectable. And because you didn't tell me they were coming. This is *my* house, Joshua."

With one fluid, cat-like motion, Joshua left the mantel and drew Fanny to him.

"No, Fanny, this is my house. You only live in it as long as I choose to keep you here. Those two ladies, Violet and Flora, are here to do exactly as they told you. To entertain. Miss

Violet is an accomplished singer and Miss Flora plays the piano in the most inspiring way. It is true, Fanny, that they have other, shall we say, talents. I want you to go on doing as you have always done . . . run this house, *my* house, which I had built just for you. Keep yourself looking beautiful in the expensive silk dresses I provide for you and be charming to the gentlemen who visit. Is that asking too much?"

"Joshua," Fanny burst out, "I will not live in a whorehouse!" Fanny stormed angrily around the room with her arms folded firmly across her chest. Fear nibbled at the pit of her stomach. The image of the sign on the Portland waterfront that said ROOMS clawed at her thoughts. Joshua had the power to put her in a place like that.

"A whorehouse," Joshua said, pulling Fanny to him again. "I don't know where you get such ideas, Fanny. And after all I've done for you. All I ask, Fanny, is that you supervise Violet and Flora, in any way you see fit. See that they are a credit to the hospitality the gentlemen of Bangor have come to expect from me. Surely, you could do that for me, Fanny."

Joshua tipped Fanny's chin so her eyes looked into his. She relaxed and laid her arms around his narrow waist. She put her forehead against his shoulder. He smelled of cigars, shaving soap, and fresh linen. She found the aroma alluring, and curiously calming.

The fact was, Joshua did not share her bed. Had that fact been common knowledge, she knew no one would have believed it. Joshua seldom initiated physical contact, and Fanny yearned for the smallest touch of his hand, the briefest of caresses.

Fanny leaned more closely into his shoulder. She hated Ellen for what she had done to Joshua. He never spoke of Ellen, but she knew that what Ellen had done had made him bitter about life, had made it impossible for him to love anything but himself. She was jealous of the touches and closeness Joshua must have shared with Ellen.

She stood with her arms around his waist and her head tucked into the soft ease of his shoulder. She was willing to risk another pregnancy if only he would show some sign of wanting her. The thought excited her. Another pregnancy might bring Joshua to marry her. But thus far, Joshua had been reluctant to accept anything more than fond embraces, as if he knew the scheme and was too wise to be caught in so ancient a trap.

What Fanny felt for Joshua was, she knew, very different from what she had felt for Robert Snow. Joshua had rescued her, had treated her like a princess when everyone else had treated her like dirt. And she had taken care of him when he was sick. She did not think that her care of him canceled her debt to him. She thought it bound them more closely. If that was love, then she loved him.

Joshua smoothed a wisp of hair from Fanny's brow and smiled his slow smile, the lazy one that gave him a boyishness that belied his thirty-five years. His youthful expression, when he was relaxed, touched Fanny very deeply. Somewhere, beneath the self-made man, the man obsessed with power, was a boy, a child, who needed her love and protection, who needed to be taken care of. Who, in turn, would love her for it.

Fanny slipped her hand under the edge of Joshua's lapel, felt his heart beat strongly and rapidly. She loosened his cravat and nestled her lips against his neck. He did not pull away as she expected. He buried his fingers in the thick coil of her hair and removed her hair pins. He dropped them, one by one, to the floor. Her hair tumbled about her shoulders in a springy orange mass. Joshua smoothed it with one hand; with the other he undid her bodice buttons and pressed his mouth to the hollow of her throat. He held her closely for a moment then scooped her into his arms and carried her to his private rooms down the hall.

11.

Joshua deposited Fanny in the middle of the bed in a room he reserved for himself. He set her down as if she were a rag doll put away in a convenient place by a bored child.

The bed was said to have once belonged to a member of British royalty. Joshua had acquired it from an English mariner down on his luck. Privately, Fanny doubted it had ever belonged to a king, but she knew Joshua enjoyed thinking it did. It was too massive and ornate for Fanny's taste. It was high and wide, curtained and canopied, and spread with deep rose silk which heightened the illusion that it had cradled the sleep of royalty.

Fanny aimed an encouraging, playful smile at Joshua.

"You will have to do something about this spread, Joshua," she laughed, "it clashes with my hair." He was very particular about the colors she wore, insisting that any shade of pink was unbecoming to her.

Joshua regarded her thoughtfully for a moment.

"I've changed my mind. The color suits you better than I thought, suits the inconsistencies of your character. Brash common orange against modest royal rose."

His words enchanted her. She had known there were wells in Joshua that ran deeper than anyone had ever dared dip into. She knew he read poetry and philosophy.

She could not read the expression on his face. It was soft, softer than she had ever seen it before, and there was a light in his eyes that wasn't wild, only hinted at wildness. Little vines of cautious excitement grew in Fanny's heart.

Fanny's bodice, open to the waist, exposed the round contours of her breasts. She knew she had a beautiful figure. The dressmakers always commented on it. She was slender without being skinny, shapely without being voluptuous. She pulled her skirts slowly up above her knees. Her bottom was bare because she refused to wear the new undergarments the dressmakers called drawers.

She pulled her petticoats a little higher, allowing full exposure of her thighs. It was a simple gesture aimed at eliciting a playful response in Joshua. He did not, she knew, know very much about playfulness. Joshua liked things to happen according to his own design. That required work and scheming, not play. This was true in all aspects of his life.

Fanny did not know where, or if, he slaked his physical yearnings, but she wanted to believe that his need to control and dominate every situation would not extend to the bedroom.

She posed seductively, a bit artfully, appealing deliberately to his carnal appetites. Her desire for Joshua had grown to immense proportions in the last few months and she had longed for this moment.

Joshua removed his clothes slowly, folded

them, and laid them on a chair. He liked things orderly, was fastidious in his habits. Fanny eyed him carefully, gauging his actions, not quite trusting this new untried aspect of him.

Joshua's body was lean and angular without sharpness. He reminded her of a wood carving with the details finely made and the edges smoothed off. Pale blonde hair tufted his chest and lay in a silken shadow on his arms, crept along his wrists, and spread like a glaze down the backs of his hands. His skin was very fair with a hint of ruddiness. His fingers were narrow and fine. Fanny's anticipation heightened as she looked at him. His hands would explore her body, soothe her, bind her to him with loving gestures. Her mind misted with the familiar haze she called love.

As if he had read her mind, Joshua slid his fingers along Fanny's arm to her shoulder, to her neck. It was a measured caress, long and slow. He drew her into the circle of his arms and brushed her lips with his, a brief teasing kiss that left her hungering for more. He moved his kisses to her cheeks, her ears, her chin.

Joy raced through Fanny's heart like heat lightning on a humid summer night. She had ached for his tenderness and caring, longed to lavish her love on him. But there was a tenseness in him, some barrier she had not breached. But it didn't matter. He wanted her, needed her, she knew he did. She floated on the pleasant passion his caresses aroused in her.

Joshua pulled at Fanny's petticoats, tearing delicate lace and silk, but there was no violence, no haste, in his action. Everything he did was calculated to produce the desired result. He removed obstacles in the most expedient way possible to get what he wanted. And now, Fanny thought, he wants me, wants to give himself into my keeping.

When Fanny was naked, the cool rose silk sleek beneath her back, she felt Joshua's passion flair and take fire. She waited for him to murmur endearments. But he was silent, and she felt a distance in him, as if he were an observer, not a participant. His fingers feathered her skin, glided and soared, sought and found until she gasped and trembled with delight. She gave herself completely to Joshua's expertise. She opened her body to him, opened her heart and soul, and reveled in the exquisite sensations his lovemaking produced.

Fanny spent her passion and Joshua eased away, slipped from her arms like a silverfish, and stood by the bed looking down at her. He did not look vulnerable in his nakedness. He wore his skin as if it were armor protecting some inner secret that he never acknowledged existed. She searched his eyes for a hint of tenderness, saw nothing but his perennial glint of amusement, his air of calculated detachment bordering on contempt. It was the same expression he wore when he had manipulated a lucrative business deal or success-fully extracted some political favor.

"Say something, Joshua. For God's sake, say something," Fanny whispered, almost begging. She was stunned by the realization that the only connection between them had been their bodies.

Joshua's expression did not change; nothing indicated he saw anything amiss or understood how Fanny was devastated by his emotional coldness.

"Very pleasant, Fanny. I knew the night I took you off the street you'd give a man a good tumble."

Devastation shifted abruptly to defiance and words hurtled off Fanny's tongue before she thought. "Is it Ellen?" she demanded.

Joshua's face tightened. The glint of amusement died. He grabbed Fanny's arm and squeezed hard enough to make her wince. She refused to give him the satisfaction of crying out.

"What the hell do you know about Ellen?" he said in a tightly controlled voice.

"You talked, you rambled. When you were sick." She spat the words out as if she had bitten into something too bitter to chew.

"Be a good girl, Fanny," he said slowly, "and I will never have cause to send you back where

I found you. You have a lot in common with Violet and Flora. And Ellen. Remember that Fanny." He kissed her lightly on the breast and went into the dressing room.

The kiss lay hot on Fanny's skin, as if she had been branded. She touched her fingers to the spot, and was vaguely surprised that it did not feel as sore as her arm where Joshua had squeezed it. She lay quietly, barely breathing, the rose silk crumpled beneath her, her hair strewn about her head like dead autumn leaves. She heard the soft, muffled sounds of Joshua changing. He would emerge as a rich and powerful merchant who made it his business to see that everyone owed him something and that he owed nothing to anyone.

Fanny reached for her ruined dress and drew it around her, covering her nakedness, sheltering herself from this sudden knowledge. Her thoughts balked. But questions formed anyway. Was that all she was to Joshua, someone who owed him a debt, someone he could use in any way he saw fit? Certainly, she owed him loyalty for rescuing her from the degrading life of a waterfront street-walker. She would have been dead or diseased or both by now if it hadn't been for Joshua. She owed him a debt of gratitude for setting her up in this fine house and providing her with every-thing a woman could ask for. Except tenderness. And love. But did she have any right to ask for those things from Joshua when he was so obviously reluctant to bestow them on her? Didn't he owe something of himself? She had saved his life when he had the fever. She had worked hard to create an atmosphere where he could entertain and dispense favors and use his influence, leading to the rapid success of his business deals in lumber and wildlands. The answers evaded her. All she understood was that he had used her body to put her more deeply in his debt, to remind her that without his protection she was nothing, had nothing. The weight of this revelation bruised her with its immensity.

What Pa had said was true. She was a bad woman, tainted, fallen, not worthy of anyone's love and caring. Not even Joshua's.

Joshua came back into the room dressed in evening clothes. He smelled of shaving soap and freshly ironed linen. She loved the way he looked in evening clothes and she hated herself for that one small loving thought.

He came to her with his usual cool approach, and something in Fanny responded. She allowed him to gather her into his arms. He searched her amber eyes with his cool blue-brown gaze. She let herself melt against him, hating herself again, but needing to try, just once more, to elicit some deeper response from him. She crashed, as surely as if she had been struck, into the stonewall of his indifference.

Joshua fingered the torn petticoats, crushed a bit of lace into his fist.

"Poor Fanny," he crooned, "you will need a new gown. Two, perhaps. Something pink. Lovely, exquisite Fanny." The wildness was in his eyes. She knew he would do something with a purpose known only to himself. This time, she did not find it exciting. It was frightening.

"Why did you do this to me, Joshua?" Fanny whispered. Her thoughts were an agony. She was bad, unworthy. Joshua did not love her and never would.

"I want to give you everything you deserve, Fanny," Joshua replied. She feared it was the only answer she would ever have.

Fanny let Joshua hold her gently against his chest. He rested his cheek on top of her head. Suddenly, crazily, she thought of Mercy and Birdie. A wave of homesickness flooded her. She wanted to go home. But she had no home to go to anymore. Her badness would contaminate her daughter. She could never go home and risk destroying the one decent thing she still had the power to help.

The next day, workmen came. By Joshua's order, they painted all the chimneys a pale shade of rose. They put a small brass plate on the wrought iron fence that enclosed the grounds. It said, PINK CHIMNEYS.

12.

After her encounter with Joshua on the big rose bed, Fanny waited anxiously for her time of the month to come around. She was infinitely relieved when it did. She sought the advice of a midwife and got the recipe for lamb's wool and olive oil pessaries. She knew, pregnancy or no, that Joshua would never marry her. She knew, too, that if she wished to remain at Pink Chimneys, as Joshua now insisted on calling the house, she would be expected to participate in other encounters with him on the big bed. *So be it,* she thought. *I've made my bed,* in a manner of speaking, *now I will lie in it.* But on my terms, she decided.

She let Violet and Flora know, in no uncertain terms, who was in charge of everything that went on in Pink Chimneys.

"Neither of you sets foot upstairs in the company of a gentleman without seeing me first with twenty dollars in your hand. Anything you can get above that is yours, including presents of jewelry. Agree to that and I will see that you're fed, clothed, and housed. Cheat me, or bother Mr. Stetson with any of this, and you will wind up in the dooryard so fast you won't know how you got there," Fanny said, bluntly.

That was the kind of talk Violet and Flora

understood best. They were, Fanny supposed, barely out of their teens, not much younger than herself. But they knew the ways of the world and were quick to see on which side their bread was buttered. Joshua had made it plain she was no better than they were. So be it.

She summoned Hod Brown, the stable man, whom she always referred to by his last name. Brown was very large, very strong, and worshipped the ground Fanny walked on. He was not terribly bright, which suited Fanny's purpose, and he was willing to do as he was told without asking questions. She fitted him up in evening clothes and stationed him by the newel post with instructions not to let anyone upstairs without her personal consent.

Joshua, noting Brown's presence, accepted Fanny's glib explanation that she was afraid some of the gentlemen would behave in too rowdy a way now that Violet and Flora were fixtures at Pink Chimneys. She said she wanted Brown around to protect the furniture and bric-a-brac. Joshua agreed, gratified, as Fanny knew he would be, that she was cooperating with his wishes and not getting all stirred up about it.

Violet and Flora were happy at being treated so fairly, and the men Joshua invited to be entertained at Pink Chimneys were pleased to have such a genteel and discreet atmosphere in which to misbehave, or not, as they chose, infinitely better than the raucous and probably unhealthy establishments of the washerwomen.

At first, Fanny did not know what to do with the money she extracted from the labors of Violet and Flora, beyond what she regularly sent to Mercy and Birdie. She accumulated two hundred dollars in an amazingly short amount of time. A bank was out of the question. Joshua sat on the boards of both banks. She thought of land or houses, but was discouraged by the thought that anyone, including Joshua, could walk into the deeds office and read of her transaction. Moreover, women simply did not make those kinds of business transactions by themselves. Men acted as their agents.

She decided to risk seeking some discreet advice.

She maneuvered Rufus Dwinel off into a corner one evening when he was among the favored invited to enjoy the musical talents of Violet and Flora. Dwinel was short in stature, dapper and handsome. He was best known for his eccentricities of business and his unabashed admiration for the ladies.

"Mr. Dwinel," Fanny said, flashing her most winning smile, "I wonder if I might have the benefit of your superior business acumen. I have put a small nest egg aside and I wish to invest it to the best advantage." She had learned the jargon from listening to Joshua; had in fact, learned a great deal about the workings of business without Joshua being aware of it.

Dwinel nodded, smiled and accepted the flattery.

"Why I'm more than willing to be helpful, Mrs. Hogan. I will be shipping a cargo of the finest pine boards this very week. If you would care to invest in a share of the cargo, I guarantee you will double your money. But tell me, dear lady, wouldn't it be more likely for you to invest in one of Mr. Stetson's cargoes?"

Fanny had anticipated the question. She leaned very close to Dwinel, so close he could look down the neck of her low-cut gown. She knew he greatly admired a well-turned figure.

"You figured me out, Mr. Dwinel," she exclaimed. "I should have known, but can I trust you with my secret? That's the question."

"Since half the town of Bangor trusts its secrets with you, Mrs. Hogan, it seems to me that you might bring yourself to reciprocate just this one time," Dwinel said in a cajoling tone.

"Very well then. But you must promise not to breathe a word. I want to buy something very special for Mr. Stetson, for his birthday. He's very interested in racing. I want to surprise him with a Morgan stallion. Mr. Stetson says anyone smart enough to organize a racing association can make a lot of money."

"You don't say, Mrs. Hogan? Does Mr. Veazie know about this?"

"I am sure he does not, Mr. Dwinel. Mr. Stetson has only just confided it to me and I have told no one but you." An air of conspiracy was exactly the right way to appeal to Rufus Dwinel.

Fanny gave him her money with every confidence. He doubled it and she received four hundred dollars in cash. He also confided that he had bought two Morgan mares. Later on, she heard he was busily organizing a racing association and bragging about how he had finally managed to put one over on Joshua Stetson.

13.

The carriage wheels whirred smoothly along State Street. It was autumn again, the time of year Fanny loved the most. The black flies were long gone. The oppressive heat of summer had transformed into chilly October mornings.

Fanny settled herself a little more comfortably against the smooth leather seat. To the consternation of the Broadway ladies, she rode with the top down so she could enjoy the pleasant weather. She had been snubbed a total of eight times since she had turned the corner at Oak onto State. She kept count, finding it amusing. She inclined her head gracefully at each Broadway lady she passed, perfectly aware that her bonnet, trimmed with glossy feathers, framed her face in a most becoming way. She thought with satisfaction of the weight of the bundle of bills resting heavily in her reticule. If things went the way she hoped, she would be as wealthy in her own right, as any of the Broadway ladies who depended on their husbands for everything—including social standing. The comparison was not lost on Fanny. She depended on Joshua for everything, they depended on their husbands. All she lacked was the wedding ring.

Brown stopped the carriage at Wentworth's Dry Goods Store. Fanny was a regular customer there. Mr. Wentworth was unfailingly courteous, grateful to have an account supported by Stetson money. Fanny believed, however, that Mr. Wentworth liked her for herself, despite the fact that his son was a mariner on one of Joshua's schooners.

When Fanny stepped inside the store Mr. Wentworth was busy waiting on a lady Fanny recognized as Hannah Bailey, whose husband had bought Joshua's Summer Street house. Their backs were to the open door which let in the pleasant autumn warmth. They did not notice Fanny.

"Oh, that's lovely cambric, Mr. Wentworth. I will have that for a cravat for Mr. Bailey. His ship is due any day now," Hannah said.

"That's a fine piece of goods, Mrs. Bailey. He will be proud to wear it. Say, did you hear old

Doc Richmond died a few days ago? In his sleep I heard."

"Why, yes, I did, Mr. Wentworth," Hannah said, shaking her head sadly. "He was a wonderful man. If it hadn't of been for Doc Richmond, Mr. Bailey and I would never have known about young Abner Giddings needing a decent home. When I think how the town might have struck him off to just anyone and him such a bright boy. I've never regretted the day I brought him home. Here, give me another yard of that cambric. Abner ought to have a new cravat, too, now that he's cabin boy for Mr. Bailey."

"I suppose with her father dead, Maude Webber will be coming home to settle the estate," Wentworth commented. "I hear she and Sam are poor as church mice and twice as happy."

"She's already home," Hannah confided. "I saw her yesterday getting off the boat. She hasn't changed much that I could see. Gained some pounds . . . like the rest of us. Mrs. Parker said Maude is going to stay here and Sam will join her next week. She heard Sam still wants to coast, which is more than I can figure out, him being a doctor and all. Well, that's neither here nor there, but I'm some sorry old Doc Richmond is gone. He was a good man, better than most."

"That he was. He doctored my Jim more than once . . . Jim was always getting himself tore up . . . and wouldn't take a penny because he knew I didn't have it. But I always saw to it Doc had some nice wool every fall for a new jacket. I think he would've gone with the holes in his elbows if I hadn't."

"He would have. It's many a time I asked him to drink tea and filled him up with a pie. Half the time he forgot to eat. Wouldn't Maude be fit to be tied if she knew that?"

"Well, he's gone now and when you're in the grave, it doesn't matter. Here's your parcel, Mrs. Bailey. Thanks for stopping by."

When Hannah Bailey had gone, Fanny approached the counter.

"Why, Mrs. Hogan!" Mr. Wentworth exclaimed when he looked up and saw Fanny. "I didn't even see you come in!" He broke into a welcoming smile.

"I was over there in the corner looking for some cashmere for a shawl. I didn't see any," Fanny said. She didn't say so, but she thought the entire stock looked depleted. Mr. Wentworth's smile faded and he bit his lip with uneven teeth.

"Now I'll tell you, Mrs. Hogan, I've had some hard luck. Made a couple of deals that didn't work out. I doubt if I'll have any of the better goods for a while. As a matter of fact, I've got a load coming in on Job Bailey's schooner, but I'm going to have to send it back. I might even have to shut the store if things don't look up pretty soon." Below his sparse hairline, a worried frown creased his forehead.

"Why are you telling me all this, Mr. Wentworth?" Fanny asked. She had noticed that Joshua always questioned what people said or did.

"I thought maybe you might be willing to speak to Mr. Stetson about a loan. The bank won't talk to me, said I wasn't a good risk. But I thought maybe Mr. Stetson, himself, might help me out."

Fanny looked carefully at Mr. Wentworth, trying to assess his honesty. He seemed like a good man, one who would keep his word and his mouth shut. She laid her reticule carefully on the counter, considering what she would say next.

"I never interfere in Mr. Stetson's business, Mr. Wentworth. However, I personally may be able to help you. How large a sum do you need?"

"I figure three hundred dollars ought to do it. That would take care of the seventy-five dollars I owe for the yard goods and the rest would pay off a few other debts I owe. Now, I'm going to be honest with you. I don't know how quick I will be able to pay you back."

"What would you say, Mr. Wentworth, if I purchased the shipment of yard goods and loaned you the balance? I'd resell the goods to you as you demanded them, at a small profit to me, of course. I'd expect the rest of the money to be repaid at the end of the year at five percent interest."

Mr. Wentworth's mouth dropped open and he rubbed his chin thoughtfully. "Why . . . I don't know. That's better than the bank would do. All right. It's a deal."

Fanny opened her reticule and counted out three hundred dollars.

"Now if you will write me a receipt containing a brief statement about our transaction, and that if you default you forfeit your store to me."

"You drive a hard bargain, Mrs. Hogan," Mr. Wentworth commented as he dipped his pen and wrote out the document.

"Of course, you understand our business is to remain just between the two of us. I'm certain that if Mr. Stetson heard out on the street that you had borrowed money from me, he would feel obliged to interfere with your son's aspirations to become a master mariner on the Stetson lines."

Mr. Wentworth looked slightly hurt and Fanny felt a little ashamed at being so unfeminine.

"I'm an honest man, Mrs. Hogan. And a lot of honest men have silent partners. Here's my hand on it."

Mr. Wentworth extended his big calloused hand and Fanny grasped it firmly, the way a man would, her momentary sense of being unfeminine forgotten.

"Now, Mr. Wentworth, I will have ten yards of that lace. And some of that pale cream silk, too. Twenty yards, I think."

Mr. Wentworth carried Fanny's parcels to her waiting carriage, a courtesy he always extended to her. This time, he even handed her up into the seat. He bowed respectfully and Fanny felt a strong current of pleasure course through her. It felt good to be in a position of power, to have something to do besides the usual female tasks of keeping house. The idea kindled within her, and she thought she was going to enjoy being a woman of business very much.

As Fanny drove away, she saw Mrs. Veazie's carriage passing. Fanny leaned way out and waved at the sour-faced lady.

Mrs. Veazie was not amused.

14.

The next week Brown brought the load of yard goods. Fanny made a foray up to the servants' rooms in the attic to see if there was room to store the merchandise. She had never been up to the attic. She had always felt it to be the personal domain of Mrs. McGuire, the housekeeper. To Fanny's surprise, only half of the great space was petitioned off into the little chambers occupied by the cook and several hired girls. The remainder was empty. It was simply one very large room finished off somewhat roughly. There was ample room for storing the bolts of fabric.

Fanny opened the crates to see just what it was she had gotten herself into. She took out finely woven calicoes, bolts of watered silk, figured taffetas, and yards of cambric and petticoat muslins. The shipment also contained reels of matching ribbons, fine laces, and sewing notions. She fingered the fabric, visualizing ways she might use it to make a little cash. Violet and Flora were always needing new garters because the gentlemen insisted on carrying them off as mementos. Bedgowns were constantly in need of repair. Each season new gowns were needed. If she required a fee from Violet and Flora each time they needed garters, or a bedgown, Fanny thought she might accumulate a tidy amount in the course of a year. She put the idea into effect immediately.

Fanny spent the rest of the week supervising the installment of shelves and a cutting table and bought dressmakers' tools. She hired a seamstress. The seamstress, however, proved to be the first of a very long series. She discovered she was sewing for Jezebels, and left in a huff.

These small enterprises, the fruits of Violet's and Flora's labor, the garter fees, the profit from the fabric as she resold it to Mr. Wentworth, brought enough money to send to Mercy and Birdie, but little more. Fanny was still dependent on Joshua for everything else. Pink Chimneys and all it contained belonged to him. She belonged to him. But she wanted to belong to herself. She knew the time had come to tell Joshua what she had been up to.

Fanny curled up on the sitting room sofa beside Joshua. She unbound her hair. She wore the filmy pink peignoir he had made for her in Paris. It dripped cascades of delicate ruffled lace and whispered silkily each time she moved. Joshua wore a quilted silk robe in a rich shade of blue which gave his eyes a gray tint. He was relaxed and in an expansive mood.

It was late December. The Penobscot had frozen over. Shipping was at a standstill and would remain so until the spring runoff. Business was quiet, but Joshua had crews in the woods cutting timber and he would have plenty of boards to ship when spring came. He could afford to relax. It had been a very prosperous year for him.

Fanny kept the conversation light, allowing him to direct its course as she always did. They talked of ships, of business, of the things that interested him. She waited for one of the small silences Joshua inserted into his conversation.

"Do you remember," she said smiling, "how I flew off the handle when Violet and Flora came here?" She watched his face from the corner of her eye. Nothing in his face tightened, none of the wildness flashed. He stroked her hair as if the motion, the contact, calmed him and helped remove some of the boulders in the stonewall barricading his emotions.

"I remember. You looked like an orange alley cat spitting and hissing. I was obliged to make you see things my way," he replied, alluding to the incident in the rose silk covered bed.

His remark stirred the hot current of Fanny's anger, but she forced a smile and pretended it wasn't anger she felt. Anger did not intimidate Joshua. Her anger merely aroused his anger. She had learned to keep herself pleasantly passive.

Joshua believed Fanny enjoyed their encounters on the rose bed. She encouraged him to believe it. What he didn't know, he couldn't use as a weapon. If you played Joshua's game, you played by his rules.

"Oh, I do see things your way, Joshua. Violet, Flora and I are sisters under the skin. We do whatever is necessary to survive."

Joshua stirred and stopped stroking her hair. His arm rested heavily around Fanny's neck.

"I'm not sure I'd take your meaning, Fanny."

"I've learned a lot from you, Joshua, about what's important," Fanny purred, ignoring his last remark. She slipped her hand into his, careful not to take too much physical liberty. He was touchy about that, preferring to be the one to initiate intimacy.

Joshua laced his fingers through Fanny's, his grip hard enough to cause her discomfort without actually causing pain. He shot her a quizzical look and she saw a shadow of wildness come into his face.

"What the hell have you been up to now?" he asked suspiciously. His guard was up, his stonewall firmly in place. But Fanny knew a few of his niches, knew where the chinks were. She had to be careful, though, very careful. She must make him believe he was in control of the situation. If she offended him, or if he thought for one instant she was scheming to find a way out from under his control, he would turn her out into the street with nothing.

Fanny relaxed her body against his, kept her face pleasant and passive.

"You asked me to supervise Violet and Flora. I know you pay them for their . . . talents, but it seemed to me, but for all the trouble and expense you've gone to, you ought to realize something on your investment. I know you said I needn't involve myself with them, but I have," Fanny said. She related the story, with certain bits of lavish embroidery, her activities of the last few months. She did not mention the deals with Mr. Wentworth or Rufus Dwinel. Both those gentlemen had kept their mouths shut and she knew they would continue to do so.

Fanny held her breath and waited. She could almost see the gears in Joshua's head turning. He rose from the sofa with a restless kind of energy and went to lean against the mantel.

"How much money are you talking about, Fanny?" he said, looking interested.

"Oh, not much. A few hundred dollars. I've kept accounts. Here, let me show you." Fanny went to her little French desk and brought an account book to show him. The figures did not reflect the total amounts, and some of the expenditures were not precisely accurate.

Joshua examined the accounts. His eyes lost the look of a hawk about to dive for its prey. A little smile played at the edges of his lips.

"Pin money. Fanny, you do the damnedest things," he said indulgently.

"But is it all right, Joshua? I had such fun keeping these figures and ordering Violet and Flora about. Could I buy a little bit of land? Or give something to a charity?"

The little smile on Joshua's face broadened to a genuine grin.

"You go ahead and play with your little pile of pin money. Buy a shop. Build a church. And if you lose your shirt, you just let me know." Joshua took Fanny's face between his hands and kissed her lightly. "But don't ever think you can beat me at my own game, Fanny."

To Fanny's surprise, Joshua laid his head on her breast. It was a rare moment. Fanny savored it, could almost make herself believe that he needed her, that he cared. She was still drawn to him like a magnet seeking steel. She did not call it love anymore, but she thought it felt something like that.

Joshua whispered into the gossamer folds of lace dripping down the front of her pink peignoir. She thought he said, "Stay here."

15.

It was New Year's Day, 1835. Brown stood in his customary place by the newel post—intrepid and silent. Violet and Flora mingled with a small company of gentlemen, all of them from away, all possessing money or political power useful to Joshua. Fanny had withdrawn to her own room after she had dined with the men. She had been witty and charming, had smiled until her face ached. She had found nothing in the men to admire; she felt, if the truth were known, nothing but contempt for them and their posturing. She cast the thought aside quickly. She wasn't any better than they were. She sat down wearily at her little French desk.

There was a tap at the door and Violet poked her head into the room. Violet always moved cautiously, like a cat on unfamiliar ground.

"If you'll excuse me, Mrs. Hogan, can I speak to you a minute?" Violet said. She was more articulate than Flora and always spoke for the two of them. For all her cat-like stealth, her manner was demure and refined. Once, to Violet's great amusement, she had been mistaken for the new schoolmarm who had just come to town.

"Come in, Violet," Fanny grumbled. She was in no mood for difficulties. Her head ached and she felt mean-spirited. "What's the trouble?"

"Oh, it's not anything serious, marm. It's just that Flora and I've been talking, and we think we need help. There's some of the gentlemen that come here regular that don't think they're getting their money's worth. Some of them are getting impatient with having to wait so long. Flora and I, we wondered if maybe you'd study on it and perhaps take on a couple more girls."

Violet's dark eyes had faint blue smudges under them. She looked pale and tired, the result, Fanny supposed, of so many late nights.

Fanny had avoided thinking about adding other girls to her establishment. Thus far, all her sins were fairly small. She had disobeyed her father, lived with a man she wasn't married to, earned money from the labors of two women who sold their bodies to men. She had abandoned her child. Well, perhaps they weren't such small sins after all. Fanny laced her fingers together. What difference did it make anyway, whether she had two women, or four, working for her? They were all fallen women, fit only for one another's company. Nothing would ever change that. And besides, two more women at Pink Chimneys meant more money in her reticule, another parcel of land to be bought with the help of Mr. Wentworth, money to send to Mercy and Birdie.

"Do you have someone in mind, Violet?"

"Why, yes, I do, Mrs. Hogan. But I'd have to go to Boston for a few days to fetch them. Friends of mine, you see, that want to better themselves."

"Then go ahead."

Violet dipped an elegant little curtsy. Her mannerisms were somewhat affected. She laid twenty dollars in the porcelain vase.

"There will be plenty more where that came from, Mrs. Hogan, once the others get here. And things will be a sight easier for Flora and me."

After Violet returned to her duties, Fanny paced the room. It was snowing outside. She stood by the tall windows and watched the flakes fill up the garden. She had not seen Joshua for a week. Though that was not unusual, the unbearable emptiness that had settled around her was. It had clung to her for days. The sound of music, laughter, and merriment drifted into the room, faint and distant. She had no desire to rejoin the party. She knew from experience that one of the guests would fancy her, and she'd have the delicate task of making it clear to him, without giving offense, that she was not for sale, that Joshua already owned her. She thought of the black reticule and how it contained the seeds of her future. But she didn't know what she wanted her future to be. She leaned her head against the frosty pane. She wondered what Mercy and Birdie were doing this day on the brink of the new year. Birdie was a big girl of four now. Fanny went back to her desk and picked up her pen. Dear Mercy, she wrote. No. That wouldn't do. Mercy didn't want to hear from her, had never once acknowledged the money sent so religiously. Mercy and Birdie were better off left to themselves. She could only bring them unhappiness and shame. Tears trickled down Fanny's face and fell in ugly splotches on her blue silk gown. She didn't care. Joshua would buy her another one.

By the time Rose and Lily arrived at the end of February, Fanny's spell of gloom had lifted. Joshua had been in constant attendance. He had taken her to see a play at the theater, and to sleigh on the river. He had told her about a few acres out on State Street, a mile or so north of Pink Chimneys, and Fanny bought the place. This cheered her and her patience improved so much she felt inclined to listen to Violet confide the histories of the new girls.

Rose, according to Violet, had been compromised by an uncle who swore he would do right by her, but left her to fend for herself when his wife got suspicious. By then, Rose was in the family way, but had, mercifully, miscarried. She had been sent to a distant cousin, a cantankerous old maid, to live and work as a hired girl, except she didn't get money for it, only room and board. Rose wasn't especially bright, but she was good looking, with a high, proud bosom, nice round hips, and that pale pink and blue complexion that men went so crazy over.

As for Lily, she had been got to by her stepbrother, talked into it by promises of extra food. In a big family, where no one ever got enough to eat, it had sounded good. But Lily's stepmother had caught them at it and threw Lily out. She hadn't been alone for long when she had been taken in by a young divinity student intent on, he said, converting her to the true moral principles, though how, Lily wanted to know, could that be done naked and under the covers? Anyway, Lily hadn't minded until the theologian had brought home a horse whip and a pair of lumberman's caulk boots. Lily hadn't waited around to find out what he intended to do with them.

Fanny listened and understood. The stories weren't so very different from her own. The image of the sign that said ROOMS swung momentarily in her head. She had the power to keep her girls fed and clothed—to let them have pretty things. She had the power to keep them at Pink Chimneys, making it possible for them to stay because they wanted to. And as long as they stayed, Fanny told herself, there would be money to ensure that Birdie was protected from poverty, and that Birdie would never be forced by circumstance into the same world as Violet, Flora, Lily and Rose.

16.

Fanny eased herself out of bed. The hired girl had pushed open the curtains and left hot water in the pitcher on the commode. Early morning sun slid into the room. Red-gold shafts of light fell in puddles on the carpeting. Usually, Fanny did not rise so early. Perhaps it was a premonition—the aftermath of the nightmare that had left her quivering even though she did not actually remember what it was that had terrified her sleep.

She splashed water on her face in an effort to wake up more fully. *It's Sunday,* she thought, attempting to organize her thinking away from the nightmare. *It's May, springtime, a little more than a year since Lily and Rose came to Pink Chimneys.*

Little wisps of the bad dream flitted through Fanny's head. It had something to do with a child crying, with being imprisoned in a huge house, of Joshua going away.

In a sense, Joshua had gone away, but Fanny hadn't expected that fact to give her nightmares. He no longer spent much time at Pink Chimneys. He had just finished building himself a stylish house on Penobscot Street, just off Broadway, not far from Pink Chimneys. He was full of ideas about how he would entertain the upper crust, talked of paying court to some respectable matron's marriageable daughter, had even got himself considered seriously as a candidate for a minor public office.

With the extra earnings garnered from Rose and Lily, Fanny had expanded her property holdings with alacrity. She had become adept at land speculation and put away quite a tidy sum in one of the new banks on whose board Joshua did not sit. As Joshua had predicted, Bangor was turning into a boom town. He continued to allow her to "play with her pin money," even encouraged her. He had not objected to Rose and Lily. He no longer asked to see her account book. Sometimes, Fanny wondered if he had grown tired of her, wanted to be rid of her. Yet, he kept coming to visit her, especially when things didn't go just right. He still sent gentlemen to be entertained, still kept track of which newly rich gentlemen spent time at Pink Chimneys, and still used that information to his advantage. But he was more discreet about it. He was, Fanny concluded, so far as he was able, carving out a niche of respectability for himself.

Fanny couldn't quite put her finger on it. Nothing on the surface seemed to have changed, yet nothing was the same any longer. What was most important to her now was not whether Joshua would ever love her, but the power she had gained, not only as a landholder, but as the keeper of the sexual secrets of a good portion of the town's male population. More than once she had used what she knew to force down the price per acre of some land she wanted.

Her dealings with Mr. Wentworth had expanded into the biggest dry goods emporium in town. Mr. Wentworth planned to build an imposing house, in the Italianate style, over on Court Street. Fanny continued as his silent partner. Mr. Wentworth had prospered so much he persuaded his son, Jim, to leave off sailing with the Stetson lines and come to work in the store. The girls at Pink Chimneys were clothed all the more lavishly from this venture, and Fanny took great pride in that. The fact was, she had done so well she could leave Pink Chimneys anytime she pleased. But she didn't. What sense was there in leaving with only enough to keep her for a few years? If she waited, she would have enough to keep her, Mercy, and Birdie, for the rest of her life.

All things considered, she should not have been suffering such strange nightmares.

Fanny had barely tied her robe around her waist when the hired girl burst in without so much as a tap at the door. Her eyes were wide with excitement.

"It's Miss Violet, marm. She says would you come *quick!*"

Fanny strode rapidly along the wide hallway on the lower floor, ran lightly up the curved oak stairway, and found Violet waiting on the landing. Violet's hair was uncombed, her dark eyes filled with fright. She hugged a thin silk kimono tightly across her chest.

"It's Rose, Mrs. Hogan. She's bleeding something awful. She's getting weak and ruining the feathers!"

Alarmed, Fanny went into Rose's room to see for herself. Rose lay on her side with her knees drawn up to her chest. She was very pale and moaned something about awful cramps.

"Get some towels," Fanny ordered, "and hurry. Tell Mrs. McGuire to send Brown for Maude Webber. I don't want anyone else. Tell Brown to bring her if he has to chase her all the way to Old Town." Fanny took the towels from Violet and wadded them between Rose's legs.

Within the hour, Maude arrived. She hadn't changed much, Fanny thought. She was still small, dark, and round. Her clothes were neat but lacking in the details fashionable women cared about. If Maude recognized Fanny, she gave no sign. With precise, kindly words, Maude made everyone leave the room and shut the door firmly behind them. Fanny breathed a sigh of relief.

Fanny sent Violet to her room and went to get dressed herself.

It was noontime before Maude emerged from Rose's room and was shown to Fanny's gold and white sitting room.

"A miscarriage," Maude said without ceremony. "Not her first. She'll live, but she'll have to stay quiet for a week or two. Another one could be fatal." The roughness in Maude's voice surprised Fanny, set her nerves on edge. She had remembered Maude as brusque, but not brittle.

"I don't suppose you remember me . . ." Fanny ventured.

"Well, you suppose wrong, Mrs. Hogan. I remember you perfectly well. Since I came back home these two years past, that's all I've heard about. Everyone whispers behind their hands about the notorious Fanny Hogan and the scandal of her pink-chimneyed house sitting cheek to cheek with the pillars of Broadway."

Maude seated herself without waiting to be asked. Fanny remained standing, uneasy. She felt tongue-tied in the face of Maude's directness.

Maude had been so kind and understanding when Birdie was born. But people changed. Circumstances were different now. She wasn't the unfortunate victim of a ne'er-do-well sailor. She was Joshua Stetson's kept woman. It was to be expected that Maude would pass judgment just as everyone else did.

Maude surprised Fanny with a touch of her hand.

"Did you ever go home?" she asked gently.

"Yes," Fanny said, relieved to see Maude's kindness, yet shying from a question that aroused painful memories. "My father wouldn't let me stay. I left Birdie with my sister when I came here."

"Whose idea was all this?" Maude asked with a gesture that included not only Pink Chimneys but the circumstances that had culminated in Rose's miscarriage.

"The house was Mr. Stetson's idea. The rest of it was mine." Fanny felt her cheeks go hot and hung her head, expecting, hoping for—she didn't know which—Maude's disapproval.

"At least you didn't end up down on the waterfront. Down in Joppa. Disease and filth and human suffering beyond anything I care to see. Everything decent is gone . . . Mr. Barker's little store, Nat Thatcher's little cabin." Maude laid her head wearily against the back of the chair. Strands of her hair fell from the coil at the nape of her neck. "I don't suppose you'd be able to find me a cup of tea?"

Fanny rang a bell. When tea had been brought, Fanny settled herself in a chair near Maude. She no longer felt uneasy.

"I heard you'd lost your father. I wanted to call, but I was afraid of what people would say."

"About you? Or about me?" Maude said. "I go where I am called, Mrs. Hogan. Rich or poor, pious or fallen, it's all the same to me. Those who object to my calling here will call someone else when they are ill. It's that simple."

"And your husband? Did he find employment?"

"Oh yes, he's still coasting. Still ship's surgeon. For Joshua Stetson. Sam gets home every six weeks or so. There's no physician alive who knows more about setting broken bones and stitching up lacerations than my Sam. Mariners are always brawling, the predictable results of too much spirits. I wasn't in favor of Sam signing on with Mr. Stetson, but Sam has funny ideas. He always felt sorry for Joshua Stetson. Old Phineas used Joshua pretty bad. Phineas Stetson is dead now, you know. His wife sold the house and went off down south. I heard she's married again. I guess she's had quite a time with all the money Phineas left her. Well, enough of this gossip. I've got other things to think about." Maude's pleasant expression disappeared, was replaced with a long look that touched Fanny.

"Is something the matter, Mrs. Webber?"

"Maude. Call me Maude. Very often, when I am called to Joppa to attend a lying-in of someone in very reduced circumstances, I'm asked to find a home for the babe because it isn't wanted. And there just aren't enough homes to put the little ones in. What Bangor needs is an orphans' home. Probably one of the churches would organize one, but it would take years for them to raise enough money for a building and have enough left to run the place. You're very lucky, Fanny, that your little girl is being brought up by your sister. You ever hear from her?"

"No, but I send money every month."

"I see. I'm sure your sister's grateful for it. Well, I must go, I've other calls to make. If you ever have an idea about starting an orphans' home, I'd like to hear it." Maude set her cup down with a soft clink and stood up. She slung her cape across her shoulders and tied her bonnet under her chin. The ribbons were wrinkled and frayed at the edges.

17.

Fanny walked alone in the rose garden situated at the rear of Pink Chimneys, beyond the flag-stone terrace that ran the length of the house. It was a beautiful house, Fanny thought, with its simple lines, wide windows, and carefully

301

tended grounds. She had heard that not even the governor of Maine lived in a place half so nice. This was her realm, hers to reign over, its servants and events hers to command. She liked that feeling. She liked it very much. Her thoughts of leaving Pink Chimneys were not as important as they used to be. For a farm girl from Fort Point, she hadn't done so badly given the hand she had been obliged to play.

The bright colors of the roses made fat splashes of pink and red in the greenery.

Fanny wore a white batiste dress delicately embroidered and embellished with restrained touches of lace insertion. She held a matching parasol over her head. She wore no hat, though she knew she should. She freckled easily and no one, according to Godey's Lady's Book, admired freckles.

Fanny strolled slowly, deep in thought, her wide skirts barely brushing the closely manicured grass. Each week she had the stable boy bring a few sheep to graze the lawn. A huge maple cast a comforting shadow into the corner of the garden. Beneath it, several wooden benches and Chinese tea tables had been placed. This was her favorite spot on summer evenings after the black flies had gone, and the fireflies lit up the deepest shadows. She paused, still wondering, after weeks of deliberation, what to do about Rose.

Rose, whom Fanny had sent for, appeared at

the double-doors that led out onto the terrace from the parlor. She made her way slowly, reluctantly, toward Fanny. She was still pale and frail looking from her illness. She did not smile, seldom smiled anymore, and that bothered Fanny more than anything about the whole upsetting business. Rose was fully dressed for the first time since she had taken to her bed. Her hair was unpinned and it fell in a blonde cloud of ringlets down her back and fluffed in little swirls around her face. The discreet paint she usually wore on her cheeks and lips was nowhere in evidence. Her doll-like pink and blue beauty had been a great favorite with the gentlemen. Fanny hated to see her go.

"Sit down, Rose," Fanny said kindly, indicating one of the wooden benches. She closed the parasol and set it aside.

"If you don't mind, marm, I'd rather stand," Rose replied in a false attempt at bravery.

It was not the attitude Fanny had hoped for, and the difficulty of what she had to say loomed large and menacing. She had chosen the garden for the interview in hopes that it would put them more at ease.

"Very well, Rose. I've spoken with Mrs. Webber and she says you are now fully recovered. But you must never expose yourself to the possibility of being in delicate circumstances again. If you do, she believes it will be fatal."

Rose's pretty pink lips trembled, and she nodded her head miserably, refusing to look at Fanny. She was not articulate and tended to keep her thoughts and feelings to herself or allowed one of the other girls to speak for her. She was good-natured and easily managed, and the other girls liked and protected her.

"I can't keep you on, Rose. I want to; I truly want to, but I just can't risk having anything happen to you. Word gets around, and it's bad for business." When Rose did not respond, Fanny continued, "I'll give you enough money for passage back to Boston or wherever you want to go, and some to keep you for a month. I can't do any more than that." The words left a bitter taste in Fanny's mouth.

Tears brimmed in Rose's china blue eyes. She hung her head. Fanny was grateful for the blonde curtain of hair that hid Rose's stricken expression.

Fanny picked up her parasol, relieved to have the unpleasant duty behind her.

Abruptly, Rose sat down and buried her fists in her lap.

"And where the hell do I go! There ain't no place. My people won't have nothing to do with me. All I know to do, marm, is entertain gentlemen."

The sign that said ROOMS swung and creaked ominously in Fanny's head. She had known it would, had been haunted with its shabby presence for days.

Rose sobbed silently. Her thin shoulders heaved and shuddered as if she, too, had seen the sign and knew what it meant.

Fanny set the parasol down again and paced distractedly. "You must have something put by, Rose. You've worked so hard. It can't be as bad as that."

"What I had I sent home to Ma for the young ones. Not that she would ever say she was glad to have it," Rose said bitterly. "But I thought if I helped out some, Ma might let me come home if I ever needed to. Guess I might's well forget about that."

Rose's words affected Fanny deeply. Over and over again, she was struck by the similarities between herself, the girls who worked for her, and their reasons for staying at Pink Chimneys. Today it was Rose. Tomorrow or next month, next year, it would be someone else. Flora, perhaps. Or herself?

"Rose," Fanny said, "I want you to listen to me, I've got an idea. I don't know if it will work, but you will have to be willing to try some other kind of work."

"Oh, God, marm, I'll try anything if you just let me stay." Rose's sobbing eased and she brushed the snarled curls out of her eyes. She was so lovely, so childlike. Without thinking, Fanny put her arms around Rose and held her as carefully as she had once held her own dear Birdie. She made soothing sounds, clucked and patted, unleashing a well of maternal feeling she never had expected to feel again. She regained control quickly and drew away, blinked rapidly, clearing the tears from her eyes, as she spoke. "Rose, how far did you go in school?" Her thoughts tumbled crazily in her head.

"I went eight terms. But I wasn't much good at it. I kept having to stay home to help Ma with the babies." Rose's face fell, then brightened. "But I won a prize once, for drawing a picture. I was always good at that, and using a needle. Nothing fancy. Mending mostly."

"Oh, that's very good, Rose, better than I hoped."

"What are you talking about, marm?"

"I'm not sure, Rose. Maybe I've lost my reason, but don't you worry. I've got an idea and if it works, you will have somewhere to go, and you won't have to entertain gentlemen. I want you to tell Mrs. McGuire to find Brown and send him for Mrs. Webber."

At the mention of Brown, Rose's cheeks grew pink and her eyes brightened into a happy expression.

"I'd be pleased to tell him, marm. I saw him over by the stable."

"You won't tire yourself? It's not too far to walk?"

"Oh, no. I'll be all right. Do me good to talk to Brown a minute. Brown and me, we understand each other." With that enigmatic remark, Rose flitted across the garden and disappeared around the corner of the house. Her step was lighter; her hair fluffed playfully in a sudden light breeze.

It was late afternoon when Maude arrived. She drove up in a chaise with peeling paint that looked as if it had seen better days. The horse looked well fed and cared for, Fanny noted. As usual, Maude's clothing was mismatched and rumpled. She wore a faded sunbonnet with a frayed brim, the kind farm women wore.

I must do something about that bonnet of hers, Fanny thought as she watched Maude climb down from the chaise.

"Thank you for coming so soon, Maude," Fanny said.

Maude wiped her forehead with the back of her forearm and fanned her face.

"I would have been here before this, but there's fever down in Joppa. Don't alarm yourself. I scrubbed myself raw and changed every stitch I had on before I set out for here. That's what took me so long. Bad drainage. Sewage running in the street. Something ought to be done. Who is ill this time?" She reached for her medicine chest.

Fanny laid a hand on Maude's plump arm.

"You won't need that, Maude. No one is sick. I wanted to talk to you. About the orphans' home you said you needed."

"The orphans' home? Nothing's come of it yet and not likely to, but if you have some new idea I haven't already thought of . . ."

"I have more than an idea, Maude, I have a place to put it. Come and sit down under the tree. Have some lemonade."

They strolled arm in arm across the grass and settled themselves.

"I bought the Sawyer place a while back. You know where I mean, the big house way out on State Street. I was going to sell it for a good profit this fall. Sawyer lost his shirt speculating in wild lands—the fool, serves him right—and he had to come down a peg or two. So I bought the place. It's a big house. Must have a dozen or so rooms. Is that big enough for an orphans' home?"

Fanny fluttered her gloved hand at a stray fly. Maude echoed the gesture.

"Big enough?" Maude asked with a dazed expression. "That place is big enough for a whole army of orphans. I know because I was called to see Mrs. Sawyer about this time last year."

"What I had in mind, Maude, is this. If you can find some church that's willing to run the place, I'll deed it over to them. But I don't want anyone to know where it came from. And you're the only one I'll deal with. The deed will have to be recorded in your name, but no money will actually change hands. You can say someone left you a fortune. Then, in six months time, you can give it to the church to run."

"Why don't you want anyone to know?" Maude asked, the question obviously calculated.

"You know why, Maude! I'm not the kind of person decent people want to associate with. No one would have anything to do with it if they thought . . ." Fanny paused, unwilling to continue.

"If they thought it was built with tainted money," Maude finished for her. Fanny avoided the intensity of Maude's gaze.

"You know that's why, Maude, now let that be an end to it. Do you want it or not?" There was an edge in Fanny's voice.

"Yes, I want it, Fanny. I want it so I can show the good citizens of Bangor there are better ways of alleviating suffering and want than casting a few crumbs to the poor once a year."

"There's a condition."

"What condition?"

"Rose. She's to have a place there, for as long as she wants. She can take care of the little ones and teach them how to draw and mend."

Maude tugged at the strings of her sunbonnet and pulled it off her head. It hung in a limp, unlovely lump between her shoulder blades. She eyed Fanny carefully.

"Playing the ministering angel, Fanny?" Maude said in a soft voice.

"I suppose you could call it that," Fanny answered tightly, not willing to admit she had been found out, though she knew perfectly well Maude saw through her motives.

"What about upkeep? Food and clothing and salaries for the staff?"

"I'll see to that for the first six months and pay Rose's way out of my own pocket as long as she stays. The church will have to shoulder the expenses after that. You will have to see to it. And one other thing. I want Mrs. Veazie on the board of directors."

Maude laughed. She had heard the stories that circulated about Fanny's skirmishes with that lady.

"You want Mrs. Veazie!" she said.

"You needn't laugh, Maude. If Mrs. Veazie gives her approval to the home, so will every other society matron in town. You know that just as well as I do."

"Yes, but I never would have thought of it, not in a million years. Well, I guess I've got my work cut out for me. It will have to be the Universalists, I think. Their membership is small, but it's growing, and attracting a well-educated congregation with the means to do good works. Won't make the Baptists too happy, I suspect, but they're pretty well occupied with the temperance question at the moment and may not take any notice of it at all."

"Then you'll accept my offer? You think it can work?"

"Of course, I accept! Work? It will work out just fine. Bangor's not the kind of place to look too closely into the mouth of a gift horse."

Maude held out her right hand. Fanny grasped it firmly, the way a man would.

"Thank you, Fanny," Maude said.

Fanny went to tell Rose. Later that day she ordered a hat from the best shop in town and had it sent to Maude.

PART THREE: ELIZABETH

1.

The house had an abandoned, forlorn appearance. Elizabeth Emerson paced the rooms trying to decide if she was doing the right thing. Her footsteps echoed sharply on the bare floor. She had sold the bright braided rugs for enough money to book passage upriver.

Elizabeth's dark hair had auburn lights and was arranged in sleek wings over her ears, looped up into a coil anchored by two wooden combs. Her eyes, an unusual shade of bachelor button blue, had ice-blue flecks. Her face was a long, pleasant oval. She was tall and usually carried herself with confidence. But on this day, her shoulders drooped. Her mouth was a sad, curved line. She carried her head tilted slightly to one side as if it were too heavy to hold erect.

Neighbors down the road had offered her a home until she could find something more suitable, but Elizabeth had declined. It had been bad enough having the whole town know the farm had been sold for nonpayment of taxes. She had no intention of living on the charity of others now that she had become a pauper. By now, everyone in Fort Point took it for gospel that she had no other choice but to go to work in the spinning mills down in New Hampshire. But this she was determined not to do. She knew how to sew. She would use her skill to earn a living.

Yesterday, in the process of separating a few personal belongings from the things she must leave behind, Elizabeth had found a back issue of the *Bangor Whig and Courier* tucked in the bottom of Aunt Mercy's bureau. At first she thought the paper was a liner for the drawer, but it was folded too small for that purpose. She was about to discard it when she noticed an advertisement heavily outlined in pencil. It said: WANTED—YOUNG LADY OF GOOD MORAL CHARACTER TO DO DRESSMAKING AND MENDING. LIVE IN. INQUIRE BANGOR HOUSE, BANGOR, MAINE, ON APRIL 28, 1852, MRS. HOGAN.

Elizabeth read the notice twice. Had Aunt Mercy intended to encourage her to apply? She didn't know, but it was the answer to her prayers.

It was just after dawn. No sails were yet visible on the Penobscot River. Elizabeth stood in the kitchen, her thoughts bound to the past. She could almost see Aunt Mercy with her cat, Daisy, in her lap rocking comfortably by the fire. The room should have been alive with Aunt Mercy's voice, the clatter of spoons and pots on the table, the clash of stove lids.

The ashes in the stove were cold and gray. The

only sound in the house was the faint rustle of Elizabeth's own petticoats. The rocking chair, the pots, the farm—they all belonged to someone else now.

The kitchen smelled faintly spicy from a century of baking and pickling, an odor so synonymous with warmth and happiness that tears pricked Elizabeth's eyes. The spicy fragrance would fade from her memory, she thought, be as final as the days of her life within these walls.

Three weeks ago, Aunt Mercy had complained of a large pain in her chest and took to her bed, declaring she would be up the next day but asking for an onion poultice in case it was the pneumonia. By morning, she was dead. And with the most ungracious haste, the town clerk had made it clear that the taxes were to be paid without delay. Otherwise, the farm would be sold to the highest bidder. And so it had been.

A wave of loneliness swept over Elizabeth like autumn fog. She and Aunt Mercy had spent much of their time in the kitchen, the way women do. Here, they had pared apples for pies, stirred fragrant grape jelly bubbling in the big copper kettle. They watched ships pass on the river and sat near the window doing the bits of mending and dressmaking brought to them by the ladies of Fort Point. Sometimes they had spun wool in the kitchen and shared the village gossip.

It was here in the kitchen, Elizabeth remembered, that Aunt Mercy had told her the melancholy story of her parents. Elizabeth's mother, Fanny, and her father Robert, had met in church and had fallen in love at first sight. Robert was a mariner from Portland, and master of his own vessel. Robert and Fanny were married within a year of meeting. After Elizabeth was born, Fanny had stayed home while Robert sailed. But she pined for him so much her health was feared for, and Robert took Fanny on a short voyage down the eastern coast. They left baby Elizabeth in Mercy's care, expecting to return within a few weeks, but they ran into a terrible gale off the coast of North Carolina. The ship went down and all hands were lost. That was how Elizabeth came to be brought up by Aunt Mercy.

Elizabeth fingered the little gold locket that hung around her neck. It had been placed there by her mother when she left on her fateful voyage. She traced the deeply engraved F with her fingers. F for Fanny, F for fate, F for forlorn.

Tears pricked Elizabeth's eyes again, and she gave into a huge wallow of self-pity and grief.

A faint mew at the kitchen door diverted Elizabeth's attention. Sometimes one of the half-wild barn cats grew brave enough to come and beg for a handout. She opened the door, unable to resist the soft insistent call. Daisy strolled in, purring loudly, just as if she hadn't been missing for days. Daisy arched her back and rubbed against Elizabeth's ankles. Twice, the cat disappeared under the shroud of Elizabeth's dark wool skirt.

"Daisy! Where have you been?"

In all the confusion of Aunt Mercy's funeral, Daisy had disappeared. Elizabeth had feared she had run away in fright. Secretly, she had been relieved by Daisy's disappearance. It spared her the additional pain of leaving the cat behind to fend for itself.

Elizabeth scooped Daisy up into her arms and stroked her warm, tabby fur. Daisy rubbed her head against Elizabeth's cheek. How could she leave Daisy behind?

It was full daylight now. The dark shapes of naked trees stood out sharply against patches of lavender and gold sky. The quick movement of light reflected against a sail alerted Elizabeth that a ship was in the channel. Time had run out. She snatched up a basket that contained her extra pair of shoes and took them out. Aunt Mercy's gray shawl still hung behind the kitchen door. Elizabeth grabbed it, held it against her cheek for one brief second, and stuffed it into the basket. Then she dropped Daisy inside and shut the lid.

Elizabeth closed the door softly behind her, painfully aware of the final click of the latch. She hesitated on the door rock, looking down across the back pasture. The Penobscot River lay at the foot of it, and beyond, the hills of Castine contoured the horizon. Upriver lay Bangor and whatever new life she could make for herself.

Daisy stirred in the basket, uneasy at being confined, but reassured by the familiar smell of Mercy's shawl.

"Be still, Daisy," Elizabeth whispered. The words were more to quiet her own racing heartbeat than to calm the cat.

The sails were closer now. There was no delaying the inevitable. Elizabeth set off down the narrow track edging the pasture. The grass, stiff and brown, caught at her skirt as she trudged. In one hand she held a much worn valise containing a few articles of clothing; in the other hand, she carried the basket with Daisy in it.

The sheep in the pasture drifted toward Elizabeth. A lamb bleated for his mother and a ewe hurried to his side to reassure him. If only life were that simple, Elizabeth thought, if only all I had to do was whimper and my mother would come to make Aunt Mercy's death and losing the farm easier to bear. But there was no family to turn to for comfort.

Elizabeth went on, running a bit, making sure she reached the boat landing before the vessel drew opposite. There was no way to know for sure if this ship would take her aboard, but she had raised the large orange flag. She was prepared to wait all day until some vessel was inclined to give her passage up the river.

As the vessel drew opposite the landing, it slowed, appearing to drift of its own accord. Elizabeth's heart hammered. This ship was going to take her aboard. She hadn't expected that of the very first one to come upriver this early in the day. She could see the sails being reefed.

Now, there was no turning back.

2.

Abner Giddings saw the bright orange flag a long way upriver, an incongruous blot of color lodged against the tender green of late April. A tall, spare figure huddled in a heavy woolen jacket, he stood on the quarterdeck of the ship, *Fairmont*, owned by Joshua Stetson. It was the custom of the farmers along this stretch of the Penobscot to hoist an orange flag when they wanted passage upriver. Local shipping often took these passengers aboard. Abner never had. But this morning the tide had not yet turned, the breeze was light, and the ship was running against only the river currents. It would cause him little trouble to do some local farmer a favor. He gave the order to Lovejoy Page, the mate.

"Heave to. We're taking on a passenger," he said.

The moment the words left his lips, Abner regretted them. He wasn't ready to resume command, not fit company for man or beast. He was better off left to brood by himself. No need to pretend to a good humor he didn't feel.

Abner stood above six feet tall—his bones slender and long. His face, weathered from sun and wind, was etched with little lines that crept out from the corners of his brown eyes even when he didn't smile. His dark hair was straight and long at the back and sides and blended into neatly trimmed sideburns. He was nearing thirty and had lost the stripling look of youth. His body had settled into the strong, solid proportions of maturity. His shoulders were broad, his hips were lean. His handsome face reflected his brooding mood in the tense lines of his cheeks and the inward expression in his eyes.

He went below. The steward rattled pots in the galley. He handed Abner a steaming mug of tea. Abner took a sip and burned his tongue. It gave him an excuse to reach into his pocket for the small flask he had carried with him since the night of the accident. He poured a large measure of rum into the tea, just to cool it a bit, he told himself. He wasn't a drinking man, but the rum had helped him through the last few weeks. He drank deeply and added more rum.

He heard the dinghy launched, the easy bickering of the crew; his men were bored with the slow progress upriver. They were eager to dock at Bangor, anticipating days of liberty before they signed on with some other vessel.

But Abner dreaded arriving at Bangor, dreaded the thought of calling on Maryanne's mother, of bringing her the details of Maryanne's death four weeks ago.

He didn't want to think about it anymore. So he sat, sipping his tea and adding rum until the tea was gone and only the sharp taste of spirits remained. The liquor settled warmly in his middle; his nerves began to relax. He had no idea how long he sat concentrating on the warm feeling in his stomach, averting all thought from the duties that lay ahead, and the pain that lay behind.

Presently, he heard Lovejoy Page give the order to get underway. Page was a competent mate, knew his job and did it well, but the responsibilities of master were new to him and he did not have the necessary experience a ship's master needed. The crew sensed this and had slacked off some since Abner had abdicated. Abner knew he should go on deck to make sure they were still in the channel and clear of the sandbar, make it look as if he were still in charge, at least for the moment. He lingered a bit longer, leaned heavily against the bulkhead, sagging slightly as if he were old.

He made a visible effort to pull himself together and went above.

Lovejoy Page had everything under control, and for some reason, irrational as it was, it irritated

Abner to see how easily he could be replaced as master of the *Fairmont*. He made it a point, as all master mariners did, to keep his relationship with the first mate strictly one of business. He had no good reason to resent Page's stepping into the master's shoes. He had relinquished his authority by his own choosing in time of great duress. Still, there was that prick of resentment. Maybe it was time to put himself to rights and send Page back where he belonged.

The *Fairmont*'s sails shook themselves out and filled away in the light breeze as pretty as a lady's petticoat on a March morning. The sight heartened him, lightened his doleful mood. He lifted his chin into the breeze, unconsciously imitating with his body the movement of the sails. He felt the power of the wind as it drove the vessel. What an exhilarating thing it was to guide the *Fairmont* through wind and water! By God! That was what he needed—the feel of the wheel under his own hand, the sure knowledge that his every order would be obeyed and the work well done.

Abner started aft, swaying slightly, not enough so anyone would know he'd been into the rum. Couldn't set a bad example for his crew, especially since spirits were now illegal in Maine. He had always run a clean ship. He gazed upward at the sails and smiled at the sight. Nothing like canvas aflutter.

Another bit of fluttering fabric distracted him. What was it? He had seen it before. He couldn't breathe, or swallow, or slow the hammering in his chest. His body recognized what his brain refused to acknowledge. That gray cloak, the graceful stance of the woman leaning on the rail—he knew them well. He had never seen the knitted blue hood, but that didn't matter. She was always knitting something—socks, mittens, scarves, warm things to shield him from foul weather. The name that escaped from his throat emerged soft as the swish of water against the ship's bow. He could have sworn he shouted.

"Maryanne."

The woman turned slightly, not enough to see who had spoken, turned so her face was in profile against the sparse April landscape. It was not Maryanne, not his dead wife.

Maybe he was drunk, after all.

3.

"Maryanne." It was barely audible, a slight motion of air that might have been nothing more than a light wind tightening a sail. It was lost on a small note of agony and joy, and when Elizabeth turned to look for the speaker she saw no one but the seamen running to and fro along the deck in response to shouted orders.

The *Fairmont* gained speed as the crew loosed

more of her canvas to the wind. If someone had spoken, he had disappeared from sight. Perhaps she had imagined it. Still, she had the eerie impression she had been mistaken for someone else.

The wind breached the folds of Elizabeth's cloak, numbing her fingers and toes. The sailor who had rowed her to the vessel was nowhere on deck. She would have to find her own way below where she could shelter from the wind. Daisy stirred in the basket and yowled.

As Elizabeth made her way along the rail toward the companionway, seamen eyed her with curiosity and open admiration. She wasn't accustomed to it, and their frank stares embarrassed her. They were a scruffy looking lot, some bearded, some toothless. She lowered her head, pretending she didn't notice how they looked at her.

The wind whipped Elizabeth's petticoats around her legs, forcing her to move clumsily. She fought for modesty, stumbled, and nearly dropped the basket. Daisy meowed a loud protest. She righted herself, took advantage of a sudden lull in the wind, and broke into a slow run. She thought she heard someone shouting a warning. But too late she saw the slippery patch of water, skidded, and lost all control of her body.

She pitched headlong down the companionway. Somewhere, very far away, a voice she did not recognize as her own screamed and was drowned by the hollow thud of boots running on the deck above. Then it was dark.

The scream harpooned Abner, tore open wounds that barely had begun to heal. He sobered instantly and arrived on deck completely in control.

As he ran, he shouted, "Mr. Page, fetch Dr. Webber!" The crew paused imperceptibly, understood that the captain was back in charge and, to a man, made certain Abner was the first to reach the woman who lay crumpled at the bottom of the companionway.

The accident struck Abner with all the horror and intensity of a month ago, but this time it wasn't Maryanne lying there. This time he could take charge, he could do something. Only for a moment, when a cat untangled itself from the woman's skirt, did he experience any desire to bolt.

"It wasn't the cat's fault, Abner, not then, not now," Sam said as he bent to examine the woman. "Nothing broke, concussion probably. Let's get her to a bunk." He signaled to a seaman.

"No," Abner said, "I'll carry her. I'll put her in Maryanne's cabin."

After he had left the woman in Sam's care, Abner returned to the deck. Within the hour the patch of water had been removed and orders given that it was to remain that way. Mr. Page deftly was relegated to tasks more usually associated with the first mate, and Abner stood at the wheel.

Elizabeth woke to find herself lying on a narrow bunk. Her shoes had been removed and a bulky bandage was wrapped around one ankle. She tried to sit up, but a steady throb in her head made her lie down again very quickly. She felt as if she had been run over by an ox team, but remembered that she had fallen.

"Daisy," she whispered into the gloom. No answering purr came; no furry body jumped up to greet her. The only sound was the creak of rigging. She wanted to get up and search, to find someone who could tell her what had happened to Daisy, but she was so weary and her head hurt so badly. She drifted off into a fretful doze, and dreamed violent dreams.

She woke again with a start, crying out for Aunt Mercy. She was not alone in the cabin. Someone had responded to her cry, had covered her with a warm blanket. She laid very still, hardly daring to breathe. A man stood in the circle of lamplight.

"You're awake, I see." The tone of the man's voice reassured her. It was deep, reminded her of Daisy's raspy purr and had the same rough gentleness. Shadows blurred the exact contours of the man's face, but Elizabeth saw that he was nearly as tall as the cabin was high. She drew the blanket up around her chin even though modesty was of no concern as she was still fully dressed.

"I'm Abner Giddings, master of the *Fairmont*." He was close enough for Elizabeth to see that his shirt was open at the throat. The light haloed his head—outlined his slender frame. She peered upwards, trying to see his face more clearly.

"I'm Elizabeth Emerson," she said with as much dignity as she could muster. It was impossible to maintain one's dignity while lying down. She poked her right hand toward Abner Giddings.

"Pleased to meet you," she said primly. Silence grew between them, huge and awkward, threatening to split the bulkheads. Elizabeth twisted her fingers in the blanket fringe. She lowered her eyes and stared at the spot where she assumed Abner Giddings' boots would be. She fought down an insane urge to pull the blanket up over her head. Desperate to banish the silence, she asked, "What time is it?"

Abner drew a watch from his pocket.

"Nearing midnight. Webber, the surgeon, says you sprained your ankle and shouldn't walk for a day or two. You hurt your head, too."

Again, Elizabeth felt herself respond to that timbre of his voice. She put her fingers to the side of her head. A large, ugly knot stood out on her skull.

"Your cat ran and hid. When it's found someone will bring it to you."

"Thank you."

Elizabeth hated the quiver in that small phrase

and felt tears gathering beneath her eyelids. Abner Giddings continued to regard her with the same neutral gaze. She felt like an insect on the head of a pin.

"Good night, Miss Emerson," he said with a stiff bow. The door closed behind him with a soft snap.

The next morning Elizabeth woke to a faint gray dawn. Her head no longer throbbed when she sat up. Her ankle ached some, but she put a little weight on it and hobbled to the wash basin. The *Fairmont*'s motion was slower, less rolling than the day before. Even the creak of the rigging was muted. It could only mean one thing. Sometime during the night they had reached Bangor! She gathered up her belongings in anticipation.

The light in the cabin grew bright enough for Elizabeth to observe her surroundings. The bunk where she had slept was constructed of a wood unfamiliar to her, carved with fluted turnings, and spread with a gray silk coverlet. Small Persian rugs made islands of color against the floor. A guitar, its neck tied with red and blue ribbons, hung on the bulkhead. A lap desk occupied the top of a slender-legged table. Beside it sat an intricately woven sweet grass basket. Surely this was not the cabin usually assigned to passengers. She stroked the blanket on the bunk with practiced fingers. It was finely spun and beautifully woven. Lamb's wool. The cabin must belong to a woman of exquisite taste.

There was a light rap at the door.

"Come in." Elizabeth fully expected a lady of great elegance to enter. She was surprised to see a small man with graying hair, a ruddy complexion, and eyes the color of summer blueberries. He carried a battered instrument case which he dropped unceremoniously on the bunk.

"Good morning, ma'am. I understand you're Elizabeth Emerson. I'm Sam Webber, ship's mate and surgeon. Feeling frisky this morning, are you? Let's have a look at that ankle. You're a very lucky young woman. I've seen stouter necks broken on sailors who have pitched down that companionway."

He examined Elizabeth's ankle gently.

"You've got a bad sprain there, but you'll be able to limp ashore when we get to Bangor. That may not be for another day or two. You'll have plenty of time to heal," Sam said cheerfully.

"What! Aren't we in Bangor right now?"

"Why, no. We're off Bucksport and likely to be all day. Two or three maybe. It happens quite regular on this part of the river. The river current is strong and the wind has died."

"I have to be in Bangor by tomorrow!" A shrill note crept into Elizabeth's voice. "I'll have someone row me ashore. I'll take the stage. I must get to Bangor!"

Elizabeth shrank from the stern look Sam fixed on her.

"That ankle won't stand too much gallivanting around, Miss Emerson. You've bruised a few ribs, too, not to mention that nasty crack on your head. Why you don't have a concussion is beyond me. You aren't in any condition to bounce around over bad roads. And besides, my dear, the mud is so bad now, you won't find a stage that could even get to Bangor."

Sam patted Elizabeth's hand. She snatched it away. She was in no mood to be comforted. All the fear, grief, loss, and pain she had suffered because of Aunt Mercy's death grew to enormous proportions. Great sobs shook her shoulders. Her chance to start a new life had evaporated with the wind.

Sam left without Elizabeth noticing. He wasn't gone long.

"Come now," he said kindly, "see what I found."

In his arms was Daisy.

4.

Sam set Daisy on Elizabeth's lap, taking care that his hand supported the cat's hind legs. He liked cats. But his life at sea had made it impossible to get well acquainted with domestic animals.

Daisy moved nothing but the tips of her claws,

kneading them into Elizabeth's skirt. She sniffed Elizabeth's hand as though making sure this was someone familiar and trusted.

"I don't think she remembers me," Elizabeth said.

"Maybe she's confused by the smell of that liniment I put on your ankle," Sam said. He liked the way Elizabeth stroked Daisy's head. Daisy did, too, and a purr of magnificent proportions swelled in her chest.

Sam laughed, glad to see Elizabeth laughing, too.

"Was Daisy hurt?" Elizabeth wanted to know.

Sam shook his head, no. He settled himself into a seat and lit his pipe, filling the cabin with a sweet, pungent odor. He was in no hurry. There was nothing much for him to do anyway. The crew was healthy; Abner looked as if he had got himself pulled together and was leaving the grog alone. It relieved Sam's mind to see Abner come out of the depression that had gripped him since the accident. Sam had worried a lot about Abner, but had, for the most part, let him be. Grief resolved itself in stages—passed of its own accord if you let it. He had said as much to Abner and now he was pleased to see that Abner was starting to heal.

"Now tell me, my dear," Sam said between puffs, "why are you in such a hurry to get upriver?"

Sam wasn't surprised to hear the sad circumstances of Elizabeth's immediate past. He had heard similar stories from Maude. He took the small scrap of newspaper Elizabeth handed him.

"Bangor House." Sam pursed his lips and smoke rose around his head in wispy circles. "That's certainly a respectable address. Lots of people by name of Hogan in Bangor . . ."

"Do you know Mrs. Hogan?" Elizabeth asked eagerly.

"No, I can't say I do. I've heard of several Mrs. Hogans. One, in particular. But I'm certain she's not the lady you're looking for." Whenever he heard that name, Hogan, he always thought of Fanny and Pink Chimneys. Fanny Hogan was known, by reputation, to everyone in Bangor, to every mariner who came up the river. Why, his own wife, his Maude, was welcomed at Fanny's as a friend. But try as he would, he never could get much out of Maude about Fanny. What Maude knew, she kept still about. He had seen Fanny, dressed in the latest fashion, driving a well turned out rig pulled by a pair of Morgans that could make a man weep for all their beauty. Hell, for that matter, so could Fanny herself. Handsome woman with that orange-brown hair of hers. At one time or another, so they said, half the lumber barons of Bangor had been in love with her. Of course, everyone knew she was Joshua Stetson's woman. But that was neither here nor there. This Mrs. Hogan advertising for a seamstress was surely not the notorious Fanny Hogan of Pink Chimneys.

Sam roused from his mental meanderings.

"Forgive me, Miss Emerson, I seem to have misheard what you just said."

"I was saying, Dr. Webber, that Captain Giddings told me he'd have Daisy found and brought to me."

The cat curled up in Elizabeth's lap, presenting a cozy domestic scene, a woman stroking a cat, the cat purring. Sam looked forward to just that sort of domesticity in his declining years. Not that he would ever get Maude to slow down much. But he had decided he wanted to stay ashore from now on. This was his last voyage.

"Giddings been here, has he?" Sam sat up straight in his seat and removed the clay pipe from his mouth. Now that was a good sign. Abner hadn't been in this cabin since Maryanne's death.

"Yes, last night. I thought he seemed . . . unsettled. Almost angry. As if he were inconvenienced by my being here." She recalled his reticence, his reluctance to say much of anything.

"No, I don't believe he was inconvenienced. You were brought here at his order. Best place for you. More comfortable than anywhere else."

"Maybe he's superstitious about having Daisy aboard." Many seamen believed a cat aboard ship brought bad luck.

Elizabeth stroked Daisy's back as the cat stretched and purred. "I kept thinking that I must have done something to offend Captain Giddings."

"You didn't offend him, and it's not really Daisy, either. The captain is just a little leery of cats, in general, right now. Especially after what happened to Maryanne."

Sam hadn't intended to give out even that much information about the accident, but there was something very kindhearted about Miss Emerson and he had spoken without thinking.

"Maryanne?"

Sam settled back into his seat, his pipe put aside, his fingers tightly laced across his navy blue jacket.

"Yes, the captain's wife. Maryanne Giddings. Pretty little thing. Her hair was dark like yours. Not so tall, though. This was her cabin." Sam tightened and loosened his fingers.

"When will I meet Mrs. Giddings?"

Sam stared at his hands.

"What about Mrs. Giddings, will I be meeting her?" Elizabeth asked again.

"No."

Sam slipped back to a memory that distressed him more than he cared to admit. As a physician he had seen much of life's inconsistencies and caprices. But nothing had ever bothered him as much as Maryanne's death. He hadn't talked to anyone about it—especially not Abner. He had been too afraid Abner would go into a decline or drink himself into a stupor and fall overboard. Or worse, pick a fight and get his skull bashed in.

"Dr. Webber, are you all right? You were telling me about Mrs. Giddings."

"It was four weeks ago," Sam began. How much should he tell this obviously innocent stranger? Would she be shocked? He met her eyes, gauging her character, saw curiosity and something else—compassion? Certainly she was compassionate. You only had to see how she handled the cat to know that. She was waiting to hear. And, surprisingly, he wanted to tell her.

"Expecting her first child, she was. I told her, stay ashore until the confinement is over. But Maryanne was never one to follow any orders but her own. Headstrong. Never knew when she would stand watch with the captain, even in the foulest weather. Crew worshiped her. So she stayed aboard. Promised she'd stay below with her cat for company and plenty of books and sewing to keep her occupied. Promised me. Promised the captain she wouldn't climb up the companionway without help, to make sure she didn't fall." Sam spoke very softly, knowing from long experience that painful memories were easier to confront that way.

"Then, the day we cleared Charleston, the cat ran off. It was a foul day, windy, no one heard

335

her call, the wind was so loud. So Maryanne went to look for her cat. She climbed up to the deck, calling the cat, soaked to the skin, the wind tearing at her hair." Sam took a deep breath and changed his position in a seat. "She caught her boot in her skirts and fell down the companionway."

Sam stopped abruptly. Must be getting old, he thought. The mental picture of Maryanne's body lying in a twisted heap was like a wound.

"You will feel better if you finish the story, Doctor," Elizabeth said. Sam saw compassion and kindness on her face and thought of Maude.

"When I saw you lying there all tangled up in your cloak, it was like Maryanne's accident all over again. The captain felt that way, too." He took a deep breath before he went on. "Maryanne died. The child, too. Nothing could have saved them. I tried. I tried . . ." Suddenly, Sam was weary. He felt every one of his fifty-eight years. He longed for Maude's generous doses of warmth and sympathy.

Sam stood up. "Well, I won't bother you anymore with my troubles. You have enough of your own." He retrieved his medicine box.

"Was Maryanne's cat ever found?" Elizabeth asked.

"Under the captain's bunk. It had never even got up on deck." Sam patted Elizabeth's hand. The gesture was meant to comfort them both.

336

"No need to trouble yourself, Miss Emerson."

"What happened to the cat?"

Sam regarded Elizabeth with a long look. Apparently, she wasn't one to shy from the bitter truth. Maude was like that, too.

"The captain threw it overboard."

Except for a slight narrowing of the eyes, Elizabeth did not respond. Whenever life holds in store for this young woman, Sam thought, she's equal to it.

5.

Elizabeth thought about the terrible circumstances of Maryanne Giddings' death for a long time after Sam Webber left. If the tragedy still lay so heavily on the doctor, then naturally, it was all the more bitter a burden for the captain. He must have been out of his mind with grief. Elizabeth understood that. Her own feelings after Aunt Mercy's death had been akin to craziness.

It was all so awful. But she didn't know the captain and there was nothing she could do or say. By tomorrow she would be in Bangor and never see him again. Besides, she had problems of her own to think about without taking on the ones belonging to Abner Giddings. If Mrs. Hogan didn't take her on, she didn't know what she would do.

Time dragged and seemed all the more interminable because the *Fairmont* was becalmed. There was no clock to mark the passing hours. Except for the steward, who brought food, Elizabeth was alone with her thoughts and tired of inactivity.

Her ankle did not trouble her much. She moved about the cabin restlessly, testing the amount of weight it would bear, gauging the amount of pain it produced. She was quite well enough to go above for a breath of fresh air, but she didn't dare to. Dr. Webber had been firm about that. Nor did she care to risk another encounter with Abner Giddings. She did not want to be a reminder of what had happened to his wife and child.

Elizabeth rustled a paper ball in front of Daisy, but the cat merely yawned, made one half-hearted swipe with her paw, and went back to sleep.

Elizabeth limped around the cabin even though Dr. Webber had said to rest and stay off her feet. She limped past the table and around and around the cabin, until she stumbled over the sweet grass basket and knocked the cover off. A few bright strands of thread spilled out from under a rumpled piece of white flannel. Her first thought was to replace the cover and move the basket out of the way. It was a lovely basket, woven, she was certain, by local Indians who peddled their handiwork to local folks up and down the Penobscot. It smelled as sweet as a hay mow, reminding her of a similar sewing basket she had left behind.

Here, Elizabeth thought, was the perfect solution to the boredom and inactivity that was to be her lot for the rest of the day. Surely, Abner Giddings wouldn't mind if she did a little sewing. The stitching would keep her happily occupied, take her mind off her trouble, make time pass more quickly. She would be very careful to return everything, even the thread snippets, to the basket. What harm could it do?

Elizabeth drew the flannel fabric from the basket and saw that it was an infant's dress, small enough for a newborn. She held it up, very tenderly, as if it were a baby, and smoothed the dress with her hands. The fabric was finely woven, soft as velvet. An embroidery had been started on it, one pink rosette worked on the sleeve. In her imagination, Elizabeth saw Maryanne reclining on the bunk, heavy with child, fashioning that one rosette. Was it then that the cat had run away?

At the bottom of the basket lay skeins of Chinese silks. Elizabeth stroked them, marveling at their beauty. There were shades of green, pink, cornflower blue, and yellow bright as the buttercups in the home pasture. A silver thimble, a carved ivory needle case, scissors, and a small embroidery hoop also lay in the basket.

Elizabeth did not stop to consider the

consequences—a trait Aunt Mercy had never quite managed to eradicate from her character.

Small patches of color grew quickly under Elizabeth's fingers. She fashioned borders of rosettes and buttercups interlaced with intricate twinings of leaves and forget-me-nots. The small spark of guilt she felt at trespassing on another's property receded into the joy of creating the designs.

The day passed; by mid-evening she had finished. She folded the dress and replaced it in the basket.

The steward brought tea.

"The wind's coming up, Miss," he said. "We'll sail within the hour. We'll be in Bangor tomorrow for sure. The captain said to tell you."

6.

In the morning, leaning lightly on Sam's arm, Elizabeth limped along the deck. The buttons on the doctor's coat shone brightly. She suspected he had polished them especially for his homecoming. His flat-crowned sailor's cap sat on his head at a jaunty angle, the narrow visor casting a shadow across the bridge of his windburned nose. The skin around his eyes crinkled as he smiled.

"We're in Hampden Narrows, Miss Emerson. This is the most notorious part of the Penobscot, you know. They say that back in the pod auger days the old mariners would send kegs of rum and molasses over the side and their mates would wait in Brewer for kegs to wash ashore. Then they would take the kegs to the Smuggling Hole and sell them. That way they avoided the customs office. I don't know how much truth there is to that story, but I've heard that since spirits have been banned in Maine, the old Smuggling Hole is doing a lively business."

"You mean smuggling is still going on?" Elizabeth asked.

"Well, I don't quite know. The sale of spirituous liquor was prohibited three years ago, but everywhere you go you still see folks who look as if they've tipped a few."

"It's a very great evil. My Aunt Mercy was very much against intoxicating drinks."

"My wife, Maude, believes drunkenness is the primary cause of poverty and disease. I'm inclined to agree with her."

As the Penobscot widened, an increasing number of wharves, sawmills, and ice cribs appeared along both sides of the river. The *Fairmont* kept to the center channel, rounding each successive bend at a steady pace. Bangor lay scattered along the riverbank, rising gently from shore in a series of rolling hills. A current of excitement gripped the crew and fastened on Elizabeth. She leaned against the rail, her eyes fixed on the town.

"Ah, it's good to be home again," Sam

remarked. "See that little cottage up there, the one with a red door? That's where my wife, Maude, and I live. Maude grew up there. Usually, when she knows I'm coming, she stands out on the doorstep and waves. I don't see her, though. This is my last time out, you know."

Sam leaned companionably on the rail beside Elizabeth and puffed his pipe.

"Will you miss coasting, Dr. Webber?"

"Probably. But I'll be busy enough. Maude's a midwife, and with my own doctoring to do, I expect I won't have much time to miss the seafaring life."

Sam puffed contentedly in silence, his eyes riveted to the shoreline. He pointed his pipe stem toward a row of brick buildings shadowed by the blurred greens and yellows of newly budding trees.

"Elms," Sam said, moving his hand in a sweeping motion that included all of Bangor. "City's full of them. Oak, evergreen, maple, the whole region from here to Canada is nothing but trees. See that crowd of people over there at the steamboat wharf? Most of them are headed for California. Gold. Now I ask you, does that make sense? Trees are where the money is. Look at all the sawmills on this river. Both sides from Old Town, way upriver, all the way down to Hampden. A lot of men in Bangor and Brewer are rich because of the lumbering. See that set of buildings over there? Rufus Dwinel's counting houses. Every unmarried woman from here to Boston set her cap for him . . . until he got to acting so odd. And those barkentines tied up over there? Joshua Stetson's. Lumber barons, both of them. Stetson has more property and more influence in Bangor than any other man around. Of course, Sam Veazie and Rufus Dwinel take exception to that."

Sam lapsed into another comfortable silence.

Elizabeth heard Abner Giddings directing the *Fairmont*'s progress with well ordered commands. She had not seen him since the day of her accident. He was very good to look at, she thought, with his sun-bronzed skin and dark hair glinting with reddish lights. Every move he made was quick and efficient; he wasted neither time nor energy, she observed.

Elizabeth's stare was open and frank. If Abner Giddings noticed, he showed no sign. Her cheeks grew warm as she realized she was attracted to the captain. It was an entirely new and unsettling feeling. She didn't like it at all. She brought her attention back to Bangor. Somewhere in the midst of this bustling place was Mrs. Hogan.

Four slender white steeples, sharp as needles, rose above solid clusters of white houses.

"Bangor folk must be churchgoers," Elizabeth remarked, quite awed by this display of public piety.

"Some are, some aren't," Sam answered." Same as anywhere else. Good and bad live side by side. You'd do well to remember that, Miss Emerson."

"Oh, look, Dr. Webber, there's a house with pink chimneys, over there on that hill. I never saw a house with pink chimneys."

"That's, ah, a gentleman's club, my dear, a place for men to conduct business and entertain their associates. I believe the chimneys were once painted red, so the story goes, but the paint was of an inferior quality and the sun faded them to this, ah, unusual color."

Elizabeth had the distinct impression Dr. Webber was not telling the exact truth.

From where they stood on the deck of the *Fairmont*, the house with pink chimneys appeared large and well proportioned, the size and style only the wealthy could afford. It sat a good ways above the harbor, yet close enough to be seen easily from the river. Except for a church steeple which rose a bit beyond, the house had no nearby neighbors.

By now, Elizabeth's excitement at having arrived in Bangor was at its peak. She was full of questions.

"Is the Bangor House difficult to find?" she asked.

The *Fairmont* had progressed into the midst of the harbor, beset on all sides by every possible kind of vessel from bark to brigantine, raft to dory. A paddlewheel steamer swept downstream, her whistle splitting the air with a rush of deafening sound.

The *Fairmont* slid by a large building, the roof bearing the legend: LANCIL'S SAIL LOFT. Harsh masculine voices drifted across the water; more than a few of the words Elizabeth could make out were profane.

The clamor of ropes and pulleys increased, and the *Fairmont* slipped alongside the wharf to her moorings.

"It's not much of a chore to find the Bangor House," Sam said. "That's it up on Union Street." He pointed directly up the street to a square brick building of four stories.

"It's much closer than I expected."

"Close enough for travelers to find easily and far enough away from the waterfront to be respectable." Sam resettled his cap on his head. Elizabeth took his proffered arm and they walked down the gangway. Elizabeth kept a firm hold on Daisy's basket.

"I will hail a carriage for you, Miss Emerson. Your ankle isn't ready for the walk to the Bangor House."

"Oh, no," Elizabeth protested, "no, thank you. I will be all right. I will go slowly, so as not to jostle Daisy." She did want Dr. Webber to know that what little money she had left after paying her passage upriver could not be spent on the luxury of a public conveyance. She would need to save every penny for food and lodging if Mrs. Hogan couldn't take her on.

"See," Elizabeth said, in an effort to convince him, "I'm not limping very much at all."

Sam gave Elizabeth a dubious look.

"All right then. I'll leave you here. Should you ever be in need of a friend, my dear, Maude and I are not far away. Just ask anyone. Everyone knows Maude Webber, the midwife."

It was frightening to be left on her own after all the kindness the doctor had shown. But Elizabeth refused to give in to the megrims. She picked up her valise and Daisy's basket, and started off for the Bangor House.

Someone called her name.

Abner Giddings strode down the gangway, his long legs covering the distance rapidly.

"And where do you think you're going, Miss Emerson?" The barely concealed fury in his voice caught Elizabeth off guard. He planted himself in front of her with such obvious belligerence she took an involuntary step backward.

"Thought you'd got away with it, didn't you?" he demanded. His eyes bored into Elizabeth. "I know you've taken the Chinese silks. They aren't in the basket. I just looked, so don't deny it." He grasped her shoulder roughly, to prevent her from running away. "Hand them over," he said between clenched teeth, "or I'll have you arrested."

His loud words and hostile manner attracted the attention of the men at Lancil's sail loft, and a few drifted over to see what was going on.

"Leave the lady be, Cap'n," one man growled, but he made no move to interfere. Rather, he seemed to find the situation amusing.

Even though Elizabeth had taken the liberty of using the silks, she had not stolen them. She did not deserve such hateful treatment. She was furious beyond words. She twisted away from Abner's grasp with surprising strength and quickness.

The men from Lancil's applauded and laughed.

"Spitfire, ain't she, Cap'n," someone called.

Abner ignored the hilarity and stepped toward Elizabeth again. She dodged, humiliated to the bottom of her feet. She drew herself up to her full height of five feet eight.

"I did not steal the silks," she snapped. "They're still in the basket." She moved away, putting a margin of safety between herself and Abner Giddings. He grabbed her wrist.

"The silks are gone."

Elizabeth looked Abner straight in the eye the way Aunt Mercy had taught her to do when confronted with a ticklish situation.

"I stitched them into the little dress in the bottom of the basket. All you have to do is unfold it."

Abner dropped her hand as if it were on fire.

Elizabeth reached into her reticule, found her last few coins, and held them out to him.

"Here," she said. "I will pay you for the silks." Her voice broke into a tiny sob. "I didn't think you'd mind."

Abner made no move to take the money. Elizabeth threw the coins at his feet. The crowd parted. Crude, boisterous laughter followed her all the way up the street.

7.

Abner's anger evaporated as rapidly as it had taken hold of him. He stood alone on the wharf. The life of the harbor clanged around him. The men from Lancil's drifted away now that the excitement was over. Drays, carts with heavy wheels, and carriages rumbled and clattered on the cobbled streets, a bass counterpoint to the shouts and curses of stevedores unloading cargo. All along the waterfront, seamen lounged in tavern doorways where rum could still be found if you knew the right people to ask. Boldfaced women competed for the seamen's attention with showy dresses and painted faces. Abner saw and heard and didn't give a damn. He had made an utter fool of himself.

Maryanne had been sewing the day she had died; the sewing basket and its contents were the last things she had touched. She hadn't been very good at sewing, but she had been very proud of the baby's dress she had made and vowed she would finish it before the child was born. Abner had made her a gift of the silks. He remembered how pleased she had been.

Abner had no wish to keep the sewing basket and its contents; they were too painful a reminder of what he had lost. He had been tempted to drop them overboard where they belonged—under fathoms of water with Maryanne, the infant, and the cat. Instead, he decided to take the basket to Maryanne's mother. It was the only gesture of atonement he could think of.

When he saw the silks were missing, something black and hateful had burned within him, canceling his ability to reason coherently. He had cursed himself for giving in to his ridiculous impulse to give the Emerson woman passage upriver. For all her reserved manner and pretty face, she had proved to be nothing but a common thief.

Abner shot one last look at the retreating figure of Elizabeth Emerson. He wanted to be glad to be rid of her, but he wasn't. He returned to the *Fairmont* and went below. The sewing basket lay on the table exactly as it had the day Maryanne died, just as he had left it after he had discovered the silks were gone.

Nothing had been stolen, nothing defiled; the silks were there, stitched up in a way that

Abner recognized as the work of a professional seamstress. The embroidery design, with its quaint sense of pastures and country innocence, made him want to weep. He had misjudged the woman. She had worked the dress with as much care as if she herself were expecting a child. Maryanne would have been delighted to see the dress so lovingly and beautifully finished.

But Maryanne lay at the bottom of the Atlantic Ocean, the child with her. He could not change that. But he could change the odds of whether or not Elizabeth Emerson found a place in the Hogan household.

Abner strode purposefully up Union Street with his jacket unbuttoned. The day had grown warm as it often did in late April. A light breeze fluffed his hair away from his ears. Later on, he would report to Joshua Stetson. Then he would go home to dear old Hannah Bailey. She would be expecting him at her inn on Summer Street.

Abner spotted Elizabeth near a window in the lobby of the Bangor House. She stared intently at the street, as if searching for someone. She looked sad and very vulnerable. Right off the farm, so Sam Webber said. Daisies and buttercups. Nettles and brambles. Anyone could see that. She would be a target for all the worst flesh peddlers in Bangor if she didn't find respectable employment.

How should he approach her? She had seemed

intimidated by his presence the night of her accident. He had called her a thief in public and had used her roughly. She had every reason to want to avoid him.

As he anticipated, she jumped to her feet the moment she saw him approach. Her fists clenched into hard balls.

"If you have come to plague me with more accusations . . . ," she began.

"No, I've come to make my apologies."

"Apologies," Elizabeth echoed. She unclenched her fists and the anxiety faded from her eyes, eyes of a deep shade of blue. Tall, autumn asters.

"My wife died only a short time ago," Abner said quietly, not sure how to launch the errand on which he had come.

"I know. Dr. Webber told me."

Abner nodded. He might have known old Sam would have paved the way for him. Sam believed in the truth, was always saying how most sickness would be cured for good if people would just talk straight to one another.

"My wife would not have begrudged you the pleasure of sewing, or use of the silks. Nor do I."

"Please," Elizabeth said, her eyes tightly closed to block out the expression of regret on Abner's face. "Please don't say you are sorry. I understand. I truly do. I've lost my aunt, my home, everything I hold dear, not so long ago." Her dark lashes lay against her high cheekbones. She lifted one gloved hand, as if to hold back the apology he felt he owed her.

"The silks aren't valuable. Here's your money." He took her hand and pressed the coins into it. "I'd like you to have the baby's dress. Webber said you're a seamstress. I thought perhaps the dress might help you to get the job you're after, as an example of your skill." He thrust a brown paper parcel into her arms.

"Thank you. I know that will help. I sent a message to Mrs. Hogan. The clerk told me to wait."

"There's the clerk now."

"Mrs. Hogan's driver is here, Miss. You better hurry. Mrs. Hogan don't like to be kept waiting," the clerk said.

"Let me walk to the carriage with you, Miss Emerson," Abner said.

Elizabeth did not reply, but she allowed Abner to take her valise. She gave him a bright smile. He grinned back. It had been a very long time since he had felt like smiling.

Abner handed her into the carriage and closed the door. The driver clucked to the horses and Elizabeth waved as she was driven away. Abner didn't wave back. He stared at the driver. It wasn't the anonymous servant of some grande dame newly come to town. It was Brown, Fanny Hogan's bodyguard and right hand man.

• • •

The forsythia bush in the front yard was bursting with pale yellow blooms. Tulips and jonquils nodded in the breeze, content with the warmth reflected from the house's granite foundation. Sam Webber looked at the flowers with pleasure. There was nothing at sea to rival a sight like that.

The house hadn't changed; it sat low and snug on the river side of the road as it had since Eli Richmond had built it back in the late 1700s. Sam walked quickly through the gate; he would have run if he had been ten years younger. He stuck his head through the front door, which he used only when he was in a hurry.

"Maude! Maude!" he called, "I'm home!"

Immediately, he heard his wife's soft tread in the upstairs hallway, and she appeared at the head of the stairs. She was rounder than the day he had married her thirty years ago. Her hair was graying some, but her dark brown eyes glowed with the same intense joy at the sight of him. Sam gathered her into his arms, swung her down from the last step, and placed her firmly on the floor.

Maude laughed and kissed him. "You smell like the wind," she said. She always said that; it was a homecoming litany.

"Are you coming or going?" he asked. Maude had on her cloak and bonnet. Her medicine chest sat by the door. Her smile vanished.

"Going, I'm afraid, Sam. I was worried I'd

353

miss you. Sarah John went to sit with a sick child so there's not a meal ready for you. I'm sorry I can't put this off. The message was urgent."

Sam put his hat back on. "Want some help?" he asked. "You always said you'd teach me the finer points of midwifing if I ever stayed ashore long enough to learn. All these years and I never did see you use those forceps you married me for."

Maude ignored his teasing.

"I wish you would, Sam. I've been called to the Bedford Inn. You know the place I mean. It stands almost where the Thatcher cabin did back in 1814. Not that I mind going alone. But sometimes I think I will go mad if I have to deliver one more young girl. Some are barely sixteen and right off the farm looking for a better life in Bangor. And what do they find? Some seaman between ships. I think I'm getting old, Sam." Maude's jaw settled into the firm hard line Sam knew so well. Maude never drew any distinctions between those she would and would not attend. She treated everyone alike. It was one of the things Sam loved about her. She had brought Veazies and Dearborns into the world as well as Murphys and Reillys.

"You could find someone else to go." It was a purely rhetorical comment and Sam knew it. Once called, Maude went.

"No one else would go, Sam. Who but me would mingle with the baser elements in Joppa to deliver a fallen woman's child? The saints preserve us," Maude said with a bit of mock humor.

Sam picked up Maude's medicine box and tucked his own instrument case under his arm. Theirs was an odd marriage, he thought, strengthened as much by their separations as by the time they spent together.

They had never had children, and he did not regret it. He was glad Maude had been spared the burden of children, that he had her all to himself.

The seedier part of the Bangor waterfront, known as Joppa, had streets lined with taverns and ale houses, where downstairs rooms catered to the rum guzzlers of the town, legal or no. The upper rooms of these establishments often were given over to the pleasures of a more basic sort. It was to one of these back rooms that Maude had been summoned.

A crowd of people clogging the narrow street slowed their progress. The crowd craned their necks and jeered at the fracas taking place outside the Bedford Inn.

"What is it, Sam?" Maude asked.

"I can't tell from here, Maude. Looks like we will have to walk the rest of the way."

Sam helped Maude out of the carriage and into the street. A few people recognized them and the crowd parted slightly to let them get through.

A group of men smashed hogsheads of rum in the street. The dark liquid trickled in the gutter and the air reeked with the sharp, sour odor of alcohol. The innkeeper screamed his outrage, but two hefty men held him at bay. Off to one side, a bit away from the melee, a member of the clergy ranted about the evils of drinking spirits and the perils of the ways of the flesh. Sam recognized the speaker as the Reverend Comfort Drummond, one of the local leaders of the temperance movement.

The crowd was enjoying the excitement and made no effort to interfere or aid the keeper of the Bedford Inn.

Sam picked his way through the puddles of rum and splintered barrels. Typically, Maude plowed through the wreckage without a moment's hesitation and no thought for the hem of her skirt.

Maude found the stairway inside the dreary interior of the tavern. She had been there before. A woman in a dirty apron met them in a dark hallway upstairs. Her hair was untidy and her front teeth black with decay. She might have been any age.

"Oh, Miz Webber," she wailed, "I thought you'd never get here!"

Maude pushed past the woman and entered the room she indicated. The place was small and bare except for a bed and washstand. A woman, covered by a threadbare blanket, lay on the bed. She was very still. Too still. The air in the room was foul and close.

"Open a window," Maude commanded. Sam was more than happy to oblige.

Maude examined the woman on the bed quickly, gently. She used her hands and her eyes, and did not hide the distress she felt.

"She's dead. Aborted herself." Maude's voice was low and even—a sure sign she was furious. She did not take the loss of life easily. Never had.

Sam held out his hand, asking to be connected to her distress, her fury, her helplessness to do anything but let this one go. Maude took his hand and they stood, linked by a sense of defeat.

"Send for the undertaker," Maude said to a woman.

"If it hadn't been for them holier-than-thous out there bustin' things up, I might have been able to get word to you sooner," the woman sniffled.

Maude laid her hand sympathetically on the woman's arm.

"No, no. She was bleeding inside. There was nothing we could do to help her."

Sam thought suddenly of Maryanne Giddings lying in a crumpled heap at the bottom of the companionway, thought of the moment her canvas-shrouded body had been committed to the sea.

"Do you ever get over feeling powerless and ignorant when something like this happens, Maude?"

"I haven't yet, Sam. I haven't yet."

8.

It was only a short distance from the Bangor House to the corner of Summer and Cedar Streets where Hannah Bailey kept her inn.

Abner walked slowly, his hands thrust deep in his pockets. Elizabeth Emerson was about to make a big mistake. What made him so sure, he couldn't say. Maybe it was the stories he had heard about the goings-on at Pink Chimneys. Maybe it was just the tight feeling in his gut. He should have said something to her, warned her, but he had made a fool of himself once because of her and was not about to repeat the performance. Elizabeth Emerson would have to take care of herself.

Yet, Abner thought, there was something vulnerable about the Emerson woman despite her spirit and determination. He liked that in a woman. She was good to look at, too, with her tall, straight figure, that dark hair and fair skin. He remembered the feel of her limp body in his arms after she had fallen, when he was carrying her to Maryanne's cabin. She was no feather. As Hannah would say, a man wouldn't have to shake the sheets to find her.

He supposed it wouldn't take long for Elizabeth Emerson to get used to the ease and luxury of living at Pink Chimneys. She would start out sewing, no doubt, but given time she would become one of Fanny's girls. The thought rankled him. Well, it didn't matter one way or the other. He would be at sea again within the week, and would never see hide nor hair of her again.

Abner walked up the familiar porch with its white Doric columns, the distinctive feature of Hannah Bailey's house. The front room was full of the home-again smells of baking pies and fresh bread. A few men, mostly mariners who nodded to Abner, sat at stout tables in Windsor chairs.

Hannah's inn was a necessary outgrowth of her own kitchen. She was a widow, and in order to make ends meet, she had turned the front rooms of her house into the most respectable eating establishment in town. She was best known for two things—the excellence of her cooking and her deep affection for Abner Giddings.

When Abner was eleven years old, his mother had died of consumption. His father had been killed by a runaway ox cart. He had no living relatives to take him in, so he became a ward of Bangor. It was the practice, back in the 1830s, to sell the cost of an indigent's keep to the highest bidder. Job and Hannah Bailey, who were childless, had paid the cost of Abner's keep. Hannah was so pleased and content to be a foster mother, she had not allowed Abner to go to sea as Job's cabin boy. She sent Abner to school, doted on him, and indulged him in every possible way. Job put up with it for a year, but on Abner's twelfth birthday, he put his foot down and insisted it was time for the boy to earn his keep.

Abner proved an able and willing apprentice. Under Job's capable and patient tutelage, he worked his way up to first mate by his eighteenth birthday. He and Job had coasted together on Job's schooner until eight years ago. Abner had injured his arm and while he was ashore waiting for it to heal, Job's schooner foundered off Mount Desert Island. The ship was lost and Job was drowned. Abner was left with two choices since he had no money for a ship of his own. He could give up the sea or hire out to one of the wealthy shipowners. Joshua Stetson took him on.

The woman who bustled into the room was short, and soft rolls of flesh padded her ample figure. Her several chins were framed by a high collar edged with lace. She wore a white muslin cap tied firmly under her chin, a style popular twenty years back and worn only by married women. The voluminous white apron tied over her dark cotton dress was spotlessly clean. The crisp rustle of starched petticoats preceded her. She reminded Abner of a deep-loaded barkentine headed against a strong river current. Her face was alight, obviously pleased to see her foster son, whom she regarded as her own. She laid her hand affectionately on Abner's sleeve.

"There you are at last, Abner Giddings. I had word of your sad loss from the captain of the *Defiant* even before you had time to get a letter to me. I can't tell you how grieved I am, Abner. Such a shame. Such a shame. But God does His will and those of us who are left have to endure." She shooed Abner to a table near the kitchen door. This spot was reserved for family, a term which included close friends as well as actual blood kin.

A mother seal herding her pup to a safe rock, Abner thought, glad for Hannah's concern.

Hannah had not, Abner knew, approved of his marriage to Maryanne Parker. Her main objections had been that Maryanne was too young and too headstrong. But Hannah had been glad for his happiness and truly looked forward to the birth of the child she had expected to grandmother with all the intensity of her thwarted maternal instincts.

Hannah disappeared into the kitchen and returned with soup and bread. She eased her heavy body into a chair and fanned her face with a small imported handkerchief quite inadequate for the job. Abner patted her plump hand. She still wore the narrow gold ring Job had placed there forty years ago.

"It's good to be home, Hannah," Abner said.

"Have you been to the Parkers' yet?" Hannah asked.

"I will go tomorrow."

"Maryanne's folks don't blame you, Abner. I went to call the minute I had the news."

"Thank you, Hannah. I knew you would."

"I didn't much relish being the bearer of bad news, I can tell you. Especially to the Parkers, who have always appeared to think they were a cut above the rest of us. But that's neither here nor there. I never made any secret that I thought you were making a big mistake getting mixed up with the Parker family. I guess I always imagined you would choose one of the Farrar girls or maybe little Abbie Patten. Good, sensible girls who know how to be useful."

Abner let her talk, knowing full well that Hannah had always wanted the best for him, and in her opinion, the best wife for Abner Giddings did not exist.

Hannah brought a pot of tea and some molasses cookies. No one ever left her table hungry.

"Heard any news since you got in, Abner?" It was a ritual question, one Abner welcomed since there were no newspapers at sea. As the keeper of a public house, Hannah was privy to all the latest word-of-mouth news making the rounds of Bangor. She knew who had died, been born, or got married; who was shipping out on which vessel and where; and all the latest scandals that occurred in the upper echelons of Bangor society. There was no viciousness in her repeating what she knew. News was meant to be told. Abner counted on her to keep him current.

"The Temperance League is stirring up trouble again. They always do before a new mayor gets elected. And this time they want one who can walk on water and drinks nothing but. There's talk of putting every illegal rum shop in Joppa out of business. By fire, if necessary. Why, poor old Moses Carson, who never hurt a soul in his life and runs a cleaner place than most, was thrown into the street and every drop of spirits he had hidden away was poured into the gutter right before his eyes. Happened just a little while ago. Poor old man like to have died right then, I heard. He's ruined for certain."

Hannah paused to collect her thoughts.

"I can't say as I don't believe something ought to be done about those dens of iniquity along the waterfront. The law says that no liquor shall be sold in the state of Maine. And I say that's the way it should be. But men will drink, no matter what. Better the wharf rats stay down in Joppa than have them crawl up here to my place with their evil habits. I want no part of it. Someone said they saw Maude and Sam Webber show up in the middle of the whole thing, so heaven only knows what else was going on. You mark my words, Abner, before this summer's done, there will be more trouble in town than there has been since the British came upriver in 1814. Come to think of it, Maude Webber, she was Richmond then, was mixed up in that, too."

"Who is running for mayor this time, Hannah?"

"George Pickering, for one."

"Who's running against him?"

"Joshua Stetson . . . on the Temperance ticket, if you can figure that one out."

"Why in the world would Joshua Stetson want to be mayor?"

"I've heard," Hannah confided, "that he's got his eye on the governor's chair. Getting elected mayor is the first step in that direction, so I'm given to understand. Old Ed Kent did exactly that back in 1837. There's some say Stetson will win it, too. Money can buy anything, Abner."

Hannah shook her head sadly and the bow under her chin quivered. Abner could see she had more to say and did not comment.

"Why, Joshua Stetson has even been down here to my place, shaking hands and telling people how this was where he got his start before he sold the place to Job. You'd be surprised at the people took in by that foolishness. Joshua Stetson got his start here all right—him and that flashy Fanny Hogan. Who does he think he's fooling? Why, the election isn't even until fall!"

"I will be long gone by then, Hannah."

They sat a while longer, Hannah reciting her large store of verbal news. Abner, with his long legs stretched out comfortably under the table, nodded and listened and wondered whether Elizabeth Emerson had arrived at Pink Chimneys.

9.

It lifted Elizabeth's spirits to know that Abner Giddings was sensitive to the needs of others. His gift of the baby's dress had touched her deeply, endeared him to her, and stirred her interest in him. She looked back to wave as the carriage drove away, but he was gone.

The carriage moved slowly along the main thoroughfare of Bangor, past wooden buildings, brick banks, and tiny shops. Signs coaxed one to buy cashmere shawls, corn, flour, salt, gingham, and cheese. The city teemed with enterprise of all sorts—stove dealers, confectionery shops, furniture stores, booksellers, and dealers in ship's plumbing and chandlery. There was so much to see, Elizabeth could barely comprehend the vastness of it all. By comparison, Fort Point was only a wide place in the road.

There were so many people. Children ran alongside the street, evading their mothers and frisking like new lambs in the spring warmth. Men in dark coats and tall hats strolled along, bowing to the ladies they passed and giving way so the women had the drier footing. A few women already had left off their winter bonnets and wore foamy confections of light straw, tulle, and silk flowers.

The carriage approached a steep hill and what Elizabeth assumed was the center of town. Traffic here was dense, but the horse pulled steadily, his hoofs making soft plopping sounds in the mud. At the top of the hill was a wide intersection which resembled a park. The carriage turned right. A brick church, so new that scaffolding still stood around it, sat on a corner. The dirt around the church was packed down, giving the area a raw, unfinished appearance. There were no other buildings on either side of the street beyond the church. A tall, cedar hedge grew thickly on the left side of the street. Presently, the carriage turned and drove through a wrought iron gate in the hedge.

At the end of a long curving drive stood a large three-story house. The grounds surrounding it were brown, but blades of grass sprinkled the lawn with a tender color. Large beds of yellow and purple crocus bordered the front walk. Flowering shrubs, still devoid of buds, dotted the lawn. The hedge enclosed the house on three sides, making it well secluded from the street.

As they rounded the ell, Elizabeth saw an orchard and beyond that a dense growth of pine which hemmed in the rear of the house.

Elizabeth stared. She had expected a large house, but this surpassed even her wildest imaginings.

She straightened her cloak with frantic haste

and brushed wisps of hair away from her face. She longed for a moment of privacy to put herself to rights, to wash away some of the travel dirt and remove the wrinkles from her clothes. She wished she had worn her good russet wool instead of her everyday navy blue skirt and severe muslin waist without lace or ribbon to brighten it.

The carriage stopped. Ready or not, she had arrived. The driver opened the door but did not help her alight or assist her with her valise or Daisy's basket, a subtle reminder of what her station in this house would be—hired help.

They were at the rear of the house where yet another ell, square and at right angles to the main house, stretched toward the orchard. The drive, even there, was paved with finely crushed rock. Elizabeth eyed the house with a mixture of dread and profound curiosity. All the windows on the second floor had heavy curtains drawn against the early afternoon light. The third-story windows, nestled under the eaves, were smaller and hung with a sheer material.

Elizabeth let her eyes travel up beyond the sloping slate roof. Four pink chimneys blushed against a bright blue sky.

10.

Hadn't Dr. Webber said the house with pink chimneys was a gentlemen's club? Had she been taken to the wrong address? Elizabeth had no time to contemplate. Without warning, a large dog of undetermined ancestry dashed from the pine woods, barking his head off. Elizabeth wasn't afraid, but the dog growled and snapped when she tried to calm it by speaking soothingly to it.

Daisy, in her basket, trembled with terror and with one swift, fluid motion exploded from her confine and bolted for the nearest apple tree with the dog in hot pursuit.

With no thought for propriety, Elizabeth dropped her valise, hiked up her skirts, and ran across the soggy ground. Her ankle hurt, but she disregarded it.

Daisy sat hissing, her eyes glowing with fire, on an upper branch of the tree. The dog yelped and launched.

"Sit!" Elizabeth commanded. To her surprise and relief, the dog sat and hung his head. Daisy retreated a little farther up the limb, for good measure. She lifted one paw and licked it daintily.

"Come on, Daisy," Elizabeth coaxed. "I won't let the dog get you. Here, kitty, kitty."

Daisy might as well have been deaf. There was only one way to rescue a cat. Elizabeth dropped her cloak on the muddy grass, tucked up her petticoats as if she were doing barn work, and swung herself up into the tree. The bark was rough and loose. It clung to her clothes and sifted into her hair. She snagged her sleeve but pulled it free and reached for Daisy. The cat sidled away. Below, the dog lost interest and wandered off. Elizabeth reached again and this time Daisy condescended to be captured. She curled regally into Elizabeth's arms and they climbed down.

Elizabeth's first impulse was to run as fast as she could in the direction she had come. She would go back to the *Fairmont* and ask Captain Giddings to give her passage back to Fort Point; she would go to the spinning mills where she belonged.

The kitchen door swung open and a woman dressed in severe black covered by a white apron with starched ruffles stared at Elizabeth.

"We don't like beggars around here. Be off with ye." She rolled her r's and her i's sounded like oi's.

Elizabeth's hand flew to her face. Her hair was a wreck and Daisy's muddy footprints blotted her clothing. Her shoes were caked with mud and her skirt was wet to the knees. Panic rose in her throat. She took a deep breath to steady herself.

"I'm Elizabeth Emerson. Mrs. Hogan is expecting me. I'm here about the seamstress position."

Disbelief registered on the woman's face, but she stepped aside and motioned for Elizabeth to follow her.

"Leave those filthy things and come with me."

The door slammed shut behind them.

The woman who sat behind the delicately-made desk was, Elizabeth supposed, forty. She had expected someone much older. In that first moment, that split second when an opinion is formed about someone just met, Elizabeth thought of the exotic Turk's cap lily that grew in the fields back home. There was a brilliance about Fanny Hogan, an orange-gold flush that shimmered from the softly fluffed tendrils of her upswept hair to the apricot and ecru tones of her silk morning gown. She moved in a graceful way, arms and hands floating in easy motions, like wind rippling leaves, bending a plant's pliable stalk. Her eyes, Elizabeth saw, were a shade of brown that in bright sunlight would be praised as amber. Something in Fanny's expression, the orange-gold aura that clung to her, made Elizabeth think of goldenrod.

Lilies and goldenrod, she thought with embarrassment, to my burdocks and nettles.

Over the years, Fanny had interviewed many seamstresses. Usually they were well scrubbed and neat, extremely biddable—until they discovered they were mending for fallen women. Often they were Irish, just off the boat.

The young woman who stood in front of Fanny's desk was none of those things. Nor did she lower her eyes when Fanny stared at her, a sure sign she was used to thinking for herself.

Fanny pushed back her brocade and rosewood chair, and stood up. The faint rustle of silk eased the silence.

"I'm Elizabeth Emerson. I've come about the seamstress position."

Fanny almost laughed. She had never seen anything like it before. And God knew she'd had her share of trouble when it came to hired help. The woman was serious! Was, indeed, the same woman who had requested an interview not more than an hour ago! Fanny's first thought was to send this one packing, but there was something in her face, something familiar. She couldn't quite put her finger on it. Obviously, she was stubborn and didn't like to be defeated. That appealed to Fanny's tenacity and determination. She decided to listen to what Elizabeth Emerson had to say.

"Yes, Miss Emerson, I am looking for a seamstress. However, you are very young. I had in mind someone who could do dressmaking as well as simple mending, someone with a great deal of experience."

Fanny waved her hand toward a nearby chair, indicating Elizabeth might sit.

"I really shouldn't," Elizabeth said, brushing at the mud on her skirt.

"Hmm, yes. Perhaps not. What experience have you had?"

With that question, Fanny expected to be rid of

the unsmiling Miss Emerson very quickly. She scanned the references Elizabeth produced and was not only impressed, but curious. From Fort Point. Could she possibly be acquainted with Birdie and Mercy? It was an idle thought, not one she really cared to pursue. Let sleeping dogs lie. At least for now.

"Very impressive, Miss Emerson. But I had hoped for someone a bit more mature . . ."

That was not exactly true. The response to her advertisement had been very poor and Fanny was faced with the prospect of doing without a seamstress, as she had the past few weeks. The reputable seamstresses in town, the ones who did the best work, refused to do her work. The whole of Bangor was getting insufferably moral what with this ridiculous election and the temperance people getting everyone to take the pledge not to drink liquor, and worse, not to associate with those who did. Well, she couldn't worry about it now. Didn't have to really. She owned as big a chunk of Bangor as anyone and could buy favors along with the best of them, but that wouldn't get the garters made and the sheets mended.

Fanny laced her fingers together and placed her hands on the satiny surface of her desk. She weighed each possibility as if it were precious metal. She eyed Elizabeth Emerson carefully, trying to make up her mind.

"Mrs. Hogan," Elizabeth said quietly, "I have

never until today had to beg for anything. All my family is dead. I have nowhere to go, no friends, no one. I have pinned all my hopes on you. Perhaps you would consider a week's trial. Then if you decide I'm not suitable, I'll find something else . . . the spinning mills or . . ."

Fanny waved an imperious hand in the air.

"I am no stranger to hard times, Miss Emerson. Perhaps if I had an example of your work, I might be more inclined to take you on." As she spoke, Fanny stood up. The interview was over.

Elizabeth pulled the brown paper parcel from her pocket and laid it on the desk.

"Please open it, Mrs. Hogan."

Fanny withdrew the infant's dress and gasped. It was exquisite.

"Is it good enough?"

"The flowers. They remind me of a place I used to live." Fanny hadn't thought of the farm in the years, not since she had read in the newspaper that Robert Snow had been lost at sea off the coast of South America. Funny how a little thing like a baby's dress could bring it all back.

"What about the job, Mrs. Hogan?" Elizabeth urged.

"I will try you for two weeks. If you don't suit, I will help you find another place. If I like your work, I will keep you on at four dollars a week and room and board."

Every instinct told Fanny that she had made a

bad choice. Elizabeth Emerson wouldn't last two weeks. As soon as she found out about the girls she'd be on her way. Maybe it was for the best. She would talk to Maude about finding some place for Miss Emerson to go. Still, that back of Miss Emerson's had steel in it. She just might work out fine.

Fanny reached for the bell pull.

The same woman who had let Elizabeth in appeared with a soft swish of petticoats.

"Mrs. McGuire, take Miss Emerson up to the attic and show her the sewing room. See that she has supper and plenty of hot water."

Mrs. McGuire set her lips into a prim line.

"And what shall I do about the cat, ma'am?"

"Cat? What cat?" Fanny looked questioningly at Elizabeth.

"My cat. Daisy. That's why I look so . . . bad. She ran away and there was this big dog and I had to climb the apple tree . . ."

"I understand, Miss Emerson," Fanny interrupted. "Take the cat along, Mrs. McGuire. Tell Brown to bring a box of shavings from the barn."

When the door closed behind them, Fanny threw back her head and laughed. Oh, wait until she told Maude about this! No, maybe she wouldn't. Because she would have to mention the baby's dress and Maude would know she had been upset by it. The trouble with Maude was, when someone felt badly, she always wanted to fix it. And as far as Birdie was concerned, nothing could ever fix that.

11.

Abner's call on his dead wife's family went more smoothly than he had anticipated. The Lord gave and the Lord took away, Mr. Parker said. Mrs. Parker was grateful for the sewing basket. Mr. Parker called Abner "son" and shook his hand, but made it clear that Abner's brief tenure as a member of the Parker family had ended with Maryanne's death. They had not approved of their daughter's marriage to him, had hoped, Abner knew, that Rufus Dwinel might notice her or that one of the sons of some wealthy family would ask for her.

Abner felt oddly relieved to learn he had been dismissed and absolved of all connection to the Parkers.

Abner walked briskly toward Joshua Stetson's office on Water Street. In a few days his business in Bangor would be concluded, the *Fairmont* loaded and ready, and he would sail with the tide. He would like to have had more time with Hannah, but she was well acquainted with the comings and goings of mariners and never grumbled about the brevity of his time ashore.

Elizabeth Emerson crossed his mind, and he toyed with the idea of making inquiries about her well-being. Maude Webber was bound to know something sooner or later and if he asked, Sam would let him know. But no, it was none of his business.

Joshua Stetson's office was one of many in the long brick buildings at the end of Water Street on the banks of Kenduskeag Stream. It was convenient to shops, mercantile banks and counting houses, and an easy stroll to the Bangor House where men met for luncheon, a cigar in the smoking room, or a discreet, though illicit, brandy in the gentlemen's parlor.

As Abner walked, he scanned the harbor. The waterfront was a tangle of rocking masts and clanging rigging, bustling with every manner of conveyance from hand cart to heavy farm wagons, steamboats to canoes, and the stylish rigs and glossy horses of the well-to-do.

This was a man's domain; respectable women rarely, if ever, ventured near. This was the heart of Bangor, the center of commerce and trade embodied in the rustle of account books and the clink of coins, the rumble of traffic hauling goods to and from the ships that jammed the harbor.

Abner breathed it all in, the fishy smell of low tide, the odor of tar issuing from the sail lofts, the ever-present, overriding tang of newly sawn pine lumber. In Abner's opinion, Bangor was the best smelling port anywhere in the world.

A small bell tinkled as Abner opened the door

to Joshua Stetson's office. A clerk, recognizing Abner, waved toward a door. Every manner of man from seaman to ship owner had stood in Stetson's office at one time or another. It was the sort of room that neither intimidated the lowly nor overly impressed the powerful. Joshua's desk, while of the finest of mahogany, was restrained in style and showed signs of use. Several nondescript chairs, legs scuffed and nicked, were placed near the desk. On one wall hung a portrait of President Fillmore and a framed sketch of one of the first vessels Joshua had owned. A small glass-fronted bookcase contained some of the better known mariners' manuals. But it was the man behind the desk who commanded any visitor's attention. His pale hair had grown paler with strands of gray threading it. His beard, the same pale shade as his hair, echoed the style of Prince Albert of England.

Abner had stood in front of Joshua a dozen times before and had never got used to Joshua's cold, almost expressionless eyes—eyes that held a man, though when he smiled, which he seldom did, his face took on an almost boyish cast.

Joshua rose when Abner entered. The hand that clasped Abner's was smooth and well groomed, making Abner acutely aware of the callouses and broken nails of his own hands. Joshua's expressions of sympathy regarding Maryanne were formal and brief. He concluded the business pertaining to the *Fairmont*'s cargo quickly and neatly.

"By the way, Giddings, the *Asia* is without a master. She's being refitted at the moment, but in six weeks or so she will be seaworthy. I need a good man. A man I can trust. Interested?"

Abner hesitated. He had no interest in the China trade. The voyages took years and required the thankless task of recruiting a new crew in every port or at least taking on a few new men. Such voyages included the onerous duty of dealing with customs officials and the necessity of shipping out with a crew that often spoke any number of different languages. Not that he didn't think he could handle it, but he was content to follow in Job's footsteps and to come home to Hannah's caring company. It took a certain kind of ability to sail in the China trade. Abner was certain he didn't have it and wasn't interested in acquiring it.

"I thought Hosea Marshall was master of the *Asia*," Abner said, stalling.

"He was, but the last time out he had a bad bout of the fever and hasn't been fit since. Not so young as he used to be. He wants to sell his share, but I don't want it to go to just anybody. I've watched you, Giddings, I think you've got what it takes. What do you say?"

"Well, I'll tell you, Mr. Stetson, I'm a man of habit and I like things to stay as predictable as

378

possible. Coasting is what I know and that's what I'd like to stick with. Not that I'm not grateful for the offer, sir."

"Hmm. I was hoping for a more positive answer. But you don't have to make up your mind right this minute. Take your time. You will have plenty of it. Lovejoy Page will be master of the *Fairmont* this time out. He did such a fine job while you were under the weather after your wife's death, I thought he ought to be properly rewarded. I'd had your belongings sent to Mrs. Bailey's. It may be some time before I can put you on another vessel. Unless, of course, you decide to take the *Asia*. The *Venerable* is due back in a month or so. I could put you aboard her."

Abner narrowed his eyes, felt his back stiffen, stunned by Joshua's words. Anger leaped inside him and fought for an outlet. But that wasn't the way to handle Joshua. You had to play his game, by his rules, as cool as he was. He sat still and pretended he didn't know the *Venerable* was one of the oldest, slowest, most accident-prone vessels in the Stetson fleet, anybody's fleet. Mariners avoided shipping on her like the plague. Word had it that her hold reeked of the Barbados rum she regularly smuggled into Bangor.

"Let me think on it, Mr. Stetson."

"Good. I thought you might want to, Giddings. I will be in touch."

Abner held out his hand, playing the game, making the right moves. His eyes caught Joshua's and held. Joshua's face contained no hint of warmth, no clue as to why he had offered the share in the *Asia*, why he had made Lovejoy Page master of the *Fairmont*.

12.

For the next few days, Elizabeth threw herself into whatever task fell her way. She earned the undying respect and admiration of the two Irish hired girls when she pitched in and helped them scrub the sewing room floor on her hands and knees. Then she undertook the general upkeep of the adjoining room which served as her living quarters.

Each day fell effortlessly into an orderly pattern, and Elizabeth began to feel reassured about her decision to work for Fanny Hogan.

Every morning at six, Elizabeth went down several flights of back stairs to eat breakfast with the housekeeper and the hired girls. She repeated the trip for dinner at noon and supper at five o'clock. The hours in between she spent mending in the attic.

Elizabeth sighed and reached for yet another tablecloth that had been burned by a cigar. Most of the mending consisted of the table linens or bed sheets, which she did not enjoy working on. She did not enjoy the intricacy of stitching darning required. She pawed through the pile, hoping for something a bit more interesting. Her hand found silk and she drew it out—a pair of red pantaloons with knee ruffles torn and hanging loose. She spread the entire pile of mending out on the worktable and discovered a sheer white batiste bedgown with a gaping seam and several chemises, large and small, in a similar state of disrepair. Elizabeth held them up and examined them carefully. A faint odor of lavender and perfume tickled her nose. Was it possible that the elegant Mrs. Hogan would wear red underwear or stir herself to such activity as to produce such badly torn seams?

Several weeks later, precisely at eleven o'clock, Elizabeth was summoned to Fanny's office.

"Can you drive, Miss Emerson?" Fanny asked without preliminaries. She was dressed in a pale blue silk dress with a wide skirt.

"Yes, I can, Mrs. Hogan." Elizabeth also knew how to harness a team to a farm wagon and on more than one occasion had driven a team of oxen, though she did not say so.

"I have a list of goods I would like you to purchase at Wentworth's store. Brown will tell you how to get there. It's not too far. Just tell Wentworth the things are for me. Brown will have the pony cart ready for you right after dinner. Will that be convenient?"

"It certainly will be, Mrs. Hogan."

Elizabeth's mood was the lightest it had been in the weeks since she had come to Bangor. A chance to be outside on such a beautiful day was more than she had dared hope for. And to be trusted with an important errand. Surely that was a sign Mrs. Hogan was pleased with the sewing that already had been done.

Elizabeth dressed herself carefully in a practical gray wool dress with lace at the collar and cuffs. She regretted having to wear her old winter bonnet and at the last minute decided to go bareheaded except for a little lace cap decorated with narrow blue ribbons.

She shut Daisy in the bedroom and pulled on her gloves. Back home, she had driven the team bare handed and bareheaded, but this was Bangor, a city, and she had been informed by the hired girls that everyone made some effort to appear genteel.

The pony pulled neat and steady along the drive at the rear of the house. Brown had told her it was the entrance used by the hired help and delivery wagons. It wound through the pine woods a short distance and exited on State Street just above Broadway.

A few shiny vehicles pulled by glossy Morgan horses whirled by. Birds chattered and sang in every tree. The little pony tossed his head and nickered softly.

Elizabeth found Wentworth's without difficulty and completed her errands.

Just down the street, a group of idlers leaned against the hitching post.

"Hey, ain't that one of Fanny's girls?" Elizabeth heard one man say.

"Naw," another replied loudly, wanting to be heard, "ain't flashy enough."

"Well, I tell you 'tis. I seen Fanny herself in that pony cart more'n once."

Elizabeth ignored the man and concentrated on guiding the pony around a large mud puddle.

"Hey, darlin', what's it like up there to Pink Chimneys? Is it true they's mirrors on the ceilings?" said the man the others called Bob. He stepped out in front of the pony and Elizabeth drew up on the reins, causing the pony to stop sharply.

Anger bubbled up to Elizabeth's lips, but she had learned, from experience, it was best to ignore such behavior. Obviously, the men had mistaken her for someone else.

"Oh, come on, little lady, no sense in lookin' so stuck up. Whole town knows about you fancy girls dancin' on the table in red silk drawers."

The men guffawed and Elizabeth felt her heart sink. Her cheeks went hot as the implication of Bob's remark became clear to her. She spoke to the pony.

Bob grabbed the pony's bridle and for the first

time Elizabeth became alarmed. The hired girls had told her stories about how the woods-queer loggers came out of the logging camps when the ice melted on the river, roared into Bangor astride huge pine logs and turned the town into a turmoil. They said the town was full of them, with their red flannel shirts and green wool pants. Most of them, the hired girls had whispered, stayed down in Paddy's Hollow or over in Joppa, but every spring a few of them straggled up to Pink Chimneys and hung around outside the gates hoping for a glimpse of Mrs. Hogan and her girls. At the time, Elizabeth had refused to believe what the hired girls had hinted at.

Now the conclusion was unavoidable. Mrs. Hogan and her girls were women of dubious reputation, and these men thought she was one of them.

Elizabeth picked up the whip.

"Take your hand off my pony, sir."

Bob roared with sudden laughter, and his cronies joined in. The pony twitched the muscles in its flanks and side-stepped uneasily.

"Now simmer down, little lady. All I want is to hear about the most famous place in Bangor. Folks like me ain't grand enough to get in there. So we'd like to hear about it first hand. You be sweet to me, and I'll show you how nice a riverhog like me can be. Ain't that right, fellas?"

A chorus of snickers and "ayuhs" fell into the street.

"You got 'er gentled now, Bob!" someone called.

Elizabeth measured with her eyes the distance back to Wentworth's. It was too far to run, even if she had been able to elude Bob's grasp. The street was mostly empty of traffic or pedestrians, unusual for that time of day. She laid the whip down, giving the appearance of compliance.

"There now," Bob said. "Now we can talk proper."

Bob sidled along the pony's side and let go of the harness. The moment he did, Elizabeth grabbed the whip and brought it down as hard as she could across the pony's back. The animal's whinny cut across the buffoonery of the men. He dug in his feet and clods of earth spattered in every direction. Elizabeth held firm to the reins, but there was no doubt who was in charge. The cart careened around a corner, narrowly missing a wagon loaded heavily with large wooden barrels. She heard shouts of "runaway, runaway," as several men jumped out of the pony's path. The cart rounded another corner and directly ahead, crossways of the street, came a chaise. The pony slowed and veered at the last possible moment, but the wheel of the cart caught the wheel of the chaise and dragged it a few yards before coming to a stop.

Elizabeth covered her eyes with her hands, not daring to look.

"I might have known it was you," said the driver of the chaise.

Elizabeth lowered her hands and opened her eyes.

"Captain Giddings!" she gasped. He was the last person on earth she wanted to witness her humiliation.

The captain stood next to the chaise surveying the broken wheel, his face wearing the same angry mask as when he had accused her of stealing the silks.

"If you don't know how to drive, Miss Emerson, you'd be better off to leave it to those who do!"

"Which most certainly does not include you, Captain Giddings, since you were taking up the whole road!" Elizabeth's retort came quickly, without thought. She glared at him, but looked away before he did. After all, he had, for all his blustering and blowing, treated her kindly when she had fallen and hurt herself on the way upriver.

"I'm sorry, sir. I lost my temper. I was scared to death. A man over by Wentworth's spooked the pony."

There was no sense in mentioning Bob and his cronies.

"You're not hurt?" Abner asked.

"No, just scared."

But it wasn't being runaway with that had frightened her. It was Bob's assumption that she was public property. She believed she deserved respect because she was a woman. That's how men always behaved toward women. With respect. It annoyed her immensely that Bob had behaved toward her in such a degrading manner.

Several men came to help pull the damaged chaise out of the road. Another man felt the pony's legs and smoothed the horse's sides with practiced hands. He pronounced both animals unhurt.

Elizabeth gave silent thanks that the cart was undamaged.

"If you will tell me how much damage has been done to the chaise, I will arrange to pay you for it," Elizabeth said.

"No need for that, Miss Emerson. I will see to it. I do not own it. It is rented."

"Please, Captain Giddings, I insist."

"Tell you what. I will forget about the broken wheel if you will agree to go to the Lyceum with me tomorrow evening at seven o'clock. A lady will be there lecturing on the early history of the Penobscot."

Elizabeth gave Abner a long look. The tense, angry expression that had been on his face was gone. He smiled at her in a friendly way. His chestnut hair glinted red in the sun. He looked very handsome in a dark green jacket and buff trousers. She thought a minute about his invitation. Her evenings were her own. Mrs. Hogan had said so.

"I can meet you at the State Street gate at six-thirty, Captain Giddings." The smile on Abner's face faded.

"Then it's true. You work at Pink Chimneys."

"Yes." She avoided his eyes, knowing perfectly well why he had asked.

He grew silent a moment, then said, "I will see you at six-thirty tomorrow evening, Miss Emerson."

"Very well. Goodbye, Captain Giddings."

Later that evening, after she'd had supper and lit the lamps, Elizabeth settled into her rocking chair to think about the day's events. Mrs. Hogan had been pleased with the goods she had selected. As for the row with the rivermen, she told Mrs. Hogan the pony had felt his oats and banged into another vehicle, but did not mention how she had been harassed. Nor did she say anything about Abner Giddings. That was her private business and had nothing to do with Mrs. Hogan.

She took Daisy into her lap and stroked the cat's silky fur. Daisy pricked up her ears and refused to settle. She darted toward the door, intent on getting out if she could. Daisy had not taken kindly to life in the attic after her many years of vast barns, wide meadows, and total independence. More than once she had run off, only to be retrieved by Brown or Mrs. McGuire.

"Come in," Elizabeth called when she heard footsteps on the landing outside the attic door.

The woman who entered was not someone Elizabeth had ever seen before. She was dressed in an elaborate evening gown.

"You the seamstress?"

"Yes, I am," Elizabeth replied, trying not to stare. Even in the lamplight it was plain to see that the woman's face was artfully painted. The dress was cut very low, framing the woman's shoulders. The gown fitted more tightly than was quite decent.

"I'm Minta. Mrs. Hogan said you'd still be up. I busted a couple hooks. Can you fix me up? Without me having to take everything off?"

"I think so, Miss . . . Minta. Are you here for the party? I heard the music start."

"Party?" Minta's blue-shadowed eyes were puzzled.

"I thought there must be a gathering of some sort because I heard music."

"Oh, there's a gathering all right. Always is except Sundays. Mrs. Hogan keeps the Sabbath. We all go to church regular. Mrs. Hogan likes to keep up appearances. That's what makes it all so odd, you know. Sitting in church with the men that was here sinning the night before. 'Course we do everything in such a pretty way, the gents don't really believe it's sinning. This is the only place in town where the mucky-mucks can have a good time without their wives finding out." Minta laughed loudly.

"Hold still, please," Elizabeth murmured, taken aback by Minta's forthright words.

"You met the other girls?"

"Girls?" Elizabeth asked cautiously, remembering the riverman's remarks.

"Lily and Flora. They've been here forever by the looks of them, but they have their following. But there's Susie and Frona. And me, of course."

"No, I haven't met anyone but the housekeeper and the hired girls. What is it you and the girls do?"

Minta let out another gale of laughter.

"You are a card, Miss Emerson. Imagine asking what we do here. We entertain the gentlemen, as if you didn't know."

"There, that ought to do it, Minta. Your dress would last longer if you had it let out a bit and loosened your corset."

Minta eyed Elizabeth carefully.

"You don't know much about men, do you? Men like a smooth-fitting dress. Gits them interested in finding out what it's covering up. Know what I mean?"

"Yes, Minta, I believe I do."

"Well, honey, I gotta go. Mrs. Hogan don't like it if the gents have to wait too long. Makes 'em pugnacious. Say, could you fix the lace on my nightdress? Old man Parker got himself all tangled up in it last night. Maybe you could make it a little shorter. It always was too long. Sort of help the old geezer out. He's one of my regulars. Nice old guy. I heard he just lost a daughter."

"Send it up, Minta. I'll see what I can do."

After the door had closed softly behind Minta, Elizabeth wandered to the window and looked down on the front drive. Lamplight spilled onto the terrace and strains of a lilting waltz drifted up to her ears.

Well, she thought, that certainly explained the red silk drawers and different-sized underclothes. She was mending for a house full of fallen women. Jezebels.

13.

"Dr. Webber said you seldom stay ashore this long, Captain Giddings." Elizabeth sat on a stiff-backed bench near the rear of the Lyceum. The lecture had not yet begun, although it was already past the time for it to start.

She and Abner had walked slowly to the gathering, her long legs easily keeping pace with his. They had talked of the weather; he had commented about the great stir the temperance movement was causing; she said she was happy with her position and thanked him again for the infant's dress.

The hall where they sat was full and a low buzz of conversation blurred the air. Elizabeth had dressed carefully for the evening, her russet wool dress newly pressed, her bonnet refurbished with matching ribbons she had found in a cupboard in the sewing room. As a mark of how special the evening was to her, she had worn her locket outside her dress. She touched it, tracing the engraved 'F' with her finger.

"Mr. Stetson has offered me a berth, Miss Emerson, but I haven't decided whether or not I will take it," Abner replied. His spotless white cravat lay like the cap of a wave against his deep blue jacket. He shifted in his seat, trying to gain room for his long legs, and in doing so, his thigh pressed pleasantly against Elizabeth's.

"Mr. Stetson is your employer?"

"Joshua Stetson is more than my employer, Miss Emerson. He is the fuel that fires Bangor. If he blacklists a man, chances are that man will never ship out of here again."

"Have you been blacklisted?" It seemed to her that this was his unspoken meaning and she allowed her curiosity to override courtesy.

"I am just between ships, that is all. It happens from time to time," he said.

She suspected, though he had not said so, it had never happened to him. She could see he was troubled and ill at ease about it. She wanted to squeeze his hand and comfort him. Instead, she sat up a little straighter and turned her attention to Miss Clark who had, at last, begun to detail the early forays of French fishermen along the Maine coast, the subsequent establishment of a colony known as Pentagoet, near Castine, and the eventual rise of civilization on the banks of the Penobscot River.

After the lecture, people milled around the hall calling to friends. A great sea of dark-colored skirts ebbed and flowed, stirred the flotsam and jetsam of greetings and goodbyes, until the eddy revealed a dapper figure with a familiar face.

"Oh, look," Elizabeth cried with pleasure, "it's Dr. Webber. And someone is with him."

"Old Webber seems to have made a great impression on you, Miss Emerson, I envy him."

His statement made Elizabeth's heart lurch and she looked deeply into his eyes. In them, she saw amusement, caring, and comfort.

"No need for envy, Captain Giddings," she said carefully, trusting that his ears would hear what her heart wanted to say.

Sam's eyes had not lost their blue twinkle.

"Maude," he said after he had shaken hands with Abner and greeted Elizabeth, "this is Miss Emerson, the young lady I told you about."

Elizabeth's first impression of Maude Webber was that she was as drab as a female pheasant—

her gray dress wasn't fashionable and her gloves were crumpled, but her manner struck Elizabeth forcefully. Maude did not immediately release her grasp on Elizabeth's hand, but held it warmly, as if assessing Elizabeth's character with a touch.

"Indeed, Miss Emerson, Sam hasn't talked about much of anything else since he got home."

Maude Webber was, Elizabeth saw immediately, a woman you couldn't keep things from. She felt herself go suddenly shy, unwilling for Mrs. Webber to discover her budding feelings for Abner Giddings. She suspected, however, it was already too late for that.

"Come over here and sit down, Miss Emerson. The men always like to discuss business without the ladies." She linked her arm through Elizabeth's and drew her to an empty bench nearby.

"I have been meaning to come see you, Sam," Abner said. "What do you make of Lovejoy Page taking the *Fairmont* out?" He could not bring himself to phrase the question to imply that he had been replaced.

"Nothing to make of it, Abner. Stetson is a strange man. You know that same as everyone else. Likes to play God. And this time he's decided to play with you. Don't read more into this then there is."

Sam shoved his hands deep into his pockets, a gesture Abner found oddly comforting.

"I've tried to figure it out, Sam, but I haven't got very far. I don't have a thing that's of any use to Stetson." Abner glanced toward Elizabeth, who looked very fetching in russet, he thought.

"Now that, my boy," Sam said, "is where you are wrong. You have got plenty a man like Stetson can use. He's making quite an effort to surround himself with solid citizens, hometown boys with integrity, like yourself. He knows darn well that rubbing elbows with a few common folk can't hurt when it comes to election time. Putting you on the *Asia* makes him look good. You get a big promotion, make a sizable chunk of money, and there you are, right in his pocket ready to do whatever he wants."

"Then he doesn't know me very well."

"Doesn't have to. It has been his experience that money, enough of it, can buy anything, corrupt anyone. My advice to you, Abner, is sit tight. He will tip his cards when he's ready."

"My husband tells me you are a seamstress of some skill," Maude said.

Elizabeth nodded. How much did Mrs. Webber know about her? Was she able to divine a person's deepest thoughts with a few searching looks and the touch of her hand? The next question did not surprise her.

"Mrs. Hogan is treating you kindly?"

"Yes, but she hasn't decided whether she will take me on permanently. She said I was not mature enough."

"Perhaps what she meant, Miss Emerson, is that you are too inexperienced to live under her roof."

"Why would she think that?" Elizabeth countered knowing perfectly well Maude Webber alluded to Minta and the others.

"One has only to look at you, my dear, to see that you have been decently brought up, taught that there are some situations which are best avoided."

It was no use. Clearly, Maude Webber's wisdom was boundless.

"You mean Minta, Frona, and the others."

"Yes, I do." Maude stuffed her crushed gloves into her equally bedraggled reticule.

"It doesn't matter. Mrs. Hogan likes my sewing. I hardly ever see the others. What they do has nothing to do with me."

"Then you expect to stay?"

Elizabeth felt her stubborn streak uncoil itself. She was doing honest work. She had a decent room and decent wages. It was far better than the spinning mills in New Hampshire.

"Yes, I expect to stay." Elizabeth glanced at Abner, and Maude followed her glance.

Maude rose. Elizabeth rose, too, in deference

to the older woman, as she had been taught. She straightened her shawl. Out of habit, she touched her locket, to make sure it was still there.

"A lovely locket, Miss Emerson."

She should have known Maude's sharp eyes would not miss the gesture.

"It was my mother's. Her initials are carved on it. An 'F' for Fanny."

Maude touched the locket gently and let it lay in her fingers. She gazed at it intently, turned it over in her hand.

"I take it your mother is dead." Her eyes probed Elizabeth's face, but it was a gentle searching.

"She died when I was an infant. My Aunt Mercy raised me. She died recently." Why was it so impossible to keep anything from Maude Webber?

"I seem to recall that Sam said your aunt's death was why you came to Bangor. Sam said that you came aboard the *Fairmont* at Fort Point."

"Yes. I grew up there, on the farm."

"How old are you, Miss Emerson?"

"Nearly twenty-one."

"Nearly twenty-one seems very young when one is past fifty, as I am. Come along, my dear. Sam has the fidgets and Captain Giddings has been glancing this way far too long."

Later, Maude lay propped against the pillows in the big bed. Sam reached to turn down the lamp.

397

He laid his warm hand on her thigh. His familiar touch was calming.

"Spit it out, Maude. Something's got you wound up tighter than an icebound block and tackle. You've been quiet as a grave ever since we got home. I know it's got something to do with the Emerson woman. And don't tell me Abner Giddings is falling in love with her. Any half-wit can see that."

Maude rolled her eyes at Sam, fixing him with what she hoped was an impatient glance but apparently failing, because he snuggled closer and the gentle stroking of her thigh continued. She clasped her hands across her stomach. Tonight she would welcome being called out. She was sure she wouldn't sleep a wink. She sighed deeply and faced Sam.

"Elizabeth Emerson is Fanny Hogan's daughter."

Now that she had said it, it didn't seem to be quite the dilemma she had thought it was. Sam stirred and rustled the bed sheets. "Can't be. Doesn't look a thing like the mistress of Pink Chimneys."

"She was wearing a locket, Sam. The same locket Fanny tried to give me after I delivered her child. Out of gratitude, I suppose. I wouldn't take it."

"How do you know it's the same locket, Maude? Twenty years is a long time."

"Women don't forget details like that. Besides,

Miss Emerson said she had been raised by her Aunt Mercy, the same name as Fanny's sister, in the same town Fanny was from. And she was born in 1831."

"But her name is Emerson, not Hogan."

"Well, neither is Fanny's."

"The point being, my dear, that you don't know what Fanny's family name is any more than I do."

"Doesn't matter, Sam. This Aunt Mercy could have changed it to protect her niece from ever discovering who her mother really was. One thing's certain, her name isn't really Emerson, or Fanny would have known right off. As I recall, Fanny always called the child Birdie. The aunt must have changed that, too. I'm not wrong about this, Sam. Elizabeth Emerson didn't lie. Her face is like an open book, no artifice nor affectation. She's Fanny's daughter. I'd stake my life on it."

Sam sat up and fumbled for the lamp. The gloom gave way to a warm, golden glow.

"Maude, if you must involve yourself in this, and I know you must, think of Abner and how he would feel to learn that the woman he doesn't even know he is in love with yet is the daughter of a fancy woman. Couldn't you just stick to the temperance crusade or the Orphans' Home, or just plain delivering babies?"

Maude slumped down further into the pillows, ignoring Sam's plea.

"Fanny will figure it out sooner or later, Sam. I'd rather she heard it from me than just have it fall in her lap. I owe her a lot. First the Orphans' Home, and now the Home for Indigent Women. All supported with her money."

"You never told me that," Sam said accusingly.

"And don't you tell anyone, either. Both places would close their doors for good if the upright ladies of town knew where the money really came from."

Sam reached for Maude and she nestled into his arms. It was good to be home every night instead of in a bunk on a ship bound for Florida. He had not realized how much they had missed all those years of being apart. Not that he regretted any of it. They both had done what they wanted to in life and loved and respected one another all the more for it. She sighed a little satisfied sigh.

"You never fail to amaze me, Maude," Sam murmured against her hair.

"Why do you say that, Sam?"

"You're the only person in town who doesn't regard Fanny Hogan as a fallen woman."

"She's not. She simply had the misfortune to believe it when a glib-tongued sailor said he'd marry her. Society did the rest—assigned the labels. She's done what she had to do with what she's had to work with. Just as we all do. It's like Papa always said, 'life turns in odd ways.' "

14.

The invitation was little more than a note, delivered by a waterfront urchin, written in flowery script. It read: You are expected for supper and a musicale Tuesday, June 8th, at Pink Chimneys at 8 o'clock.

Abner turned the note over in his hand and read it again. He lay in his room in Hannah's house on the big cannonball bed built specially to accommodate his height. A fresh, late-May breeze fluttered the white curtains at the open window like a sail filling away.

He had been idle more than a month, but time had passed agreeably enough. In the company of Elizabeth Emerson, he had attended lectures, gone on evening walks and drives, listened to the Bangor Band at outdoor concerts, and canoed on the river. Their acquaintance had blossomed into friendship, and something more. Try as he would, though, he could not get her to talk much about Pink Chimneys. He had tried to convince her it wasn't proper for a young, unattached woman to work there, but she had silenced him with a hard look and a clamping of the jaw, saying that Mrs. Hogan had given her a chance when no one else would have, that she was doing honest work, that it was her business, not his. He had retreated, admittedly with little grace, and accepted the fact she wasn't going to change her mind. She was not easily led. Still, he worried. What if Joshua Stetson got his hooks into her, dazzled her with silk dresses and gold chains? The thought disturbed him. He was very fond of Elizabeth, had even told her so, and her eyes had gone all misty blue, the color in her face as pretty as a wild rose.

He had wandered around the waterfront, too, watching the destruction of barrels of demon rum as attacks on the illegal grogshops became more frequent. He had hung around in some of those smoky, thick-aired dives listening to the talk and scuttlebutt that flitted like moths in the dim light. He didn't like what he heard. They said Joshua Stetson was smuggling rum like it was water, yet his ships were never searched, nor were the taverns that sold his kegs ever attacked. Ugly talk about showing Joshua for what he really was had bubbled up, but no one volunteered to organize such action. The general consensus was that the temperance movement was the real culprit, because Joshua used it as a lever to get his hands on the mayorship. This contradiction didn't seem to bother anyone. Joshua was known to tack his course even when there wasn't any need for it and to veer from the main channel when it was least expected.

Abner lay back against the pillows which Hannah had plumped for his comfort. She had sputtered and fussed when he had told her about being replaced by Lovejoy Page.

"You mark my words, Abner, there's trouble brewing. If I were you I'd ship out on a garbage scow before I'd hook up with Joshua Stetson again. Why the very idea! Lovejoy Page the master of the *Fairmont*!"

Abner accepted Hannah's concern as motherly flutterings. She loved him dearly, he knew, and still tried to protect him despite the fact that his boyhood had passed many years ago.

He had thought seriously of going up to Boston and finding a vessel there, but that would be construed as running away, a smirch on his integrity as a man. Bangor was his home. Job had set a path for him to follow. He would stay the course.

There were other cargoes to ship besides lumber—bricks and pottery from Brewer, or ice from both sides of the river. But all his inquiries had been hemmed and hawed at, set aside, or refused. No one cared to risk Joshua's ire. Business was risky, they might need a loan, and Stetson sat on the board of the bank, the merchants said. He realized he had been blacklisted. It was the *Asia* or nothing.

Abner placed that note on the washstand by the bed and lit his pipe. Like a majority of Bangor's male population, he had never been to Pink Chimneys. One only gained entry by personal invitation. But he had heard stories of its opulence, the Chippendale mirrors, Hepplewhite furniture, crystal chandeliers, and velvet draperies; of singers and musicians who performed there; of elegant, beautiful women who mingled with the guests and were available for more private entertainment. Everyone knew that railroads, steamship lines, even the Penobscot Boom itself had been built, on paper at least, in the best whorehouse in Bangor.

Indeed, local people talked of little else, and not all the talk was negative. There were merchants who were more than glad to fill Fanny's orders for satin sheets, silver cutlery, and French wallpaper. Without the income generated from Pink Chimneys, many people would have starved.

Abner chuckled to himself. Invitations to Pink Chimneys were sought after by anyone who had even the smallest claim to fame, wealth, or political influence. Once inside Pink Chimneys, you had reached the pinnacle of success as measured in Bangor, Maine, in 1852. And all he had was his mariner's skills, as common as alewives in Kenduskeag Stream in May.

He puffed thoughtfully, his thoughts drifted once more to Elizabeth Emerson. Someday, he supposed, when this whole mess was straightened out and he was back to coasting, he would ask her to marry him. But first he had to do something about the bind Joshua Stetson had him in.

He rose, dipped his pen into the inkwell, and wrote a brief acceptance to the invitation.

15.

If anyone had said, right after Aunt Mercy had died, that she would be happy by the time summer came, Elizabeth would not have believed it.

Everything had fallen comfortably into place. She was a permanent employee at Pink Chimneys. She had received her first month's wages. She belonged somewhere. And though it wasn't precisely what she had envisioned when she had arrived, it would do. She was happy because of Abner, with his slender bones, warm hair, and bristly moods. Whenever she was with him, she thought of copper pots, bleating sheep, and the tide lapping at the river's edge. He felt like home. After they had spent time together, she would savor the details of each moment, like a child sucking on a peppermint drop. She loved him, and she hugged that knowledge to herself, telling no one but Daisy, who merely blinked her yellow feline eyes and kept quiet.

Elizabeth shook out a bedgown and matching robe that lay in a heap of foaming lace on the work table. It was the one old man Parker kept getting tangled up in. She had left it until last, trusting that Minta would return for a fitting as she had said she would.

Supper time came and went. There was no sign of Minta.

Elizabeth lit the lamps. She settled into the rocking chair and threaded her needle. Minta had left instructions that the garment was to be finished as quickly as possible.

It was the most beautiful bedgown Elizabeth had ever seen. It was a delicate shade of blue, like bachelor buttons, a color that was, Elizabeth knew, most becoming to her eyes. She held it up to see the effect it made. Her imagination glided like a hawk over a meadow. Would Abner think her beautiful if he saw her in it? She imagined herself on their wedding night, wearing the bedgown, seeing the fire of passion kindled in his eyes. She stroked the fabric with her fingers. Minta had said make it shorter, but Minta had not stood still long enough for the hem to be marked.

The moon had risen and hung round and golden just beyond the window. The fabric caught the light and shimmered like the evening surface of the river. Elizabeth swirled the bedgown around her feet, holding it with one arm against her waist. She and Minta were about the same height. She could kill two birds with one stone. If she tried it on she could estimate how much to cut off the bottom . . . and see how she would look in the moonlight wearing a silken bedgown as soft as a lupine petal.

The fabric slithered silkily over Elizabeth's head, fell in cool folds against her arms. The neckline was cut in a low V, revealing, yet also concealing. She slid into the matching robe and tied the ribbons at her waist.

She preened in front of the mirror, turning this way and that, allowing the yards of material to cascade around her bare feet. She pulled the pins from her hair and let it fall to its full length down her back. The gold locket gleamed around her throat.

Music drifted through the window and Elizabeth executed a few waltz steps, slowly and gracefully, pretending she was in Abner's arms. She closed her eyes and turned and swayed until the skirt flew in a great circle away from her legs.

Daisy crouched under a chair, her eyes wide and nervous at such strange goings-on. The skirt swirled closer and the cat darted to the door and scratched at it until the door opened a crack. One well-practiced paw pried the opening to cat width, and Daisy trotted, not down the back stairs, but down the passage that led to the hallway to the bedrooms of Fanny's girls.

Elizabeth stopped abruptly in mid-swirl just as Daisy's tail disappeared through the door.

"Oh, Daisy," she called, "not again!" and sped after the cat. Mrs. McGuire would not be pleased.

For a brief instant, Elizabeth thought of how

she was dressed, that Mrs. Hogan had said specifically she was not to visit the second floor. But Mrs. McGuire had said if she found Daisy roaming the house one more time, it was out in the barn for Daisy.

It was mid-evening and Elizabeth knew everyone would be on the first floor eating a buffet supper. They only came upstairs later. Much later. No one would ever know. No one would see her wearing Minta's finery. She tiptoed along the dimly lit hallway, her steps padded by the Persian runner.

Daisy crouched near the landing leading down to the first floor. She lashed her tail perversely as if she had been into a bed of wild catnip. Elizabeth bent to pick her up, but Daisy scampered halfway down the main staircase.

The music was louder now, more rollicking, and a female voice sang a snappy tune. Elizabeth could not make out the words. Laughter punctuated the music and Elizabeth guessed the song must be a humorous one. The hallway below was empty. The door to Fanny's office was closed. Brown was nowhere in sight.

Elizabeth's heart pounded in her throat, her armpits suddenly damp, but she descended the stairs one careful step at a time. It would be easy to sidle quickly down to Daisy, grab her, and run back to the attic. But Daisy sidled, too, all the way to the bottom step, and sat purring in

408

the middle of the hallway perfectly content with herself.

Poised on the bottom step, Elizabeth saw that her effort was useless. Her courage faded and she turned to go back to the attic.

The door to Mrs. Hogan's office snapped open, and there stood Mrs. Hogan, a small man with pale hair, and Abner Giddings.

The man with pale hair, clearly surprised, recovered first.

"Well, Fanny," he purred, striding to Elizabeth and taking her hand, "you certainly have outdone yourself with this one. Quite a beauty."

Elizabeth tried to draw back, but to her horror, he cupped his hand under her chin, and kissed her lightly on the lips.

"Welcome, dear lady, to Pink Chimneys."

His breath smelled of spirits.

Elizabeth stiffened, panic rising. Before she could react, Abner seized the man and swung him around.

"Get your filthy hands off her, Stetson. You swine!" he spat out. He used a few words Elizabeth had always associated with sailors, stevedores, and teamsters.

Sanity returned and Elizabeth found words forming in her mouth.

"Abner," she cried, "you've made a mistake!" She grabbed Abner's arm, but he shook her loose and smashed his fist against Joshua's mouth.

Doors opened, the hallway became flooded with light, voices, people, confusion. Elizabeth grabbed the banister as her knees buckled.

"You will never be mayor in this town, Stetson, I'll see to that," she heard Abner say. He turned, and the look he threw at Elizabeth was dark with bitterness and betrayal. It was as if he had struck her, too.

She watched with a sinking sensation as Abner tore open the front door allowing it to crash against the wall. He strode, with rage in every step, out into the night.

For a moment, Elizabeth was too stunned to move. She clung to the banister, anchored to the floor as if she were suspended in some strange half-world where nothing registered except the fact that the man she loved thought she was a fancy woman who had made a fool of him.

Her feet regained movement. She flew out the door after him. She had to make him understand that it was all a mistake, that it was Daisy's fault.

Darkness hindered her view. She ran a little way toward the main gate, saw nothing but the moon laughing in her face. Then she heard footsteps and knew he had gone out the rear entrance. She reversed direction, her bare heels pounding furiously in the dirt, keeping time with the drumming of her heart.

She was glad she was a farm woman, used to heavy work, to walking long distances, used to running across hilly pastures in search of tardy cows. She would catch up with him, explain how he had been mistaken. She would quit her job, she would beg his forgiveness.

She reached the gate. It stood wide, yawning into the night. She stopped running, stumbled, and fell. Seams ripped, her hair matted around her face, sweat trickled everywhere. She wept silently, violently.

The voice, when she finally heard it, she only dimly remembered. She opened her mouth to scream but a hand smelling of pine pitch clamped over her teeth.

"Now, little lady, you're gon'ta show old Bob what a Pink Chimneys fancy woman is really like."

16.

"They found her an hour ago, Maude. In the woods behind the house. She hasn't said a word, has barely blinked her eyes. She just stares at nothing," Fanny whispered. She kept her voice low. The atmosphere in the room was like a funeral. She averted her eyes from Elizabeth's blank face.

"Shock," Maude said tersely as she bent to work.

Brown had roused Fanny shortly after dawn to say that he had found Elizabeth in the woods.

411

It was now Fanny's nerve-wracking task to try to keep the incident quiet.

Fanny dabbed with a damp cloth at Elizabeth's face where an ugly bruise discolored her temple. There were scrapes on her arms and legs. The lace nightgown was in shreds. Fanny glanced again at the smear of dark blood on Elizabeth's thighs, found it too unsettling and left the area to Maude to tend. She let the ugly word form in her mind. Rape. Visions of the sign that said ROOMS leaped into her thoughts. She pictured tight-laced ladies in black dresses whispering behind their proper, gloved hands. If it became known that Elizabeth had been raped, she would be blamed; accused of inciting her attacker to passion with immodest dress; painted as a woman of depraved instincts; in short, be branded a fallen woman. Ask any of the girls at Pink Chimneys. They knew.

Fanny sat straight-backed in a chair by the bed. From the moment she had laid eyes on Elizabeth Emerson, she had known she meant trouble. Women like Elizabeth didn't belong in a place like Pink Chimneys. She was decent. She should have been a farmer's wife raising sturdy children, tending animals, and going to church every Sunday with a man who appreciated her.

With shaking fingers, Fanny reached for the basin of water, intending to empty it. She sloshed water on the floor.

"Get hold of yourself, Fanny," Maude said brusquely, "or leave the room."

"It's all my fault," Fanny said, dullness in her voice. "She's ruined. If this gets told around town, and it will, the Temperance Union will use it as one more excuse to descend on me like a plague of black flies. They would like nothing better than to close me down. And what will Joshua say?"

The thought of Joshua pained Fanny more than she cared to admit. Once, she had seen in him glimpses of the man he might have been, the man she had fallen in love with, still cared for. But those glimpses were rare now. Joshua's money and power had corrupted him. The irony of it was not lost on her. Joshua, who had sought to corrupt, had become his own victim. He still came to visit her. For comfort? For friendship? She did not believe so. Because he needed her? Ah, yes, Joshua needed her. She was a stand-in for Ellen, whom Joshua loved and hated, adored and abused, petted and punished. She had known that for years and she had stayed. Out of hope, she supposed, hope that he would change, hope that he would forget Ellen, hope that someday he would want *her,* Fanny, for herself. But she knew, now, that would never happen. She had been thinking seriously of going to California. She had heard that the gold miners out there didn't see women for months on end and were inclined to propose matrimony to the first one they saw, no questions asked. She could go out there, get married, just disappear. But she had done nothing about it. Maybe she wasn't ready to leave yet. Maybe it took the rape of an innocent young woman to make her take a long look at her own life.

"Here," Maude said, "lift her shoulders and help me get this bedgown over her head."

Deftly, Maude arranged Elizabeth neatly in bed. It always impressed Fanny how devoted Maude was to those in her care, the tender way she handled them and mended their ills. *Everyone's mother,* Fanny thought. *Tucking people in bed like Ma did when I was a girl.* The thought was a stray one and prompted her to reach for the brush on the washstand. Ma had always brushed the tangles out of her hair at night. It was relaxing, she remembered. Perhaps the motion, along with the sleeping powders Maude had administered, would soothe Elizabeth, help ease the stricken look on her face.

"Prop her up a little more, Maude," Fanny murmured. "I'll brush the pine needles out of her hair."

Fanny worked carefully, separating the long strands of dark hair with her fingers as she worked, picking out bits of moss and dried grass. The brush caught in a dense tangle.

"Hand me your scissors, Maude, there's something shiny caught in her hair. I think it's a gold chain."

Fanny snipped the lock of hair away and bent toward the window to examine it. Perhaps it would offer some clue to the identity of the attacker and pave the way for the administration of private justice since public justice was out of the question.

The only sound in the room was the soft swish of Maude's skirts, and the barely audible whisper of Elizabeth's breathing.

Fanny smothered with her hand a little cry.

"It's my locket!" she gasped, "the one Joshua gave me, the one I gave Birdie twenty years ago!"

Fanny closed her eyes and opened them again quickly. The locket felt heavy in her hand, familiar yet remote, like her memories of her mother. As she stared at Elizabeth, the girl Fanny had been at 1831 merged with the woman she was in 1852. It wasn't possible. Her mind pulled down a shade.

"How do you suppose Elizabeth Emerson got Birdie's locket?" She saw the answer written on Maude's face.

Fanny was glad for the chair she sat in. She clutched the locket to her breast, swallowed the tears rising in her throat. She touched Elizabeth's hand. It was cool and still. She stroked the smooth skin, remembering when that hand was as tiny and soft as a rose petal.

"You knew, Maude," Fanny whispered. It was an accusation.

"I was going to tell you this very week."

Fanny had never seen Maude look so distressed. "How did you know?"

"The locket, same as you. She wore it to the Lyceum one evening, more than a month ago. When she was with Abner Giddings."

"Abner Giddings! You mean he, she . . ."

"Very attached to one another I'd say. Sam thinks so, too."

"Oh, my God," Fanny breathed. Now it all made sense, was even worse than she imagined. Abner Giddings thought Elizabeth was one of the girls. Elizabeth had run after him to explain. And some filthy wharf rat had made her a fit resident for Pink Chimneys. The sins of the mothers, she thought ruefully. She choked back a hysterical laugh. The hateful irony of it struck her like a hammer blow. Rage, bitter and black, roared up her throat, came out as a laugh that dissolved into a strangled cry unleashing twenty year's worth of tears. She let them flow and, with a savage swipe of her hand, accepted the handkerchief Maude offered.

So be it. But she wasn't going to let her child suffer any more humiliation or degradation. She had abandoned Birdie once, but not again. She had money, knew people who owed her favors. She would see that Birdie—no, Elizabeth, she must remember that—Elizabeth had the respectability she had never had.

"She will mend, Fanny," Maude said in her soothing way. "She will mend."

"You're damn right she will. I will make sure of that."

It was late when Maude went home. Fanny had cried herself dry. Elizabeth lay limp and sleeping. How she would react to her attack, Maude dared not to predict.

Sam met her at the door, his dear face full of concern. He took her cloak and untied her bonnet's strings. Sarah John produced a pot of tea and generous slices of apple pie.

"Hannah Bailey was here today, fit to be tied," Sam said. He jabbed at the pie, as if it needed dissecting, with his fork.

Maude braced herself. She knew she didn't want to hear what Sam was about to say. He had that look on his face. She stirred her tea noisily, chopped viciously at her pie.

"What did Hannah want?" she asked reluctantly. She was tired. She was angry at herself. She blamed herself. If only she had told Fanny sooner.

"Abner didn't come home last night. They found his jacket on Harlow Street. There was blood on it."

"Hell and damnation, Sam!" Maude exploded.

The teacup rattled on its saucer. "If you are telling me Abner Giddings has been accused of rape . . ."

Sam laid a steadying hand on her arm.

"No, Maude. Listen. I went down to the waterfront after I talked to Hannah and asked around a little. Looks like Abner's been shanghaied. At least one person saw him carried, unconscious, aboard the *Venerable*. In irons."

Sam's face was grave. Maude reached for his hand.

"Joshua Stetson's ship. We have to do something, Sam. Tell the sheriff, the harbor master . . ."

"I've done that, Maude. But it's a tricky situation trying not to drag Elizabeth's name into it. Anyway, won't do a bit of good. The *Venerable* sailed for Barbados in the night, so they said. Could be headed anywhere—Liverpool, South America. All we can do is wait."

"And pray."

17.

Elizabeth sewed with furious concentration. She did not care what Mrs. Webber or Mrs. Hogan said, she would not leave the attic. Someone would see her and they would know she was different. She was safe in the attic, nothing had ever happened to her there. She didn't have to talk much, or smell the pine needles. She could pull the black curtains she had made across the windows so the moon wouldn't intrude.

She had not said so, but a pain was centered in the pit of her stomach, a pain that got worse whenever anyone mentioned going outside. It was very odd, this pain, because it was her heart that should have hurt, not her stomach.

They had brought Daisy back to her, hoping to cheer her up, she supposed, but she had made them take the cursed cat away, she didn't care where. If it hadn't been for Daisy . . . she blocked that avenue of thought quickly. It led to the gate, and the gate opened on memories she had chained to the cellar of her mind. She kept sewing, with greater concentration.

She thought a lot about Abner, but it was with grief, as if he were dead, had died along with the pieces of her soul that lay buried out by the gate. That was why she wore the gray dress, to mourn Abner's death, the death of love. She and Abner had died together, out there. They had tried to talk to her about Abner, but she wouldn't let them. She couldn't bear to hear them confirm what she already knew.

She wore the dress because it protected her. She understood what had happened to her. It had put her on the same path as Minta and Flora—even Mrs. Hogan. But they never wore gray. Gray was an inconspicuous color. People who wore gray were left alone. Cool and distant.

One night she had a nightmare and woke screaming. She knew what was happening. The seeds of the nightmare were growing inside her.

The attic door opened, but Elizabeth did not look up. It was easier not to look into anyone's eyes. Cool and distant. But she knew it was Mrs. Webber. Mrs. Webber always came softly, wearing her wisdom like a magic robe. But she knew how to fight Maude Webber, how to turn aside the probing knife of her eyes. Cool and distant.

Elizabeth stabbed the needle firmly into the towel she was mending. If only they would leave her alone, she would be all right. They were spying on her, trying to make her expose her pain. But they would never penetrate her defenses. Every day for three months it was the same—Mrs. Hogan in the morning, Mrs. Webber in the afternoon, Mrs. McGuire in the evening.

"Good afternoon, Elizabeth," Maude said.

She was always pleasant, as if everyone ought to be pleasant, as if the world out beyond the attic walls was pleasant.

"Hello." Monosyllables had become a part of Elizabeth's armor. They worked well in keeping the distance.

"Mrs. Hogan says you have been unwell the last few mornings."

"Yes." She didn't mind admitting that. Mrs.

Hogan had seen her vomit. She couldn't lie about it even if she had wanted to.

"Can you describe how you feel?"

"A pain."

"Where?"

"Stomach."

She had to be careful about Mrs. Webber. Mrs. Webber was smart. She knew about other people's armor and how to use it to her advantage.

"Vomiting?"

"Yes."

"When?"

"Morning."

"Every morning?"

"Yes."

"For how long?"

"Week, two, longer."

She bit the thread off with a vicious bite of her teeth, rethreaded the needle, and picked up another towel. Mrs. Webber would give up soon, would retreat as pleasantly as she had come.

"Are you nauseated during the day?"

"Sometimes." If Mrs. Webber did not give up soon, she would go to her bedroom, lock the door, jump out the window. No. Cool and distant. That was the only way. They would only hover more if she tried to run away from them.

She tightened her grip on the needle, poised it to pierce the towel, but Maude pulled it gently away. Surprised, Elizabeth glanced sharply at

Maude's all-knowing face. She looked away again quickly.

Maude's actions fluttered on the periphery of Elizabeth's senses. Paper rattled, fabric was shaken out, a soft flannel garment settled onto the worktable.

"Here, Elizabeth, I'd like you to mend this first." Still that pleasant voice.

Elizabeth reached for the garment, let her eyes center, a cool distant stare at the thing Maude laid before her.

The pain in Elizabeth's stomach ground to a new intensity. The cool, distant stance vanished. The iron gate across her mind swung open on creaking, rusty hinges. The gray armor she had girded herself with fell away.

She screamed a curse at Maude, and with a fury she had never known, swept to the floor the baby dress Abner Giddings had given her.

18.

Eventually, Elizabeth's screams gave way to sobs, the sobs died to a small shuddering, cushioned by Maude's comforting arms. The cool distance around Elizabeth melted away, leaving her with the stark reality of her situation. She was pregnant by a man who had assaulted her, employed by a woman of dubious reputation, and Abner Giddings had left her. Now that Maude had yanked her back from the brink of madness, all that was left was a black depression filling her with irritability and listlessness.

Within the week, she had been removed from the attic and brought in Fanny's closed carriage to Maude's house. They installed her in the parlor with its old-fashioned furniture and large hearth. It was not so different from the one at the farm at Fort Point.

Elizabeth lay on the bed they had set up for her, feigning sleep, listening to the soft talk drifting like wood smoke into the parlor from other parts of the house. The most frequent topic of discussion was the recent election. Joshua Stetson had lost it by a narrow margin.

Maude talked much of the infants she delivered to Irish immigrant families, arrivals that created a great degree of want and poverty. In spite of herself, Elizabeth pricked up her ears at this kind of talk. She knew little of childbirth, less about caring for an infant. Part of her did not want to know, part of her did. So she listened and pretended she hadn't. The weather was discussed, too, and the sensation caused by the Reverend Comfort Drummond, the temperance leader, when he had remarked publicly that Joshua had lost the election as a punishment from God. Joshua in retaliation, revealed that the Reverend Drummond had, on more than one occasion, spent the night at Pink Chimneys.

There were frequent visitors to the Webber house. Fanny called every week, bringing exotic foods to tempt Elizabeth's appetite and bits of mundane mending for her to do. Elizabeth never quite knew when she first noticed the difference in Fanny's attitude toward her. The elegant remoteness Elizabeth had been accustomed to was now replaced with something akin to reverence. Fanny tucked afghans around Elizabeth's feet, inquired after her needs, her likes and dislikes, took every opportunity to pat her hand, or adjust the bedcover. Elizabeth thought it odd, at first, but found Fanny's gestures comforting. She began to look forward to Fanny's visits.

Sam Webber, in his quiet, kindly way, spread the greatest balm on Elizabeth's tender soul. He gave her bright ribbons for her hair, read poetry to her even when she turned her face to the wall in moments of despair. Often, he carried on a one-sided conversation with her, apparently not caring that she didn't respond. He brought her little things no one else thought of—a seashell he had found many years ago on a beach in South Carolina, a red maple leaf, dried weeds, a pretty rock. These treasures lined the windowsill by her bed.

The household, commanded by Sarah John Thatcher's efficient ways, revolved around Elizabeth. She felt safe within it, a wounded thing forced back into a womb, just as the child within her had been forced into her womb. She recognized the parallel, knew that she must emerge from it, or die.

Sometimes, Elizabeth felt like a mushroom growing in the dark corner of the Webber's parlor, round and misshapen, cultivated by Sarah John's kindly care. Her increasing pregnancy was a reality she could not hide from. The revulsion she had felt in the early months, for herself and the unborn infant, had softened as the infant took on an identity of its own. It rolled and thrashed beneath her belly button, kicking and poking, as if it were furious at having been forced into existence. Elizabeth found the idea oddly comforting, acceptable even.

Elizabeth stared at the great lump in her middle. Like a chrysalis, she thought, stroking the mound of her belly. Once, she had brought home a chrysalis to ripen in Aunt Mercy's kitchen. She remembered how a yellow and black butterfly had emerged from it, a poor dumb creature with no knowledge of its beginnings. She had felt a kinship with the butterfly, its beginnings as obscure as her own.

The child within her fluttered and Elizabeth's abdomen rippled with the movement. Soon, the child would emerge, wet and wingless, into the world. Maude had suggested, with great care and tact, that the orphans' home might be the place for the child. At the time, by saying nothing,

Elizabeth had implied that she agreed, glad to have the decision so neatly removed from her hands. But as she lay in the parlor, thinking of the butterfly, of her own tenancy in the womb of the parlor, she went through a change of heart.

Maude interrupted Elizabeth's thoughts as she came into the room, her skirts whispering against the floor. She carried a large book under her arm. She sat down near Elizabeth. Uncharacteristically, she hesitated before she spoke.

"You have been idle long enough, Elizabeth. There's no reason for you to continue dragging yourself from bed to chair and back again. You've lain abed since September, doing nothing, saying nothing, allowing your misery to rule your life. If you are to put this tragedy behind you, you must find something useful to do. As you know, Dr. Webber and I are childless, but we have come to look on you as a daughter. We both greatly regret not having someone to pass on our skills to. We want to pass them on to you. Midwifing is not in as high demand as it used to be, but there's still a living to be made from it. That, and the simple doctoring Dr. Webber can teach you will assure that you will never starve. As for your reputation, which has suffered a blow, Mrs. Hogan has seen to it that the incident has not been connected with your name. She has smoothed it over. And once your infant is placed in the orphans' home, nothing can hinder you except yourself."

Elizabeth sat up clumsily. Maude could not have chosen a better time for her proposal. The confines of the parlor were now too small to contain the new Elizabeth Emerson who was beginning to emerge. She looked at Maude with a new respect, admiration, and gratitude.

"You are quite right, Mrs. Webber. The time has come. I've decided to keep my infant." Now that the words were spoken, Elizabeth felt easier, was glad to see approval on Maude's face.

"There are miseries in this world far greater than yours, Elizabeth. It's time you learned that. Midwifing with me will teach you that."

"I will try, Mrs. Webber." She owed the Webbers more than she could ever repay. How much easier it would have been for them, for Fanny, if they had simply sent her to the town farm.

"Life turns in odd ways, my dear. My father used to say that. It's a useful thing to remember."

"You spoke of protecting me from the gossips, Mrs. Webber. How can I possibly visit the sick in my present condition without causing talk?"

"You will go out with me only at night, and only to the homes of poor women who will not know you or care to. It will be all right." Maude handed Elizabeth the book she had brought. "My father's anatomy book. Study it. Learn. It will be all right. You will see."

It was as Maude said. The wives of Irish

immigrants or mariners' abandoned doxies cared nothing about Elizabeth Emerson's troubles. All that mattered to them was that Maude delivered their infants with the help of her apprentice, always referred to as Lizzie, and charged them only what they could afford.

It was a strange time in Elizabeth's life. She felt as if she were a child exploring the possibilities of grownup life for the very first time. In a way, she believed, that was the case. The Webbers had become the parents she had always dreamed of; she had become the child they had never had. The arrangement suited them both. But she knew once the birth of her child was accomplished, things would change. She would change. Life in the chrysalis had seen to that.

February arrived with a blizzard that tore about the eaves of the house and piled drifts ten feet high. It was, Elizabeth thought, a fitting night for her child to be born.

Elizabeth gave birth with a minimum of fuss, made easier by the knowledge she had gained from assisting Maude. There was only one troubled moment. Maude held the infant up for Elizabeth to see. But for a long moment Elizabeth could not bring herself to open her eyes, and the image of the gate formed behind her eyelids. She reminded herself that she was a butterfly now, not the pale larval creature of a few months ago. She opened her eyes quickly. The child was a girl.

Her hair was red-brown. She looked exactly like Aunt Mercy. Elizabeth named her Mercy Maude.

19.

The time had come. May had burst into a soft plume of green and pink. The windows in the parlor were thrown wide as Sarah John Thatcher scrubbed away all traces of the winter months, all evidence that mushrooms and butterflies had once lived there.

Sarah John paused in her flurry of dusting and bent over Mercy Maude's cradle, the affectionate look on her face making Elizabeth want to change her mind and stay.

"Can't make head nor tails of you, Elizabeth Emerson, wanting to go off by yourself when you know you'll always have a home right here with us," Sarah John said.

"Life turns in odd ways, Sarah John."

Sarah John shrugged and resumed dusting.

"Guess you're right about that one. Who would ever have thought I'd have ended up keeping house for the woman that delivered me? Always did think the sun rose and set on Maude Webber."

The rattle of carriage wheels in the yard slowed Sarah John's housekeeping pace.

"Looks like Mrs. Hogan. Now that's an oddment. It's been a while since we've laid eyes on her. Guess I'd better go put the kettle on."

Shortly after Mercy Maude's birth several months ago, Fanny's visits stopped abruptly with no explanation. She had resumed her cool, elegant attitude toward Elizabeth, and her clumsy attempts at maternalism ceased. Elizabeth assumed she had tired of the role of benefactress. When she remarked of the change to Maude, her reply was equally enigmatic.

"There are some things I cannot discuss with you, Elizabeth," Maude had said.

Fanny wore an uncharacteristic melancholic look about her eyes, as if she had suffered some secret sorrow. She was as elegantly dressed as ever, nary a hair out of place. But something about her was different, something Elizabeth couldn't identify. It gave her a prickly feeling, like stepping barefoot on a thistle.

"Mrs. Webber is out, Mrs. Hogan," Elizabeth said pleasantly, hiding behind civility.

"It's you I've come to see." Fanny, appearing ill at ease, placed herself rigidly in a side chair. "From the day I first set eyes on you," she went on, "I knew you'd cause me an endless amount of trouble."

Fanny did not look directly at Elizabeth, glanced instead at Mercy Maude.

Elizabeth knotted her fingers together in her lap. A little surge of resentment nipped at the pit of her stomach.

"I'm very sorry if I've caused you any trouble,

Mrs. Hogan. I had no idea when I came to Bangor . . ."

Fanny cut her off in mid-sentence.

"No, no, Elizabeth. I'm not talking about then. I meant the day you were born."

The nibble of resentment vanished and another emotion swept into its place. Elizabeth could not name it, but it made her mouth go dry, her palms go damp.

"The day I was born? I don't understand."

"No reason why you should." Fanny's beautiful eyes met Elizabeth's.

Turk's cap lilies, Elizabeth thought, frantically blocking any other thoughts.

"Please go on," she said in spite of herself.

"I've spent the last two months fretting about this, trying to decide if I should tell you or not. Maybe you will think I'm cruel, but I have to tell you because everything that's ever happened to you is my fault. I think if you know, then you will be able to make a better life for yourself than I could ever have given you."

"Please, Mrs. Hogan . . ."

"No, don't stop me, I've made my mind up."

Fanny raised an imperious hand and took a deep breath.

"My name isn't Fanny Hogan. It's Frances Mary Abbott."

Silence settled into the room; a bit of dandelion fluff drifted through the open window and settled on Elizabeth's lap. The curtains made a sudden flapping noise in the breeze.

"Abbott," Elizabeth breathed, stirring the bit of dandelion fluff.

The story flowed from Fanny's lips in a rapid stream of words, and with each sentence, Elizabeth felt her brain grow numb with the enormity of it. She neither moved nor spoke; the unnamed emotion curled in the pit of her stomach and chained her to the chair. It was a fairy tale, a figment of the imagination, but little by little, Fanny revealed the details of Elizabeth's early life and closed the gaps Elizabeth had always wondered about.

It had cost Fanny a stiff emotional toll to reveal her past life and how it was connected to Elizabeth.

"Now, you know," Fanny said so softly Elizabeth could barely hear her. "I don't expect love or loyalty from you, nor friendship, or even for you to like me, considering how I've lived my life. But I made the best of a bad situation. I decided to tell you because I'm leaving town next month and I'll never see you again, never have the chance . . ." She faltered and tears welled up in her eyes. She reached for a dainty handkerchief trimmed with tatted edging.

Fanny's tears jarred Elizabeth into action. She rose and bent over Mercy Maude's cradle, adjusting blankets that didn't need it. She

432

shut one window with a sharp bang, flicked an imaginary speck of dust off a small cherry candle stand. She was in perfect command of her external surroundings. Inside, chaos had full rein. She didn't know, as Aunt Mercy would have put it, if she were afoot or on horseback.

Gradually the chaos in her mind sorted itself out. She felt no hate for Fanny Hogan. After all, Aunt Mercy's life had been made happier for having a child to love and bring up. Nor was she angry because she had been abandoned. She had never felt abandoned. Aunt Mercy had fabricated a wonderful romantic tale of the death of her parents. She had never questioned it. What baffled her now was the suddenness of being required to think of Fanny Hogan as her mother instead of a benefactress. It was too vast a chasm to leap all at once.

"I believe this will take some getting used to."

Fanny stuffed her wet handkerchief into her black leather reticule.

"All I want is to see that you are provided for. I've purchased a dress shop over on Union Street. Respectable neighborhood. Maude said you had decided you would rather be a seamstress than a midwife. The shop has rooms above where you and the baby can live. Here's the deed." She handed Elizabeth several folded documents. "I've deposited money in the Bangor Bank in

433

your name. Sam and Maude have agreed to act as your financial agents if you need them."

Fanny rose stiffly, retreating into the old formal elegance Elizabeth was accustomed to.

"I don't blame you for being ashamed of me, Birdie. I never meant you any harm," she whispered as she turned to leave.

At the sound of her childhood nickname, the unnamed emotion in Elizabeth's heart uncurled and fled. Life turned in odd ways, indeed.

"I've heard your story, Mrs. Hogan. Perhaps you would like to hear mine."

Fanny sat down abruptly, as if her knees had suddenly given way.

Elizabeth told of growing up happy and poor, with never enough to make ends meet, of taking in sewing.

"But I sent money," Fanny interjected. "Lots of it."

"I remember letters from Bangor arriving every so often," Elizabeth said. "I was never allowed to read them. Aunt Mercy would be very agitated. She would talk a lot about the wages of sin and how I must always do honest work for honest pay. Then she would pay a visit to the preacher and be herself again. She must have given him everything you sent, for the church."

They talked on until Sarah John came to light the lamps.

Elizabeth turned the sign in the door of her shop so it said CLOSED. She leaned against it, feeling slightly smug knowing she had earned nearly twenty dollars that week alone. Her success, over that last few months, she believed, was due, in part, to the new mansions being built on Bangor's West Side and the shop's proximity to the Bangor House. The Bangor House drew all manner of important people, and it was quite common for their wives and female connections to need a new bonnet or some essential repair made on a ball gown.

Local women, however, made up the bulk of her business and if any one of them had the least suspicion that Elizabeth Emerson was Fanny Hogan's love child, they never let on. They did, however, hand on whatever news they happened to hear.

Pink Chimneys, Elizabeth learned, had been the target of picketing by the Reverend Comfort Drummond and the Temperance Union in retaliation for a slur Joshua Stetson had cast on that gentleman's character. As a result, gentlemen with reputations to protect had reduced drastically their visits to Pink Chimneys. The house, more often than not, was dark and empty now. They whispered that Joshua Stetson spent a good deal of his time drunk, but that rumor was dispelled when he appeared, sober as a judge, at several public gatherings. Others whispered that Joshua was gravely ill. Some said it was God punishing Joshua for his sinful ways. That story was the one most of Elizabeth's informants preferred to believe. This was reinforced when news arrived that the *Asia*, the star of Joshua's fleet, had gone down in the middle of the Atlantic with all hands lost. Then, to add fuel to the fire, word came that the *Fairmont* had run aground with a hold full of rum bound for the Smuggling Hole on the Penobscot River. No amount of money could prevent customs officials from swarming Joshua's office asking pointed and embarrassing questions.

Earlier that day, Maude had stopped by to visit and to bring several garments that needed mending. She said Fanny intended to leave for California in a few weeks. Fanny had not yet told Joshua of her plans. Maude was worried that there might be consequences.

A muffled wail pulled Elizabeth away from her musings. She bent over the wooden packing crate that served as Mercy Maude's daytime cradle. The child had been fretful all day. Teething, Maude had said.

Elizabeth nursed the child back to sleep. She resumed sewing on the last of a long row of hooks on a black mourning dress. Usually, she did not stay so late in the shop, but the demand for mourning dresses had risen after the recent outbreak of a fever had struck down a number of people.

The door opened and closed. Annoyed that she had forgot to lock the door and that someone had disregarded the CLOSED sign, Elizabeth rose to ask whoever it was to come back tomorrow.

A tall, slim man dressed in the dark navy blue wool of a mariner stood near the door, his face in shadow.

Elizabeth's heart lurched, the memory of being attacked always just below the surface of her conscious thoughts. She felt sweat break out on her brow and her heart began to beat rapidly.

"I'm closed for the day, sir," she managed to say in a calm way. "If you'd care to come back tomorrow . . ."

The man stepped into the light and Elizabeth's knees turned to jelly. The floor swayed like the deck of a ship on rough sea. She backed slowly away from the man, found the counter with her hands, gripped the edge. She hated the way her face flushed with shame as the man's eyes traveled from her face to Mercy Maude's improvised bed, and back again.

"Abner," she whispered. There was only despair in the sound, none of the joy of more than a year ago, none of the hope.

The one thing she had never been able to bring

herself to discuss with the Webbers was Abner. Whenever they had broached the subject, she had cut them off or became so agitated they did not press her. She believed he was dead. It was easier that way.

Now he was here, all long bones and navy blue, his hair tumbled across his brow, his skin deeply tanned, a new scar angling from eyebrow to ear.

She uttered his name again. There was nothing else to say. His face registered a series of emotions, none of which Elizabeth dared to identify, and settled into an unreadable mask.

"I've heard," Abner said quietly, gently. He removed his hand from his jacket pocket and pushed hair away from his eyes. "I got in this morning. I went to Sam Webber's house. He told me where to find you."

There was no reading his face. Was he angry? Had he come to castigate her? What did he want? She wanted to die from shame.

"You've found me, Abner, now go away. I'm not fit company for you anymore. It's over and done. All I want to do is forget."

But it wasn't over and done, and she had never forgotten. Her heart raced with relief to see him alive. She had been so wrong to think that her love for him had died. But it was too late, too late.

She saw hardness in his face, a ruthlessness that had not been there before. She did not understand it, did not understand why he had come to her except to torment her. She felt as if she had been torn up by the roots.

"Please leave, Abner," she pleaded, "go back to wherever it was you ran to that hideous night." He did not move, his look did not soften. "Why are you here?" She was almost shouting now. Mercy Maude stirred and whimpered. "To gloat? To see what a fallen woman looks like up close?"

Her words stung him, she saw, and she took a perverse pleasure in seeing him upset. She strode angrily to the door and flung open.

"Get out! Leave me alone!" But even as the words left her mouth, she regretted them.

Abner closed the door gently and leaned wearily against it, his eyes closed. He opened them and said, "Then you didn't have anything to do with it. Sam insisted you didn't, but I wouldn't believe him, didn't want to. I thought, I was so sure . . ."

"What, Abner, what?" Elizabeth urged.

"That you put Stetson up to the idea to shanghai me. I thought you were in it together."

The enormity of his words took the wind out of her sails, immobilizing her thoughts.

"Shanghaied," she said in disbelief.

"Yes. Forced to work like a slave all the way to South America with a crew of cutthroats fit only to run a garbage scow like the *Venerable*. All the way around the Horn. God only knows how we ever survived it. The weather was that fierce, but we made it to California. I jumped ship there, lucky for me, or I would have died of scurvy for sure. As soon as I felt well enough, I signed on with a schooner bound for Chile. From there I traveled back around the Horn on a bark carrying guano, bird droppings used for fertilizer, a stinking, filthy cargo. The only thing that kept me going was thinking how I'd have my revenge on you and Stetson when I finally made it home."

The bitterness in his voice struck Elizabeth like a lash. She made no attempt to hide the tears that trickled down her cheeks.

For a long moment there was no sound in the shop except for the insistent ticking of the clock and Mercy Maude's soft stirrings. Elizabeth closed her eyes in an attempt to block it all out.

Abner stepped close to her and she felt him brush away her tears. And without thinking, Elizabeth flung herself into his arms, as wanton and shameless as any of the women at Pink Chimneys. The brass buttons on his jacket bruised her ribs; his unshaven face scratched her cheeks and neck. He smelled of foreign places, of the wind, and the open sea. Here, at last, was the safe harbor she had longed for all those long, unhappy months. She clung to him like a barnacle, but he pushed her gently away. The air between them cooled.

"I will come back for you, Elizabeth," he said,

brushing her face with the tips of his calloused fingers. "I have an old account to settle."

The door clicked shut behind him. She made no attempt to stop him. She watched until he was out of sight, terrified that she would never see him again.

21.

The crowd outside the Oak Street gate at Pink Chimneys milled as restlessly as June bugs near a lit lamp. The sound of scuffling feet, a sharp cough, the clearing of several throats marred the serenity of the evening. Daylight had just begun to turn to dusk, but Abner spotted a familiar face here and there among the crowd—businessmen, a few between-ships mariners, idlers with nothing to lose. The taste of excitement was in the air.

The Reverend Comfort Drummond stood on an overturned soapbox, his face pocked by the dim flair of torches held aloft by some of his most loyal followers. In one hand he held a spirits bottle, in the other an open Bible. He waved the bottle over his head, and the liquid sloshed out of its top.

"Look at this, my friends, and remember my words! This is the devil's brew! Concocted by heathens and idolators on wicked islands in the Caribbean. This, this poison corrupted my soul, debased my integrity, made me unfit to minister the Word of God! The fires of hell and damnation are waiting inside this bottle, waiting for you, waiting inside this bottle, inside the walls of this den of iniquity called Pink Chimneys!"

Cries of "Amen" rose from the rear of the crowd along with a few enthusiastic cheers.

The Reverend Drummond smashed the bottle to the ground and held his Bible aloft.

"I have been redeemed! This is the Way!" he shouted. "This is the Light! Repent as I have repented! Save yourself from the torches of hell as I have been saved! Together, we will destroy the evil in our midst!"

The crowd stirred restlessly and edged closer to Reverend Drummond.

Abner skirted the extreme edge of the crowd, making his way toward State Street and the rear entrance to Pink Chimneys. No one took any notice of him or appeared to recognize him.

He had slept little the past few days. The closer he got to Bangor, the deeper his need to settle accounts with Joshua Stetson—and Elizabeth—became. Even now, it whirred within him, a deadly engine powered by the fuel of revenge.

In the months of believing Elizabeth had deceived him, he had blotted her from his mind, had forgotten her pride, how her eyes were the color of asters, how his heart quickened and sang at the very sight of her. Tonight, it had all come back to him. They still had a chance for happiness together, no matter what she said, despite what happened to her, and to him.

He wasn't yet sure how he would have his revenge. It would have to be an eye for an eye. Perhaps he would arrange to have Stetson shanghaied and forced to work in one of the camps in the far north. That idea was most appealing. The mental image of Joshua Stetson obliged to fend for himself in a louse-infested, rough and tumble woods camp amused him to no end. Still, he had sharpened the knife he always carried in his pocket. Maybe he would cut off Stetson's ears. There was also a piece of stout twine in his pocket. He wouldn't mind seeing Stetson hanging by his thumbs in Haymarket Square.

His thoughts were very calm, too calm, Abner believed. He recognized a capacity for violence in himself that went far beyond the amusing idea of giving Joshua Stetson a taste of his own medicine.

Joshua had attacked the very core of Abner's manhood—had deprived him of liberty, stripped him of dignity and self-worth, had changed all his guideposts and taken away his direction in life. It very nearly had been a mortal blow. There would be no forgiveness.

Abner fingered the knife in his pocket.

Pink Chimneys was dark except for a light in the window of Fanny's office. The stableyard was deserted. No horses stamped in their stalls.

Not even a cricket chirped. The only sound was the distant murmur of the crowd gathering force by the front gate. The only sign of life was the bright orange glow of lamplight spilling onto the terrace.

Abner made his way cautiously around to the front of the house where things were more familiar to him. It seemed a century since he had stormed out of that door stung by the humiliation Elizabeth had heaped on him, bent on destroying Joshua's chances of becoming mayor. But Joshua had lost the election on his own; Abner never had a chance to say a word about it.

Life turned in odd ways. He had heard Sam say that. Now its turnings had brought him back to the steps of Pink Chimneys just as it had brought Elizabeth and Maude Webber—even Fanny herself.

He peered upward into the darkness, his eyes barely able to discern the roofline. A few stars twinkled cold and distant. There was no moon. He shivered involuntarily. What was it about this place that drew some and repelled others? He was not prone to philosophical thoughts, but he could not help but wonder, and it disturbed him.

The rumble of the voices of the crowd drifted over the hedge, louder and more menacing than before. Someone yelled, "Burn it! Destroy the evil among us!"

Abner hurried toward the heavy front door, grateful for the dark that concealed his presence. The crowd was getting nasty; there was no time to lose.

He had no clear idea of how he knew he would find Joshua Stetson at Pink Chimneys. Something in his gut told him that. He trusted his gut; every mariner worth his rum ration did, except when it came to women. It never worked with women.

Abner turned the doorknob with no intention of knocking. He wasn't surprised when the door swung open on silent hinges. His gut was always right about these things. He moved stealthily into the entry. The place was quiet as a church on Monday morning. The newel post was ornamented with a naked marble cupid whose outstretched arms held a lit oil lamp. Shadows flickered up the stairwell as a current of air disturbed the flame. The house seemed to hold its breath.

Abner's eyes adjusted to the light. He left the door ajar, wide enough to catch any change in the tempo of the Reverend Drummond's harangue. He stood very still a moment, his ears bent with the effort of listening, sounding the atmosphere of Pink Chimneys as if it were a dangerous river channel where one false move would bring danger, perhaps fatal.

An almost inaudible patter of sound led him toward the slightly opened door of Fanny's office. With caution in his fingers, he opened it a crack more and peered inside.

Joshua lounged casually in an overstuffed leather chair, near Fanny's desk.

Every cell in Abner's muscles urged him to pounce, but with a will of iron, he held back and listened.

Fanny stood behind her desk, her hair in disarray, her face tear-stained, her elegant bearing only barely sustained.

"I'm going, Joshua," Fanny said, the bitterness in her voice like a lash.

"Then you will go in a coffin, Fanny, my dear. I decide what you do. I've decided that from the moment I fished you out of the gutter in Portland twenty-odd years ago." He laughed nastily and Abner clenched his fists. "Thought you could sneak out, didn't you, Fanny," Joshua continued. "Thought you could beat me at my own game, speculating in land, collecting fees from the girls. Money hasn't made you any better than you are, Fanny. You were born on a dung heap, Fanny. You will die there. It's what you deserve."

"What I deserve, Joshua? Or what you deserve?" Fanny said, the expression on her face deadly calm.

Joshua laughed again, without mirth. The sound grated against Abner's nerves, but he stayed where he was.

"Oh, come now, Fanny, we've had our differences before, but you have always grown to see it my way. California is no place for you. You have responsibilities. To me. To Pink Chimneys. I lost the mayorship. That doesn't mean I will lose the governorship. You'd make a splendid first lady of Maine. You can be a big help to me, Fanny."

"No, Joshua."

"I understand that delicious Emerson girl has a place over on Union Street. I wonder if she's happy. Perhaps she needs the protection of an older and wiser man?"

Rage surged in Abner's chest, but he did not betray his presence. His gut held steady. Something told him that Fanny could handle the situation, but she was visibly rattled and he was worried.

The color drained from Fanny's face, her eyes amber pools and reflecting—fright? Indignation? Despair? Abner could not tell for certain. He only knew the time wasn't yet right for him to burst into the room.

"Elizabeth Emerson has nothing to do with you, Joshua," Fanny said, her back steeled, her words barbed with ice.

Joshua lounged a little more deeply into the chair. He extended his legs to make a barrier between the chair and the desk. If Fanny decided to leave the room, she would have no choice but to step over them. She did not move.

Abner held his breath, chafing with indecision,

hating himself for not acting, for hesitating so long.

"Thought I wouldn't find out about her, didn't you? You and that frumpy Maude Webber. If you want your bastard child and her misbegotten brat to stay in good health, you would do well to see things my way, Fanny."

Joshua was almost purring.

Defeat was written on every part of Fanny's body. Her face was haggard, her shoulders sagged, dark circles of perspiration stained her pale mauve gown. She eased away from the barrier of Joshua's legs and sat down heavily behind her desk.

Abner waited, mesmerized by what he had seen and heard. It was as if he were caught up in the action of some diabolical play, a play in which he hadn't known he had a part. His concentration was so intense, he was only dimly aware that the commotion out at the front gate was growing steadily louder.

"All right, Joshua," Fanny said. Her voice broke as she went on, "I'll stay. I'll do anything you want. The deeds to my properties are in my desk. I will give them to you."

Fanny rummaged through the desk drawer. When she withdrew her hand, it did not contain documents. She held a small derringer. With a sudden rustle of silk, she stood up and pointed the gun at Joshua.

For one long breathless moment, Joshua did not move. When he did, it was with snake-like precision, with extreme caution. He eased to his feet.

"Come now, Fanny," he purred. "Our little game has gone far enough."

"Our game, Joshua," Fanny said, her voice expressionless, "is over."

Before the words were out of Fanny's mouth, Joshua's hand flew toward Fanny's wrist. She threw herself sideways to avoid him, pulling him over onto the floor. Bric-a-brac crashed and clattered.

From where he stood, Abner could not see exactly what happened next. He heard Fanny and Joshua struggle, a stifled scream, a harsh groan, a quick report as the gun went off. Then silence.

"You can stay . . . ," Abner heard Joshua say. Then nothing more.

Fanny, standing now, dropped the gun and buried her face in her hands.

The sound of Fanny's weeping broke the spell, releasing Abner from his part in a play he had not chosen to take part in. His first coherent thought was of the crowd. They were roaring now, moving closer. He realized with a start they meant to burn Pink Chimneys. He did not stop to think whether or not it was right or wrong to rescue Fanny. He only knew he wouldn't allow Elizabeth to be hurt again.

449

Abner burst into the room just as Fanny pointed a second gun, a mate to the first at her heart. When she saw Abner she dropped it in surprise. He kicked it under the desk.

"Let me do it; let me die!" Fanny moaned.

Abner grabbed her by the shoulders and shook her until hairpins flew. If he didn't keep her quiet, they didn't have a chance. He knelt next to Joshua, felt for a pulse, found none, confirming what he already knew.

"We can't stay here," Abner said. "Comfort Drummond has a gang headed this way and they won't stop until Pink Chimneys is in ashes."

Fanny's eyes focused on a plane just beyond Abner's shoulder. Her face was whiter than a sheet. He shook her again, gently this time.

"It's Abner Giddings, Mrs. Hogan," he said.

"I've killed him. Oh, dear God, I've killed him," Fanny whispered, collapsing against Abner.

"Mrs. Hogan. Fanny. Listen to me. How do we get out of here? Where's the back door? No one has to know what happened. It was an accident, Fanny."

"But I wanted to kill him, I wanted him dead," she said with a strangled croak.

"If you hadn't killed him, Fanny, I would have," Abner said bitterly.

Fanny gave him an odd look and pulled away.

There's steel in that lady, Abner thought, more grit and determination than anyone ever gave her credit for. He felt himself feeling something akin to admiration for Bangor's most notorious lady.

With a visible effort, Fanny took command of herself. She did not look at Joshua as she led the way out into the hallway. She stopped and let her gaze travel to the mahogany staircase, the silken wallpaper, the exquisite carpets.

"No one will ever know the price I paid for all this," she said.

"Hurry, Fanny," Abner urged. "The mob is halfway up the drive. If they discover us with Joshua, they might lynch us right on the spot." He grasped her arm, but she shook him off.

"Damn Comfort Drummond and his hypocrites. I'll see them in hell before they destroy what I paid for with my self-respect."

She reached for the lamp held by the marble cupid. With one swift, defiant motion, she hurled it against the wall. Little licks of flame sped along the trail of spreading oil, traveled along the parquet floor, and swooped up the velvet drapery.

Abner grabbed her hand and pulled her roughly after him until they were out of the house and running along the rear drive. When they emerged onto State Street, they turned back to look. Already, a heavy shroud of smoke billowed upward and angry tongues of flame lapped against the night sky.

The clamor of the mob rose to a crescendo of

surprise and excitement, then turned into cries of "Fire!"

Abner reached into his pocket and drew out his knitted watch cap.

"Put it on," he said tersely. He swung his jacket around Fanny's shoulders. "Lean on my arm and pretend we've had a few. Quite a few."

Fanny was shaking, not from cold, Abner knew, but from the shock of having killed Joshua Stetson.

"I can't," she said through trembling lips.

"Do it for Elizabeth, Fanny. How would it look if my future mother-in-law were hanged for a crime she prevented me from committing?"

It was not the time for humor. Neither of them laughed. Fanny linked her arm in his. They affected a staggering, drunken walk and struck up a chorus of "Drink To Me Only With Thine Eyes."

Their raucous voices drifted crazily into the night. All around them people ran toward Pink Chimneys to watch it burn.

22.

Elizabeth heard them before she saw them. And when they finally arrived at the shop, she stared at them in disbelief.

Abner's shirt, untucked and rumpled, was caked with grime. He reeked of cheap spirits and by the looks of his pants, he had crawled some of the distance to her shop on his hands and knees.

She peered carefully at the woman leaning on his arm, shocked to recognize Fanny Hogan. Fanny's grimy silk dress, tucked up in front, revealed a wide expanse of lace petticoats and quite a bit of trim ankle. Her unbound hair fell in snarled hanks down her back. She, too, reeked of rum.

Elizabeth bristled, too shocked to speak.

"Hold on," Abner said as he deposited Fanny in the nearest chair.

Elizabeth held her tongue, waiting, knowing that something happened, that Abner in his perverse way had tried to make it right. She knew, too, without his saying so, the account with Joshua Stetson had been settled.

The story Abner told Elizabeth was brief—Fanny and Joshua had argued. Joshua had become violent and had fallen, knocking himself senseless. Fanny had panicked when she heard the mob at her door and had overset a lamp, setting the place afire. Abner had found her running for help. She had begged him to save Joshua. But it was too late, the fire had spread too rapidly. He was afraid the mob would harm her if they found her, that they would accuse her of harming Joshua.

"So you pretended to be drunkards out having a

good time," Elizabeth said, interrupting the story.

Abner nodded. "Something like that."

Elizabeth did not press for details. She suspected there was more to the story, much more. For now, it was enough that he had come back to her.

Elizabeth helped Fanny upstairs to bed and soon she slept. She poured water for Abner to wash in. When he had dried his hands, he held out his arms and Elizabeth moved into them eagerly. She laid her head against the soft ease of his chest. He still reeked of rum, but it didn't matter. She would have wanted him near even if he had smelled of guano.

She felt no need to talk. Whatever talking they must do would come later. For now, touching him was enough.

They stood a long time by the window watching long fingers of flame stab the midnight sky, the ruddy glow blotting out the stars. Elizabeth watched it, knowing that a part of her life was going up in smoke along with Pink Chimneys.

As they watched, a wind came up and blew sparks toward the river, igniting a rickety wooden building on the waterfront. Soon, the entire waterfront was ablaze and constables began going door to door asking for volunteers for the bucket brigades.

"I have to go, Elizabeth," Abner said against her hair. The thought of leaving his warm, safe embrace was distasteful and filled her with tension. She rested against him a moment longer, then let him go.

"You'll be back," she said, needing to extract a promise from him.

"I'll be back," he answered firmly, kissing her roughly on the lips. She did not cling to him, though she wanted to.

After he was gone, Elizabeth stayed by the window. It was a hallowed place now, the place where they had spoken to one another without words, where they had looked for love in one another once again and had found it.

The fire spread rapidly, working its way down-river to Joppa. It hesitated at Kenduskeag Stream, leaped across, and swallowed up more buildings.

Another constable rapped on the shop door.

"We're taking anyone we can get now, Miss. Men, women, and children. About all we can do is keep the surrounding roofs wet down. So far, that's doing the trick."

There was no danger to Union Street or the shop. Mercy Maude and Fanny would be safe. Waiting for Abner would be easier if she were busy.

Elizabeth knelt by the bed and roused Fanny.

"Mrs. Hogan. Fanny," Elizabeth said. Using her mother's first name for the first time felt strange on her tongue. "Fanny," she said again, softly, making the word more familiar by repeating it.

"I'm needed to fight the fire. Take care of Mercy Maude for me."

Fanny opened her bleary eyes and Elizabeth saw that the effects of the rum had worn off.

"Be careful, Birdie," Fanny whispered, "you are all I have left."

A heavy, acrid smell of smoke bit Elizabeth's nose when she stepped out into the street. The roar of a fire out of control filled her ears. It was a short walk to Water Street and within minutes someone thrust a bucket into her hand and she took her place in line.

She lost all track of time. The buckets passed from hand to hand in an endless procession of sloshing water. The fire snapped and sizzled as buildings collapsed with great belches of flame and smoke. Her back ached and her hands grew blistered.

There were few injuries. The fire had given people plenty of warning. Men and women worked side by side, their collective energy galvanized to save what they could of Bangor's waterfront.

By mid-morning, Elizabeth decided she had done enough. She needed to nurse Mercy Maude. She walked wearily back to her shop. Fanny had bathed the baby and put fresh clothing on her.

Elizabeth settled into the rocking chair to nurse Mercy Maude.

"As soon as I can hire a horse, I will be

leaving," Fanny said without preamble. All traces of the rum-sodden harlot of the night before had vanished. She had pinned her hair into a severe knot. The gown she had borrowed from Elizabeth was demure. Gone, too, was her aloof elegance.

Elizabeth barely recognized the woman who sat opposite her. There was nothing to indicate that Fanny had ever been connected with so infamous a place as Pink Chimneys.

"Will you go to California?" Elizabeth asked. The thought of Fanny leaving did not trouble her. At best, whatever association she and Fanny might achieve would always be clouded by the events that had shaped them into the women they were. They were mother and daughter, but they were strangers.

"No," Fanny said, "Fort Point. I bought a farm there a few months ago."

"Starting over again?" Elizabeth asked. It was a rhetorical question. She had learned from Maude that life doesn't allow for new beginnings, it only allowed for growth, for new leaves to sprout from old roots.

"No, Birdie," Fanny said wistfully, "to find Frances Mary Abbott."

EPILOGUE

THE GUESTS in Hannah Bailey's parlor were few in number. Sarah John Thatcher bounced Mercy Maude on her knee. The baby giggled and drooled.

Sam and Maude Webber had agreed to sign the marriage certificate as witnesses. Maude, for once, had a bonnet that matched her dress and the lace jabot at her throat wasn't rumpled. Sam looked dapper as ever in his navy blue mariner's coat.

Hannah bustled back and forth from the kitchen to the parlor, determined to supervise every aspect of the wedding breakfast, but equally determined not to miss anything going on in the parlor. Her cap ruffles quivered with her activity and she kept repeating, "Dear me, I'm all aflutter!"

Outside, the thud of hammers and rasp of saws created another kind of din. The ashes of the fire were barely cool, and already new buildings were going up along the waterfront. In all, a mile along the river, from Oak Street to Joppa, lay level and blackened.

Joshua Stetson's charred remains had been found in the cellar hole where Pink Chimneys had stood. Stories made the rounds speculating about the circumstances of his death, but Elizabeth turned a deaf ear. Whatever had happened that night at Pink Chimneys was over and done with, and best forgotten.

The only person missing from the gathering in Hannah's parlor was Fanny Hogan, now Frances Mary Abbott. Talk about what had become of her had been rife. But only Elizabeth and Abner, and the Webbers, knew she now lived quietly on a farm in Fort Point.

Fanny had sent Abner and Elizabeth a letter of congratulations in the form of a business proposal. She had bought the controlling interest in a small lumber schooner. She wanted Abner to be the ship's master. He could name it whatever he chose. The excitement of that communication still clung to Elizabeth as she stood beside Abner and repeated the vows that made them husband and wife.

Maude was the first to kiss Elizabeth and wish her happiness.

"Sam and I have a little gift for you, my dear—nothing to compare with the one from Fanny, I'm afraid. Wait," she said as she disappeared into Hannah's kitchen.

She returned with a basket. A cat's yellow eyes peered over the rim. It jumped out and made straight for Elizabeth.

"Daisy!" Elizabeth cried, tears stinging her eyes.

"She has been the star boarder at the orphans' home," Sam said. "Maude figured it was as good a place for an orphaned cat as an orphaned child."

Daisy wove in and out of Elizabeth's skirts as if she hadn't been absent for months. After she had been petted and praised, she jumped back in the basket making little chirring calls. A chorus of tiny meows answered.

"Daisy has a family!" Elizabeth exclaimed. She let her eyes meet Abner's and he touched her cheek with one long, calloused finger. He reached for Mercy Maude and took the child from Sarah John. He cradled the baby in the crook of his arm. With the other he circled Elizabeth's waist.

"So do I," he said proudly, "so do I."

DISCUSSION QUESTIONS

1. What character do you most admire and why?

2. In what ways has the status of women changed since the era in which Maude, Fanny, and Elizabeth lived? How has it stayed the same?

3. Maude's relationship with her father is loving and supportive, Fanny's father is distant and judgmental, and Elizabeth has no father—how do father-daughter relationships determine the choices each woman makes, and what they turn out to be?

4. Maude, Fanny, and Elizabeth also grew up without mothers. How does that impact their lives?

5. In the early to mid-1800s, women had few rights. Discuss how that has and has not changed.

6. Abner and Elizabeth get off to a rocky start. What attracts them to one another?

7. Maude has made up her mind to never marry, but Sam Webber changes that. Discuss their relationship.

8. Fanny and Joshua have a complex relationship which, today, would doom them to long years of therapy. If you were their therapist, what would you say to them?

9. Joshua is bright, educated, and wealthy. He could have turned out better than he did. Why didn't he?

10. Did any scene in the book cause tears to come to your eyes? Which one and why?

11. If you could write a sequel to *Pink Chimneys* what would your storyline be?

12. What did you learn from reading *Pink Chimneys* that you didn't already know?

Books are produced in the United States using U.S.-based materials

Books are printed using a revolutionary new process called THINKtech™ that lowers energy usage by 70% and increases overall quality

Books are durable and flexible because of Smyth-sewing

Paper is sourced using environmentally responsible foresting methods and the paper is acid-free

Center Point Large Print
600 Brooks Road / PO Box 1
Thorndike, ME 04986-0001 USA

(207) 568-3717

US & Canada:
1 800 929-9108
www.centerpointlargeprint.com